BLOOD
— AND —
CIRCUSES

ALIYA SMYTH

VARLET VERTUE

Blood and Circuses

ISBN: 978-0-9948908-2-5

First Edition

Publisher: Varlet & Vertue
varletandvertue.ca

Books may be purchased by contacting the publisher or author at info@varletandvertue.ca.

To Kevin, who believed first,
Erin, who believed best,
And the cynics, who didn't believe at all.

The Calpurnii

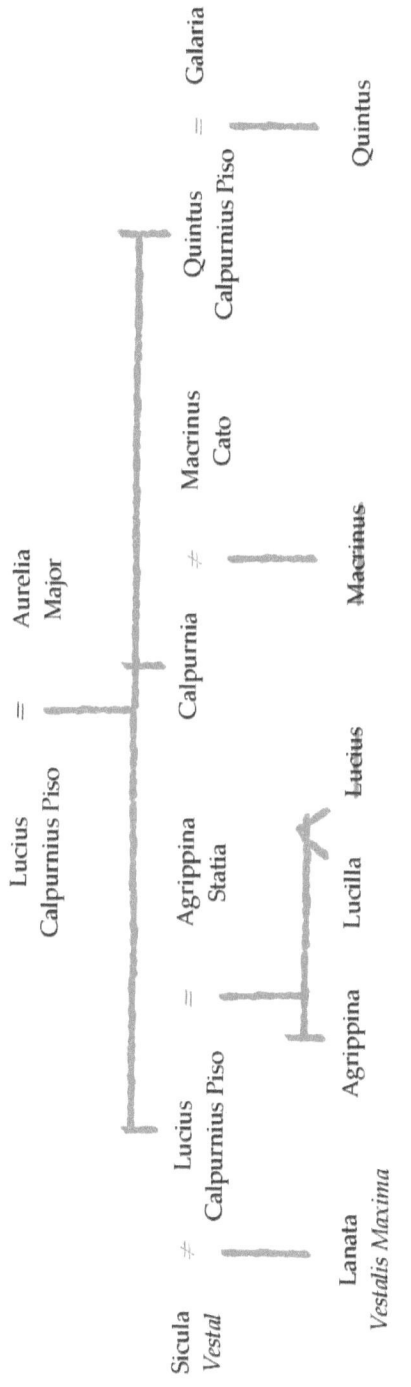

Sicula
Vestal

Lucius
Calpurnius Piso
≠

Lucius
Calpurnius Piso
=
Aurelia
Major

Lanata
Vestalis Maxima

Agrippina

Agrippina
Statia
=

Calpurnia

Lucilla

Lucius

Macrinus
≠

Macrinus
Cato

Quintus
Calpurnius Piso
=
Galaria

Quintus

"Each man makes his own shipwreck."
Lucan

PART I

DECEMBER

By Decree of the Senate of Rome: Year 1 of Emperor Vitellius

or

By Acclaim of the Legions of the East: Year 1 of Emperor Vespasian

… depending on who you ask.

ONE

ROME WAS ON FIRE, YET FATHER HAD NOT RETURNED. Even from where I hid, nestled between life-sized statues of Minerva, Hercules, and that hideous Minotaur, smoky tendrils tainted the winter air. The Lady of Wisdom stared into the distance, her painted expression unfazed. She didn't belong here in the atrium. None of them did. Fortunately, garden remodeling had created an unnatural—but ideal—hiding place. And I would *not* allow Eudocia to force me from the city without Father; nurses made notoriously bad generals.

Her sandals *clopped* around the atrium yet again. "Spiro, I can't find that foolish girl anywhere. Agrippina is packing for her instead."

"Lucilla won't like what her sister leaves behind," Spiro answered, voice raised to be heard above the sounds of the city. Bellows from people and animals echoed through the open ceiling in the centre of the atrium, an exodus fed by the flames. "And she certainly won't like missing Pherenike's honey cakes."

I almost snorted crumbs up my nose, and carefully swallowed my mouthful of pastry. Spiro should know better—I'd never go into hiding without provisions.

From a small opening between Hercules's club and Minerva's shield, I could just make out Eudocia's faded grey skirt and Spiro's leather sandals as they neared. I pulled my bare feet deeper into the shadows.

"Has the fire spread?" Eudocia asked in a sharp whisper.

"Last report, it was still contained to the Capitoline Hill."

"The gods protect us," she muttered. "I refuse to believe the Emperor's own forces would destroy the Temple of Jupiter. It's barely five years since Nero's fire—have they lost all sanity?"

"Vitellius is no longer emperor, and after this he'll be lucky not to be thrown into the Tiber." Spiro's cold resolve made me shudder. Trapped in a bag, sinking helpless beneath the waves would be bad enough, but drowning in the same river where all of Rome threw its waste was the ultimate disgrace.

I took a bite of cake, dissolving it on my tongue so I could still hear.

Eudocia let out a puff of breath. "Surely Gener—Emperor Vespasian won't want such a merciless start to his rule. The dominus wouldn't support that, not even to end civil war."

"Dominus Lucius wants peace and trusts Vespasian to bring it. Eventually. I should have gone with him." His voice dropped lower, filled with frustration.

"He ordered you to protect the girls, and I've never known you to disobey an order."

Spiro snorted softly. "Not from him, in any case. The fire changes everything. We can't hold out here if it spreads ... He should have been back by now."

Her skirt swayed closer to him, and I slid to my knees, inching forward to peer out. Father said our familia could weather any storm, even one caused by Emperors, surely Spiro wouldn't doubt that. He'd been Father's shadow since childhood; through countless battles.

Eudocia put a hand on his arm. "Gavius is with him. Four other soldiers. Another dozen around this domus. Everyone will be safe—"

A squeal from outside shattered their muted conversation. My heart leapt at the sound, taking my body with it; I cracked my head into Minerva's buttocks. My yelp of pain turned into a sigh of relief as the braying repeated—just a distressed donkey. Then a hand latched onto my ankle and dragged me from between the statues.

I stared up into Eudocia's severe scowl, her frizzy hair a halo in the sunlight. Her cheeks puffed out as she struggled to restrain her temper, eyes darting between me and the cake crumbs now scattered over the mosaic floor. "I see," she said, voice notched higher than normal. "With the whole of Rome burning around your ears, you think to hide and eat sweets!"

I stood, defiant, heart still sputtering. "I was waiting for Father to get home. And Spiro said the fire is only on the hill—"

"There is no *only* when a sacred temple burns, child! Would that

Jupiter took a lightning bolt to your backside for such disrespect," her Greek accent faded as her voice returned to its normal pitch, checking her anger as she always did.

Spiro rubbed the stubble on his shaved head. With a subtle jerk, he motioned for me to escape down the corridor.

I hid the mushed remains of cake in my hand and eased toward the kitchen instead. Pherenike would have another batch out now, and they'd be warm …

"Where do you think you're going?" Eudocia asked, taking my arm and leading me down the opposite corridor. "No more cakes — go pack."

"I'm still hungry. And we're not leaving without Father." I popped the last bite in my mouth.

"If you pack now, I'll bring some for when you act like a child of noble birth, instead of an urchin. As I always say —"

"Hunger robs us of reason," I mumbled, spraying a few crumbs.

"And do *not* talk with your mouth full. Agrippina somehow manages to chew and swallow before speaking."

Gods above. The only time my sister *didn't* talk was when her mouth was full.

A surge of shouts came from the atrium and Eudocia paused her marching. Spiro's answering call ordered the front door to be opened.

She let go of my arm and nudged me towards my room. "Stay and pack. This is not your concern." She hurried out.

I only hesitated long enough for her to turn the corner before following. Anger. Shouting. Fear. *All wrong.* My heart pounded faster with every smack of my bare feet on the chilled tiles.

The entrance was a chaos of people and sounds. Slaves rushed from the corridors, helping Gavius and Spiro as they struggled to lay something near the shallow pool. It nearly slipped from Spiro's hands, and it seemed no one wanted to grip it tight — holding it at a distance as though it might foul their clothes.

"No." The gasp came from behind me. Agrippina neared, brown eyes wide and dazed. My sister shook her head from side to side, dark curls bobbing in disarray.

My confusion vanished in an icy gust of understanding.

Father.

I pushed my way to the centre of our clustered familia. They let me pass. Some spoke in muted voices. Others sobbed, or stood in silence. At their feet lay my father, head cradled in Spiro's lap. Grief had chiseled Spiro's face, every line harsh in the sunlight. I dropped to my knees beside them.

Father's embroidered tunic had been reduced to rags. Blood covered the front, staining the blue silk a deep purple. Part of his throat had been torn free and pale tendons glistened in his neck, laid bare to the light. I struggled for breath.

"He fought," Gavius said, laying a wide-palmed hand on Spiro's shoulder.

"Of course he fought," but my rebuke was barely a whisper. Father still refused to wear a senator's toga instead of his military tunic. Always a solider. "How ...?" I turned my angry gaze on Gavius, and searched for the rest of Father's guard.

"They're dead. All four," Gavius answered, eyes clouded with confusion and dismay. "The general chased the attacker into an alley. I was too slow ... by the time I got there the others were dead."

"But how did it come to *this?*" Spiro asked, holding a shaking hand over Father's face.

At last I saw past the bloody tunic, past the mangled flesh of Father's neck, to the part my eyes had refused to accept. His entire body, every bit of skin, was covered in open sores. Small and raised like gooseflesh, they'd burst apart; brown and black fluids mixed with oozing red, turning his handsome face into a mask of decay.

The sores seemed to pulse with a life of their own, but Father lay still. I reached for his cheek, hand trembling, then snatched it back at the last moment. If I touched it, it would be real. Nightmares weren't real.

"Come away—" Eudocia's voice broke. Her prodding forced me to rise and she guided me to where my sister cried against Minerva's broad shield.

Spiro's head snapped up, gaze fixing on Eudocia. "We must get the girls to Quintus. Now. Only poison could have this effect. This is not just a political move ... it's malice." His lip curled, a wolf's snarl I'd never seen him wear.

She narrowed her eyes, considering, then nodded. "Girls, collect your bags—whatever is packed will do."

Quintus? We couldn't retreat to Uncle Quintus at a time like this.

Father's murderer was getting away.

Spiro began shouting orders, and the atrium went from stunned silence to focused activity. Only the statues remained steadfast. Goddess, demigod, monster. Not one of them would stand for such insult. No true Roman would either.

Agrippina put a shaky hand on my arm, but I jerked away and ran ahead. *Pack. I have to pack.*

I reached my room. A clean green dress and tunic were draped over the back of a chair—I stuffed them into my bag. Jamming my feet into sandals, I gave a last look around. My doll lay crumpled in a corner, combs and beads neatly laid out on a small table. What I needed wasn't here.

Agrippina blocked my way down the corridor. Whatever she saw in my face made her eyes widen. I pushed past her.

"Lucilla, stop!" she cried. "Eudocia ... Spiro! She's gone mad," her voice rang in desperation behind me.

I raided the kitchen. Bread, pears, figs. Whatever came close to my fingers was flung into the bag. At last I found it.

A knife. Wide, for butchering meat. I grabbed it off the table.

Spiro burst through the door, his red-rimmed eyes fastened on the knife at once. "Who's that for?"

"Who did it? Who killed Father?" I tried to draw a deep breath, but it hurt.

"I don't know. How could I?"

"You know what Father planned. You know who'd want to kill him!"

Spiro frowned. "Do you want to find out, or do you want to wave that knife some more?"

The blade glinted between us. *What am I doing?* "I want to kill him. We need to find him."

He took a wary step towards me. "We won't let this injustice stand, but the time must be right."

"But he's escaping—"

"Lucilla, the city burns." He took another slow step. "Armies clash, yet are desperate to keep citizens safe. It's no time for a ten-year-old to run into the roads shouting murder. Or do you doubt me?"

The knife grew heavy in my hand.

"You can't do this alone." Spiro's gaze took in my unlaced sandals, soles soft for parties, not travel; my bag, overstuffed with fruit and clothes mashed together; then to the knife.

Fingers protesting, I placed the blade back on the table. "Will you let me help?" I choked back the sob burning my lungs. I shouldn't have to ask. Spiro was a slave. But I was a child—I had no power to control my fate.

"Could I stop you?" Spiro opened his arms, and I walked into his embrace.

My father's arms had been stronger.

Two

WE WERE GOING THE WRONG WAY. I pushed back the shutter, peering out the window of the carriage as we jostled along. A short marble milestone, inscription only half-visible, stood at one side of the paved road. I leaned out to see how far we'd travelled, but could only just glimpse *Capua*, the nearest town, and *Roman Forum*, the only destination that mattered. Home—a long four days behind us.

"Stop wiggling and get off my dress," Agrippina snapped. "You're interrupting my prayers."

I closed the shutter with a thud and pushed the hideous yellow fabric away from my side of the bench. "I'm not on your ugly dress. And the Lares can't hear you now anyway, they're where they belong—back at our domus."

Agrippina glowered while she smoothed out her skirt, her face framed by lanky, dull-brown ringlets; lack of hot baths had added to my sister's foul temper. "We have four walls and a roof, don't we? This is home for now."

I eyed the carriage's cramped interior. Two benches front and back; window and doorway on either side. It might have curtains, pillows, and carvings, but it wasn't even ours—Spiro borrowed it after we fled the city. "I'm pretty sure it needs a hearth to be a home."

"Lady, give me wisdom," she muttered in frustration. "It's my responsibility to protect you now, Luce. Stop arguing with everything."

"Just because you're almost of age, doesn't make you the empress." She'd been dangling her upcoming twelfth birthday as though she'd be mystically transformed into a lady. The gods were sure taking their time about it.

Agrippina sat a little straighter, staring down at me. "Remember what Father said. A family is like the army — only victorious if the chain of command is followed." She clasped her hands in front of her again, and I realized she'd brought the small bronze statues of our ancestors.

"You're not allowed to take those! The Lares belong in their shrine." I tried to snatch one from her hand but she moved to the forward-facing bench, next to our napping nurse.

"They belong with us, and nobody else remembered to pack them. If we're going to live with Uncle Quintus, then the Lares need to protect us there."

"The Lares are Uncle's responsibility. He's the head of our family now … and higher up the *chain of command* than you," I countered.

"He may be our guardian, but we're still the daughters of Lucius Calpurnius Piso. We have a responsibility to our ancestors … and that includes Father."

I kicked my heel against the wooden bench beneath me, wishing I could stop the image of Father joining the shades of our family. And Agrippina was certainly the last person I wanted to answer to … though maybe that was a bit unfair. I'd never met Uncle Quintus; he might be worse. After all I knew his son, and *he* was more pompous than a slave during Saturnalia, when all roles were reversed. "Do you think Quintus will be at the villa?"

Agrippina sighed, looking up from the tiny figure she clutched. "I don't think so. He was still living in Rome with his mother. Aunt Calpurnia will be though, she wrote a while back that she'd come home from her journey."

"Oh no. I was sure she'd be married again and moved away for good. Eudocia said —"

Eudocia snorted awake, blinking her eyes like a confused owl. "What did I say?"

I frowned at her uncanny ability to interrupt at the worst moments. "You said Aunt Calpurnia wouldn't want to live with Uncle forever."

She fixed me with a steely gaze. "That is *not* what I said. I said your aunt has been living with one brother for years, and may be ready for a change. For example, she may have come to live with the dominus."

I tucked my legs to my chest and leaned into the corner. "She can't come live with Father now, can she." It wasn't a question. The shutter tapped softly against the window frame as the carriage rocked.

Eudocia's knees cracked as she rose and made her way past the curtained door to sit beside me. "Do you know what I remembered?"

"I don't care," I mumbled into my knees.

"I remembered," she went on, undeterred, "you once asked what happened to Spartacus, at the end of the Gladiator War."

I glanced at her, suspicious. "And you said I wasn't old enough."

"That was some time ago, and I think you've learned enough to understand the terrible price he paid."

"What price?"

"Think on this: we've travelled the road between Rome and Capua for more than three days in the comfort of this carriage." She patted the cushion beneath us. "But Spartacus and his remaining men—"

"After they were crushed by Crassus!" I ground a fist into my palm.

"Yes, yes, after that. Spartacus, and the gladiators and slaves who dared follow him, were crucified. One man at each mile down that stretch of the Via Appia. Three days' ride. Longer on foot."

Agrippina was staring gape-mouthed out the arched doorway, as though trying to imagine an unending line of rebels, each a milestone of warning.

I frowned. "They had to expect that, didn't they? They broke the laws and had the army after them."

"Perhaps," Eudocia said. "But often people live in hope, not realizing until the end that it was all flour and no bread. And what you girls must remember—"

"Ha." Agrippina's dimples flashed with her self-satisfied smile. "I knew you were going to make a lesson out of this."

Eudocia puffed out her cheeks, trying to school her expression, but couldn't quite hide her amusement. "Then hush and learn. The dominus … your father … was trying very hard to make bread. To make something of substance. His death does not diminish that, and it does not diminish him."

The firm press of Eudocia's hand on mine turned into a mighty yank as the carriage lurched sideways, a splintering crack echoing from outside. The horses snorted as we ground to a stop.

Spiro's bald head appeared, bobbing beneath the widow while he checked the wheels. The metal reinforcement around one had sprung loose, and the wooden rim had cracked. Spokes and shards littered the ground.

"There's no fixing this," he said, looking up at Eudocia, Agrippina, and me clustered in the window. I elbowed my sister to give me more space.

Gavius grunted as he descended from the driver's seat, where he'd been trading off the reins with Spiro. "It's the same distance forward to Neapolis or back to Capua. We might find help nearby. Someplace smaller."

Spiro picked up one of the long spokes. "But it's less likely we'll find someone to fix this type of wheel. We shouldn't have bothered with Senator Rusticus's offer. No matter how comfortable."

"Then you should have listened to my first suggestion," Eudocia said with a hint of heat. "It would have been safer to go to Ostia and take a boat down the coast. And faster."

"And predictable. Whoever murdered Lucius knows what they're doing. We couldn't risk the girls by playing into their hands. Boat captains can be bribed."

Eudocia glanced at us, lips pressed in a thin line. "Since we're now stranded here, what do you suggest next?"

Spiro rubbed the stubble on his head. "We only have the two dray horses—too few for all of us and too big for the girls to ride. Our best bet is to find another wagon. Gavius will stay with you. You have provisions for the night, and the carriage will be comfortable enough."

Gavius nodded, though Eudocia didn't seem impressed. We climbed out and stretched our legs while the men nudged the horses into action, pulling the maimed carriage off the side of the road, under a small copse of trees. Spiro slung a waterskin over his shoulder and took a look through his satchel, withdrawing several knives.

"You had the right idea." Spiro passed me one of the smaller kitchen knives. "Your father wouldn't want you to be unarmed. It shouldn't come to this, but a small blade can be just as effective as a large one, if you strike true. Remember?"

The stories sprang to mind. Father, the proud Roman soldier; Spiro acting the part of whichever hapless barbarian fell before Father's sword, or dagger, or drummer's stick. That was the best story, even Agrippina agreed. Whenever Father told it we went to bed threatening each other with all the things that could be thrust up a nose.

I held the knife as Father taught me—the metal hilt was cool, and I missed the way his warm hand would adjust my grip. "I remember." I recited Father's drill, "Eyes, throat, heart."

Spiro's face twisted into a melancholy grin. "Perhaps those are too high for a small girl. But if you strike his balls, you'll have a chance to get away."

Eudocia gave a disgusted cough, chivvying us back in and following him as he got ready to leave. "What nonsense. The girls will be staying in the carriage, not ravaging the marshland ..."

I tucked the knife into my corded belt and leaned against the doorframe, trying to make out the rest of their hushed conversation. But Agrippina began humming behind me, using her knife to prop up the small Lares, which kept toppling over on the now-tilted surface of the bench.

"Shh. I'm trying to hear what they're planning."

Agrippina rolled her eyes, continuing her wordless melody as she unwrapped items from an old grey dress she'd been using to protect them. "I need to see if the shaking broke my perfume bottle."

"If it had, the whole place would stink like roses," I muttered.

Eudocia bid Spiro farewell, and he mounted one of the stocky horses Gavius had unhitched for him. With a wave to me, he started down the road toward Neapolis.

"What do we do now?" I asked Eudocia when she climbed in.

"Perhaps some food?"

"I'm not hungry." Besides, we'd finished the honey cakes days ago.

"More Odyssey? We were at the part when Odysseus encounters the witch, Circe."

I groaned. "We've heard that a thousand times. She turns his men into pigs, but he manages to overcome her wicked ways. Skip to the part about Penelope tricking her awful suitors."

Gavius nudged open the curtained door. "Riders approaching fast. Likely messengers, but stay hidden." He let the curtain fall back into place, his silhouette standing sentry outside.

Eudocia softly closed the shutters. "Quiet, girls."

Agrippina stopped humming as we listened to the fast clatter of hoofbeats approach. They slowed. A low voice spoke in a sharp snap, though it was too muffled to make out.

"Girls—in the cubby." Eudocia thrust Agrippina's knife back into her hand. "Stay hidden no matter what happens. And Lucilla—you have a choice. Choose to obey." She pried open the panel to the compartment under our bench and hustled us inside. I pulled the knife from my belt. A stale darkness overwhelmed us as she closed the panel. Heavy footsteps rocked the carriage, but I couldn't hear past the thundering of my heartbeat.

Agrippina pressed close, her breath hot on my neck as she whispered, "What can we do with a knife, anyway?"

A knife. *What can we do with a knife?*

"This saved my life once in Britannia." Father passed me the leaf-shaped pugio.

I held it awkwardly, but he firmed my grip and moved my arm through several jabs.

"Let's see. You're such a little opponent, I think your best chance will be to lunge and thrust the blade up, under the ribs and into the lungs or heart. Like this—" he demonstrated on an invisible enemy. "Most times you'll have surprise on your side, but that's temporary—you must make deadly use of it. Don't forget, little love, you always have three weapons. They are?"

"Eyes to see, a mind to think, and hands to act," I chanted.

"Good. Each part is important. Leave one out, and you'll rely on the Fates, instead of yourself."

"Lucilla!" Agrippina's frightened whisper snapped in my ear. "They're yelling—for us."

"Come, girls!" The voice coaxed. "There's no need to be afraid. Nothing bad will happen."

"They aren't here," Eudocia said loudly. "You've wasted your time. They stayed with friends in Capua."

She sounded so certain. He must believe her. Then I heard another voice, deep-pitched and slow, the words too low to understand.

"We know you're in there," the first man yelled out again. "If you're not, you have no need of your nurse. I'll count to ten, then slit her throat.

"One.

"Two.

"Three."

He's going to kill Eudocia.

"Four."

We had no choice—no matter what Eudocia said.

I shifted the panel open. Agrippina grabbed at me, hands fumbling. "No, no—"

"Five."

I folded the knife into my skirt and stumbled out of the carriage. Agrippina trailed after me. I blinked quickly, trying to get my bearings as the bright sunlight stung my eyes.

At the rear of the wagon, a man clutched Eudocia in front of him, a long knife pressed to her ribs, puckering the fabric of her grey dress. Her eyes widened as we came out.

Desperate, I searched for Gavius, but he was at the front near the horse, forced to his knees by the second man, whose left eye was nothing but a dark hole. Not even a scar. Just an empty socket, smooth and hollow. He had no weapons I could see, but Gavius was white-faced with pain, arms rigid in the man's grip. My throat grew dry, as though I'd screamed myself hoarse. Where was Spiro? *Was that Father's last thought, too?*

Observe. Think. Act. I studied the man holding Eudocia. He wasn't tall, only a half-head more than her. Several weapons were strapped to his hips over his simple brown tunic. A trimmed beard covered his lower face where a jagged cut slashed down his cheek and into his jawline.

Eudocia was motioning with her eyes for us to run deeper into the scraggy trees. But Agrippina was slow, and there was no way we could hide with her in that awful yellow dress.

We couldn't run. We couldn't hide. I began to inch away from the carriage. Agrippina grabbed for my hand, but I batted hers away. I needed both hands free.

I took two steps, then everything changed. Without a word the attacker thrust his blade between Eudocia's ribs. She gasped, and he dropped her. Agrippina let out a mangled scream.

He walked towards us, blade down, relaxed. A drop of blood hit the dirt at his feet. He gave his accomplice a smug grin, exposing missing teeth in the depths of his beard.

"Prove your worth first, then smile," the one-eyed man said from behind us. "Or do you need more scars?" His tone was severe; commanding. But I didn't risk shifting my gaze from the man approaching.

His thrust his chin out as he stalked closer, a fiery resolve kindling in his eyes. Daring us to run. Eudocia lay helpless, struggling for breath.

I whispered to Agrippina, "Run when I say."

She looked at me in horror, but blinked understanding.

I had to act before he knew I could, or we wouldn't survive. He was only a step away, his knife held lazily at his side. I had two weapons he didn't know about: surprise and a blade. Father said they made a deadly combination.

He stopped. "Kneel. I'll make this easy for you, children."

The knife nearly slipped from my trembling hands and I clutched it tighter. I looked up into his face, then sideways at Agrippina and whispered, "Go."

The man's expression lit with surprise and he reached out to stop her from running. I lunged, both hands on the hilt, thrusting my knife upward into his chest with all my strength. The dagger shivered as it plunged deeper, grating against something hard. Shock etched his face. He stumbled sideways. I clutched the blade as it slid free of his body, blood spilling onto my hands and arms, hot and thick. He collapsed to the ground.

Agrippina ran to Eudocia, but I spun at a noise from behind.

Gavius was a crumpled heap at the base of a tree twenty feet down the road. I frowned, bewildered. It looked like Gavius had been thrown. But the blond man still stood beside the horse. Staring at me.

His single green eye transfixed me—turned my muscles to stone. I couldn't have run a step. I could barely breathe.

Then, between one shallow gasp and the next, he closed the distance between us, towering above me.

I swallowed a shriek and raised the knife, its bloody point inches from his body.

He knelt with deliberate slowness, green eye narrowing as he looked me over. I couldn't make sense of his expression—both angry and pleased. Thwarted yet satisfied.

His nostrils flared and he glanced at the knife. "That will not save you." He spoke each word with care, as if I might not understand him.

"It did already." The words squeaked out before I could think.

He bared his teeth in a twisted smile. "You are ... unexpected. I do not often misinterpret the signs." He reached for my face.

"What signs?" I lifted the knife higher, inches from the black hole where his eye should be. He stopped moving his hand.

"He was not worthy." He pointed indifferently at his companion, no more concerned than if the man had lost a bet on a coin toss. Heads you win; ships you die. "We will see if you are worthy."

Fear spiked through my body.

In a blur of silent movement, he disappeared into the trees, branches shivering in his wake.

He had left his horses behind.

The knife fell from my trembling hands.

"Lucilla!" Agrippina's panicked voice broke through my terror.

I turned and forced my legs to move, slow and clumsy, to where Agrippina cradled Eudocia's head in her lap. She held her wadded shawl to the wound. Eudocia's jagged breaths spattered blood from her mouth. So much blood. I collapsed to my knees beside them.

Eudocia lifted her hand, floundering as she tried to reach my face. I pressed her palm to my cheek, as she'd done every night when tucking me in to sleep.

She gave me a weak smile. "The sun has not yet set forever."

"That's what you always say." Tears tracked down my cheeks.

"And I'm always right."

"Spiro will be back. Please hold on. It's our fault! We didn't do enough to protect you." I held her hand tight against my face as she struggled for words.

"You did the right thing … You girls were not mine, but love is not bound by blood." Her eyes found Agrippina, then me.

Then she was gone.

THREE

I woke alone in a small sleeping room, sunbeams streaming in through a large window. The plastered walls had been painted to mirror the lush pastures and orchards of Campania outside. Uncle's villa.

My body felt as stuffed as the cotton mattress beneath me. Faint memories trickled in of Spiro's return and the sombre end of our journey. How I'd held Eudocia's hand until her fingers were too cold and limp for me to stand. Our arrival under black night and bright stars, with only the flickering torches at the door to guide our last steps.

I wished it was all a dream, but if it had been a dream, Eudocia would be here, chastising me for sleeping so long past dawn. *The day is half-done, lazy girl.* I pressed my palms over my eyes, but there were no more tears.

A noise outside the door had me scrambling to my feet on the far-side of the bed. *My knife! Why hadn't I kept it?* When the door didn't open, my pulse slowed again, and Spiro's hushed voiced from the other side drew me over.

"… your back still pains you, someone else can take over."

"This is my post," Gavius responded. "I won't leave it."

Spiro grunted agreement. "He's just had word that Senator Rusticus is arriving to offer condolences."

"Odd, isn't it? Him coming here during client hours."

"Considering Rusticus, yes."

Gavius took several loud gulps followed by a low belch, leaving me time to wonder at their suspicion. Established senators like Father never made early morning visits, the time reserved for clients to beg favours of their patrons. Only junior senators would admit their lower status in order to bind alliances. I'd met Senator Rusticus—he was definitely not *junior*.

"Is he bringing *her?*" Gavius asked.

"You know Junilla goes wherever she wants. But be on your guard. It might be a planned distraction."

I yanked the door open. "Why would he need a distraction?"

Spiro's bushy eyebrows came together. He put down a tray and glasses on a small gilt-edged table. "You should still be sleeping."

"I'm not tired. Tell me why you're worried about Senator Rusticus."

"We're being cautious. That's all."

I folded my arms. "Doesn't sound like all. Why is he coming now? He should leave us be after Eudocia's death."

Spiro exchanged an unreadable look with Gavius. "Senators don't fret over the deaths of slaves. And he's coming because he wants his carriage back. Does that satisfy you?"

It didn't, but if he was lying, I wouldn't get more from him now. I frowned at Gavius instead. "You told me in the carriage that the man I killed was the one who attacked Father. How about the other man? With one eye?"

Spiro stepped in front of him as if to stop our conversation, but Gavius laid a hand on his shoulder and Spiro sighed with resignation.

"The night your father was killed," Gavius said, "I only saw the man with the scar on his face. I'd been scouting ahead but ran back when I heard the calls. The general used the man's own knife to slash his face, then he and the others gave chase. By the time I got there, the guards were dead and the general—your father—poisoned." Gavius looked down, adjusting his sword belt.

I knew what he saw. The rot now masked my own memories of Father's broad smile. It seemed to spread within me each day. "The man with one eye must have been there. He's the only one who could have killed Father."

Gavius cleared his throat. "If he was, I never saw him."

"He was so fast—" I shuddered. "And strong. He threw you down the road!"

"I told you before, no one threw me." Gavius's face paled and his throat worked as he swallowed. "We grappled and he won."

"But you—"

"I think that's enough," Spiro said, glancing sidelong at Gavius, whose knuckles were turning white as he gripped his belt tighter. "You should meet with your uncle."

I planted my fists on my hips. "Yes. I'll meet him. He'll explain everything you're not telling me."

"Lucilla, you have to let us take care of you," Spiro said.

"Take care of me? *I* was the one who had to take care of Agrippina. And Eudocia—"

Spiro's expression dropped and he reached for me.

"I'm hungry." I turned on my heel and stalked down the corridor. Gavius's footsteps trudged behind me.

I passed room after room, barely noticing the dim halls. A flood of light drew me onward into a vast garden, far bigger than ours in Rome. Perfectly square, it was surrounded by two storeys of columns and open to the corridors at the centre of the villa. A large loom sat beside a skinny, reed-shaped pond that ran almost the entire length. Statues peeked from between well-tended bushes and trees. Vines curled on their trellises, climbing for the sun. It was stunning. But it wasn't home.

Though the main rooms must open to the halls around the garden, noises in other parts of the villa were muted. *Where is everyone?* I peeked through doorways, unsure where to go, but unwilling to look to Gavius for direction.

A slave carrying a jug of wine startled me as he emerged from a dark hall. He gave me a skeptical glance, but kept on his errand. I followed him through a study which led from the first garden to another, more than four times larger. The slave made his way down the long, colonnaded walkway at the garden's edge, me in his wake.

Open windows set in the outer wall framed the entire Bay of Neapolis, water glistening in a hundred hues of blue. Large, square-sailed ships crisscrossed in the distance and brightly painted rowboats bobbed close to shore. Father once promised that we would watch the sun set over the bay together. He'd smiled, telling me how he could name all the towns dotting the crescent, and knew all the villas nestled between. He'd never broken his word, before now.

I turned from the view … and thought I'd wished Father's spirit into form. From behind, the man's posture was identical, straight and proud. Then I caught myself, disappointed as I realized who it must be.

Uncle Quintus swivelled on the stone bench, studying me as intently as I did him. He resembled father, but with softer features. His eyes turned up a bit at the corners, as if about to laugh. Dark, curly hair was carefully combed, but not styled. And though I'd heard him called a philosopher, he didn't wear a beard, like statues of the old Greeks.

"Lucilla," he said, with a sad smile. "You won't remember me. You were a baby the last time I saw you." Hand wobbling, he placed his goblet on a small table. The slave refilled it before collecting the pieces of two other jugs, broken on the ground.

"Why is Senator Rusticus distracting us? How do we catch the man with one eye? And what's happened to Eudocia?" It was too rude, I knew it from his narrowed gaze. But there he sat—looking so much like Father it made my chest hurt—and I couldn't seem to stop the questions from tumbling out.

He rubbed his forehead. "That's a lot of questions for your old uncle. But a better reaction than I feared, after what you've been through."

High-pitched chittering made us both turn. Agrippina strolled into the garden, feeding figs to a ball of grey fur perched on her shoulder. "Look, Luce, it's a monkey!" She stroked its little head while it nibbled.

"I can see it's a monkey." I recognized it at once from Eudocia's descriptions. Using nimble hands and feet, the monkey hopped into the tree next to us and suspended itself upside-down from a branch.

Agrippina *oohed*. "Isn't he adorable? Aunt Calpurnia bought him for my birthday, but since we're here already, she said I might as well have him." A flicker of emotion crossed her face, though I couldn't tell if it was sorrow for the lost, or for her ruined coming-of-age party.

"My sister has excellent taste in gifts." Uncle watched the monkey hop onto the shoulder of his slave, who had finished collecting the broken pottery.

"Oh yes!" Agrippina said. "They're all the rage in Pompeii. Cincinnata told me in her last letter."

If Cincinnata said it, it must be so. I frowned. "It's peeing all over Uncle's slave."

The man endured the monkey's abuse in silence, the front of his brown toga now streaked with urine, and his gratitude was obvious as Uncle waved him away.

"How can you even care about a stupid animal?" I snapped at Agrippina. "Where's Eudocia? What's happened to her body?"

Uncle patted the bench next to him and I plopped down. "Your loyal nurse is being cared for," Uncle said. "Her ashes will be returned to the city when we know Rome is secure—it appears Vitellius has been killed and Emperor Vespasian's forces are in full control. And Quintus is safe, you'll be happy to hear. I've just had a letter from him."

"That's good," I mumbled, wanting to speak more of Eudocia, and less of Quintus. Though Uncle had a right to worry for his son, I supposed.

"Yes." Agrippina put a tentative hand on Uncle's shoulder and he patted it. "I'm glad to hear that."

"But why is Spiro suspicious of Senator Rusticus? Is he the one trying to kill us?" It was the only question that mattered any longer—Eudocia was gone; Father was gone. I couldn't help unless I knew who was responsible.

Uncle frowned. "You must be careful voicing such accusations. When you give words to something, you also give it a life of its own. And as for Spiro, as a slave he's now my property, but he'll always be loyal to Lucius first. He wants to protect you, and may be jumping at shadows to do it."

"Yes," Agrippina said, plopping down beside me. "It's not like you kill someone for having an affair anyway. Just divorce them—I mean, if Junilla didn't divorce him first."

Uncle paused in his sip of wine. "Affair?"

"Junilla and Father?" It made sense, now she said it. It would be a mad woman who didn't fall for Father, even without Cupid's arrow. "Probably because Senator Rusticus is so—" I wrinkled my nose. "Well, he has fish lips."

Uncle rubbed his forehead and ignored my comment. "What makes you think they were having an affair?" he asked Agrippina.

Her dimples appeared, and she played with the ends of her corded belt. "Well I ... I saw them kiss in secret after a party. Spiro knows about that because he found them when her litter was ready. But Senator Rusticus wouldn't care. He's her second husband anyway."

Gods were angered by mortals who bragged too much; senators and their honour were even worse. I'd wager all the shades in Hades that Rustics was jealous. I opened my mouth, but Uncle cut me off.

"Relationships are often more complicated than they appear. One thing is certain: there is a deeper plot here. I've written warnings to Quintus and also Lanata. It would be difficult for someone to target the Vestals, but I couldn't leave your sister uninformed."

"Half-sister." Agrippina sniffed with distaste.

Uncle ignored that too. "Trust that I'm doing what I can to find the person behind this."

"The man with one eye should be easy to find." His bottomless gaze still chilled me. "He's faster and stronger than any normal man."

Uncle nodded. "Ah, yes. Gavius told me of his conversation with you. Understand that in the heat of battle, it's easy to … make mistakes."

"It's not a mistake." I tried to remember my foggy argument with Gavius late last night. "He's lying because he's afraid. He was thrown—Agrippina you saw it!"

Her eyes were hard. "I was helping Eudocia."

"Then Gavius must have hit his head and doesn't remember. But the man told me—" One green eye; one dark hole. *We will see if you are worthy.* What did it mean? Why wasn't I dead?

"Luce, I didn't see anyone talk to you." Agrippina sat beside me, arm around my shoulders. "The other man was a coward in the end and ran away when his partner was killed."

"This assassin is a man, Lucilla," Uncle said. "Just a man. And from his description we can start searching. Though it's not easy to find someone in the city who doesn't want to be found." He fixed me with the same stare that Father used to quell any argument. Even his eyes were a match for Father's—rings of yellow, green, and brown that seemed to know exactly what I was thinking. "I'm the head of this family now. To have justice, we must proceed with caution. If your temper is high, you'll see the need for revenge in every slight."

Agrippina bobbed her head in agreement, but revenge sounded fine to me. Force the senator to confess, and kill him. Find the man with one eye and kill him too. With a legion if necessary. No matter what Uncle said, I—we—wouldn't be safe until that man was dead.

Agrippina pinched my shoulder. "Stop it, Luce."

"Stop what?"

"Whatever you're thinking, you're making my whole arm tremble." She pinched me again, then stooped to collect her monkey.

I rubbed my shoulder. "Go on and take your pet! It's like you don't even care about Father. Or Eudocia!"

"Lucilla," Uncle warned.

"I'm used to it," Agrippina said with a sneer. "If you don't yell and get angry, Lucilla thinks you don't have any feelings at all. I'm going to spend some time with Aunt Calpurnia. She wanted to see you when you woke, but I'll tell her you're being an ungrateful brat." She held her chin high and sauntered from the garden.

Minerva, please let that monkey pee all over her dress.

"You should rest, Lucilla. Spiro informed me you barely slept in the wagon. But if you'll indulge me first, there's something I don't want to forget." Uncle fumbled a bit as he pulled a ring off his forefinger and handed it to me.

It bore a gold ram's head, and was far too big for any of my fingers. I spun it around and read the engraved inscription. *Usque ad finem:* to the very end. A soldier's ring. This may not be a battlefield, but the lines were drawn. If Rusticus was behind these deaths, then I had a duty to end our feud.

Uncle took another deep drink of wine. "Since Agrippina received a present early, I thought you'd also like one. I know what it's like to be the younger, and get passed over. And I'm afraid I sometimes made a fuss—Lucius was the Stoic, not me."

I frowned. "Father always said you were the philosopher."

"Not by nature, not by nature. But we become what we practice." He drained the last of his glass. "I am now a collection of other people's wisdom, Lucilla. I wonder if that makes me wise."

Footsteps crunched across the gravel and I hated the way my heart ran ahead before my mind could catch up. At least it was only Spiro, approaching from the villa.

"Senator Rusticus and Junilla have arrived. He required to be seated in your study."

Uncle stood and gave his toga a little shake, gazing at Spiro thoughtfully. "Persistent, isn't he? I would keep him waiting longer, but since he can see me from there—no, don't look Lucilla—it might be taken as rude."

I stopped trying to peek around Spiro and crossed my arms. "He shouldn't have come."

"Quite right," Uncle said. "Senators make the worst guests.

Always wanting to be fed and watered like an exotic animal. Lucilla, please remember your manners in any case. There's no use poking a bear if you're not ready to fight it."

Spiro's stern expression softened with a slight smile. We let him lead us to the study, a statue of Minerva looming large between the high columns that opened it to the garden. Uncle's desk was scattered with piles of scrolls and parchment, a plate of fruit and olives balanced to one side. Two cedar chairs were positioned on the facing side; in one sat Senator Rusticus, his short white hair curled with care, drumming his fingers on the carved armrest; the other was vacant—Junilla stood with Agrippina, both cooing over the frolicking monkey.

I leaned against Minerva in the background, trying not to be distracted by the eerie snake-haired Medusa carved into her cloak.

"Greetings to you both," Uncle said. "I am Quintus Calpurnius Piso, and my nieces I believe you've met before." He gestured to each of us in an offhand way. "My apologies for keeping you waiting, but I don't invite many visitors here." His tone was distinctly unapologetic.

Rusticus splayed a manicured hand over his chest. "Gaius Commidius Rusticus, and my wife, Junilla of the Grania," he said with formality, his puffy fish-lips overemphasizing each syllable. "I was saddened to hear of your brother's death. Senator Piso was a good friend to me, and in times like these we must stand with our friends."

Junilla gave the monkey a last pat, and came over. Her hair was pinned up in a coil of dark braids, with tendrils trailing down over her shoulders. "Yes, Lucius was a good friend. We both regret his loss."

My stomach turned when she called Father Lucius. She wasn't family; it wasn't proper.

Rusticus shifted in his chair. "I came to offer my condolences. And of course to have my slaves collect my carriage, which was no doubt instrumental in bringing your nieces safely to you."

"No doubt," Uncle said. "Though unfortunate how a wheel broke at such an inconvenient time for the girls."

Rusticus didn't like that—he coughed and patted his plumped curls. Combined with his heavy jowls, his face seemed strangely square. "I'd heard about the attack. Mercenaries wasn't it? Awful." His gaze slid to me, a slight smirk stretching his lips. *Bragging.*

That's right. I killed your man. What had Uncle said? Poking bears? A brass stylus lay next to a wax tablet, and I wanted nothing so much as to jab it into that fleshy smile.

"Yes, awful," Uncle said. "But the Fates spin; we merely wear what they weave."

Junilla blinked several times, eyes glistening. "You're as eloquent as Lucius described."

"I find it interesting my brother mentioned me at all."

"For weeks, all he's talked about were his army days with you and our new Emperor. Though Vespasian was always 'the general.'" She gave a slim smile.

"It's a hard habit to break." Uncle gestured for her to take the vacant chair, before taking his own seat.

Junilla lowered herself with a graceful swish of skirt, her silk shawl sliding to expose her pale shoulders. "I, for one, found Lucius's loyalty endearing."

Rusticus had been eying them as they talked, and now coughed again. "How right you are, my dear. Such loyalty should have been rewarded." He began droning on about Uncle taking up Father's responsibilities; how the Senate needed him to give up his self-imposed exile here on the Bay. Sounded like the same fishing for votes that had made Father's day so dry. Apart from drumming his fingers, he barely moved, but his eyes kept darting my way, forehead wrinkling with each sullen frown. *Wondering how I survived, no doubt.*

I made my way past Uncle's desk, nabbing a few dark olives off the tray. I popped one in my mouth, working the flesh off the pit with my teeth; trying to savor the taste over the bitterness of having to listen to Rusticus. The longer he talked, the more I worried. After all, he had the nerve to come here, to our home, and call my father his friend.

I needed to talk to Spiro, and wished I'd walked towards him on the other side of the room, instead of Agrippina. She seemed lost examining every item the elegant Junilla was wearing—from gold rosette pins sprinkled in her dark hair, to the gold-beaded ribbon wrapped around her slender torso.

"We're wasting time," I whispered to Agrippina. "We can't just stand here and pretend he's not to blame."

"You can't really think the senator ..."

I squeezed the olives in my hand, frustrated she could be so oblivious. "He's here to brag!" I hissed. "We should make him confess. Now."

She rolled her eyes. "And how would we do that?"

"How about we get him drunk? Father always said *wine tells hard truths*."

"That's a terrible idea. And don't you dare cause a scene," Agrippina warned.

That's exactly what we need. Surprise him into giving himself away. Mentioning his accomplice would probably do it.

I shrieked. Loud. Everyone turned. Agrippina's gaze was a barrage of poisoned darts.

"The man with one eye!" I pointed toward the garden's far gate. "He's here!"

Spiro took off down the path, calling for Gavius.

"How extraordinary." Rusticus tilted his head to examine me as a child would a beetle. "A man with one eye?"

Uncle rubbed his temple, and I worried I'd poked an unintended bear. "One of the mercenaries was of that description."

"Brazen to attack you in your own home." Rusticus's cool gaze was still fixed on me. Not even a hint of worry—he knew the one-eyed man wouldn't attack without his order.

Junilla stood with a jerk, hand to her throat. "Are we in danger?" She sidled along the edge of the desk, closer to Uncle, as though she'd forgotten Father already. And she'd dared talk about loyalty. *May the gods below curse them both.*

Guards had run in and Spiro ordered them to scour the garden. While everyone was distracted by the ruckus, I waved the crushed olives under the monkey's nose and tossed them into Junilla's high-towered hair. He scampered after, mussing up her braids and sending hairpins *plinking* to the ground. Junilla *eeped* and waved her hands, trying to knock the animal off.

"Don't hurt him!" Agrippina dashed forward to pull him free.

Rusticus resumed drumming his fingers, lips pursed in deep wrinkles while he observed their dilemma. "Friend Piso," he said. "A drink if you please, and perhaps some delicacy or other, while the ladies collect themselves."

Uncle managed to call for wine, have a squint-eyed slave help Junilla with her hair, and order me back to bed, all without raising his voice.

It was worth it. I knew my enemy.

FOUR

"LUCILLA, DON'T CUT YOUR FINGERS OFF WITH THOSE SHEARS." Aunt Calpurnia glanced at me while weaving the shuttle through the vertical threads of her loom. She sat in a low-backed chair, legs blanketed to obscure their deformity, and had to stretch to reach the fabric's edge.

"You'll get blood on the new cloth," Agrippina chided.

I glared at her and snipped the shears threateningly. She didn't seem very afraid, turning with a superior sniff to help Aunt lift the heddle bar and tighten the newly-woven thread against the chevron pattern. Aunt didn't like to draw attention to her infirmity, so she waited with infinite patience while Agrippina fumbled somewhat, before lowering the heddle into her reach.

I went back to flipping the small shears in the air, catching them by the curved handle. It wasn't even dangerous—so long as my finger didn't get caught between the open V of the blades. Single flips were easy ... now for doubles.

A few steps took me to the edge of the long pond. Bright afternoon sunlight warmed the inner garden, though the trees and shrubs weren't quite ready to bloom.

"When can I weave with you in the mornings?" Agrippina asked Aunt Calpurnia. "I've been practicing for weeks and I won't embarrass you in front of Uncle's clients the way Lucilla did."

It's not like the monkey peed on Junilla. And Uncle had smoothed it all over—I was only a *child*, after all, and had been through *so much*. A little brown bird chirped in a disgusting display of happiness. I lofted the shears up toward where it perched, and sent it fluttering onto a second-storey railing.

"My dear, you're a proper young woman and I'm certain you would behave beautifully," Aunt said. "But I'm not sure you understand why I weave in the garden while my brother has visitors."

Agrippina crinkled her nose. "Because it lets Uncle's clients see we have a traditional household, even if his wife isn't living here?"

"Where your Aunt Galaria lives is not your concern. And young Quintus benefits from maintaining close ties to her family in Rome. They have no other grandchildren, after all." Aunt's matter-of-fact tone didn't quite hide her irritation with her sister-in-law. "Though you're right that it's important for our visitors to see a proper household. More importantly, *I* will also be able to see *them*. I can see who is upset; who is groveling and asking for favours. And I can provide my brother with some gentle advice without him having to ask me for it." Aunt gave a little wave of her hand, as though banishing trouble from sight. "It would be much easier if men would not be so very conscious of appearances. Prideful creatures." She resumed weaving. Agrippina's nose was still twisted as she puzzled through Aunt's advice.

I hadn't realized Aunt was so devious, but the inner garden really was the best place to see what happened in the villa. Every main corridor started here. The atrium at the front entrance, dining room, and even Uncle's study were all visible from Aunt Calpurnia's favourite spot. Right now Sidonia, Agrippina's young slave, appeared from the kitchen corridor.

"There's a letter for you, domina Agrippina," Sidonia said, handing over a small scroll of parchment.

"Is it another from Cincinnata?" Aunt asked.

"No, it's from Quintus. I recognize his handwriting." She cracked the wax seal and unrolled the letter.

"Why is he writing to you?" Quintus never did anything without some kind of plan. Like the time he tricked me out of three gold coins in a flip-game.

"Likely because he knows I'll open it, instead of burn it." Agrippina read aloud, "'Dear cousins, I hope this letter finds you in good health. Forgive my late message, but there has been so much to do in Rome since the fire last month. Please make yourselves welcome in my father's home. Though our fathers had the misfortune to be at odds, I would hate to think of you feeling like outsiders while you are under our care.'"

"*Our* care?" I fumed. "He's not the head of our family yet."

"Quintus is trying to be friendly. And responsible." Aunt pinched her lips together, but turned back to her weaving.

"'Uncle Lucius had a sizeable estate and, despite having barbarian ancestry, your mother also left you both substantial resources. Father would not go into the details with me at this sensitive time, but I'm certain your parents have ensured you should have no difficulty finding husbands in the near future.'"

"I knew it. He's only writing to tell us we have to get married." *Gods below, save me from ever becoming Quintus's responsibility.*

"Of course we'll get married—" Agrippina started.

"Of course you'll get married," Aunt said in near-unison.

Their amused expressions made me frown. "Well does he have anything interesting to say that's not about our money?"

Agrippina's gaze trailed down the letter. "There's a bit about Jupiter's temple being destroyed during the fighting—"

"We know that already. And they cut Vitellius's head off—"

"Heavens, girl," Aunt said. "An emperor's death should be discussed with dignity."

"I'll remember to do that when Emperor Vespasian dies."

She fixed me with Medusa's glare.

"Oh! Here." Agrippina said. "'You will be happy to hear that mother was recently able to visit Lanata, and that the Vestals were in no danger during this turbulent time. The city was made safe in just a few days, and your half-sister was privileged to be invited to join the Vestalis Maxima at a banquet in honour of the Emperor's son, Domitian. She remains a model of honour and virtue for our family, and I would encourage Lucilla, in particular, to follow her example in all things.'" Agrippina's frosty voice was not directed at me this time.

Quintus's admiration for Lanata always irked Agrippina. An odd competition had brewed between my sisters ever since Lanata visited two years ago and explained how, as a Vestal, she was sacred. Doubly blessed even, since her mother, Father's first wife Sicula, had also been a Vestal. We rarely saw her, as she'd been taken when seven to live with the chosen of Vesta: six in training; six priestesses; and six mentors. Lanata could be as snobbish as Quintus, but she was family, and I knew even Agrippina was glad she was safe.

"That's good advice," Aunt Calpurnia said, with a nod in my

direction. "It's a relief to hear the soldiers respected the sacred temples as much as possible. Now, I have other things to attend to this morning." She shooed us toward Sidonia, who still stood at Agrippina's shoulder. "Go and let Sidonia take care of you."

"Yes, Luce." Agrippina pulled at my arm. "I want to talk to you."

Torture time. I trudged up the stairs after Agrippina. Sidonia followed behind, ready to apply everything she'd just learned from Aunt Calpurnia's aging ornatrix about styling hair and painting faces.

"Not again," I groaned, dropping down at the dressing table in Agrippina's room. Sidonia entered, followed by stoop-backed Opelia who always emerged from the plaster scenery whenever something needed to be poked or plucked or pinned.

"Well?" Agrippina reclined on her sofa, head propped up on the high arm, and waited for Sidonia and Opelia to finish their preparations.

"Are you jealous Lanata had a chance to meet Domitian? She can't marry him you know." Not until the thirty years of her vows were over. She'd be old by then—close to forty.

"I am not jealous." Agrippina hesitated. "But *you* should be angry. You should be yelling about when Quintus got you in trouble for pushing him in the pool, and …" She frowned and started chewing on her smallest fingernail.

Why was she upset? True, everything Quintus did usually made me angry. His bragging. His obsession with family honour. And especially when he thought he should give me advice. But this letter had washed over me, as though it were from someone I didn't know.

"Luce, how many rooms are there in the villa?"

"What kind of question is that?"

"You knew every one of the thirty-three rooms in our domus—even the storage rooms. So how many rooms are there here?"

I stared at the glass perfume bottles lined up in a row. Light glinted off their many colours—red, blue, gold flecked. "I don't know. Why does it matter?"

"You … you're not being … normal," there was a tremor in her voice.

I found myself staring at the hand mirror on the dressing table. My face was pale and thin, dark rings under my eyes. *Not normal.* Normal was Eudocia stuffing me with food; forcing me to sleep.

Normal was Father's stories and mock battles in the garden. It hadn't been that way for weeks. It would never be that way again.

I clutched the gold ring—Uncle's gift—threaded on a cord around my neck. Father would be ashamed of the way I was acting—as though I'd given up.

"I'll try, Agrippina."

She smiled, thin but hopeful.

Opelia shuffled forward, leading Sidonia, who held a pair of tweezers. "Domina?" She squinted at Agrippina, who lay back on her couch and gestured for them to begin. Opelia turned to Sidonia. "Now is not the time to be timid."

Sidonia screwed up her face, firmly grasped a hair in the tweezers, and pulled—hard.

"Ooh!" Agrippina gasped as the tiny hair was ripped from her eyebrow.

"You do not have to yank it, Sidonia," Opelia chastised. "Pluck it briskly in the same direction as the growth. If a little blood is drawn, dab it with a piece of linen. Do not let it scab on the surface. Try again."

Sidonia moved back in with the tweezers, scrunching her nose and sticking out her tongue in her effort to grasp another elusive hair. Agrippina was careful to remain still and keep both eyes. The next pluck seemed gentler and Agrippina barely twitched, only a little *hic* to her breath.

"That was much better," Agrippina said.

"Now, more quickly," Opelia said, "taking care to shape the brow from the area nearest the eye first."

Sidonia nodded and continued her work.

I tossed the letter on the table, where it clinked against a glass jar.

"You should try that perfume, Luce. Aunt Calpurnia bought it for me when she was in Herculaneum yesterday. Lemongrass and jasmine. Aunt said it's from somewhere beyond the Indus River but I can't remember those eastern countries. It might suit you."

"You don't like it?" I pulled out the blue decanter from the mess of cosmetics lying on her table and dubiously lifted the stopper. Instead of being sickly sweet, it had a fresh scent.

"It's nice, but I prefer my rose—" Her response turned into a hiss of pain as Sidonia pulled something the wrong way.

"Don't you think you're overdoing it a little, Agrippina? You don't need to be getting your brows plucked or your legs honeyed yet, you know." The slave should have practiced on someone else, but it seemed pain was no obstacle in the pursuit of beauty. I could only image how awful it would be when Sidonia started ripping out leg hair.

"You may not have been paying attention to anything lately, but I did have a birthday. Now that I'm twelve, I need to be thinking about my future."

"So what?"

"Well, Uncle had me review my accounts and prepare my will, now I'm of age. And Aunt Calpurnia said I could be meeting potential husbands this year. You know how Uncle is always having visitors down from Rome. Some bring their families to Herculaneum or Neapolis for the summer. And there are even a few acceptable families nearby. There may be … you know …" She coloured a little as she finished. It could have been from shyness or from the effort of keeping still under Sidonia's grasping tweezers.

"You wouldn't want to get married right away, would you?"

"If it was a good match. I'd love to be mistress of my own household, maybe back in Rome. I miss the city. And I would finally have something over Lanata." There was satisfaction in her voice. She sobered suddenly and turned to stare at me, face withdrawn. "Do you think Lanata was attacked, too?"

"Someone would have told us, wouldn't they?"

"They haven't told us very much at all," she pointed out.

"Spiro would have told me. He said I could help—"

Agrippina snorted inelegantly and gestured for Sidonia to resume her work. "Help? Lucilla, really. Look what you did when Rusticus was here. You're a child. What in Juno's name do you think you're going to do to help?"

Stay calm, stay reasonable. Show her you're not *a child.* "What should I do? Let us get attacked until the whole family is dust in our tomb?"

Her hands clenched on the fabric of the couch and her lips pinched together. "I want revenge, too, you know. For Father. For Eudocia. But there's nothing we can do except trust Uncle and Spiro to live up to their duties. And we should live up to ours. You need to start acting like a lady and quit being such a child."

"You just told me I *was* a child," I said, tired of her ever-changing arguments. "And if I was Quintus, I would be expected to help."

"But you're not Quintus. You're a girl and you'll be a woman. Not a general. Not a senator. You can't pretend to be something you're not."

"If I had pretended to be like you, we would both be dead."

She sat up with a jerk and Sidonia gasped as my sister batted the tweezers away. Agrippina glared at me. "If you had been like me we would have stayed hidden and Eudocia would be alive."

Heat crept up my neck and face. "You're wrong. Gavius told me the man with one eye knew we were in the wagon—he'd told the other man we were hiding."

One green eye, one dark hole. I was breathing fast and fought to let out a slow stream of air.

Agrippina persisted. "Eudocia told us to stay in the wagon—"

"You were there. You heard her. She said what we did was right!" I slammed the jar of perfume onto the desk, cracking the base of the glass. The scent of citrus wafted into the air.

"That can't have been what she meant. She would never expect you to kill someone."

"She said a person is judged for their actions. I had to try to save her. I couldn't let her die and do nothing!"

"Lucilla, stop talking this way. I don't want to fight with you." She struggled to keep a shrill edge from her voice. "Now, sit down here and let Sidonia take care of you."

I glared at my sister. Behind her, Sidonia stood with the tweezers upraised, looking shocked at the turn of our conversation. Opelia squinted at me with tired eyes. Why did I think Agrippina could understand? She didn't want normal. She wanted me to be like her.

Stalking from the room, I brushed past Gavius in the hall. He seemed torn as to which of us to stay with. When I didn't hear his footsteps behind me on the stairs, I broke into a run.

"Ladies don't sprint!" Aunt Calpurnia said as I passed through the inner garden. *Good thing I'm not a lady yet.*

A startled slave eyed me as I raced out the door. I ran faster once I reached the long walkway on the outside wall of the grand garden. Following a gravel path, I cut away from the cliff and reached an orchard of young trees. The farther from the villa I ran, the better I felt. A stitch in my ribs made me stop, huffing, near the stockyard. A chicken clucked angrily as it scuttled past. And then another. More and more squawks. *A fox in the coop?* I might only be a child, but at least I could chase a fox away. I pushed my way through the small door and saw the cause of their distress.

A boy was crouched in the corner, trying to blend in with the scenery behind him. The inside had been painted by some misguided slave with—of all things—stories of Roman chickens. Unfortunately most of these, such as the one with Claudius Pulcher, involved killing them. The artist had perfectly captured the terror in the birds' eyes as they were being thrown overboard Pulcher's warships.

The boy looked a bit like a terrified chicken himself, with his wide, scared eyes and dirty dark hair standing on end like a comb. He was near my age but painfully thin, and backed away as I approached. I understood his fear as soon as I spotted the iron collar around his neck. Only a brand on his forehead would have more clearly marked him as a slave.

Father always said you must speak to a slave as you would a dog. Firm, but not angry. "What are you doing here?"

He didn't answer.

I took another step forward, the few chickens still in the coop squawking as he disturbed their nests, backing right into a corner. He didn't seem like a killer, but the collar around his neck was a sure sign he'd run away before, and been caught. Of course, he could be lost. "Did you lose your master?"

He continued to stare and I wondered if he had no Latin. "What's your name?" I asked in Greek, the only other language I knew.

"Rafa," he mumbled.

"Don't you know any Latin?"

"Of course, but I do not answer your questions." Rafa stood up straighter, gaining confidence as he spoke. "You will go get me some food, then I will leave. Tell no one I am here."

"Or what?" I demanded. "I'm not going to help you run away and get in trouble. You could be killed."

We stared at each other. Chickens clucked softly around us. Shifting from foot to foot Rafa narrowed his eyes.

"I am a slave by mistake. I must get to Rome and everything will be put right. If you help me, I will make sure you are rewarded." His bold speech was betrayed by the worry in his eyes.

"How can you be a slave by mistake? Either you were born a slave or your people were conquered. Now you'll have to earn your freedom, if you can be dutiful."

"Are you dutiful?" he said with an edge, looking me up and down, taking note of my embroidered sandals and silk dress. "Do rich Roman girls always come get the eggs? I think no. Or are you a hen, to live in this place?" His accent became heavier as his temper flared.

I clenched my teeth. *Even in a chicken coop there was someone to point out my faults.* "At least I know how to get food."

His eyes lit up. "How? Tell me."

"Just open your eyes!" I scooped up the egg at my feet and flung it—it spattered a sticky mess against his face. He retaliated, sending me ducking against the wall. Soon the entire coop was awash with egg drippings and flying feathers. Rafa tackled me with a grunt of frustration and we scuffled in the dried grass.

A large red hen charged, slicing open my forearm with her talons as she jumped onto us. Her angry screeches mixed with mine and Rafa's yells. I shoved the hen away, narrowly avoiding her plunging beak.

"Out! Get out!" I pushed Rafa towards the door, throwing my shawl over the hen to distract her. Before we could get away, the large torso of Gavius wedged its way into the coop, sword drawn. Rafa and I came to a sudden halt. Gavius was staring at us in bafflement, no doubt certain he'd been charging in to stop a murder.

Rafa caught my eye. "You are a very ferocious hen."

"You're an ass." I brushed the worst of the grass from my hair, wincing at the pain in my arm. The red hen had gone screeching from the coop, so I picked up my fallen shawl and wrapped it around the long gash on my arm.

Gavius struggled to keep a straight face as he marched us down the gravel path and through the grand garden where Agrippina was now sitting with Aunt Calpurnia. I didn't think it was funny at all. My face burned at their astonished glances, Agrippina's eyes widening as she took in my appearance, covered with egg, chicken droppings, and grass. I stuck out my tongue at her, but I was worried.

How was Uncle going to react to *normal*?

FIVE

GAVIUS BROUGHT ME AND RAFA into Uncle's records room, the shelf-lined walls stacked with wax tablets and parchment. Thank the gods I wasn't to be scolded in the study, visible to both gardens. Gavius mumbled something in Uncle's ear. Uncle pressed his lips together and gestured for Gavius to wait in the hall.

The silence stretched. Uncle stared at me, a scroll open on the table before him. "Making some new friends, Lucilla?" He approached Rafa and brushed grime away from the boy's neck, inspecting the iron collar. "You're a slave, but not mine. Where are you from?"

"It's my fault, Uncle. I found him in the chicken coop and I should have gotten help—"

"Not now, Lucilla."

"But—"

"Quiet now or step outside."

I closed my mouth.

"Boy, tell me where your master is." Uncle Quintus spoke with soft authority.

Rafa hesitated. He searched the room, looking for a route of escape no doubt, his eyes finally settling on me. Even though he was a slave, even though he'd smeared chicken shit in my hair, I recognized his fear. He was alone, even more than I was, but that hadn't stopped him from defying me. He hadn't given up to Fate. I held Rafa's gaze, and nodded for him to speak.

He bit his lip, eyes flicking to the door then back to my face. At last he took a deep breath and said, "I am from Judea. Captured during the fighting and brought here as a slave. But it is a mistake! My family is loyal to Rome, to Emperor Vespasian. If I am returned, they would be very grateful." He spoke in a sincere rush of words.

"Where did you arrive and when?" Uncle asked.

Rafa stared at his bare feet, black with dirt. "Pompeii. Three days ago."

"I have difficulty believing your story. Most commanders avoid sea crossings this time of year. The emperor himself has yet to leave Judea."

Even I knew the Emperor hadn't made it to Rome, letting his generals and son rule in his stead until he'd finished with the revolt in the province. I held my breath, wondering if Rafa was truly ignorant, or lying.

Rafa's thin face pinched tighter. "We left in the autumn. Making stops in the Aegean and also, I think, Greece. I was not captured by a Roman soldier, but a mercenary. I tell you I am no slave but you won't believe me!" Rafa made a turn to run from the room but Uncle Quintus shot his hand out and caught his shoulder.

"I may believe you, but you must be completely honest with me, boy. Otherwise I can't help you." He gave Rafa another assessing look. "Lucilla, please wait in the hall."

I nodded, glum. Whatever had happened to Rafa, I wasn't going to find out. I trudged into the hall, but Gavius still stood guard at the door so I couldn't even try to listen in. Pacing the corridor, I waited to be called back for some sort of punishment. Father had me whipped only one time—for breaking the death mask of a famous ancestor, Calpurnius Piso Caesoninus. I'd been chasing Agrippina with father's scabbard when it knocked the mask from the wall and the brittle wax had broken. The slave had struck me three times with the rod, and I couldn't sit for days afterward.

Finally, Uncle's voice called, "Gavius, bring Lucilla."

Rafa turned away when I entered and moved to a corner of the room, tears tracking down his grubby cheeks. Uncle spoke a few words to Gavius, who escorted Rafa out the far door. As Rafa left, he looked back at me with a little smile. I didn't know what it meant.

"Lucilla, Rafa told me he provoked the fight. Is that the truth?"

"Well … I know I should have come for help when I found him, but he said I was like a hen and wasn't dutiful. So I threw an egg at him because he told me to get him food and …" My excuses trailed away under Uncle's gaze. "I'm sorry, Uncle. What are you going to do?"

"Rafa wasn't quite sure who his master was, as he'd just been sold while in Pompeii. I'll be making some discreet inquiries. For now, anyone who needs to know will be told he's a slave from your household in Rome, arrived with a few others today. I'll be taking care everyone understands. Including you. Do you understand, Lucilla?" Uncle waited for me to respond.

I nodded, surprised—it seemed drastic to hide Rafa's identity. I didn't know what to make of it. "Are we going to keep him?"

"You may have gotten off to a rough start, but you won't have much to do with him. And yes, we'll keep him until I know what's best to be done." He walked back to his table, shuffling through some documents.

I wasn't sure Uncle was making the wisest decision. If Rafa kept insisting he wasn't a slave, he may try something desperate to escape or—I sucked in a breath. "But what if he's spying on us?"

Uncle looked up. "Why would you think that?"

"Because it's strange, isn't it? Him coming here just after we did, and his story doesn't seem right."

"You're a clever girl, Lucilla, but I'm a reliable judge of character. Rafa is not a threat."

Spiro thought we would be safe if he left. Eudocia thought she could keep us hidden. Adults weren't as smart as they pretended to be. I needed to keep a close eye on Rafa until I knew if Rusticus had sent him.

He walked over and brushed off a bit of grass stuck in my hair. "Calpurnia told me you had a genius for mischief and I've seen how right she was."

I sighed. *Lucilla has a talent for trouble* was one of Aunt's favourite sayings, though I was sure she was the one to bring misfortune—it was only when she'd visited that the worst seemed to happen.

"You must swear you won't put yourself in danger. You are to let Gavius, or whoever is in his place, keep watch."

"I promise, Uncle. But I still don't understand why Senator Rusticus wants to kill us. No matter what Father did, Agrippina and I haven't hurt anyone."

"I have no proof against the senator—or anyone else for that matter. Until I do, I can't be certain of your safety. And enemies of the father are often enemies of the children."

"Like Germanicus," I said sadly. Father had brought us to a party in honour of then-Emperor Vitellius's son, Germanicus. Slightly older than me, with curly chestnut hair and wise eyes, he had politely returned a flower which had fallen from my braided hair. I heard he'd been killed after his father lost the city to Vespasian's legions.

"I will protect you," Uncle said, "if you let me."

"And will you tell me? When you find proof?"

"I will, if you uphold your promise to me."

A clamor at the door made me groan. Aunt Calpurnia was being borne in on her litter. Even though this one was styled as a chair, instead of a couch, her four lecticarii struggled to get her through the smaller door to the records room.

"Why is Lucilla covered in remnants of the chicken coop?" Aunt Calpurnia sat very erect, hands flapping in irritation. "I have tried to give our brother's children the opportunity to settle in, especially after — well," she cleared her throat. "Agrippina has been lovely, trying to take care of Lucilla." Aunt pointed at me. "But she seems to think being dirty is an accomplishment."

This was unfair. Before now, the only mess I'd made was the wine cellar. And when I fell into the water off the dock — but that's because Agrippina stepped on the hem of my dress. I wanted to speak but Uncle shook his head at me and I didn't interrupt. As though I could. She was still holding forth like an orator in the forum.

"… and how am I supposed to raise an eligible young woman — a child of one of the most noble houses in Rome, I daresay — when she would rather appear in public looking like …" Here she faltered, gesturing at my straw-matted dress. My shawl, orange to match, was wrapped around the stinging gash on my arm.

"Calpurnia, you are quite right," Uncle said. I glowered at him, certain he would put up some sort of defence, but he was looking at his sister. He held out his hand to her and knelt so she wouldn't have to crane her neck from where she sat. She took his hand with a sigh of resignation. "I know how difficult it has been for you," he said to her. "Having Lucius's children thrust upon you. How seriously you take your responsibility to raise them." He turned a frown on me. "Lucilla, you must be more considerate of your Aunt's instructions."

Even though he said *instructions* his careful glance at Aunt's condition made my insides squirm. I didn't want to stare, but my eyes slid to Aunt's crippled leg extended on the litter, foot clearly contorted though she kept her dress draped over it. I could imagine few things worse than not being able to walk, forced to be carried from place to place. Not that it ever seemed to slow my aunt's progress.

"I don't have the time to watch Lucilla day and night," she said into the pause. "I must be in Baiae tomorrow, Herculaneum on the Ides, I have accepted an invitation from Poppaea to visit Rome for the Lupercalia—" If her lungs had held out I suspected her schedule could be listed for a number of months ahead.

"Which brings me to make a most fortuitous announcement." Uncle stopped Aunt Calpurnia's next tirade just as she opened her mouth. "We have visitors arriving in several weeks. I received a reply to my letter to Diagoras. You might remember him, Calpurnia. From Rhodos. He was here briefly when we were boys, just before Lucius joined the army."

"Diagoras. Yes, perhaps I remember him. A tall boy with blond hair?" She busied herself twitching the skirt of her dress back in place.

"Yes. But it's not Diagoras who's coming."

"Oh, no? Then who?" she snapped. "You know I dislike your riddles, Quintus."

"Very well, since you refuse to rise to my bait." He smiled to himself as Aunt Calpurnia gave a huff of disapproval. "A man named Nikandros, and his wife who journeys with him. Diagoras had written a while back that his library was in complete disrepair. Scrolls stacked and piled and with no organization whatsoever. I told him that's what comes of pillaging the libraries of the conquered—you may take their knowledge, but it will drown you before it can be put to use. As it turns out, he employed this Nikandros to put the place to rights, and then recommended I do the same. So I've invited him, and he has accepted."

"This is all very well for your library, Quintus—which I might add is in a woeful state. But I don't see how this solves the problem of Lucilla's behaviour."

"It's an easy solution. I'm hoping Nikandros can be persuaded to spend part of his time acting as grammaticus for Lucilla and Agrippina." He turned to me. "You do know how to read and write, Lucilla?"

"Yes, Uncle. Eudocia taught us both Latin and Greek."

"There you have it." Uncle laced his hands together in satisfaction. "They're too old now to need a nurse, and too young to be giving marriage serious thought for at least a few more years. A little structure is what's needed."

"Well, certainly we don't want the girls to be uneducated, but I'd assumed we would buy someone locally. And they will still need to be taught the proper arts for young women. Lessons in the morning. Weaving and spinning in the afternoon. Music. Yes … we can create a very efficient plan for their days …" she was now talking more for her benefit than ours.

I groaned when she said *efficient*. Whenever she had come to our domus in Rome she complained of how the roads were much too inefficient. And our slaves. And the marketplace.

Aunt Calpurnia was lost in thought, no doubt planning all the most efficient ways possible of keeping me inside the villa.

Uncle Quintus took me by the shoulder and led me from the records room to the inner garden. "Don't despair too much. You couldn't expect to run around forever without any responsibilities. I'm not yet looking forward to your marriage, as your aunt is, and there are many things for you to learn that I don't have time to teach. I'm sure you'll find a way to make your lessons fun." He smiled. "Your father and I always did."

"Yes, but you had a brother. I just have Agrippina."

"Don't whine. You're too old for that now. Quintus has an excellent grammaticus and quite enjoys his studies." His expression softened as he spoke of his son. I hadn't seen Quintus in almost a year, and wondered how often Uncle saw him. "He's showing a real aptitude for mathematics." His chest puffed in pride.

"He would," I mumbled. Quintus always seemed to know the cost of everything he touched. "That's fine for Quintus, but what am I going to do with mathematics?"

"Perhaps if I showed you the vast amount of money and property you've inherited, you would take a little more interest. I won't allow you to manage your own affairs when you're older if you persist in acting like an ignorant child." The words stung, but then he gave me a hug, grimy dress and all, the tart scent of his breath filling my nostrils before he pulled away.

I realized my dress smelled much worse than old wine, and my suspicions about our new slave returned. "What are you going to have Rafa do? If he's telling the truth and he isn't a slave, then he probably wouldn't be good at anything, right?"

Uncle considered me carefully. "For now, I think tending the birds would be a fitting task for him. They do tend to wander. When Nikandros arrives, Rafa will attend lessons with you and Agrippina. Some of my overseers are getting older and need help with the record-keeping. It might be the best use for a young boy."

"But what if he's working for the senator?"

He rubbed at his forehead as though it ached. "Whatever Rafa was before, he's a slave of your household now. It's your duty to take care of him, and his to obey. And yours to obey me. Lucilla, you must behave as your status requires. Let the slaves — Rafa included — do their own work. You'll be a lady one day, and you'll never be successful at it unless you practice." He looked over my shoulder, and when I turned I saw Sidonia standing in the doorway. "To your bath now — and an important lesson: ladies do not wear egg."

SIX

AFTER THREE MONTHS OF AUNT'S *EFFICIENT* AFTERNOONS—including one when I got tangled in dangling threads and was forbidden touching the loom ever again—I was ready to lose a finger to my shears and escape weaving. *Four flips should be no problem.*

I walked a few steps away from where Aunt sat, Agrippina at her side. Today all pretense of weaving had been given up in favour of gossip while we waited for our new grammaticus to arrive.

One of the peacocks had found his way here from the grand garden, making a slow strut through the beds. I took two honey cakes from the small table behind Aunt and, crushing one, tossed the crumbs down the path, hoping he would find his way over so something interesting might happen. I stuffed the other cake in my mouth before Agrippina could notice. I'd been overjoyed when Pherenike finally made it from Rome to the villa—even though Uncle's expensive chef thought her pastry recipes weren't fashionable enough. Savoring the sweet, I went back to trying four flips and no lost fingers.

Rafa appeared, slowly tracking the peacock through the garden. I watched him out of the corner of my eye. The sun glinted off the shears as I flipped them with enough force for four rotations—or almost four. I snatched my hand away before the points could nick me, and the metal *pinged* as it hit the tiles.

When I straightened from picking them up, I caught Rafa staring at me and frowned. It wasn't the first time. He quickly turned his attention back to the peacocks, part of his duties as bird-keeper. Peacocks, geese, a few doves. And the chickens. At least it was a kind of justice that he was the one to collect the eggs. Ever since our scuffle in the coop, the biggest red hen, Eris, attacked anyone who came near.

He snuck another glance at me, eyes dark-rimmed as though he'd been up all night, then quickly looked away. Was he reporting back to Rusticus? Planning an escape? Thanks to Gavius's constant following, I wasn't able to find out if Rafa was up to anything. Yet.

"Well, they're here." Agrippina said, resigned, and pointed toward the atrium.

"Cheer up, Agrippina," I said. "You always liked poetry. And now that you're older, you can read the poems Eudocia wouldn't allow before about the *mysterious arts of love*." I mimicked Eudocia's drawling tone. I'd caught more than one pair in dark corners of the villa, and couldn't see anything mysterious or poetic about it.

Agrippina's eyebrows arched skeptically.

"Or how about geography?" Now I was really grasping. "Then you could know more about the value of trade, so when you go to the marketplace you'll know if you're being swindled."

"Lucilla," she sighed, "you are so odd."

I couldn't disagree. She'd filled the long hours of our days with hairstyles and gossip, but Eudocia's absence made my days hollow. Gone were her soft-spoken poems on rainy afternoons, when you could feel the force of the wind that kept Odysseus on his long journey. Or tales told around lamplight at night, her eyes sparkling as she found humour in the folly of heroes, or tearing up at their tragic demise. Her stories combined with Father's of his times in Germania and Britannia, forming a great mosaic in my head—each one a small part of something greater—connecting me to her, and to my father, and our past. I wanted that again.

From the inner garden we peered through to the atrium as Uncle greeted his guests. Or was guest the right word when you were paying someone? They certainly weren't servants; no one could mistake Nikandros or his wife for anyone subservient.

Nikandros himself was tall, taller than Uncle, with light brown hair cropped in loose curls. He seemed fit, though he wore the robes of a philosopher and was unusually pale, likely from long hours indoors surrounded by scrolls. His long nose in a longer face bore an expression of polite civility as he exchanged greetings with Uncle and Aunt.

His wife was almost as tall as he, her black hair tied back in a waist-length braid. She looked Egyptian, perhaps, with a deep bronzed complexion and dark eyes. She seemed to notice everything in the room, and beyond. Her curious gaze found Agrippina and me, and she inclined her head in silent greeting. Considering they'd been in Greece several years with Uncle's friend, they were younger than the middle-aged couple I'd expected—perhaps not even thirty.

Uncle Quintus came toward us with the visitors while Aunt Calpurnia arranged the unloading of their belongings.

"My nieces, Agrippina and Lucilla." He gave us each a gentle pat on the shoulder.

"Yes. You had written you were guardian to your brother's children," Nikandros's voice was a deep rumble, with a bit of a rasp.

"I was going to impose on your abilities and ask you provide them with instruction, as well as tending to the onerous job of organizing my library," Uncle began in his lighthearted way, smiling down at us. "I understand it may take longer to accomplish the task I brought you here for. However, I feel the children must be given at least as much consideration as my scrolls."

"In my experience, what is contained in scrolls is far more valuable than what is contained in the minds of most people," Nikandros said, somewhat impatiently.

Uncle's eyebrows shot up, the corners of his mouth lifting. "Surely it is important the right person be put in charge of providing young minds with thoughts which have value? Then, like a good wine, they can continue to improve with age."

"Ah, but will they be able to comprehend the gift they've been given? Or will their minds be nothing more than a sieve to let the wine flow away, leaving only the dregs behind?" Nikandros scowled, but seemed more annoyed than angry.

Agrippina and I exchanged an apprehensive look.

"Perhaps I have a solution." Nikandros's wife stepped forward. Her gold bracelets jingled as she tucked her arm under her husband's— and gave a near invisible pinch to the inside of his bicep. It twitched.

"Hamitra, my dear, what have you devised?" He looked at her with the closest he'd come to pleasure.

"If our new friend is amenable, I could provide instruction to the girls. Better than spending all day in a dusty library with you." She gave him a mischievous smile. "Trailing after Nikandros for so long, I've had nothing much to do besides study all the volumes he's cared for. If you're uncertain of my competence I would be willing to take any test you devise. But this way Nikandros can continue his work, and your lovely nieces can have their lessons."

Uncle gave Nikandros a questioning look.

"I have no doubt Hamitra would be an excellent grammatica. She is as educated as any man I've known," he volunteered graciously. His arm twitched again.

"Then I'm very happy with this arrangement." Uncle turned and gave us a parting wink, before he led Nikandros and Hamitra through the small garden.

"They aren't what I expected at all," Agrippina whispered.

Even though they were already most of the way across the garden, Hamitra glanced back and smiled.

Curiosity hooked me and I dogged their progress from a distance as Uncle and Aunt introduced them to the villa. Aunt showed them their rooms on the upper floor near the family's quarters, her lecticarii confidently negotiating her small litter on the stairs. Then the main level for dining and lounging and impressing visitors of all classes. Beneath us, though rarely visited, were two levels of cellars, where slaves and freedmen maintained the supplies for keeping our sliver of the empire fashionable. Seventy-six rooms altogether.

Hamitra admired the statues tucked in the gardens, some bronze, some painted in bright colours. Nikandros was diligent in pointing out the stories depicted in mosaic floors and plaster murals—tales of gods and monsters, and the human heroes who tried to defy both but mostly just died for their troubles.

Then Uncle Quintus took them to the small library. It faced toward the sea, and though it was only four or five paces to cross the entire room it had been jammed with scrolls and scroll boxes, many tossed in piles and left to collect dust and mould.

"This library was the personal collection of a certain Philodemus. I'm not sure if you are familiar with his work." Uncle ushered Nikandros and Hamitra into the small amount of available floor space by the door. "He resided here for some time, oh, more than a hundred years ago now. It hasn't been used much in the decades since his death. I've only ever looked at a few of the scrolls. I'm glad you are here. It seems such a waste to let them rot without knowing what could be buried here." He seemed apologetic at the state of the room.

Nikandros cleared his throat. "It would be a shame to lose something valuable. I should have the cataloguing, mending, and copying completed within the year." There was no mistaking the disappointment in his voice.

"Is there a problem?" I could have sworn Uncle's eyes smiled, though his face radiated concern.

"Not at all. Only from your letter and the conversations I had with Diagoras I expected—" Nikandros's gaze swept the room. "More." The contempt on his face marked our home as beneath his notice.

"Ah," Uncle said. "If you'd follow me, I want to be sure you're entirely comfortable during your stay." He led them from the room and through the inner garden, to the side of the villa facing the mountain. I followed behind quietly, suspecting what he was up to.

He pushed open a wooden divider, floor to ceiling height, which folded back on itself in sections to reveal a huge room—more than five times larger than Philodemus' library.

Expensive, ceiling-height scroll shelves lined every bit of wall, leaving only a gap for the large double doors framing the bulk of Mount Vesuvius. And the shelves were full. Bulging. Like one of Pherenike's stuffed chickens on a feast day.

Nikandros looked like a man greeted with an opulent spread. His eyes sparkled, a smile breaking his stern expression. Slowly, he walked the room, peering up at the overflowing shelves, crates, and tables piled with scroll after scroll. A few hundred were carefully arranged on the lower tiers of one of the shelves—the ones my uncle read most often. But hundreds, thousands more, remained in disarray.

"Perhaps this is better?" Uncle asked with good humour as he watched his guests survey the chaos.

"A truly spectacular collection," Nikandros replied with satisfaction. "I look forward to setting this to rights."

"Perhaps it will even keep you busy for a little while." Hamitra picked up a scroll that lay on a table near her and glanced at it. "There aren't even tags on most of these."

"I've never been afraid of the unknown, my dear." Nikandros pushed parchments together in a pile to clear some space at one of the overflowing desks. He started talking quietly to himself.

Hamitra turned to Uncle Quintus. "He won't notice anything until it's time to eat," she said with a laugh.

∞

"He's late. Again." Agrippina lifted her chin and stared at Rafa as he came trudging across the inner garden.

"It's not your place to comment," Hamitra said, with only a touch of annoyance.

How did Hamitra stay so calm? Rafa was often late and Agrippina always mentioned it.

"I can comment on the behaviour of a *slave* any time I choose." She addressed Hamitra, but I could feel my sister's eyes on me.

I shouldn't have defended Rafa when he first started lessons with us, but Agrippina had been so snippy, demanding to know whose slave he was, that I'd claimed ownership and told her to stop jabbering like her monkey. Comparing her braided hairstyle to Medusa's snakes hadn't helped either. Now, months after our lessons began, she still picked on Rafa whenever she was upset with me. As if she thought it would bother me.

"You don't have to be rude to Rafa, just because I broke your mirror." I tried to sound bored, staring at my scroll and concentrating on copying the lines of poetry to my wax tablet.

> With all the others came Camilla of the Volscians,
> Leading mounted troops dressed in gleaming bronze,
> A lady-warrior, hands not trained for spindle and wool,
> But for Minerva's other craft, toughened for the fight—

"He shouldn't be at our lessons. It's inappropriate." My sister's *tongue* was toughened for the fight. Agrippina was like a charioteer circling the racetrack—*this* time around she'd be victorious.

"Maybe you should stop complaining and work harder," I said with a prim smile. "Then Rafa won't beat you again."

"I know you helped him just to make me look foolish."

"He didn't need help for that." The truth was, Rafa was far better at memorizing passages than either of us. Agrippina hated to be shown up, especially in front of Hamitra, who seemed to appreciate his intelligence more than my sister's excellent grooming. Though it marked yet another strange thing about Rafa. Where had he learned to read and write, not just in Latin, but Greek too?

Agrippina opened her mouth, fire in her eyes, but Hamitra raised her hand for us to stop. "Your uncle requires Rafa attend lessons, and that he be permitted to arrive after his morning duties."

"Ladies." Rafa gave a small bow when he reached us at the small tables and chairs set out next to the thin pool.

"What *are* your morning duties?" Agrippina rounded on Rafa.

"I wouldn't want to bore you, domina." Rafa let out an enormous yawn—I'd been expecting it. Whatever these duties were, they were not being done in the morning.

Agrippina glared at him and he covered his mouth hastily. "Look at him!" she said. "He doesn't have any manners."

Hamitra massaged her temple. Her patience couldn't be endless; if Agrippina complained too much, Rafa might be forced out after all. Desperate, I tried to turn the conversation.

"Do you really think Camilla could run across water?" I raised my voice to get Hamitra's attention over Agrippina's nattering. They both looked at me, confused. I pointed at the scroll. "Virgil says she could run across the sea and not get her feet wet. Could she?"

"Of course not." Agrippina interrupted Hamitra. "She would at least have had wet feet, just from touching the water."

"Very sensible." Hamitra gave her a polite smile, covertly gesturing for Rafa to take his seat. "So assuming a slight exaggeration, do you think it possible she could run fast enough to avoid falling in?"

"I suppose, but it doesn't seem likely." Agrippina gave a dismissive sniff and picked up her stylus.

"Why not?" I asked.

"He also writes that she was a warrior, skilled at the spear." She sounded more skeptical of Camilla being a warrior than of her running over water.

"Women can fight. They do all the time. There are the Amazons, and Minerva, and Diana with her bow."

Agrippina pointed her stylus at me. "Minerva and Diana are goddesses. They can do whatever they want."

Hamitra stepped between us, eyebrows raised high, as if struggling to keep her expression serene. "Anyone can learn to fight well. Have you never heard stories of the Spartan women?"

I shook my head. Eudocia had told us about the Spartan army's strict training, but not about their women. "Did they fight in the army?"

"No," she said. "But they did train as rigorously as their men. The Spartans thought if a weak woman could have a strong son, strong women could have even greater sons. So they encouraged their women to learn to fight and withstand hardships, much as the men did."

"But they were wrong, weren't they?" Agrippina said.

Hamitra's eyebrows snapped together. "How do you mean?"

"Spartans don't rule the world. We Romans do. So what they did doesn't matter. Roman women don't fight and the Roman army is the greatest in the world."

From behind us, Nikandros let out a spurt of rough laughter. It startled me, and seemed to surprise Hamitra as well. "You should never discuss history with children, my dear." He passed Hamitra several scrolls, his face settled back into his usual frown. "Or Romans. It's always the army with them. Roman children are the worst of all. They fail to remember anything that happened before breakfast. What about Kynane, sister of Alexandros—a warrior and a ruler in her own right?"

"People can't remember what they've never learned," Hamitra said gently, placing a hand on his arm.

"Then they should remember their ignorance," he snapped.

"I think Camilla could do it." I looked up at Nikandros. "I've seen a man run faster than I thought possible." The memory came as it always did—his movements a blur. Feet not making a sound as he fled.

"Not again." Agrippina moaned.

Nikandros looked at me with reservation; Hamitra, with concern. She crouched and laid her hand on my arm. I hadn't realized how chilled I was, but her touch was hot. "Unusual things do happen," her voice carried sympathy, "and they can be hard to explain."

A violent snore broke the silence. We all turned. Rafa lay on the desk, head on his arms.

Agrippina stood with a huff and stormed from the garden.

Hamitra exchanged an amused look with Nikandros, then she gestured for me to continue my work.

I turned back to my tablet, glancing at Rafa out of the corner of my eye. The one-eyed man might be hard to explain, but Rafa's odd behaviour wasn't. He was doing something late at night, and I was going to find out what.

SEVEN

FROM THE LIBRARY DOOR, a small form slipped away from the villa and down the path toward Herculaneum. I followed, trying to keep my footfalls silent and staying near walls as long as I could. He reached the crest of the bridge over the narrow river, and his silhouette against the town's lights confirmed my suspicion.

Rafa was up to something.

It had taken me weeks to work out the signs, because he didn't go out every night. When he did, the only clue I noticed was that he'd work alone in the library after Nikandros retired. But Gavius would always catch me lurking downstairs when I should be in bed. Sneaking away from him had been the hardest part, but tonight I'd done it, leading Gavius out into the orchard, then backtracking into the kitchen garden and waiting outside the library.

Glad for my dark shawl, I pulled it over my hair and used it to hide my face. Rafa moved with confidence into town, never hesitating or stopping to check his direction. I stayed a careful distance behind. When he turned a corner, I rushed silently after him, peeking from behind the wall to be sure he hadn't entered a nearby doorway.

The few people in the streets paid little attention to either Rafa or myself. Aunt Calpurnia once said Herculaneum was quieter than the Via Appia. She was right. There would have been far more excitement in the tombs outside Rome than in the town on our doorstep. No wild dogs. No parties. Probably not even a pickpocket in this place …

I groaned, spinning in a circle. *Where was he?* I hadn't been paying attention.

Eyes to see, a mind to think—I should never skip that second part.

I hesitated at an intersection. Left or right seemed equally unhelpful. The sky was pitch dark and only a few small lamps shone in scattered windows. Buildings rose tight together and high over my head, leaving me at the bottom of a ravine. I couldn't see either mountain or bay as landmarks.

Daydreaming had gotten me lost, and maybe worse. This may not be Rome, where even the lowest social climber needed bodyguards flanking them at night, but it was still unsafe for a young girl to be wandering alone after dark.

The prickle began at the base of my spine and tingled up to my neck, hundreds of tiny pins jabbing me.

Someone's watching. My heart thudded against my ribs. *Why didn't I at least bring a knife?*

I stepped back and pressed myself to a wall, looking up at the windows overhead. Taking soft, shallow breaths, I tried to focus on my options. I could wait here until someone came by and then ask for directions—but it could be someone unsavoury. I could try to retrace my steps—but then I would lose any chance of finding out what Rafa was up to.

Or … I had to guess which way he went.

I squinted, trying to see down the street to my right, which seemed the likeliest. Soft light filtered out onto the paving stones from half-shuttered windows. Occasional bursts of laughter echoed in the distance. Maybe a taberna? If people were drinking it could be dangerous to get too close. But Rafa might be meeting someone.

Back to the wall, I inched down the street toward the light. Each step seemed louder than the last, my sandals shouting *come and get me.*

At last I caught sight of Rafa's thin frame pressed up beside a large wooden door, which stood open for patrons. With a deep breath of relief, I hurried toward him, my feet scuffing clumsily. He turned with a start and his eyes widened in surprise. Rafa crept away from the taberna and pulled me into the alcove of the next entrance.

"What do you think you're doing?" He was angry.

"I'll ask you the same question!" I hissed back. "What is my slave doing outside a taberna in the middle of the night?"

"It's not the middle of the night and I'm not your slave!"

"Uncle registered the documents. You're part of my household and you answer to me."

"How can you take that seriously? You know I'm not really a slave," he said, with a growing edge in his voice.

"I know nothing of the kind. You've never told me. But if you want to deny you're my slave we could take this to the magistrate. Maybe you'd tell *him* who you really are!"

Rafa lunged at me and we went down hard on the pavement. I managed to roll on top and slapped at him when the doorway behind us sprang open and a voice called out, "*Ad oculos!*"

The contents of a chamber pot drenched us.

"Oh, *merda!*" I groaned.

"Bless His Name. It's *not* shit," Rafa said with relief.

It could have been much worse, but even in the dim light from the doorway I noticed my hands stained with something blue. My skin began to tingle.

"Oh. I didn't see you there," a girl said in a soft voice, eyes wide with shock.

"Justa!" a woman called from inside. "What are you doing—" A tall woman, thick black hair tumbling in loose waves, came to the door. She scrutinized us. "You don't live nearby."

I shook my head, trying to place how I recognized her.

"Please forgive my daughter. Come in and clean yourselves up."

I looked the woman over, then glanced at Rafa—he nodded.

∞

"What in the name of Hygeia is this stuff?" I was scrubbing my skin raw with a pumice stone. It wasn't helping. Rafa stood, a soggy blue mess, dripping onto the packed dirt floor.

"It's dye," the girl, Justa, finally volunteered.

"Obviously." I gave up with a frustrated splash, nearly knocking over the basin, and tossed the pumice to Rafa. "This is all your fault," I muttered as he dunked his head into the water.

"Why are you tossing blue dye into the street?" I turned to face Justa. Her blue-green eyes drooped sadly, and I tried to remember my manners. "I meant to say, why do you have a basin of blue dye in the first place?"

Justa perked up a little and showed me to a corner of the small front room. "I'm trying to make a less expensive purple dye. It's usually from murex shells, but they cost a fortune to import and are almost impossible to raise. I thought if we could make a cheaper kind, we could get some trade with richer—" She gave me a timid smile. "I mean a better class of people. I'm just glad it wasn't a try at making soap. The last time I made that, I scarred myself with the lye." She showed me her hand, the back mottled with pinkish skin amidst her burnished tone.

"This is Justa's shop. She sells dye and fabric—all kinds." Her mother, who had introduced herself as Vitalis, gestured to the other side of the small room. Shelves were stacked with a modest collection of linen, and even a few lengths of cotton and silk. "Justa makes most of the cleansers and dyes that we—she—is practicing with to lower costs." She smiled proudly at her daughter, who didn't look much older than me.

I reached out to touch one of the deep red silks but stopped before my stained hand could do any damage. The silk and cotton alone were worth more than the shop.

Perhaps my puzzlement at their situation showed, as Justa softly confided, "Mother convinced my father to invest—for my future. But Stephanus is her former master, and his wife doesn't appreciate his generosity to me. She'd be in open revolt if Mother owned any of it." She glanced at her mother, who was pouring water into several clay mugs. "She's working hard to keep me respectable."

"It's what every mother wants, isn't it?" I said with a nod.

Rafa finished toweling off, though by the state of him I didn't hope we'd return to our normal colours anytime soon.

"At least you can wash piss away," Rafa said with frustration.

"I am sorry," Justa said for the tenth time, bringing Rafa a cup of water. "I normally dump the failures down the latrine in the back."

Rafa and I exchanged a look.

"The latrine is clogged," Vitalis explained. "Which usually means there's some body or other stuffed down there."

"We told the vigiles, but they said it wasn't their job to clean the latrines, only to recover bodies or stop fires," Justa said.

"I'll go and speak with an aedile tomorrow. One of the council's slaves will have to go down there and find where it's blocked up."

I wrinkled my nose and looked at Rafa in disgust. "Don't ever run away again or I'll make that your job for all time!"

"I wasn't running away," he said. "I've come to town before on errands for your Uncle and always returned."

"Are you going to confess, yet? What were you doing?"

Rafa took a deep drink from his cup, then fixed me with a serious gaze. "Not much, just waiting at the taberna for someone important."

"But—oh." I shut my mouth, feeling my face redden. Could Uncle be using him to collect information on someone in town? But who? The senator, I hoped. Now I knew he was watching someone, maybe I could convince him to tell me more.

"Lucilla needs to get home," Rafa said. "Thank you for your hospitality."

Vitalis wrapped a shawl around her head and shoulders and followed us out the door. "I can't let you walk home in the dark unescorted. I know almost everyone in town, my presence will keep you safe. I wouldn't want something unfortunate to happen."

I was too blue to argue.

∞

It was worse than I'd thought. The entire household was awake, torches ablaze and lights in every window.

I glanced at Rafa as we walked up the gravel path to the entry. The crunch of stones underfoot was louder than a drumbeat. Vitalis followed us into the bronzed light under the portico and wrapped the knocker. A brief scuffing of hurried footsteps came from inside.

Uncle pulled open the door. His expression of relief when he saw me lit a fire of guilt in my stomach. Then his eyes widened as he took in my appearance, and he sucked in his lips. Aunt Calpurnia in her litter sailed up behind him.

"By every name of every god—she's blue!" Aunt Calpurnia bemoaned. Her glare fell on Rafa, hunched at my side, as we were drawn into the atrium. She tore her astonished gaze away and raised it to Vitalis. "Excuse my rudeness in not greeting you properly. Thank you for returning Lucilla to us …"

"Calpurnia," Uncle said. "This is Petronia Vitalis, freedwoman of Petronius Stephanus."

At last I placed why she seemed familiar. She'd visited Uncle before, probably on behalf of her former master, too proud to go door-knocking himself. Piecing together Uncle's endless stream of petitioners and clients was more complicated than weaving.

"I see." Aunt's short reply conveyed her contempt for Vitalis's status more clearly than if she'd turned her out of the house.

"I'm pleased I could help." Vitalis swept back a lock of unbound hair, eyes drifting around the high-ceilinged atrium. "A young girl out at night can quickly be in more trouble than she expects."

"You have our gratitude." Aunt pursed her lips and turned her glare on her brother.

Uncle Quintus gestured for Vitalis to accompany him. "How is Petronius Stephanus?" Uncle asked as he escorted Vitalis to the door. "I've not spoken with him since his lovely wife and I had that … slight disagreement … over ownership of a slave. Fortunately, Stephanus is a reasonable man and agreed that it wasn't a matter for the courts."

Vitalis cleared her throat. "Yes. He takes great pride in his capacity for reason, though Themis doesn't care so much for it, herself." Her face tightened, eyes narrowing with distaste.

"It often happens that husbands and wives don't see eye to eye," Uncle said. "Please know we *are* grateful you've brought our niece back. I would be even more grateful if this incident weren't well-known in town."

She gave a small nod. "I don't see any reason why it would be. My daughter was so distraught at damaging Lucilla's dress, I don't think she would ever speak of it." She paused, lacing her fingers together. "Would it be possible for her to call on your niece in the future to apologize?"

Uncle's smile seemed forced. "That would be delightful."

"Quintus!" Aunt Calpurnia called. "We will be waiting in your study." She snapped for her lecticarii to move her litter. "Lucilla, come. And bring that boy."

Rafa and I trudged in her wake, Uncle following after seeing Vitalis out the door. We marched into Uncle's study and were given the appearance of privacy, though far more gardening and cleaning was happening beyond the columns than seemed necessary at night. Rafa and I stood before Uncle's desk while he settled into his chair, Aunt's litter lowered to one side.

"That one was doubtless the cause of this mess," Aunt began hotly, pointing a bony finger at Rafa. "He must be sent to the fields, or sold. We can always buy another literate slave. He's far too ungrateful of the opportunities he has with a family such as ours. Anything could have happened to Lucilla—in town! At night!"

Uncle pinched the bridge of his nose. "I would rather discuss this in the morning, Calpurnia."

"Nonsense! I'm leaving to take the waters in Baiae tomorrow, or had you forgotten?"

From the look on Uncle's face, it was clear he hadn't forgotten at all. "Lucilla, how did this happen?"

I scratched at my arm, still tingling from the dye. The fact that I followed Rafa out of the villa was bad enough, but I knew Aunt would demand to know why. If she learned he was a runaway, she'd sell him faster than Jupiter throws lightning. There was no good reason for me to be following him, but … "I snuck out and Rafa tried to stop me."

Rafa was staring at me, gape-mouthed, so I stepped between him and Aunt Calpurnia's narrowed gaze. Uncle regarded me with a curious expression. "And how did you end up," he cleared his throat, "… blue?"

"Well, when Rafa and I were fighting, a girl threw a basin of dye on us and—"

"You were fighting?" Aunt sucked in a breath and pointed at Rafa again. "He attacked you?"

I stared between her and Rafa, who'd gone pale, and slowly realized what she implied. "It was only—"

But she spoke over me, addressing Uncle. "Quintus, you must see him punished at once. A beating may not be enough. A slave raise a hand against his master? This can't be allowed—Gavius!" Her voice was shrill, her hands fluttering.

"No!" I yelled at her. "You're not beating my slave or executing him either!"

"You still have much to learn, girl! We live in the shadow of Vesuvius, where that barbarian Spartacus dared lead a slave rebellion. We cannot allow our family to appear so weak that even our slaves take advantage of us."

"No one saw." I kept Rafa behind me. "And you don't have the right. He's mine, not yours."

She opened her mouth, but Uncle stopped her. "Lucilla's right, Calpurnia. You're upset, but only Lucilla or her tutor—who is me, and not you—has the right to decide about her property. And the boy did make sure Lucilla was found before any serious harm was done."

"It was my fault," I said. "I'll take the punishment." I deserved Aunt's anger for being so impulsive, and I wouldn't allow Rafa to bear it for me.

Aunt refused to look at either Uncle or me, but instead flicked her hand to be carried from the room. "I will deal with you when I've returned," she said through a thick sniff. "Or whenever you're no longer such an unnatural colour."

I slumped with relief as she left, but when I turned to Uncle, his disappointed expression made my guilt flare fresh.

He sat wearily back in his chair, the wood creaking. "Lucilla, you gave me your word to keep safe. This is not what I expected of you." He gestured for Rafa and me to leave.

Outside the study, Gavius waited to escort me. Exchanging a last glance with Rafa, I went upstairs and he went down.

EIGHT

"I'M NOT SUPPOSED TO TALK TO YOU ABOUT IT," RAFA SAID. He tried to step around me, but I stayed fixed in the doorway to his small room, blocking him in. I crossed my arms, examining the tiny space. Cot against one wall, with a sliver of floor space beside it. He was fortunate to have a room of his own.

"It would be a shame if you had to share a room with some smelly Thracian, like Cisseus." It seemed a good threat.

"Lucilla, stop being such a pest. You wouldn't break an oath to someone, why expect that I would?" He scratched at his right ear, which was still blue, along with most of the right side of his face. The left had escaped decoration.

"Can you at least tell me if you were spying on Rusticus?"

He heaved a sigh. "You're not going to let it be, are you?"

"Of course not. I need to know if he murdered my father so I—" I stopped, knowing it sounded foolish.

"You want to kill him?" Rafa asked in a whisper.

I nodded, not wanting to say the words aloud.

He looked down at his hands, shoulders hunched to his ears. "I know how you feel."

"Then tell me. Did the senator murder my father?"

"I don't know. Your uncle has me following the senator whenever he comes to Herculaneum." His face was carefully expressionless. "Almost none of the conversations I've overheard seem worthwhile. When he was here last he mostly talked about his gambling debts, complaining Fortune deserted him." Rafa rolled his eyes, disdain for Lady Fortune clear.

"You've been doing this for so long, that can't be everything."

He shuffled his feet, gaze lingering on the blue streaks covering my arms. "Once he was talking to an older man—his father-in-law I found out—who mentioned your father's name. Rusticus said, 'told him she would be the death of him. But he persisted, so I knew I had to end it.' Then a crowd got in my way and I wasn't able to learn more. I've told all of this to your uncle. You must trust him."

The words spun in my head. *She would be the death of him.* "That's it then—he did it."

"No. It's not proof of anything. There are other—" He stopped, a pained expression on his face.

"Other what? Other people? Who?"

Rafa grunted. "I heard your Uncle talking to Spiro—he's been searching in Rome the way I've been searching here. He asked if it was possible Vitellius could have been behind the attack."

"The old Emperor?"

"Apparently he'd done it before. Killed a senator who made him an heir under his will." Rafa's face twisted into a lopsided sneer. "The Emperor was very short of gold at the end."

"He was after our money?" I felt sick, legs collapsing under me. I thumped down on Rafa's cot.

He sat next to me. "No. Spiro said there was no way for Vitellius to claim any of it. So unless there was another motive, they ruled him out. But I only know a bit of what your Uncle has been doing to search. This was why—" he stopped again, muttering to himself in frustration.

"Why *what*?" I had to speak slowly to keep from shouting.

He mumbled something.

"Tell me or I'll sell you after all!"

Rafa frowned. "Why your uncle told me not to tell you. He said you'd get carried away when there was no proof."

"No proof? The senator is the only person who needed Father dead, and he all but confessed it! What more proof do we need?"

"What about the man who attacked you? With one eye? If we connect him to the senator, that would be proof."

I let out a slow breath. "You won't believe me—no one does."

He waited, eyebrows knotted with concern.

"I don't think he's human."

Silence lingered a long moment. "You mean an animal? Or a

giant?" He asked with confusion.

"No. He looks like a man ... but ... just not ..." At least he wasn't laughing. "He threw Gavius farther than I could throw ... well ... anything. And he moved fast—too fast. What kind of creature is that?"

Rafa ruffled his hair, eyes wide. "I don't know, but I've been spending a lot of time in the library. Maybe I'll find something there." He let out a slow whistle. "Your uncle didn't explain it that way."

"I told you. Nobody believes me."

"He might not believe you, but trust your uncle. I do." His openness put a stop to my creeping anger.

"Tell me why. Why do you trust him?"

"I gave my oath I would tell no one." His voice held regret, but I didn't care.

"Then I can't trust him, or you."

"We're only trying to protect you."

"Perhaps Uncle is trying to protect me. Or perhaps he's the one trying to kill me." The idea was sudden, but it could very well be true. "No one will tell my why he and Father refused to meet." I'd asked Uncle, that first day, but he never told me. And refused every time since until I'd at last given up.

Rafa looked at me with deep disappointment, but passed me a bowl of dried figs from under his bed. He took one and began chewing loudly. My fig was tough and I chewed louder, glaring at him; willing him to tell me why I should trust people who kept things from me.

Could I really trust anyone?

My uncle? My aunt? Rafa had been annoyed with my accusation, but I'd dismissed the idea as quickly as I'd voiced it. Either of them could have had Agrippina and me killed in many ways, with no one the wiser. And I didn't feel their affection for us was false. Aunt Calpurnia would be much more pleasant if she was trying to kill me.

Who else? Any of our slaves or freedmen? I wondered again at Spiro's withdrawal from my life when we'd been so close. But he had nothing to gain—he hadn't even been freed by Father's will, and I knew his grief was real. I shook my head and took another fig. Not Spiro.

Surely a slave or freedman would have just poisoned our food, or slit our throats in the night, not hired murderers to attack us. And no one, it seemed, knew about the poison which killed Father ... the shock of his rotted face never faded. I could barely swallow the last bite of fig.

"Lessons," Rafa mumbled.

Giving up on plots I couldn't unravel and figs I couldn't chew, I trudged upstairs with Rafa to the inner garden. I tried to focus on my Greek hexameters, but it was hard to care about Aeneas and Aphrodite with my mind in such turmoil.

Bit by bit I uncoiled the lines before me. The Greeks had gotten past the gates of Ilium by hiding warriors in a massive wooden horse. It was a good plan, but only because the people of Troy didn't listen to anyone with sense and brought the horse inside the city. So now the city's being sacked and Aphrodite steps in to protect her son Aeneas during the fighting ... except she gets a cut on her wrist and can't go on. *What sense is that?* She's a goddess, and immortal besides.

I tapped my stylus on the wooden table, irked at wars and heroes and temperamental gods. "Is immortality boring?" I asked Hamitra.

"Pardon?" She started, whipping her head to stare at me from where she was working with Agrippina.

"Do you think the gods are bored? Is that why they care so much about what mortals are doing?"

Hamitra tilted her head to one side. "I wonder if it's not boredom, so much as humanity." She neared and looked over my shoulder at the verses of the *Iliad* I'd been reading. "The gods are so remote, sometimes cruelly indifferent to the lives of mortals. Yet here Aphrodite interferes to protect her own son. I don't think she would have cared to visit Troy for the next century if it hadn't been her own family being threatened."

"She certainly didn't care that she started the bloody mess in the first place, causing Helen to fall in love with Paris," Rafa said.

I nodded agreement.

"Perhaps the gods worry that if they don't stay present in the mortal world, they'll lose all compassion," Hamitra said, with a melancholy expression.

"I'm not impressed," Rafa said.

"You have many reasons to feel that way. As the histories show, humanity has long struggled to find goodness. Power, glory, and gold are all much easier to obtain." She fingered the bangles on her wrist. "If the gods had wanted a perfect world, they could have made it so. Perhaps this world is perfection for them, just not for us." Hamitra laughed gently, her mood seeming to lighten in an instant. "One day I hope to have a better answer."

An old slave hobbled toward us. "A visitor for domina Lucilla."

Hamitra waved us away, bracelets tinkling.

Sunlight shone through the wide opening in the atrium's ceiling, the water sparkling in the pool underneath. Justa hovered self-consciously next to the pool, her eyes widening when she noticed Agrippina and Rafa behind me.

"Lucilla," she greeted me. "I came to offer my apologies again for the damage I caused you. And," she rushed on, "you should know they did take a body out of the latrines this morning—his head was almost clean off!"

Agrippina made a strangled sound.

"As amends I would like to make a gift of some fabric, to replace the dress I ruined." Justa pointed to several bundles on a hand-cart by the door.

"Agrippina, this is Petronia Justa, who owns a fabric shop in town," I introduced. "My sister, Calpurnia Agrippina," I continued for Justa's benefit.

Agrippina, smiling as though she'd found another pet, patted Justa's slender shoulder. "That is a very appropriate gift, and more than my sister deserves after her reckless behaviour." She glared, still upset I hadn't been punished before Aunt left. I thought being blue was punishment enough.

I sighed, expecting Rafa to share my annoyance, but he was staring at Justa with a rapt expression. *Well, she does have beautiful eyes.* Blue-green, bright against her bronze skin. Dark hair hung in loose waves, except for a simple braid pinned around the crown of her head.

Justa gave Agrippina a timid smile. "I would be honoured if you'd choose something for yourself, too."

Agrippina raised a red scarf to her cheek, *oohing* at its softness. Rafa's gaze never wavered.

"You didn't tell me," I whispered to Rafa, "did you find the senator last night?"

"I—I was looking in the taberna. But he might not be here for several more days."

"The taberna? You mean next to where Vitalis and Justa live?"

"I guess so."

"You were spying on her, weren't you?"

His eyes flew to mine and, though half of it was still blue, I saw his nose turn pink. "Is it that obvious?"

"You could blink once in a while. Hadn't you met her before last night?"

"I have no business talking with her. I'm just a slave." Rafa rubbed his nose again, the bitterness in his voice unmistakable.

"Not forever. Just until you're thirty and I can free you legally." It didn't sound as encouraging as I'd intended, and an itching unease filled me, as though I was tangled up in Aunt's loom and didn't have shears to cut my way free.

Agrippina squealed. "It's absolutely decided!" She clutched Justa's hands. "I am going to be Justa's patron."

Justa beamed, excited and embarrassed at the same time, and I tamped down my annoyance, not wanting to spoil Justa's happiness when I didn't even know why I was upset. Patronage from a family like ours could raise her far beyond her current status. She shouldn't have expected to look up higher than the likes of Stephanus—her father— who'd freed her mother. We only looked up to the emperor.

Agrippina pointed a menacing finger at me. "You're not to buy fabric from anyone else, Lucilla. I forbid it."

Raising my hands, I gave a weak smile. "I wouldn't dare."

∞

"Ow, ow!" Agrippina slapped Sidonia's hand. "Stop pulling!"

Sidonia shook out her fingers with a pained expression, then continued to work Agrippina's hair into a spiraling tower. The front was being elaborately curled and pinned, which was the source of the pulling. The back had already been coiled into a high, braided bun, the work of the last hour.

"It looks very … tall," I told Agrippina.

"It's supposed to be tall. But how does it make me look?"

"Grown up." It was the only nice thing to say. It seemed a waste to spend so much time on something that wouldn't last the night.

Agrippina patted the back.

"How are things with your new client? Justa will expect you to help her if she needs it. Father had so many—"

"Just because Father took you everywhere doesn't mean I didn't pay attention to what he did." She took on Father's tone. "A patron's duty is to use their influence to benefit the client's wealth and status. A client's duty is to support the patron's politics and prestige."

"I'm trying to make sure things work out for both of you." Not like the monkey, who'd been sold when he used Agrippina's new slippers as a latrine. "Justa might need you to loan her money to grow her business."

A dreamy look crossed my sister's face. "I have an idea. We should all buy fabric for new dresses from Justa for your coming of age. It's less than two months away you know!" I knew my birthday was coming, clearly she had forgotten. "And you should start having Sidonia dress your hair in the mornings."

Oh no. Next she would start using the word *efficient*.

"Not on your life." I was happy with my hair tied back in a simple queue. But I sighed inwardly. No doubt Aunt would require me to wear my hair up after my birthday.

"You're still blue, brat." She glared at me through her hand-mirror.

"I am not." I snuck a look at my hands. Though had I still been *unnatural*, Aunt wouldn't have let me attend Agrippina's birthday dinner. Somehow, without even noticing, a year had passed since Father's death. And Eudocia's. It felt like betrayal to celebrate without them. As though we sailed on, stranding them on a shore in our wake.

"I almost forgot," Agrippina said. "Quintus sent a note for you with his last letter."

Just what I needed. Another lecture. But if I went to bed without reading it, I would toss and turn all night wondering what he thought important enough to write about. "Ugh. Where is it?"

Agrippina leaned forward to reach it on her dressing table, but Sidonia let out a squeak of terror, hair sliding through her fingers, and my sister stopped.

"Never mind. I'll get it." I found the small scroll and made for the door, mood souring further with every step. "'Night, Agrippina."

"Goodnight." She gave me an absent wave.

Passing between the twin pillars of Gavius and our new guard Sylos, I left Agrippina's room. Sylos followed, and I felt a twinge of frustration. Sylos was even more imposing—and far better at keeping up with me—than Gavius had been. It was no more than I deserved, after making Gavius look a fool the night I snuck away.

I made my way down the stairs; the villa quieter than usual. Aunt

Calpurnia had already retired, planning to visit acquaintances in Pompeii tomorrow and so sailing early. Uncle had gone to a dinner in Herculaneum. Rafa was … I didn't know where Rafa was. But as I was trying to obey Uncle's rules, that was none of my concern.

Reaching the inner garden, I sat on the low wall of the pool and unfurled the scroll.

L

Aunt Calpurnia was reluctant to inform my mother of your latest disobedience, and I must say I was shocked when I heard. I would be failing in my duty if I did not make clear that your actions are not only unsafe, but compromise the honour of our family. Your selfishness cannot continue.

Quintus was angrier than I thought, he didn't even bother to ask after my health.

You are surrounded by ladies of the highest order. Our aunt, Calpurnia, remained dedicated to our family even after such setbacks as the loss of her child and divorce.

My stomach churned. Only Quintus would refer to such losses as *setbacks*. He hadn't even lost a parent.

Lanata is held in high-esteem by her sisterhood. Even Agrippina has chosen to behave in a way which will certainly secure a husband of both wealth and nobility. When I, myself, take a wife, I cannot have your name to be an obstacle to that union.

"You should wait until your voice drops before planning marriage," I muttered. Feeling foolish talking to the scroll, I glanced over my shoulder at Silos, but he didn't appear to have noticed. I pressed my lips together and read to the end.

I do not want to carry our fathers' dispute into another generation. But if your behaviour is anything like what your father's had been, I can understand why my own esteemed parent moved so far away. You must avoid any further trouble at all costs.

Q

Crumpling the parchment, I flung it into the water. *How dare he? How dare he blame my father for what happened?* Quintus didn't know any more than I did, otherwise he would have said so.

I paced around the narrow pool, trying to let the cool breeze drive away my anger.

It was just a letter. Just words. I shouldn't let it bother me.

But it didn't help that he was right … at least about being selfish. I'd cared more about discovering what Rafa was up to than remembering my promise to Uncle.

Halfway around the pool I made up my mind. *Straight to my room, no distractions, no trouble.*

Except I didn't walk to my room, I kept going. Through the atrium. Out the door. My feet had a mind of their own, my anger with Quintus—with myself—spurring them into action. Past the open pavilion, its red curtains turned brown by the near-darkness of the night. Past the swimming pool, overlooking the bay. Down the stairs cut in the rock-face of the low cliff. At the waterline of the beach, I stopped. Waves lapped gently against the shore, soaking my sandals. Before me were the sea and the sky.

I couldn't go any farther.

In the distance, Agrippina screamed. A piercing note, like a javelin cast from the villa above me straight to my heart. The same sound as the day Eudocia died.

I whipped around.

The man with one eye stood on the stair behind Sylos.

Please no—not again.

I wanted to cry out, but my voice was gone.

Sylos looked at me in confusion, as though he thought I'd been the one to scream. With agonizing slowness, understanding spread across his features. He turned to face the danger behind him.

I blinked and they were gone from the stairs. A crunch sounded. The man pressed Sylos into the face of the cliff walling the beach. Sylos thrashed and cried out, but the man's hand covered his mouth and nose and muffled it to a strangled grunt. Snakelike, the man struck, biting into the exposed flesh of Sylos' neck.

Heart hammering against my ribs, I backed down the beach, away from the stairs. Over the rush of surf, it seemed I could still make out the gulping swallows of the man feasting on Sylos. He drank and drank; my stomach heaved. Then, like an animal, he ripped his head back and spit a wad of flesh to the sand.

The man pulled away, letting Sylos fall. His attention fixed on me.

The world grew sharper. Strange details sprang to life. The heavy gold buckle of his sword-belt. His blond hair, carefully combed and bound into a low queue. His eyes—far enough away that both were fathomless black holes.

Gods above, I won't die a coward. This was my chance to know. I forced myself to stand still; to stand straighter. "Was it you who killed my father?"

He took one soundless step after another. "Your sister's fate hangs by a thread, yet you ask after a dead man?" It was clear that for him *dead* was the same as *forgotten.*

"Why did you poison him?"

"I did not poison him."

"But you …" I glanced at Sylos, crumpled in the sand. Blood pooled in a dark puddle under his head.

"How could I not? What could be sweeter than the nectar of life? I am too old to deny what I am."

"What are you?"

He smiled, teeth bared. Mouth and chin dripping with blood.

My breath wouldn't come. I had nowhere to run. No way to fight.

"I wanted to wait," he said, "but the gods don't care for our plans." One good eye shone in the moonlight, alight with anticipation. He drew his sword. "This will be painful, young one. But quick."

I'd been rigid with fear, certain he would kill me the same way as Silos, but now I dropped to my knees with relief. Somehow, the sword was better. The strangeness of it made me smile.

"What an odd child you are. No one smiles at the end."

I clenched my fists. *Why couldn't I have a brave reply?* But my mind was wiped clean.

Then a tall form dropped from the cliff and a swirl of sand and air rose around us. Dark fabric and long hair streamed behind the glint of a curved blade. The man raised his own sword and the harsh clang of their impact echoed from the rock walls. They circled—the man and Hamitra—moving so fast there seemed four swords instead of two.

The hairs on my arm stood on end and I scrambled away, trying to keep them in my sights. Like flickers of lightening crisscrossing the beach, it was impossible to see where one began and the other ended. Sand hung in the air like fog as first one, then the other, would fall but avoid defeat.

Black spots coated my vision before I remembered to breathe.

Crack—the man's blade spiraled into the water and he tumbled the opposite way, landing hard on the rock stairs. Hamitra ran toward him, but he sprang to his feet and fled into the night.

Hamitra turned to face me, breathing deeply, her expression shrouded. She looked from Sylos' body, to me. "Are you all right?"

I nodded, but my legs shook as I got to my feet. Brushing down my skirt, I tried to hide my trembling. Mortals were always punished when they witnessed things they should not. Actaeon was turned into a stag just for seeing a goddess naked. I stared at Hamitra's feet.

"Did he tell you what he wanted?" Her sandals came two steps closer.

Your sister's fate hangs by a thread. "To kill me and Agrippina—" My voice broke and I looked up toward the villa.

Hamitra reached a hand out toward me. I stiffened, and she pulled it back. "Nikandros went to protect your sister. I believe she is safe. I came to find you."

My mind was ablaze with questions and I looked in her eyes for the first time. "You followed me into Herculaneum, didn't you?"

Her lips twitched. "You seem very fond of trouble."

"Are you going to punish me?" I asked in a whisper.

She frowned. "For what? Being attacked?"

"No. For—I mean, like Diana did to Actaeon."

Hamitra gave me a sympathetic smile. "I am no goddess. I have no power to transform you into an animal or a tree or a flower. But you must be more careful, and think before you act." She sounded upset. "And so should I."

I grabbed her hand and she looked at me in surprise. "Thank you. I … I thought he would kill me."

"Fortunate for you, he wasted his opportunity." Her eyes strayed back to Sylos, heavy with speculation.

"What is he?"

All expression left her face as she considered me. "There are many stories where people are gifted by the gods. But gifts and curses are two sides of the same coin."

"But what—"

She raised a hand. "I've just broken one of two rules I live by. You know of my secret, but I cannot tell you more or risk breaking the second."

"What's the second?"

"I don't kill children." Her gaze was hard and serious. "You must never speak of this to anyone. Nothing happened on this beach. You weren't attacked. I'll make sure Sylos' death looks like the work of the man who attacked your sister."

"If I keep your secret, will you protect me?" I had no power to bargain with her, whatever she may be, but I had to ask.

"For as long as we can stay, yes, I will protect you."

Stay silent, and she would protect me. Expose her secret and …

I let out a slow breath. "I understand."

∞

I knelt at the shrine to the Lares—guardians of our home, guardians of my family. My offering of honey cake sat on the altar with the other gifts they received, daily reminders of our devotion.

This night they'd repaid our devotion. I'd been protected. Agrippina had been protected. Though all I knew was Nikandros had arrived in time to throw the second man out Agrippina's window, his body broken by the fall. Sylos was found in the kitchen garden and I'd overheard the slaves whispering about his severed head. I didn't care to know how Hamitra would clean the mess on the beach, but I'd no doubt all traces of the one-eyed man's attack would have vanished.

Aunt had sent me off to bed, four slaves acting as guards. She'd been too busy fussing over Agrippina to notice I hadn't been in my room earlier. They guarded me still, their forms barely lit by the lanterns at the four entrances to the atrium.

I eyed the brightly painted shrine. Carved columns held the triangular roof which protected the altar. Small statues of the Lares seemed to dance in the flickering lamplight. The doors to the altar stood open, only to be closed and locked when our family left for another residence. But the Lares would come with us. Not for the first time, I wondered if my Father had joined them. Or did his spirit wander, restless?

Restless—I was restless.

I had a hundred questions to ask Hamitra. Yet I could not ask even one. I had to hide it all, even from Rafa, and be careful to never let on that there was anything strange about Hamitra and Nikandros. But I was relieved to know I hadn't been mad, seeing the man with one eye for what he really was. *Other than human.*

All I had were eyes to see, a mind to think, and hands to act.

I had seen, and would now be more aware of the danger.

I could think, and perhaps in time gain Hamitra's trust. Maybe enough trust that she would tell me how to defeat such a monster.

But I still didn't know how to act. How could I protect myself if Hamitra left? How could I get revenge on a creature who moved faster and would always be far stronger than me? And until I could, how could I risk confronting the senator?

Lifting my shawl over my hair, I took one of the small figures and clasped it tight.

"Lares, protect us. Guardians, guide me," I whispered.

Asking was easy, but the spirits demanded payment in return. Honey cake wouldn't be enough. I rubbed my thumb over the clay face, gently tracing the outstretched arm.

All I had left were oaths.

"I swear to be dutiful."

A start, but Agrippina was far more dutiful than me.

"I swear to uphold the honour of my family."

Even Quintus was more likely to do that.

"I swear—somehow—to end this threat." Our family would suffer no more at the hands of this adversary. The weight of the lost had made an anchor of my heart, binding me to their memory. It hadn't been possible for me to save Father. I hadn't been strong enough to save Eudocia. But the call of the wrongful dead couldn't be ignored. And they called to me.

In my heart, I feared they would have no peace until justice was done—and neither would I.

NINE

THE DECK OF THE YACHT HAD PLENTY OF SPACE, even with Aunt Calpurnia in her bed-sized litter. Aunt lounged, framed by the billowing blue curtains of the canopy. Her six lecticarii, dressed alike in belted blue tunics, stood silent at their posts. There was an odd uniformity to them, from their close-cropped blond hair to their evenness of height. Though I supposed if their heights weren't matched, the litter would tilt in an unrefined fashion.

Our carriers wore brown, and were not so well matched. Agrippina sighed in contentment, humming and batting at the green curtains of our litter. She seemed almost unaffected by the attack last night.

Of course, no one had been eaten in front of her. Agrippina's scare had been limited to Nikandros charging into her room, stopping the attacker from even drawing a knife.

I rested my head against a curtain post, closed my eyes, and tried to focus on the gentle sway of the ship. *Why did Aunt insist we come?*

Hamitra's encouragement to go with Aunt smacked of being a test. If she was testing my ability to keep her secret, I would test her ability to protect me. Pompeii was still on the bay, but a distance from the villa. I doubted she'd follow.

"It would be so nice if we could visit Cincinnata today," Agrippina said in a breathless rush. "She said in her last letter that Nonius would be here and she knows he's hoping to see me again."

Aunt Calpurnia gave my sister a considering look. "I know your father was good friends with the elder Nonius Arrianus, but you shouldn't form an attachment too young, Agrippina." She paused, taking a deep breath and twitched her skirt over her legs. "There are many noble families who will value you and your connections."

"And our money," I blurted out. Aunt Calpurnia and Agrippina gave me matching looks of disgust.

"Don't be vulgar, Lucilla." Aunt turned back to Agrippina. "Do you understand me, my dear?"

"Yes. But can't we visit? I haven't seen Cincinnata since we lived in Rome." She set her mouth in a firm line. Once my sister fixed on an idea, it was nearly impossible to steer her in another direction.

"I see no reason why we shouldn't continue your relationship with the Nonii. Even though their father doesn't get along with his relatives in Herculaneum, they are still a powerful family. A connection with them would be acceptable. But the younger Nonius Arrianus is only one of many options." She reached over to squeeze Agrippina's hand. "There's no harm in waiting for the right match. You know, the emperor has two sons." She said it lightly, but I could tell the idea held appeal.

"Everyone knows Titus Caesar is infatuated with the Jewish queen." Agrippina sniffed. "Though how can you be a queen without a kingdom?" The gossip about the Emperor's eldest son and Queen Berenice was potent enough even the slaves talked about it, likely because she was older than him. They said she was even living with him in Rome.

"If you can moon over Nonius, why shouldn't Titus love a queen?" I challenged.

"It's not right—she's foreign!" Agrippina countered. "She can't become Empress of Rome."

"Of course not." Aunt gave me a look of warning.

"Domitian is married too," I said to Agrippina in mock sorrow. "So perhaps you should settle for Nonius after all."

"What does it matter if Domitian's married? His wife divorced so they could be together instead. Marriage doesn't last forever."

True enough. "Emperor Vespasian has no wife. It would be easiest if you just marry him. But he's rather old."

"What does that matter? An old man can be just as tender as a young man," Agrippina said.

Aunt Calpurnia snorted softly, the lines around her eyes softening. She seemed … relieved. I hadn't considered that Aunt may have been frightened for us. My gaze flicked to her distorted leg, always hidden. *Had she felt as helpless as I had?*

"Whichever you choose, I wish you much happiness." I tried to keep my tone light, as though this were any other day and my mind was not in turmoil over unknown, murderous creatures.

"You girls are beyond ridiculous." Aunt's lips pursed with a suppressed smile. "We're nearly there. Lucilla, don't rock about on that litter when you're being carried. Remember your status. I don't want to explain why you've fallen into the street."

∞

Good Goddess. This must be how poor Tantalus feels standing all day in water, parched with thirst, only to have it vanish when he bends to drink. I flopped back on the litter's pillows.

Agrippina and Cincinnata had talked of nothing but jewellery since we'd picked up her friend at her villa. Every time it seemed the topic might change—when Cincinnata pointed out a bath or market or temple as we were carried through Pompeii's bustling streets—it somehow transformed back into colours of gemstones, or innumerable styles of fan-shaped earrings.

At least her mother, Matidia, travelled with Aunt. In the time it took her to emerge from her villa and enter Aunt's litter, she'd managed to complain about the frescoes in her dining room taking *forever* to complete, and how the price of *this* and the stench of *that* were absolutely intolerable. Aunt's eyes had glazed over even before the curtain was lowered.

I closed my eyes, letting the sounds and smells of town surround me. The crowd burbled like a river, breaking around the rocks of our guards and lecticarii. Scents hung heavy in the air: peppered sausage being grilled in tabernas; fish sauce stinking in the sun; animals penned in the marketplace. In the distance, sound of hammers on wood and chisels on stone.

"Oh!" Cincinnata let out a pitiful sigh. "And poor Umbricius Scaurus was found ripped apart just over there!"

I jerked upright to stare at her. Agrippina's mouth dropped open.

"Maybe you haven't heard, it *was* just two days ago. But these murders … I'm surprised it's not as talked of in Herculaneum as here.

At first Father thought it was gangs fighting over territory. But almost a dozen people have been found now. Tradesmen, freedmen, slaves." She lowered her voice and confided in a loud whisper, "Even some women—and not just prostitutes. And now Scaurus." Cincinnata's cheeks paled, her slender hands trembled in her lap.

Agrippina propped up higher on her elbow. "But what's so special about him?"

"He was rich—it's not right! His family owns nearly all the garum trade."

"But why couldn't that be gangs, then?" Agrippina asked.

"Is fish sauce a risky business?" I was still lost.

"Every business is risky if you own too much of it," Cincinnata said. "It started a few months ago. People found with their throats torn out, pale as chalk. Some were even …" she swallowed, "… ripped apart entirely. Mother thought it was one of those jungle cats escaped from the amphitheatre, but none were missing."

"And then? What changed?" Agrippina pressed her.

"Nothing."

"What do you mean?"

"Nothing changed. The attacks were all the same. No one gets away from whatever it is. No survivors," she finished in a hushed voice, brown eyes wide.

I wasn't surprised. The man with one eye had likely been prowling the bay, waiting for the senator's order to strike. Brushing the curtain open a crack, I peered into the street. "So no one has any idea what's doing it?"

"Or who is doing it." Agrippina frowned. "I wonder … it does sound like what happened to father. Except he was poisoned also."

"Maybe your father was poisoned and then some animal attacked him when he collapsed." Cincinnata clutched Agrippina's hand. "It's hard to feel safe anywhere."

Agrippina gave me a fleeting look. I shook my head. *Don't do it. Aunt wouldn't want the gossip.*

"What is it?" Cincinnata asked. "What happened?"

"We were attacked again. Last night." Agrippina blurted out.

Opening and closing her mouth several times, Cincinnata at last found her voice. "But it's been almost a year! Why now?"

I snapped the curtain closed. "Why attack us in the first place?"

"Uncle will discover who it is." Agrippina was at least smart enough to avoid mentioning Rusticus. "I'm just grateful Nikandros happened to be walking past and heard me scream. He burst through the door, and pushed that vile man out the window. I was never so happy to see anyone so unpleasant in my whole life."

"He might have been lucky once, but you can't rely on a librarian to protect you." Cincinnata nodded her head decisively. "If I were your uncle, I would hire some mercenaries or gladiators to guard you. That should frighten off whoever is behind it."

"Why not soldiers?" I asked.

"By the time they retire, they're so feeble even Mother wouldn't fear them. *You* would probably be more frightening than some old soldier." Cincinnata gave a tinkling laugh that hurt my ears and turned back to Agrippina.

I would be more frightening. I killed the first attacker, didn't I? If I saved us once, why couldn't I do it again?

The rightness of the thought struck a chord deep in me. This must be what the Lares intended—the way to fulfill my vow. And now that there had been another attack, Uncle couldn't pretend the danger was gone, or that we were truly safe. Father wouldn't have wanted me to leave my fate to Lady Fortune. He'd always warned against such blind trust. Plus, I had a feeling She didn't like me much.

"There he is!" Cincinnata said. She and Agrippina broke into giggles, peering at a group of youths, some in their first adult togas judging by the self-conscious readjusting of their folds. One of the young men separated from the group and walked toward our litter.

"Ladies, I'm pleased I happened to see you today." He gave an awkward bow and I barely recognized Nonius from the last time we met. He was a foot taller and had sprouted fuzzy facial hair. Combined with his blotchy complexion, he resembled an overripe peach.

He helped Cincinnata and then Agrippina off the litter and they went to speak with Aunt. I clambered down the other side after them. Guards surrounded us like a living wall.

"Aunt Calpurnia, I would like to introduce Gaius Nonius Arrianus," Agrippina began the introductions. Cincinnata exchanged a grin with her mother.

"Ah, yes," Aunt said. "We are having a dinner next month to celebrate Lucilla's coming of age. Your mother wasn't sure if you would be returning to Rome, or would be able to attend."

"I would be pleased to come." Nonius bowed his head.

Aunt nodded and directed her lecticarii to continue on. The four of us couldn't all fit in the second litter, so we followed behind, Nonius walking between Agrippina and his sister. Agrippina's dimples grew deeper as he began a story about his recent stay in Rome.

My eyes darted around the crowds and shops, an uncomfortable feeling settling over me. We passed a taberna, men and women jostling for table space to avoid eating in the street like beggars. A grimy child grabbed a scrap of bread that fell to the stones, receiving a kick as he scurried away with it into the alley. And there, in the shade of the alley, a tall figure stood stone-still under a tattered awning. She clasped her hands near her waist, gold bangles flashing.

Hamitra.

The histories spoke of those who were gifted beyond the ordinary: Hercules, with his mighty strength; Helen, the most beautiful; Romulus and Remus, founders of Rome and sons of Mars. Whatever else she was, Hamitra had lived up to her word. Her presence bound our bargain. But even if she protected me now, she couldn't do so forever. I had to find a way to do it myself.

I stared too long, and tripped over a large stone in the roadway. I fell against Agrippina, who toppled into Nonius' arms. After a string of apologies, we continued our walk.

When I glanced back, Hamitra was gone.

Agrippina's gaze met mine and I expected annoyance, but her expression was pure gratitude. In a daring breach of decorum, Nonius held her arm, helping her along as though she might sink into the paving. *Next time I'll throw her at him. Maybe she'll forgive what I'm about to do.*

TEN

I waited two whole days after returning from Pompeii before approaching Uncle. I'd planned my strategy. First, remind him someone was trying to kill me. Then, persuade him it would be best if I knew how to defend myself.

But as I approached him in the garden, almost dizzy with nerves, my mouth blurted out, "Uncle, I killed someone."

He looked up from his reading, eyes round in mock-surprise. "What, just now?"

"When we were coming here—Agrippina and I."

"Yes, I remember." He rolled up his scroll and placed it on the bench beside him. "Is it bothering you?"

"Not really." I winced a bit at how cruel I sounded. "It's just … he was going to kill us, and he killed Eudocia, and I don't think I should feel guilty about killing someone like that."

He gave a slow nod. "Sensible. What do you want to discuss?"

For a moment I was speechless; I hadn't intended on being so blunt. "I want to learn how to fight."

Uncle seemed bemused by our conversation—the way I'd felt when Eudocia was first teaching me Greek. I tried to keep up, but was always a sentence behind as I translated her words.

"Quintus hasn't even started weapons training yet, and he's fifteen. Aren't you a little young to be planning on joining the army?"

My heart sank. He wasn't taking this seriously. Why would he? What proper girl wanted to learn how to fight? I rallied. "The Spartans trained their daughters."

A huge smile cracked his face. "So those lessons are paying off already, are they? Spartans—what a good subject. The Battle of Thermopylae was always an inspiration for me."

I nodded, afraid to say anything that would reveal my complete ignorance of Thermopylae.

"I have a lesson for you as well. It's a saying I have lived by for some time and perhaps will do you good. A friend of mine once said, 'What cannot be changed, must be endured.' So tell me, what is it to be? Can I take you off this path where I see only obstacles? Or do I endure it?" His eyes were deep with an emotion I couldn't name.

I looked at my sandals. "Don't change me."

"You must consider one more thing: Can you endure it? It's not easy to follow a different path than the one expected of you. There is comfort for most people in being like others. Think on it." He gestured for me to leave.

I left, not sure if I'd gotten what I'd asked for, or something more. *Could I endure it?* Endure Agrippina's disgust and Aunt's dismay? Endure gossip and speculation from our slaves and freedmen? Endure the work that lay ahead?

I must endure it; it was the only chance I had to survive.

∞

I paced the large garden, switching between views of Uncle's study and the bay. At last I heard footsteps approach. One set echoed loud, the other a soft shuffle.

They came into sight—a bent old man with a wild shock of white hair, leaning on the arm of a middle-aged warrior. The old man let his younger companion guide him, his heavy-lidded eyes without focus. They passed through the garden and stopped in front of me.

"Ah, Lucilla," the old man said. "Your uncle has told us much about you."

He didn't look at me when he spoke and I wasn't sure if he knew where I was. I glanced up at the younger man in question.

"Look at me when I speak to you," the old man reprimanded. "*I* am your tutor. This lumbering bear is simply my instrument." He pointed, and the unnamed fighter moved to lean against a tree. "For your first lesson, you'll attempt to strike me."

This was a farce—to hit a blind man wasn't a lesson. *Uncle hadn't been serious.* I'd asked for too much; he thought I wasn't ready. That I was too young or too weak.

Almost of its own will, my hand flew out to slap the old man's face, which was not much higher than my own.

Smack. His hand connected with mine, knocking it away. I rubbed my smarting knuckles and stared at his innocent expression.

"Is that all you can muster? Hilarus and I had been led to believe you had spirit. Come now—again!"

I hit out with my left, then my right, then my left again, but every move I made was blocked by a quick flick of his arm.

Groaning in pain, I inspected the red marks on my hands and forearms. I huffed out a breath and looked up at him—he stared right into my eyes. *He's no blinder than me.*

I took a step back.

"You cheated," I said.

"I did not. You did."

"How did I cheat? I didn't pretend to be blind!"

"No. Much worse. You refused to see."

I opened my mouth, but didn't know what to say.

He continued in a kinder tone. "Don't feel aggrieved, girl. This trick has worked on many opponents, all of whom were older and wiser than you. Sit down near Hilarus there. It's time for our proper introduction."

We moved into the shade of the tree where Hilarus stood, and sat on a marble bench facing the pond. A fountain trickled nearby.

"I am Petrus. I was a soldier, then a gladiator, and then an actor. I have been many other things as well, I might add. However, once you have incurred infamia there are very few career options open to you."

"Is that where you learned how to pretend to be blind, acting?"

"Ah, yes. I was the finest Oedipus to grace the stage at Ephesus for two generations. But don't distract me from your lessons, girl. The first and most important lesson of any fighter is to observe your opponent. This must become as easy to you as breathing, for you won't have time to reflect on what you see. Only to act. Your body must be ready to move without your mind interrupting. Your opponent will try to deceive you in many ways, though few will be as cunningly displayed as my blindness, which is very well done if I say so myself. But they'll show you false weakness, or false strength. If you're unwilling to see past their facades then it's your fault when they put the knife in."

"How will I know these things—about false weaknesses?" This is not the lesson I'd been expecting.

"Haven't you been listening? You will observe. You will begin now and practice every day. You will observe everything around you, but most especially people. Watch them waking, and sleeping, and talking, and eating. Find all the ways they're deceitful." He ran his hands across the white stubble on his chin as he observed me. "You look doubtful and so you should—it's a mighty task to see all the instances of deceit in people. We seem to lie even more than we … well, perhaps that analogy may wait until you are older."

From behind us, Hilarus let out a grunt of laughter.

I didn't understand the joke—but I would when I was older. *Always when I'm older.*

"Ah, you are getting angry again."

Curiosity cut through the creeping heat. "How did you know?"

"I have eyes that are still good enough. Your body tightened, like a cat about to spring up a wall, and your breath stopped for a heartbeat. Also you frowned—usually very telling." He smiled and I laughed, just a bit. "So that is your task—to observe all you can and learn what it means. This will be difficult and will take many years, but luckily you are still young. Also, I think you'll enjoy secretly observing people."

"Why?"

"Even before I was a soldier, I was a child, and it was my favourite pastime. Just watch you're not caught at it. People won't be easy around you if they think you're too interested." He slapped his hands together and reached for his cane. "Well, Hilarus, I had my doubts about training a girl, but this one may be acceptable. We'll return tomorrow and see how much of today's lesson has taken root."

Petrus sprang to his feet and I realized the appearance of being old, while not exactly false, was a deception too. He walked easily from the garden. Hilarus gave me a last skeptical look before he followed.

I wasn't sure what to think.

∞

Aunt Calpurnia was horrified when she found out. I tried to follow Petrus's instructions and observe their conversation undetected, but there was no chance of that. I was hauled into Uncle's study.

Vulgar, *undignified*, and *scandalous*, were said quite a bit. To my relief, Uncle held firm and eventually all that was left was for Aunt to proclaim, "If you insist on this ridiculousness, she will learn to fight respectably — dressed like a proper lady!"

"Calpurnia, what are you talking about?" Uncle asked.

"Do you intend our niece to fight in the amphitheatre, or join your old legion?"

"Neither of course. This is for her protection. Lucilla will feel safer if she knows how to take care of herself. And I will as well. Someone has killed our brother. Has tried to kill our nieces more than once." He paused and sighed, shoulders slumping. "Lanata has also been targeted."

Aunt sucked in her breath, more shocked than I was.

"They would kill a Vestal?" she said in a hush, as though voicing it was criminal. Aunt held out her hand for mine and I walked to where she sat, letting her pull me down beside her on the litter.

"Some are saying it was divine judgement," Uncle sounded skeptical. "An interesting proposition, given the turmoil since Nero's suicide. Though it appears Vespasian may bring stability at last."

"Is Lanata …?" Aunt's question faded away.

"She is safe. Fortunate for Lanata the poison meant for her was wrongly delivered. It was the Vestalis Maxima who drank it."

Not so fortunate for the Chief Vestal.

Aunt Calpurnia whispered to the gods for protection and gripped my hand. I clutched hers back, relieved Lanata had been spared. The one-eyed man was a powerful opponent, but he and the senator weren't invincible. They failed last year, and failed again this spring.

"Lanata has been elected by the college of Vestals to be the next Vestalis Maxima." Uncle didn't seem impressed. "She's young, but she has much to recommend her to the position."

Aunt shot him a withering look. "Her mother, her fortune, and this latest twist of Fate, is no doubt what you are referring to. You're an old cynic, Quintus."

"Others have called me far worse, sister."

I thought of my own sister. Agrippina was going to be beyond jealous. Not even twenty and Lanata was the Vestalis Maxima? Of course, there were only six possible candidates for Vestalis Maxima at any one time, and Aunt was likely correct—Lanata's wealth combined with her mother's influence as a past Vestal would have been a powerful combination. Agrippina might actually have to marry the emperor to top this.

Uncle laid his hand on Aunt Calpurnia's shoulder, then turned to me. "The poison was the same as the one which killed your father."

I didn't want to remember, but the vision of Father's rotting face couldn't be stopped. I sat next to Aunt, forcing myself to focus on Minerva instead. *Look at the statue. See her beauty.* The Lady's eyes gazed into the distance, cold and impassive. The gods were always impassive. Why did we think they cared about us mortals? We died so easily and caused so much grief—it would be like me caring about Eris the chicken. I refused to let my tears fall, blinking until they faded.

"This cannot be a coincidence and we cannot ignore the threat." Uncle's calm voice worked to soothe some of Aunt's aggravation.

She took a few steadying breaths. "Very well. Such cowards won't be the ones to lay our family low. But," she held up a finger, "I insist Lucilla learn to fight respectably, wearing proper clothing—" she waved her hands as Uncle tried to interrupt. "Dresses, shawls. She won't fight barefoot, or in tunics and things that legionaries wear. She won't be attacked wearing armour so she won't train that way."

Even Uncle couldn't dispute this logic. He nodded, giving me a half-smile.

I smiled back. *If that was the cost, I could pay it.*

Aunt Calpurnia re-adjusted her veil and seemed to regain some spirit. "And you will not interfere with how I explain this to people. I'll do my best to ensure Lucilla's—and our—reputation is protected. This must not become well known if she is ever to make a decent marriage."

Uncle nodded as she was carried away, though as I snuck out after her I heard him mutter, "Fight respectably."

I walked out to the garden and leaned against a column, relief flooding my body. This was just the beginning. If it hadn't been for Uncle, it would be back to weaving for me. The older I became, the more I felt out of place. Lanata was a Vestal; Agrippina would be a matron; Quintus would become pater of our family one day. Why was it so hard for me to imagine a place for myself?

On one of Aunt's visits to Rome I'd overheard her lighthearted laughter with Agrippina. I'd not heard what amused them, but she'd told my sister that they'd been woven from the same thread. It was obviously not so with me. They were both ladies, from perfumed hair to manicured toe. Women a Roman would be proud to have as a wife.

I'd asked Uncle not to change me, but why was I this way? If the gods had answers, they were being irritatingly tight-lipped.

∞

Petrus returned the next day. Hilarus followed behind, leading slaves carrying bundles of wooden posts and weapons. Petrus directed the slaves to set up the wooden palus as an opponent, along with other pieces that seemed to be obstacles. Off to one side Hilarus was laying out the weapons.

Rafa sat under a tree, watching. I'd asked him to train with me, reasoning it would be better to practice together so I could spar with someone close to my size. He refused, saying Aunt or Agrippina would see it as outright rebellion. He had a point. Aunt would take any excuse to make a case against Rafa, and I wouldn't risk his safety again.

I looked over the swords, blunt-tipped spears, and shields. "Why are the weapons all made of wood?"

"You don't know what you're doing yet. Wouldn't want you to kill yourself on the first day," Petrus said in a deep tone, but his eyes glinted. "Also, wooden weapons are heavier than metal ones. Once you're used to fighting with wood you'll have better stamina and strength with metal."

"A tree needs roots before branches," Hilarus put in. *Lumbering bear, indeed.* I shouldn't have been surprised Hilarus, also, was more than he appeared.

A disc of wood hit me in the leg.

"Ow!" I yelped and swung around, rubbing at the tender impact. I only just noticed Petrus take another disc from a pile and flick it at me. I dodged. He threw more and more and I darted behind trees and over benches to avoid getting hit. I laughed even as I took a stinging blow to the shoulder with the last disk.

"Not bad for a first try," Petrus said.

I panted, rubbing my shoulder, and Rafa shot me a grin. "When do I get to use the weapons?"

"We will get to all the weapons in their own turn, but first we work on your two big failings."

"I only have two?" He wasn't really so rude, if you looked past his gruffness.

"You are weak, and you are small."

The unexpected insults cut deep. "I can't help it! I'm a girl, and I'm not even twelve!" I started to stomp away.

"Three failings—your temper will get you killed," Petrus called after me. "And if you leave now, you'll never learn to be any better."

I stopped, but didn't turn around.

"Time won't improve these failings. Anyone you fight will likely be bigger and stronger than you. And if you allow your temper free rein it will be easy to goad you into uneven fights. Provoke you into making mistakes."

He's right. I turned back and he gestured with a snap of his wrist for me to come closer.

"You'll have to be faster than they are." He flicked his cane at me and I dodged away. He nodded. "You'll have to be precise in your attacks and deadly in more ways than they're expecting. And you'll have to outwit them."

"Yes, I know. 'Eyes to see, a mind to think, and hands to act.'" *Would father have given me these lessons if he were alive?*

"A good saying to remember." Petrus raised an eyebrow in question.

"Father sometimes told me about his time in the army. But how can I hope to win with so many problems other fighters won't have?" I kicked the dirt.

"Because most people think once they have won a few battles, overcome a few opponents, they have mastered survival. They don't work to get better once they're *good enough*. It's a mistake. Large fighters rely on strength and don't develop speed. Fast fighters refuse to learn multiple weapons because they don't want to feel slow with something unfamiliar." He was speaking with passion now, some of his roughness slipping away, and I could see how he would have been as an actor on the stage. "But you—you're young and have time to learn. And you have an excellent tutor, to keep the laziness away." Petrus lowered his voice, one long finger extended toward me. "And something more. You have fire. You know the thin edge between life and death. You want to walk on this side as long as possible, I think." His eyes burned bright.

I took a slow breath and realized we were alike. Fire—Jupiter had punished Prometheus for giving man the one gift which was forbidden. Bound by chains, an eagle fed on his liver every day, only to have his immortal flesh regrow it during the night. An eternal torment for one act of defiance. There were no stories of the gods being punished for other gifts. Minerva gives us weaving, Mars gives war, Venus gives love. All those gifts are free. But fire has a price. If I wanted to live as long as Petrus, I would have to trust him.

"What's your question?" he asked. "The one I see in your eyes." He was too observant.

"How many deaths have you caused?"

"Fifty-seven that I know of. Pick up that sword and follow Hilarus, or it will be fifty-eight." But the nudge of his cane was gentle as he prodded me down the path.

Eleven

FOR ALL OF AUNT CALPURNIA'S MANAGING WAYS, I was happy enough with her routine. At dawn were lessons with Petrus and Hilarus. Petrus had approved of Aunt Calpurnia's order that I train in my regular clothing and took it one step further. As it was unlikely I would ever have a shield nearby, he decided I would learn to fight with a sword in each hand. It would be easier for me to have weapons in both hands, rather than the weight of a shield, and easier for me to find something to substitute for a blade.

Easy it was not.

On days they didn't come I practiced on my own, striking the palus with my wooden gladius first with one arm, then the other. The ache never left my arms now. Not just my shoulders and forearms and joints, but all the way down my back and across my chest. I felt leaden and heavy after, but every day I could train longer.

In the later part of the morning I would join Rafa and Agrippina as we studied under Hamitra's gentle gaze—or endured a well-earned rebuke if we lost our concentration. Even though I fell asleep more than once during our afternoons with Aunt, she seemed to appreciate my improved behaviour. Agrippina wasn't so pleased about my *morning lessons*, as she called them, and refused to acknowledge me if she happened to be in the garden during my training.

Hamitra found me the daybreak before my birthday. The first rays of sunlight had broken over the mountain, throwing the vineyards and groves snaking up the summit into crisp relief. She watched me stumble through a difficult sequence of strokes, with an upward thrust following hard on the heels of a downward parry. Petrus wasn't here today, but his command of "Practice!" haunted me.

When I'd gone through it several more times, I turned to get Hamitra's opinion. "Well?" I demanded.

"I don't want to interfere with your training," Hamitra said, apologetic, and reached for a pinch of fennel seeds from my breakfast tray.

I came over and rolled an apricot slice in the fennel before popping it in my mouth.

"But ..." I tried to not dribble juice down my face.

She handed me a napkin. "But, if you would bend your knees more and keep your body centered, you wouldn't need to rely only on the strength of your arms."

She led me back to the open space at the end of the long porch and positioned me as she suggested. A hint of fennel from her breath tingled in my nose as her face came close to mine. Pressing down gently on my shoulders, she rocked my body back and forth between my planted feet. "Stay on the balls of your feet as much as possible, to shift position quickly."

I lifted my heels a bit and felt as though I'd topple over. "I can't strike with enough force."

"Try." Hamitra plucked a wooden sword for herself off the ground and worked me through the moves, one stroke at a time. "Don't lean back when you bring your foot forward ... Pull your shoulders over your hips ..."

After the ninth time, it felt easier. After the thirtieth, it felt right.

"Good," she said at last.

My arms hung boneless and I dropped my practice sword at the feet of a waiting slave. Hamitra inclined her head toward the path and I shook out my cramped hands as I followed. We walked through the grove and sat with our legs dangling over the edge of the cliff. The sun behind us cast long, pointed shadows over the beach below.

Hamitra pulled her braid over her shoulder so it wouldn't trail in the dust, and leaned back on her hands. "I didn't expect you would learn to fight."

"Why not? Someone's trying to kill me."

"It's unusual."

Looking out over the water, I pressed my lips together to stop my thoughts from tumbling out. *Everything about this is unusual.*

"It can be difficult to be unusual," she said, and I realized she was worried.

"I didn't tell anyone."

"I know."

I didn't question how she knew.

"Why?" she asked, her intense stare making clear how important my answer would be.

I swallowed. "Because of Pandora and her jar of evils. She released evil into the world just for the sake of her curiosity. If I try to find out more, or tell your secret, it won't help me. But it will force you to leave." *Or worse.*

"So you're choosing to *not* be curious?" Her eyes flashed with something I hoped was humour.

"Yes."

"The very fact you know we have a secret may force us to leave."

"No one would believe me, even if I wanted to tell—and I don't. Let Nikandros know I'm just a simple girl who hasn't realized anything that can hurt you." If I hadn't been misreading her, I suspected Nikandros was more concerned about what I might do.

"Simple?" She gave a soft snort of amusement. "I think you're wise beyond your years. And you don't care what we are?"

She'd protected me. Saved my life. Was one of the only people in the world who could. *Whatever she was, was less important than what she did.* "No, I don't care. I need you to stay."

"You're very single-minded." Hamitra smiled, white teeth peeking from behind her lips. "So you've decided to learn to defend yourself?"

I nodded. For now, it was defence.

She looked at me from the corner of her eye. "I'm awake very early in the mornings, if you find yourself with a spare day."

"You could always join me and Petrus."

"I don't think that would be wise. He's far too observant."

Rustling in the bushes made me start.

Eris strutted into view, scratching at the ground with her sharp talons every few paces.

"I hate that chicken," I said. "She mocks me."

Hamitra's eyes shone with mirth. "Don't waste your time hating a bird for being a bird. What would you expect her to do? Let you trample her eggs and torment her?"

"She's vicious. The other hens aren't so miserable."

Eris chortled, plunging her beak after a small lizard. Scanning the ground, half-bent, Rafa trailed after her. He was so intent on searching under the bushes, Hamitra had to lift her hand to get his attention. His frustration turned to resolve when he saw Eris.

"Sorry," he whispered, creeping near. "I closed the gate behind me. I don't know how she escaped."

Slow and silent, he lifted a branch off the ground, then flicked it toward the massive red hen. Eris screeched, but ran a few steps in the direction of the stockyard. He tossed a handful of rocks and she ran further. I watched Rafa drive Eris until they were both out of sight within the grove.

I stood, but when I turned to excuse myself, Hamitra still gazed toward the stockyard, eyebrows pinched in a thoughtful expression.

"She may be a miserable chicken," she said, "but she makes the others feel safe."

I walked away, shaking my head. *Stupid chickens.*

∞

Petrus was late, so I spent the early morning of my birthday in the kitchen, where Pherenike was planning cakes and sweets for the party. She whisked from oven to table to cabinet, muttering under her breath, her wheat-blonde hair pulled into a long queue that swished like a horsetail behind her. I was surprised when she said flamingo tongue — I hadn't realized it was used in any deserts.

Norbanus, Uncle's chef, grumbled when she walked in his way, but thankfully a *pax culina* had been established between the villa's slaves and our Roman household. They didn't start yelling as they had when she first arrived.

The kitchen was a haven of mouth-watering aromas. Herbs, fresh picked and stuffed into all manner of meats. Sauces and stews slowly thickening. And best of all, Pherenike's deserts. *I could survive on just her honey cakes.* She passed me one, hot from the oven, then started cracking open walnuts with the flat of a large knife. With a wink, she rolled one over to me, the lumpy meat exposed inside the shell. I usually found walnuts too bitter, but was surprised how well it tasted with the cake.

A blonde slave carrying a jug of water snickered as she noticed me. Self-conscious, I stopped licking my fingers.

"Slaves talk, same as anyone," Pherenike said to me. "Some don't understand why you train like a boy." She raised her voice, "But it seems right to me a woman should know how to take care of herself." She brought her knife down hard on the wooden table. The activity in the room quickened. A blonde head quietly disappeared down the hall.

"You do?" I asked.

Sweeping the shelled nuts into a pile she chopped them vigorously with her knife. "The day they took me from my village I was thirteen — just older than you. I was a lucky one, bought by a rich merchant, and for more purposes than just a bed-warmer."

"Did you want to kill him?"

"Sometimes yes. Sometimes no." Pherenike gave a wry smile. "I learned many things — some things brought me to your family." She rolled me another walnut and scooped more to chop. "But on that day, I would have fought."

"You know, I own you now." It had been a strange meeting, when Uncle helped Agrippina and I decide which of father's property we were to inherit.

"I know, little domina," she said with a grin.

"Would you leave me if I freed you?"

Pherenike looked at me, face cautious.

"Wait," I said. "It doesn't matter."

"No?"

"No." I avoided her gaze and snatched another honey cake, watching the activity around us instead.

The kitchen was always a good place to practice observing deceit, so much was going on. At first I'd caught little things … a slave dropping a cut of meat on the floor, but quickly brushing it off and feigning competence before being caught by Norbanus; others sneaking undeserved tidbits, carefully wiping juicy drips.

Then I noticed the secret glances — between women and men, men and men, women and women — a gleam of shared memory, or with a seductive shifting of the body. Some were nearly hidden, a flicker of anger or resentment. But Petrus had been right, so many were deceitful. Hiding an action, a thought, a feeling.

Even though Norbanus and Pherenike's rivalry meant they kept their separate domains in the kitchen, it was surprising how often they seemed to be in the other's way. Brushing past with a sigh of annoyance. Reaching for the honey at the same time. Bickering over a pot. I hoped their mutual hatred wouldn't affect the food.

The blonde slave returned. "Domina, your *teacher* has arrived."

Pherenike turned on the girl. "If you ever speak to the domina in that saucy tone again, I will puree your tongue."

Eyes threatening tears, the girl nodded and hurried away.

Pherenike wiped her hands on her apron with a hearty *thwap*.

∞

Crack—crack. My poor attempt at sparring with Hilarus was agonizingly slow, though the clack of wood was satisfying. It echoed down my arm and into my body like a second, strange heartbeat. Petrus had complimented me on my observations of kitchen slaves and then yelled at me to "Practice!" Even though I wasn't sparring with Petrus, I could imagine.

"You look like David and Goliath." Rafa chuckled from his spot under the trees. He noted my puzzled expression. "David was a shepherd who became a mighty king, but Goliath was a giant, twice as large as any living man."

I looked up, way up, at Hilarus' grin.

"And who won this battle?" Hilarus asked, lowering his sword and turning to Rafa.

"Me!" I slapped the broad of my sword on Hilarus' exposed thigh. He boomed with laughter.

"This is exactly what I was afraid of," a voice said in severe disapproval. My cousin Quintus strode into the peristyle. His eyes darted between Petrus, Hilarus, and me.

I was conscious all of a sudden of how comical we would look. Petrus, with his white hair standing on end, wrapped in his dark robes. Hilarus and I, opponents of such unequal size.

"Nice to see you, too, Quintus." I turned back to Hilarus, wishing Quintus had ignored this birthday like he had the last. The sight of him, with his shiny brown hair carefully combed and oiled, his tunic cinched at his waist, made me want to give him a slap with my sword.

"I hoped our Aunt would have a better influence on you." He walked around us, eying my appearance with dismay.

"She has. I'm wearing a dress aren't I?" Anger bubbled, as it always did when Quintus was around.

He made a fastidious circuit of my training area, nose wrinkled as though in the presence of a bad smell.

A hand on my shoulder made me jump.

"Breathe deep and slow. Let your blood cool," Petrus whispered. "It'll do no good to have your lessons taken away over this … *boy*."

I realized he was right. Quintus was a man the same way I was a woman—we were trying it on, still waiting for it to fit. I took a breath and let it out. Then another.

Quintus turned, and I saw his confusion that I hadn't lost my temper, as I had the time I pushed him in the pool.

He frowned. "Yes. At the very least you're properly dressed, thank the gods. You've never had a mother, after all, to teach you how to be a lady." He said it in an offhand way, as though explaining the sum of two and two.

It shouldn't bother me. I knew it shouldn't bother me. But I couldn't smile any longer. So I held myself stiff, wooden sword down at my side.

"I don't know what I can say to convince you to end this madness. What would your father think?" Quintus eyed me with a mixture of concern and disgust. "The shame of seeing his daughter train like a savage."

My foot stepped forward of its own will.

The garden erupted with feathers and squawks. I whipped around and saw a flood of chickens and geese scurrying in through the open door to the grove. Rafa followed, kicking out at a brown hen and stirring them all into a frenzy. Fat, feathery bodies swarmed around us and we tried to avoid the thrusting beaks and flapping wings.

"You!" Quintus pointed at Rafa, who was now doing his best impression of innocence. "Get these birds under control."

"Of course, dominus," Rafa said, but his tone reeked defiance.

Quintus set his jaw, walked the two steps to Rafa and backhanded him across the face.

I raised my sword, but Hilarus' large hand clamped around my arm and held me still. Hilarus took my glare stoically but Petrus jabbed a bony finger into my ribs.

"Breathe. Practice!" He and Hilarus returned to the villa.

Rafa had ducked away from Quintus. Enough chickens pecked at his legs that my cousin decided to flee the garden, shaking a brown hen free of his toga as he high-stepped away.

∞

It was only fair for me to help Rafa round up the poultry, since he'd saved me from my foolishness. Quintus would have run fast as Mercury to his mother. Somehow, even when Quintus caused a problem, his explanations left no one in doubt that I was to blame.

At last only Eris remained loose. In his haste to get the chickens into the garden, Rafa had knocked down the gate to their enclosure. Eris didn't need a further invitation to make chaos.

We tracked her trail of destruction. Ends of curtains shredded. Garlands decorating doors for my coming of age had flowers and berries plucked free and scattered. She'd made a circuit of the porch, left a smear of droppings on the mosaic floor in the atrium, and was now clucking angrily in Uncle's study.

We peeked in—she perched on Uncle's desk, shredding his most recent letter. Rafa and I tried to flank her but she struck out at me and gashed my palm. I sucked in a breath at the slicing pain and, retreating to the door, wrapped it with a strip torn from my shawl.

I grabbed a wax tablet. "I'll try to knock her off the desk."

Uncle came in, face grave. "Lucilla, lower that bit of memoir. I'd rather not lose that particular incident. Rafa, take off your outer tunic."

Rafa wiggled out of the heavier over-layer, shivering as the winter breeze ruffled the thin cotton one.

Uncle flung the cloth over Eris and bundled her as though in a sack. It jerked in his hand. "Lucilla, come."

With a last glance at Rafa, the side of his face still red from Quintus's slap, I followed.

We walked out through the garden, past the grove and the stockyard, and beyond most of the outbuildings. The bundle kept spasming, Eris complaining in a throaty *bak-bak-bak*.

We stopped at the slaughterhouse.

"It's time for you to keep the peace in our home," Uncle said.

My stomach dropped like an iron weight. I knew what he demanded. He was giving me the freedom to train with Petrus. It was more than I should expect, and it came with a cost. I'd given Eudocia little enough peace during my childhood—hiding at bedtimes, fighting with my sister, underfoot in the kitchen. And I'd done no better at the villa, going so far as to break my word and wander alone into town. To keep the freedoms Uncle was willing to give, I must pay the price.

The Lares had heard my promise to be dutiful and uphold the honour of my family. That included obeying my uncle.

"I will."

With sure hands, Uncle unbundled Eris. He grasped her body in one hand, wings held tight. With the other, he stretched her neck down onto the chopping block, then jerked his chin at the axe. Eris's eyes rolled in her head, but Uncle held her body now with both hands, leaving her neck exposed. She didn't have the strength to break away.

I picked up the small axe and stood over the block, looking down at Eris. She was far more vulnerable than in the study. Her life was in my hands and it felt … right.

I raised the axe. *But she makes the other chickens feel safe.*

"It's just a chicken, Lucilla," Uncle said, seeming to sense my hesitation. "This is her fate whether you swing the axe today or not."

I swung.

I missed her neck and broke her head. Her body spasmed.

"Again!" Uncle ordered. I'd forgotten he'd been in the army.

Sight fixed on her neck, I cleaved the axe through and into the block. Her mangled head came off and Uncle held her body away from us as blood spurted. He hung her twitching carcass over a large bowl, draining in a steady stream, then slowing to a patter. Her talons opened and closed, opened and closed.

Uncle took the axe from my hand and struck it into the block. "Come. Calpurnia will be waiting. Let's get you changed for your party."

I looked down at my red-spattered dress. *How had I forgotten my coming of age?* That's why the family were here, after all. Aunt Calpurnia. Quintus and his mother. Agrippina, Cincinnata, Nonius. At least I had time to change before dinner.

I let out a slow breath.

Time to keep the peace.

"There are some remedies worse than the disease."
Syrus

PART II

JANUARY

Year 5 of the Emperor Vespasian

Twelve

His fist struck my jaw. I dropped hard.

"Lucilla ... Lucilla?" The words swirled around me like birds circling the sky.

Who's asking my name? I know who I am. The tree roots beneath my hands were hazy and I blinked with exaggerated care, trying to clear my vision. I groaned.

"Lucilla?" Hilarus asked again.

"I'm all right." I forced the words out my aching jaw.

"I shouldn't have followed through." He was only mildly apologetic. It wasn't the first time he'd landed a real blow, and it wouldn't be the last. We started sparring in earnest after I turned fourteen last spring and I demanded he take it seriously. If I couldn't learn to take a hit, my enemy would have yet another advantage. Though we hadn't been attacked again for nearly two years, the long delay had increased my agitation instead of soothing it. I was more than willing to endure a few bruises while I waited.

"It was my fault. I should have seen that coming." I reached for his outstretched hand. "Or rather, I saw it coming but couldn't do anything about it."

As he hoisted me to my feet, my spotty gaze fastened on a silver ring he wore. I'd never noticed it before.

"Is that a griffin?" I asked. The flat bezel of the ring was stamped with a rearing beast, half lion, half eagle.

"Yes." He steadied me under my elbow when I swayed.

"Was that me or the ground?" The earth was prone to tremors in Campania, so it was possible I wasn't a complete mess.

"The ground," Hilarus replied with a grin, but he helped me to sit on a large boulder while the last of the rumblings—and my unsteadiness—died away. Taking off his ring, he examined it briefly before passing it to me. I was grateful for the excuse to focus on something that didn't seem to be spinning.

Hilarus sat next to me, hunched forward. His tunic gaped to expose two parallel scars running along his collarbone, nearly shoulder to shoulder. He caught me looking and traced a finger along one puckered ridge.

"Was that from a lion?"

Disgust twisted his mouth. "Gladiators don't fight animals. That's for the venatores."

"But when Petrus was explaining, he said the beast hunts happen in the amphitheatre."

"They do, but only in the morning, and only against the venatores—they even train in a different ludus than we do. Then executions at midday. Gladiators fight after the rest. We don't kill for sport—we fight for pride, and honor."

I nodded. Beasts and criminals were executed for the host of the games to demonstrate their power. But there was no honor in butchery.

"There are three kinds of gladiators," Hilarus went on, thoughtful. "The first pray to leave the sand alive. Often slaves in their first year. They see a match as a death sentence, and fight like caged animals."

"You sound disappointed."

"They're no worse off than a coin toss. No lanista—the organizer—wants to lose a valuable fighter, so we fight opponents of equal rank. A match doesn't have to end in death, only victory."

I pondered that. I'd never been to the amphitheatre but Petrus, Hilarus, and occasionally even my uncle spoke of it. Death was always possible when one opponent was outmaneuvered by the other, or when a defeated gladiator had not earned the love of the crowd. But most defeats weren't deadly. Hilarus was right—gladiators were too expensive to train and keep. One of Uncle's clients constantly complained how risky an investment his were.

"You said three kinds?" I prodded.

He rubbed at his scar. "The second show off their power, to intimidate opponents and impress the audience. When they win, they yell, to be sure everyone has seen. I've noticed many worship the sun, by whatever name he has in their land."

"What's wrong with the sun?" I suppressed a smile at his explanation. He'd never spoken so much at one time, and never with such candour.

"It's only in the sky half the day."

I flicked the ring back to him and he snatched it from the air.

"So the third?"

"The third know that if you're deserving, you'll be given victory; if you're arrogant, defeat."

"You put your faith in Fortuna?"

"Lady Fortune is often blind to a man's worth." Hilarus touched his thumb to the griffin before sliding the ring over the large knuckles on his first finger. "But her sister, Nemesis, has granted me many victories. The more boastful my opponent, the more I feel her wrath in my blade."

"Now I know how to defeat you," I said. "Stop my bragging."

"No. Stop thinking you should lose." His direct gaze pierced to the spot in my heart I'd thought well hidden. The spot which knew I would lose against the man with one eye. Any other outcome was impossible.

I crossed my arms. "Why would I bother with all this, if I don't think I can win?"

"You tell me."

I'd only ever spoken of it to Rafa, for fear of being mocked. But Hilarus also knew me well. "Vengeance."

Hilarus raised his eyebrows, thankfully with no trace of a smile. "Then remember you have a reason to win. And you're in luck. Vengeance is my Lady's specialty."

"What are you going on about over there?" Petrus muttered with irritation, waking from his spot under the tree. He'd taken to napping more often of late and I wasn't sorry. I didn't miss the discs he threw at me or the sly jabs he took with his cane when I sparred with Hilarus.

"Hilarus was teaching me about gladiators."

"He shouldn't be teaching you anything. He doesn't speak. And you," he said, pointing his finger at me, "should be training."

Hilarus shrugged his shoulders, dismissing the old man's carping.

I looked Hilarus up and down, impressed at his indifference. "I'll have to learn to bite my tongue and shrug like a gladiator."

"You're too small to shrug properly," he said, stone-faced.

Petrus rapped his cane on the tree. "I am tired of this discussion. If you're done warming up, we'll continue with the spear before you're required by your aunt."

I gave an inward groan, trying to squash my frustration. The rest of my day was needed to prepare for dinner this evening. Which meant hours of bathing, plucking, braiding, and dressing. The cost of keeping the peace had been higher than I first thought.

Petrus ambled stiff-hipped to the equipment and selected a wooden spear with a blunted tip. "Effective at disabling an opponent from a distance and useful for hand-to-hand defence. Unless you are as prodigious as the glorious Achilles, I suggest you practice."

I walked over to take the weapon, nimbly blocking the swift jab of his cane as he yanked the spear out of reach.

He nodded approval.

I shrugged, and grabbed my spear.

∞

The swimming pool overlooked the bay, on a terrace a storey lower than the main house. Though I enjoyed the bay during summer, heated water was much more pleasant in winter. I dove in, shedding the grime and ache of practice. A bit of freedom before beginning the long process of dressing for dinner.

After a few lazy laps, Rafa appeared on the terrace above. He spotted me and beckoned to someone to follow. I had a feeling I knew who it was—Rafa didn't normally escort visitors, Eron did. And Numina from the kitchens brought refreshments; Korax waved the fan and plumped pillows. Not to mention Gavius, my ever-expanding guard, who right this moment seemed to be napping on his feet in the shade of the pavilion.

Resting on the pool's tiled stairs, I made a quick count of which of my familia were nearby. Twelve, to be exact—Lenoria, my new handmaid, singing absently to the clouds while holding my towel, six in the gardens pruning and weeding, two sweeping the terrace, and the rest on the shore repainting the railings of Aunt Calpurnia's yacht. Until I'd started observing others, I hadn't realized how many observed me in return. It might have felt safe, except not one of them could thwart my enemy, and so I merely wondered who would be lost next.

Rafa approached. As I suspected, Justa accompanied him. She wore a new shade of pale blue, no doubt of her own creation, with a matching shawl pinned at the nape of her neck to expose her dark hair. Braided into a simple crown, her hairstyle couldn't be more different than the elaborate towers Agrippina still adored.

Justa smiled, settling on her knees at the pool's edge. "I came to deliver some fabric for Agrippina, but needed to speak with you as well. I was hoping you would consider a business proposal."

"What sort of proposal?"

"I need help managing records and suppliers. Mother's been so busy with Stephanus and Themis—" She broke off, always reluctant to speak of her father and his wife, and how they controlled her mother's actions.

"Has it been bad, lately?"

"Worse all the time. They're worried about the upcoming elections." She sounded tired.

"Another scheme?"

"Stephanus and his never-ending and never successful political ambitions," Rafa said with scorn.

She gave him an appreciative smile. "Yes. He relies too much on mother and his other freedmen to get him in office. She's campaigning all day, trying to win over citizens who don't have patrons. Or who are angry with their patrons. But she's exhausted." Justa sighed. "I wanted to trade for use of Rafa's services. He already knows the business somewhat, and I can't afford to purchase anyone who'd be competent."

The twitch of Rafa's fingers, as though reaching for Justa, made his longing obvious. "Wouldn't hurt, me being in town more often," he said in an offhand way, though I understood his meaning. *Easier to find out anything about Rusticus.* Not that we'd managed to learn much more.

I sank under the water, holding my breath in the calm. While Rafa and I still attended lessons together in the morning, our once-easy friendship now seemed as perilous as a rutted road. Afternoons had been reduced from shared hours, to scattered moments, until only the occasional word in passing remained. Instead, I spent my time as Aunt ordered, weaving or playing the lyre; he took instruction from Uncle or the overseers, and visited towns along the coast on mysterious errands. We both avoided mention of my preoccupation with the one-eyed man or his with Justa—and I dodged outright any conversation that might veer into the territory of Hamitra's secret. Too many hard truths we had no appetite to share.

Yet how could I grudge him the chance to find a place for himself? He'd had a life once. A home and a family. Now he was a slave in name; lived as one in our household. For his own safety — and apparently for mine — he was willing to suffer that fate. But that fate didn't have to last forever. Of course, since Uncle had required I be responsible and make my will, there *was* a way Rafa could be freed before he turned thirty — I just wasn't ready to die for his release.

Thoughts still knotted, I emerged, sucking in air and plastering on a pleased expression. "He has my permission, so long as it doesn't disrupt his duties. You don't even have to pay him," I said lightly.

"No. I can pay him something — I mean, he deserves to be paid," Justa stumbled, looking flustered.

I might have been the only person alive who could see how Rafa's straight face filled with delight.

∞

I couldn't move. If I leaned forward my piled hair would slide and become a braided blindfold. Keeping my torso rigid, I carefully shifted my legs, stretching them a bit on the couch where I reclined for dinner. I should have more faith in Lenoria's handiwork, but the bitter smell of singed hair still tickled my nostrils. To Sidonia's dismay my dreamy handmaid had burned off a lock with the curling irons. Agrippina's hair, under Sidonia's masterful hands, would likely survive a thunderstorm. My sister rested on her elbow with confident elegance.

The couches in the dining room formed three sides of a square, surrounding a circular table. Aunt Calpurnia had been moved from her litter to share a couch with Quintus. Uncle and I were on the second. Agrippina and Uncle's wife, Galaria, on the third. Though three was the ideal, it was much more pleasant when there were only two to a couch. With three, you inhaled far more perfume from guests, than aroma from food.

"It's gratifying to spend an evening with family on such a happy occasion," Uncle began formally, lifting his glass. "We are to celebrate not only Agrippina's sixteenth year, but to congratulate her on the announcement of her betrothal to Nonius Arrianus."

Agrippina gave a dazzling smile as we toasted her accomplishments. And so they were—four years ago our lives may have been cut short. Now she was a woman, and to be married to the man of her choosing. I was glad Agrippina's choice had Aunt's approval at last.

Knowing it would be my only glass, I took a small sip of wine, its bite softened by honey and spices. My senses couldn't be trusted if I had more than one, though the rest of my family weren't as concerned about overindulging.

"Thank you, Uncle," Agrippina said. "I'm pleased to have it settled at last." She flicked her gaze to Aunt Calpurnia and I hoped the two of them wouldn't continue their dispute. Nonius had made his formal offer last year, before he'd left with his father for Pannonia. But Aunt had forbidden the marriage until he returned.

"He's had the chance to prove his abilities," Aunt said. "You wouldn't want to marry a man who doesn't know himself." She waved her hand for the musicians to begin. The soft strumming of a lyre floated in from the porch.

"And you wouldn't have enjoyed Pannonia," Aunt Galaria chimed in. Her wide-spaced eyes made it appear as though she could see the entire room without moving her head. "I've heard it's barely civilized—filled with trees and savage mountain men."

How do trees make a place less civilized? I took another sip of my wine, knowing Aunt Galaria wouldn't care for my opinion. *Keep the peace ... keep the peace.*

"Mother," Quintus said. "When someone begins with 'I have heard,' reasonable people don't bother listening to the rest."

Aunt Galaria gave an injured sniff. "My son is so very reasonable he doesn't have use for his own mother any longer."

"The Empire could stand a few more reasonable men at its helm, don't you think?" Quintus ran a hand over an errant curl above his ear.

"You will have plenty of time to establish yourself," Uncle said with amusement. "Vespasian and his sons appear to have things well in hand. There should be no immediate need for you to step in."

"Great men rely on money and influence to remain so. It can never be too early to gather both." Quintus gave a decided nod.

Fortunately for my stomach, the procession from the kitchen began and conversation drifted into the safe waters of fashion, chariot racing, and gossip about our neighbours. Slaves passed us plates of food laden with bite-sized morsels of each dish: oysters with cumin and olive oil; lobster broiled scarlet, dripping with butter; and Agrippina's favourite main course—braised peacock, dressed with its tail fan spread open and stuffed with mint, plums, and raisins.

When the platters of fruits and sweets arrived at last it was clear it had been a successful feast; the mosaic beneath us was blanketed with bones, oyster shells, fruit pits and lobster claws. Norbanus came from the kitchen to receive our compliments, glowing with silent pleasure. Then the scraps were swept away and bowls of rose water brought to clean our hands.

I'd finished my wine, so sipped my lemon water, enjoying Aunt Galaria's struggle as she clumsily discarded the white pulp of a pomegranate, her plump arm extended off the couch so as not to splatter Agrippina beside her. My sister was nearly comatose, part satisfaction at having an evening in her honour and part having stuffed herself silly with honey and poppy-seed dormice.

Uncle Quintus emitted a loud belch. Holding his greasy fingers over a bowl of scented water, a slave washed and dried his hands. He clapped them together once and everyone turned their heads at the unexpected sound.

"And," he began, as though continuing some previously silent conversation, "I'm happy to tell you all that we'll have a new addition to our family before the summer."

Everyone whipped surprised faces to Aunt Galaria. Quintus's mouth hung agape as he eyed his mother's mid-section. But she looked as shocked as everyone else, wide eyes blinking.

"Ah. Not that," Uncle Quintus said, but it had clearly been his intended effect. Aunt Galaria flicked her napkin at him. "We have a cousin of Agrippina and Lucilla coming to stay with us. From Britannia. His mother is a second or third cousin to Agrippina Statia."

Mother. Her lineage was still a mystery to me, though Eudocia had explained it more than once. All I recalled was that her own mother had been of a Britannian tribe, while her father had been Roman.

"Why are we being imposed on this way?" Aunt Calpurnia snapped to the girl behind her, who began to fan more vigorously.

"Besides being family," Uncle said, "his mother was recently deposed as ruler of her tribe and barely escaped with her life. She has been a staunch ally of Rome. This is considered a personal favour by both her and the emperor."

Aunt Calpurnia sniffed, somewhat mollified.

Quintus's eyes narrowed and darted back and forth, as though calculating the future value of this favour. "Should he not stay with us, then, in Rome?" he asked his father.

"He may, for part of the year. You're similar ages and he can benefit from your rhetor, at least until you're done with your studies. I thought perhaps both of you would enjoy taking the summers here." Uncle glanced at his wife, who shrugged noncommittally and chose another pomegranate. "The city is deserted of people worth knowing in the hot months, and most come to the bay." He lifted his cup of wine and sipped with a great deal of care.

"What will he do?" I asked into the silence. Uncle looked over at me. "Our cousin, what will he do now that he has no place in his homeland?"

"Rely on his connections," Aunt Galaria said, mouth full of pomegranate pips. "Eventually he will have to make his own way." She reached for a fig.

"We will take care of him until this tribal rebellion is suppressed," Uncle said.

"So he's a hostage?" Quintus asked. It wasn't unusual for high-born hostages to be taken to ensure a rebellious group came back under the protection of the empire. But this tribe was fighting among themselves, not Rome.

"He's not a hostage," Uncle said to Quintus with exasperation. "He's a guest and will remain a guest until the Emperor and his own mother decide what should become of him."

Sounds like a hostage to me. The only thing worse than being a hostage, was being one when you should have ruled a kingdom.

Agrippina hiccoughed and tilted her head, considering me. "A barbarian cousin is probably the best match you could get, Luce."

"Or maybe he would be a better match for you than Nonius," I shot back. "Our cousin was a prince after all. It might be as close to being an Emperor's wife as you'll ever be."

"Girls." Aunt Calpurnia lifted a hand. Agrippina had to be content with sticking out her tongue. I caught Aunt Calpurnia glance momentarily at Uncle, raising her eyebrow. He gave a slight nod.

"Lucilla." Aunt Calpurnia turned to me, her softer tone all the warning I needed. "When this cousin arrives, try to be polite. We must do whatever we can to help the Emperor's friends." *And get you married to whoever will take you.* I could finish her thought without effort.

"Will he even care?" I snapped, rising to go to my room. "He might have no manners at all."

"That will still be more than you." Quintus tapped his cup for more wine, while his mother continued to stuff honeyed fruits into her mouth.

"Then you'll just have to sell me to some old gladiator." I gave Quintus a slim smile, enjoyed the sound of Aunt Galaria choking her shock, and strode from the room. *Meddlers.*

THIRTEEN

"YOUR COUSIN IS VERY …" Justa's words trailed off and Agrippina and I looked down the shoreline to where Quintus and Bricus were talking. It wasn't difficult to know which one she spoke of. Quintus was … well he was Quintus. Hair combed, tunic cinched, trying not to get sand between his toes.

Bricus on the other hand—Agrippina raised her eyebrows at me and I struggled not to grin. Bricus's long orange-brown hair whipped about in the breeze. Bare torso and arms were dotted with freckles. Though about the same height as Quintus, our cousin from Britannia was significantly more muscular. *Not that it matters.*

"Wild?" Agrippina suggested, poking Justa in the arm as we lounged on carpets protecting us from the coarse sand.

Bricus gave Quintus a playful shove, which Quintus stonily endured, then flopped into the water. *Like a bear. A very exuberant bear.*

Agrippina lounged back on her elbows. "You know, Nonius is just so *proper* all the time. It can be like talking to a statue—you never really know what he's feeling. These barbarians aren't so stoic." Both the spring weather and my sister were in fine form today. She'd bloomed since winter, throwing herself into her role as Justa's patron, and introducing her to friends among the families nearby.

She and Justa continued itemizing Bricus's fascinating differences. Rafa, holding one side of the canvas awning shading our heads, stifled a groan. I batted my eyelashes at him; he glared back.

Squinting into the bright sunlight, I looked south past the mouth of the Lyrinis, the small river separating our villa from Herculaneum. The beach on the other side was packed with bathers splashing in the shallows and lounging on the shore. Above, on the terraces overlooking the bay, small groups ambled, the fresh breeze fluttering brightly coloured dresses and shawls like banners. Boats sailed into and out of the small harbour, decorating the water like a scattering of jewels.

Turning north, the stretch of coast where our villa sprawled was almost as long as the entire sea frontage of the town. Needless to say, our beach was much less crowded.

Bricus had swum the few strokes to reach us and yelled from the water. "Come on, cousins! The water is warm enough to bathe in!"

"What do barbarians know about baths, anyway?" Agrippina teased.

"I know I can see naked girls there. What else is there to know?" Bricus wiggled his eyebrows.

"Scandalous." Agrippina's dimples flashed as she bit her lip.

Justa laughed, and Rafa's glare, which had never quite faded, deepened into an outright scowl.

It had taken less than two days for us to realize Bricus was not only a merciless tease but seemed to have no sense of proper etiquette. Aunt Calpurnia had difficulty spending more than a few moments at a time in his company. I'd tried to dislike him; tried finding fault with his lack of manners, or his halting Latin, or his too-easy grin. That lasted only until he'd picked up a rudi to spar with me in the garden.

Glancing at Agrippina and Justa, who both shook their heads to decline, I unfastened the ties at my shoulders. Sidonia urged Lenoria forward, and my handmaid unwrapped the ribbons belting my dress before shaking it out and folding it over her arm. She flitted about, tweaking adjustments to the linen band around my chest.

I made a face at Rafa, who took his turn smirking at my discomfort. Aunt had finally conceded that I didn't need a tunic when swimming in public. Another glance over at Herculaneum's beach proved she was still the most conservative guardian on the bay. With the wrap over my breasts and a linen loincloth, I was more covered than most women at the baths—and many on that beach.

Lenoria nodded, and I dashed to the water. "Where did you learn to swim?" I asked Bricus.

"I was fostered to a family who lived on the coast. It was a little like this, but greyer, rockier, and without so many trees. Actually," he said, laughing, "it was nothing like this except that it had water." For an exile, Bricus was surprisingly cheerful.

I walked into the calm shallows until the waves bumped my knees, enjoying the coolness on my sun-warmed skin.

"Don't ruin your hair!" Agrippina warned.

"Don't worry," Bricus reassured her. "She won't." Then he picked me up and threw me under.

I spit a jet of water at him as I emerged, grateful for the excuse to swim freely without aggravating my sister. We went a short distance from the beach to where I could barely reach the bottom.

Bricus wrestled his drenched hair away from his face. "Look there! Let's claim that little boat." He pointed at a small red hull bobbing out in the bay. The boat was farther than I'd swum before, but there were other vessels rowing and sailing, and the day was calm.

"Don't barbarians sink in deep water?" I taunted, swimming away with long strokes. He chuckled, then dove beneath the waves.

Even with a head start I could hear him surface closer and closer behind me, taking huge gulping breaths before splashing back under. Fighting the foamy crests and taking in a mouthful of water I understood why he liked being below the unpredictable churning.

The little boat was almost within reach, closer than I had thought from shore, when I realized I couldn't hear him behind me. I stopped, twisting my body in the rough tide, searching for his bright hair.

"Bricus!"

No answer but the slapping of water. I paddled in a circle. Nothing. I felt a sudden chill, my arms and legs stiffening.

"Don't Romans know anything about strategy?"

I whipped back around and there he was—one hand on the boat, his broad smile only slightly dimmed from exertion.

Heaving a breath, I closed the distance between me and the boat and grabbed the rim. It was tacky to the touch. Grimacing, I jerked my hand off the boat. Bricus caught my arm and we both tread water, staring in puzzlement at the red stain on my palm.

"Is that blood?" he asked.

I nodded, eyes spinning, and thrust my hand in the water to clean it off. We pulled ourselves up to peer into the boat.

A pool of pink sloshed in the bottom. Bloody hand-prints smeared the inside like a macabre mural. But there was no body. No ropes or nets either. Only two oars—one of which was clutched by a hand. Part of the forearm was intact, the white bones protruding, their jagged edges pointing like accusing fingers.

"I don't understand," Bricus said.

"I'm going to swim around. Keep an eye out." It wasn't a fishing boat, as it was missing the fish tank in the middle for keeping the catch fresh. When I saw the opposite hull I realized why. *Persephone* was painted in blue under the lip of the red rim. It belonged to a larger ship, perhaps a trading vessel or a quadrireme from the fleet at Misenum.

"It's from a ship called *Persephone*," I said when I rejoined him.

"We should row it back to shore." It sounded like the last thing he wanted to do.

It was in no way appealing to me either, but I knew he was right. Uncle would know who to inform, and they may need the boat to piece together what had happened. Visions of sea-monsters surfaced in my head but, as I only half-believed in fish stories, I guessed murder was more likely. Trying to avoid rolling myself in blood, I let Bricus push me up over the rim. Then he splashed in. Sitting cross-legged on one of the slats, I lifted my feet out of the wine-coloured water. The boat was wide enough we could sit side by side and each take an oar. But there were only two—and one was still being held.

"Should we keep the hand?" I didn't want to pry it off.

"They may need it. Maybe the person can be identified."

We looked at each other.

I lifted the oar and squeezed the paddle between my knees so the arm extended out toward Bricus. With one hand he held the upper part of the shaft and with the other tried to free the thumb from its grip. It wouldn't let go. Bricus jiggled the handle, trying to shake the fingers loose. Bloody water spattered from the mangled end of the arm.

"Is it terrible that I want to vomit and laugh at the same time?" I watched as he worked at the hand, his brow furrowed in concentration.

"Don't," Bricus said tersely.

At last the hand came free of the oar.

He threw it into the bow, where it landed with a thump. At least we wouldn't have to look at it as we rowed. But with every stroke, I imagined a man clinging to the oar to save his life. Rowing away in fear, or using the oar to defend himself. But it hadn't worked. Fight or flee— he'd been helpless.

Breathing in time with our strokes helped keep my mind

distracted; reduced the heaving in my stomach. We were almost to shore, just a few more pulls.

"Isn't there some kind of joke about a Roman, a barbarian, and a rowboat?" It was a miserable stab at wittiness, but I needed to break the silence.

"Not one that ends happily."

∞

I found Bricus again in the evening. The sky was dark indigo, with only a sliver of gold peeking over the horizon. He stood on the beach, bare feet half buried in sand and pebbles, watching the silhouettes of sails cross in the distance. Lantern lights set at each prow and stern flickered like low-hanging stars.

I came up beside him but didn't know what to say that wouldn't sound hopelessly childish. So I said nothing, and we watched in silence as the light faded.

"Do you think they'll find out what happened?" he asked.

"We know the name of the boat, so it's possible. It was probably expected nearby. Pompeii, here, maybe Baiae." I wasn't hopeful. Rafa had been sent to Misenum with a message for the fleet commander. If the *Persephone* was a navy ship, the commander would know of it.

"Strange, though, don't you think?"

"Yes." Uncle said a ship's boat was usually launched to land a party or because the vessel was in danger. What had happened to the rest of the crew? Had they suffered the same fate as the man in the boat? Or was he a deserter? "Perhaps the person or people in the boat suffered some sort of delirium, and ..." I couldn't finish my half-formed suggestion.

"Perhaps. I heard people can go mad from drinking seawater. I haven't seen it myself, but the sailors talked about it on the ship leaving Britannia." His voice was sombre and he glanced at me quickly out of the corner of his eye. He was holding something back, and it made me wonder what else the sailors told him.

I huffed out a small breath, tired of the honey-coated stories people thought I could handle. The villa we lived in was a world apart; almost a strange dream. But it was not the only world I knew. *Bricus doesn't really know me yet. I need to be patient.*

An unusual flicker in the water distracted me. "What's that?" My skin prickled with unease.

"What?" Bricus squinted into the dark. Clouds hid the moon. Only the lights along the bay and on the ships broke through the dark.

"There was a shadow over that ship's light. As though another ship crossed its path. But I didn't see any other lanterns." Even as I explained, I had a horrible premonition. *Something's wrong*—I watched these waters day and night for years.

"Just some lax commander."

"No ship is allowed to sail in the bay without lights, they get fined. There's too much traffic to be sailing blind, and accidents still happen." I paced slowly along the shore, twisting my head and trying to catch an angle that would illuminate what I suspected, hoping for moonlight to break through. "Yes. Look." I pointed.

Bricus came up behind me and lowered his head, looking over my shoulder down the line of my arm. "You're right." His warm breath tickled my ear and I could smell the peaches he had gorged on during desert. "It's a ship. I think it is headed for us. But—"

I turned to him, his eyes were wide and close to mine. I knew we both had the same thought. There was no rhythmic splash of oars, no fullness in the sails.

"Go back to the villa. Get your uncle." Bricus jogged for the little row boat moored to our dock.

"No. I'm coming with you." If the ship wasn't manned, he'd need help to avoid it crashing into the harbour of the town. There wasn't time to find someone.

"Help! On the water!" I yelled out as we clattered onto the wooden dock. If Gavius hadn't fallen asleep somewhere, perhaps he would hear.

Bricus had already unmoored the boat when I hopped in behind him, taking up an oar. His face set in an uncharacteristic scowl but he didn't waste time arguing. I rowed as fast as I could and he kept pace. We hadn't needed to row out very far. The ship glided toward the shore on the wind and incoming tide.

At last, moonlight. The ship was a large merchant vessel, which explained the lack of oarsmen. But my dread doubled when I saw the painted stern.

Persephone.

Our little boat rapped against the side of the *Persephone*. Someone must have heard, but no voices came from above.

"Hello on board!" Bricus called up.

A scream ripped free on the air—mind-numbing and anguished— followed by a drumroll of cracking.

I stared at Bricus, heart in my throat. On the deck above us a dark form appeared. Something was flung from the *Persephone* and broke through the stern of our boat. Water spilled in and we tilted under the strain. Wrapping his hand around one of the *Persephone's* dangling ropes, Bricus pulled me out. I clutched at another rope, fumbling in the dark before clamping both hands around it.

Our boat sunk under the waves and I realized the *something* had been a body, its limbs gnarled at unnatural angles. My hands convulsed on the rope, and I clenched them tighter around the rough weave.

A second splash echoed, this time from the other side of the ship. Another body? Or someone making his escape? Bricus and I exchanged frightened glances. *Climb or swim?* I didn't want to be in the water with whatever did this. I pointed up.

We paused at the top, listening intently. Bricus motioned for me to wait. I nodded. He slid over the edge and muttered a shocked oath, but the names of his gods were muted and unfamiliar.

A hand grabbed me. I barely bit back a scream as I realized it was Bricus who had reached down, almost yanking my arm off as he hauled me up onto the deck.

It was a battlefield of broken wood and bodies. The mast groaned and I could see it was split, a large jagged rift running up from below deck all the way to the cross-piece for the sail. I was surprised it was still standing. Ropes were lashed around the mast, as though someone had tried to keep it pieced together. And the deck—

Arms. Legs. Chunks of stringy flesh.

Heads.

My stomach roiled and I vomited over the side, clutching the railing as my body heaved.

"Stay there," Bricus said, hand on my arm. "I heard—"

Then I heard it too. A low whimper, like a dying animal. Bricus stalked toward the stern, moving along the railing so as not to walk barefoot through gore. Spitting out the last of the foulness in my mouth and wiping my face with my skirt, I followed.

A man was just visible at one of the rudder shafts. We glanced around, but nothing else moved. The man was tied to the shaft, hanging limply over the railing at his side. Hands shaking, I moved to untie him, but the ropes were unknotted. He must have wrapped himself there as a last attempt at steering the ship. Bricus eased him to the ground. It was impossible to tell where he was injured—all his clothes had been soaked with blood and were crusted onto his body.

"I saw lights," he said, feeble voice quivering. "Only darkness, he said." He moaned again.

I looked toward the lights of town and recalled just how much danger the boat was in. Most ships rode so high it was possible the *Persephone* could sail right into the harbour and destroy docks, ships, even low-built harbour buildings. We couldn't let it crash.

"The anchor!" I called to Bricus.

Bricus moved swift and sure to the anchor, made of iron and stone, and swung it into the water. The rope lengthened. I held my breath and braced against the railing, waiting for the drag. Finally, the rope tautened and the ship slowed. With a small jerk it pivoted slightly as it rode the tide, then stopped. We sighed with relief.

I turned back to the injured sailor, but his eyes were fixed, sightless, on the stars.

Fourteen

"DON'T THINK ABOUT IT ANYMORE," Bricus said in my ear, startling me.

I turned away from the view of sails skimming peacefully on the bay. "I wasn't." But it was a lie, the *Persephone* was anchored in my mind.

Bricus and I had given our account of the *Persephone* time and again. Aunt and Uncle were the first to know, followed by the fleet commander, arrived from Misenum in the morning. Then the magistrates from Herculaneum, who were extremely grateful Bricus avoided a disaster in the harbour. It was an honour I let him claim.

"You'll never know what happened," he said. "No one will."

"I'm not sure about that. If it's happened once, it must have happened before. Someone knows what creature did this." *And I know who to ask.* Except … I could not.

"Perhaps it was a sea monster, or something the sailors captured. They told us she sailed from the Black Sea. I've heard tales of bears with horns and giant eagles that swim." Bricus shrugged. "Or it could have just been a lion."

"A lion?" I couldn't believe his audacity.

"Not the best theory, but the simplest answer is often right." Bricus picked up a large wooden rudi and swung it around, whacking the trunk of the nearest tree.

What we'd seen aboard the *Persephone* didn't seem to bother Bricus as much as it did me. The problem was the simplest theory was the most frightening: that it was a man. Or at least, looked like a man. I knew the man with one eye could have savaged the crew of the *Persephone,* but I couldn't voice this fear aloud. Was this a message? A warning from him that he was still watching? But if it had been him, he could have killed me if he'd waited on board. Were there others like him? Strange I'd never considered it before … and unsettling.

Bricus finished smacking the tree and turned back to me with a frown. "Why is Agrippina's wedding in June? It seems like a long time to wait, now that Nonius has returned."

"Everyone knows that May is an unlucky month for weddings."

"The whole month? I'll never understand you Romans, no matter how much I try."

"I don't know why you bother. You'll be going home one day." I took one of the smaller practice swords and faced him.

Bricus gave a wistful smile. "I used to think so. In the earliest days of our exile, Mother swore she would reclaim her throne and put her traitorous consort to death." He balanced his sword on the back of his hand, trying to keep it level. "But after we'd been a few years in Germania, she began speaking of her legacy—meaning me and Corra. By all rights it should be my sister who succeeds, and I think that's why Mother sent me away. To learn what I could, to see if Rome would be our ally again. To help my sister if the time is ever right."

"You don't sound very hopeful."

Bricus looked at me with a peculiar expression, amber flecks glinting in his brown eyes. He raised a hand against the sunlight. "I'm not hopeful that our family will rule again. But perhaps there are better ways for me to serve them. I would bring home some of this …" Bricus gestured back toward the villa, and toward the ships in the harbour bursting with trade from around the world. "My people aren't poor, they aren't ignorant. This wealth, though, the luxuries of baths and libraries. Those things they don't have."

His selfless ambition stunned me, and I didn't know what to say. *You're mad* seemed a bit insensitive. I raised my sword. "You'll have to fight me for them."

By the time Petrus and Hilarus arrived we were both breathless and, my strength giving out at last, Bricus knocked me to the dirt with a wicked swing of his shield.

Petrus *tsked* as he walked up. "You are still too impulsive. You see the thing, but you do not understand its meaning."

"I don't like riddles, Petrus, you know that." I brushed grit off my forearms.

"Describe this enemy of yours." Petrus jabbed his cane in Bricus's direction.

"Taller than me. Longer reach. Almost twice my weight and about three years older."

"Meaningless," Petrus spat.

I looked Bricus over again, not understanding. "He has freckles."

"Let me try," Bricus said with a smile.

"You couldn't do any worse," Petrus said.

"She's a girl and not some brawler, so if she considers herself a fighter it's because she's trained. I would expect at least basic skills."

I stuck my tongue out.

"And," Bricus went on, "if she's trained, she may be concealing weapons, since she's not carrying them openly the way a soldier or mercenary would."

"Are you?" Petrus asked me.

Gods above, I hadn't thought anyone would find out. Ever since the *Persephone* I kept a small dagger strapped to my thigh, hidden by the draping of my skirt. It wasn't the best place to keep a weapon, but it was better than being unarmed.

"How did you know?" I asked Bricus.

"Just a guess," he said, pleased.

"All right," I said, gaze flicking over Bricus. "He wears a short tunic and breeches, and a gold torque around his neck, none of which are Roman. He also doesn't have Roman colouring." Bricus made a show of tousling his orange hair. "And he doesn't act civilized," I said, smiling. "Which means he may know how to use weapons I'm unfamiliar with and I should be watchful for different techniques."

"Better," Petrus said. "What else?"

"He hasn't killed anyone yet—"

"How do you know?" Petrus demanded.

"His eyes." I stared into Bricus's brown eyes, still laced with humour and soft around the edges. "Whatever else has happened in his life, he hasn't killed yet."

Bricus frowned, staring at me.

"Is she right?" Petrus asked.

"Yes." For some reason he wasn't happy admitting it.

"So he may not be trying to kill me outright," I said. "Maybe just wound me or get away. He'll be preoccupied with too many options, while I'll be more focused. Less distracted." My voice had faded as I realized this was not a game. Practicing was one thing. Considering how to overcome and kill the man in front of me was another. Because that's what I was looking for. Not how to disarm; but how to kill.

"From now on when you observe someone," Petrus said, "consider how what you see affects how they'd act. What sort of opponent would they make? What is their temperament? What weapons would they favour and how would they wield them?"

"It would help if I could see the tactics others use," I said, though it was a worn-out discussion. I'd been begging for months to watch a real match, but had always been denied.

"I'd hoped to take you to Pompeii to see at least one day of games," Petrus said. "They're starting in a few days and a troupe from Rome has been added to the entertainment. It should be better than the usual provincial fare."

My heart jumped. Petrus wouldn't have brought it up unless it had already been allowed by Uncle—or rather by Aunt Calpurnia.

"But we won't go if you're unable to complete your lessons. Seeing your enemy clearly is only the first step."

"What are you going to hit me with now?" I asked.

"Those lessons you know. You only need to practice more." But he threw a disc at Bricus for good measure, who ducked his head, laughing as it flew past. Then Petrus nodded at me, and pointed toward Hilarus. "Control your enemy."

I blinked. It seemed an impossible task, to control someone more than twice my size. Another riddle. "This is your lesson?" I asked impatiently. "Control my enemy? How am I supposed to do that?"

"Control your surroundings, as much as possible. Pick a spot for your battle that will favour your strengths." He opened his arms wide and turned in a circle on the path.

To my right—some loosely spaced trees, then the chickens. In front, down the path, was the stockyard filled with other animals. I ruled out both those directions, full of mud, muck, and obstacles. Plus animals—too unpredictable. To my left was the remainder of the grove, thinning out toward the cliff. Behind me was the wall to the garden with a small vestibule, so it had inner and outer doors.

"Where?" Petrus asked.

I pointed to my left. "If I fought over here, I could use the trees to hinder my opponent. I would move faster than Hilarus and could maybe force him over the cliff."

"Why not take it to the wall and try to escape into the garden?" Bricus asked.

"You're thinking like a defender," Petrus replied for me, "relying on your belief that others would be in the villa to assist you. Lucilla is on attack, as though she is alone and must end this fight now, or never."

That is what I was thinking. End the fight.

"You wouldn't get me over the cliff," Hilarus said.

I gave him a wink.

"So," Petrus said, holding up one finger, "you control your enemy if you control your ground, and force the fight on your terms." He held up a second. "You can control him by learning his weaknesses. If you can trick him into believing those weaknesses are his means of victory, you control his actions."

"Like using size against a large opponent?" I eyed up Bricus.

"Yes. Let him become overconfident in using his strength." Petrus gestured for Bricus to advance on him, pretending to fall back under his attacks. "Then, make yourself small and quick and use his force against him." When Bricus chopped down, Petrus stepped sideways and grabbed Bricus's sword hand, yanking him off balance and onto the ground.

"And against a short, fast one?" Bricus grinned and looked up at me in challenge.

"Be smarter," Petrus said.

"You lose," I said to Bricus, smiling at his mock-outrage—but then sobered as I considered the opponent against which my every battle was waged. He was large, but fast. Experienced and ruthless. "What about against a smarter, faster, more experienced opponent?"

Bricus and Petrus both stared at me, blank as new slates.

"Swim," Hilarus said, pointing down the cliff and to the sea.

Fifteen

The amphitheatre. Finally. Petrus's grumblings about the heat made no dent in my excitement. Though after I parted from him and Hilarus, I was glad of the cooler breeze at the top of the auditorium.

Hamitra had accompanied me so neither Petrus nor Hilarus was forced to give up a better seat lower down—Petrus was far blinder these days than he wanted to admit, and I would have felt too self-conscious sitting with the other senators' families on the low podium.

More women were here than I expected, the top seats speckled with bright shawls and shimmering ornaments. Several local troupes made the rounds in Campania, but the imperial class of gladiators had attracted quite a following. Pompeii had been buzzing, crowds in every plaza wagering on the advertised pairings.

"There is nothing like the emperor's gladiators," said the lady to the right of Hamitra as we took our seats.

"And why is that?" Hamitra asked.

The woman narrowed her eyes—clearly one shouldn't question the superiority of the emperor's stables.

"You'll see." She tipped her chin, then turned to her companions.

Hamitra smiled and adjusted her shawl, bracelets tinkling. I lifted my own higher to shade my eyes from the sun. Overhead, the amphitheatre's massive awning billowed in the breeze, but even under its shade the heat was merciless. The stink of mingled sweat wafted through the sun-baked crowd, and would only worsen as people returned after the lunchtime lull.

Trumpets sounded below, and our attention focused on the bowl of the amphitheatre. We'd not arrived early enough in the day to watch the animal hunts, but instead were midway through the noon-hour executions. The first round had been carried out and cleared away. The second was beginning.

Jeers rose from the crowd as five men were prodded from the tunnel beneath the auditorium's stone benches. Dressed in animal skins, they wore the heads of the beasts as crude helmets. Two were tigers, white and orange. One was a lion. One, a bear. A bull was last—he stumbled as he entered, weighed down by the horned headpiece.

The nuntius bellowed the name and crime of each. When the tigers were announced as arsonists, cabbages, apples, and other spoiled fruit rained down from the stands. Crouching low to avoid the worst of the onslaught, the condemned looked even more bestial. I wasn't surprised by the crowd's anger—arson affected everyone.

Doors to the tunnel opened again and the executioners, marching in unison, came in to a swell of applause. They were costumed as soldiers, brightly polished helmets flashing in the light. Two carried bows, two carried spears. If these had been the true venatores Hilarus described, ready for an animal hunt, the four of them may have been outmatched. A spear against real claws would be a challenge. But these animals were defenceless, their claws and teeth a parody. There was no place to hide. The only choices were run or stand. *Run or stand.* My heartbeat echoed the words, faster and faster. The crowd held its breath.

Cymbals crashed.

The bull sank to his knees, too feeble or guilt-ridden to avoid fate. An arrow flew and lodged deep in his thigh. He cried out and fell onto his hands. The lion turned to run, but the second archer caught him in his shoulder. Cheers from the crowd marked each impact, as though the voice of the audience guided the arrows to their targets.

The bear, hide flapping around his pumping legs, ground to a halt when a spear impaled him from behind. As he fell, he clutched the spear-point protruding from his belly, and tripped the unfortunate orange tiger who'd been running at his heels.

My gaze snapped to the archers as they downed the bull with arrows to his throat and back. The lion, struggling with the arrow in his shoulder, took another in the calf and fell, sending up a dusting of sand. He scrabbled in the dirt, dragging his lame leg behind him. Calm and confident, a spearman stalked over and swung the shaft of his weapon into the lion's head, knocking the animal helmet free and exposing the man's face. The lion raised his hand, as if to ward off the blow, but only succeeded in having his hand as well as his face pierced by the spear.

Cheers for the death of the lion turned to gasps. The orange tiger, ignored in the initial rush, had pulled the spear from the bear's back. Uninjured and now armed, he approached the executioners. The spearmen had only daggers left. Locking shields, they marched towards the orange tiger. *Run or stand … or fight. But did he know how?*

His accomplice, the white tiger, who'd avoided the stampede by running sideways, inched his way along the wall to flank the archers. With a mad shriek he ran for the nearest, who fumbled nocking his arrow and couldn't loose in time. They fell to the ground in a tangle, rolling. Half the crowd screamed, *"Yes!"* the other, *"No!"*

My eyes burned with grit and heat; I blinked several times, trying to moisten them. Orange tiger hesitated, spear raised. *He's only got one throw.* I held my breath, waiting for him to decide. He cast long with the spear—one of the spearmen lifted his shield, deflecting the blow. I groaned at the waste.

Running in unison, the first spearman landed a ringing blow with his shield, and the orange tiger fell sideways. The other landed on him, slitting his throat.

Only the white tiger left. I had to stand to see him rolling with the archer in the sand before the archer managed to half-kick, half-throw him. The second archer was ready—an arrow streaked like lightening into the white tiger's exposed chest. He twitched on the ground, then lay still. The downed archer reclaimed his helmet. Saluting the cheering crowd, the four executioners marched back down the tunnel.

I sucked in a shaky breath and sat. Hamitra glanced at me as I tore my gaze away from the sand—away from the bodies being hooked and dragged away by a man masked as a god of the underworld.

She put a gentle hand on my arm. "Perhaps we shouldn't have come so early."

"I'm fine." I'd wanted to come. And the *Persephone* had been worse. Much worse.

"Yes, *Persephone*." Hamitra shifted on the stone bench to face me, and I realized I'd said the name aloud. "I'm surprised you haven't come to speak to me about it."

My gaze darted to the people nearby, but none seemed interested in us. "I made you a promise—a bargain. And you've upheld your end. I'm alive, aren't I?" My smile felt weak.

"That's been easier than you make it sound."

Even as I turned my attention on the pair of clowns emerging from the tunnel, the weight of Hamitra's gaze lay heavy on me. *I'd kept her secret, what more did she want?* I let out a breath, concentrating instead on the praegenarii—one in red, one in blue. Each wore a polished helmet with a massive feather, and a brightly coloured loincloth. Coloured padding around legs and arms was so overstuffed their joints could hardly bend. But then, that was the point.

Blue took a wild swing at Red with his long wooden sword, sending him tumbling to his back. He rocked like a tortoise on its shell. Blue whacked at the dirt, unable to bend his elbows or knees to land a blow on Red. Laughter bubbled in the amphitheatre like soup at a simmer, but the amusement didn't reach me. *She's still staring.*

Slaves trotted in to rake out the sand, forcing the praegenarii to make bumbling exits, stumbling over the last bodies being dragged away. A large chalk circle was drawn in the centre—the limit of the field of combat. The audience hushed as weapons for the first gladiators were borne in to be inspected by the summa rudis and his assistant.

Still staring. I glanced at Hamitra. "What have I done wrong?"

She spoke softly, barely moving her lips. "Nothing. You've been so good at keeping your word, you won't even approach *me* with your worries. Perhaps I've been a bit … unfair … to continue hiding everything from you. You're not so young anymore."

I opened my mouth to speak, but bellow us, the nuntius announced, "Victor of seven matches, Hanno of Carthage." The crowd broke into loud applause and I tamped down my impatience—Hamitra dangled answers and I wasn't about to pass up my chance to ask.

Hanno emerged, his bristle-like brown hair uncovered, chest exposed. His entire armour was only a belted loincloth and a bronze manica protecting the length of his left arm, topped with a flared shoulder guard. He sheathed the dagger handed to him by the assistant and armed himself with the net and trident. *A retiarius.*

"His opponent," the nuntius drawled. "Victor of fifteen matches, Celadon of Thessaly!"

Cheers deafened as Celadon strutted onto the sand, his bearing triumphant. He raised his helmet in acknowledgment of the crowd before donning the sleek dome. I couldn't imagine fighting in such a trap, with no opening for mouth or nose. Only two, round eye-holes. It was little better than fighting with a sack over his face. Celadon took up a gladius and his large concave shield before facing his opponent.

"Impeccable physique," the woman beside us muttered to her friends as they craned for a better look. Celadon was built like Hilarus, his torso a mass of muscle.

Speed against strength. Hanno was more exposed, but could move freely. Celadon was heavily protected—even being able to hide most of his body behind a secutor's large shield—but could barely see or breathe. The longer the fight lasted, the more likely Hanno would win. Long or short, it would be hard to question Hamitra during the noise of the match. I forced my foot to stop tapping.

The summa rudis raised his baton in the air and the crowd hummed with excitement.

He lowered it with a flourish.

The gladiators circled. Hanno feinted with his trident, a shallow poke left, then long thrust right. Celadon's heavy shield blocked each.

I couldn't contain myself any longer and leaned toward Hamitra. "*Persephone.* You know what did it?"

She gave a sharp nod. "Yes."

"Should I be afraid?"

Hamitra's eyes sparked with amusement. "Would you not be afraid of a creature that could do such a thing?"

"I mean, was it the one-eyed man? Is he back?"

"I haven't seen him, and he wasn't on board the ship."

The crowd shrieked—Celadon had stepped on Hanno's net, and the strap connecting net to wrist had trapped Hanno like a fish on a line. He whipped out his dagger, and in one smooth motion severed the strap, dancing away from Celadon's sword.

"So there are more creatures like him?"

"Yes," she said, voice bleak. "Not many, but enough."

"And you ... fight them?"

All the softness vanished from her face. "When necessary."

"Could I learn to—"

"Never."

My flesh prickled. I swallowed my next question as hundreds of days of *normal* were swept away. Hamitra sat with an unnatural stillness in the vibrant crowd. I yearned to know her secret. To fully understand the world she lived in, but which I'd only glimpsed in moments of terror. *There must be some good in it. She and Nikandros lived among us. Protected my family.*

Her taut expression made me worry I'd pushed her too far, and I turned back to the fight. Celadon had pressed his advantage and, with a final sword thrust, knocked Hanno's dagger away.

Hanno knelt and lifted an arm into the air, index finger raised, acknowledging defeat. Celadon placed his blade at the base of Hanno's throat. One of Pompeii's magistrates stood and opened his hands, waiting for the crowd's verdict. Jeers came from some, but most turned their thumbs in favour of Hanno. The magistrate followed their lead.

The summa rudis lowered his baton between the fighters, then raised Celadon's hand in victory. Removing his helmet, Celadon accepted his wreath. The applause of the crowd followed him like a wave as he made a lap of the amphitheatre. With a final salute he left the sand, following the defeated Hanno.

The women around me talked a great deal about the fight, though none of the comments were about the quality of the match; it was the qualities of the fighters that piqued their interest.

Hamitra arched an eyebrow, though whether amused with the ladies near us, or inviting me to continue my questions, I wasn't certain.

"I didn't think the fight would be over so soon," I said, trying to return to a safe topic.

"That was quite fast, but others, particularly between swordsmen, will be longer."

"Have you been to the amphitheatre many times?"

"Enough that occasionally I find it more interesting to watch the spectators, rather than the spectacle." She glanced at the woman beside us, who was now talking earnestly to her companions and fanning herself with her hands.

Six matches followed and Hamitra was right, most were far longer than the first. I saw familiar weapons wielded by masters and novices alike. Curved blades and straight, spears and daggers, shields of all sizes and shapes. Except when Hilarus sparred with Bricus, I was always one of the fighters. Watching two fierce competitors increased my appreciation for how blades could be swung, blunted, thrust, and once by a daring provocator, handled from the wrong end.

Beside me, Hamitra let out a gentle huff. "All this time, and all this opportunity, and you still haven't asked what we are. You're the least curious human I've ever met. And perhaps the most trustworthy."

The word hung between us. *Human*—I'd never expected her to make such a confession. I risked reaching for her hand, hot where it rested in the sun. "Thank you—for trusting me. I won't betray your confidence, especially not where Nikandros might hear."

Hamitra laughed gently. "Yes. He has excellent hearing, and even after many years together, worries too much for my safety."

I returned her grin. *Hard to imagine Hamitra in danger.*

My smile disappeared as her attention snapped with alarming precision to the last pairing, her gaze fixated on the fighters. I'd not heard their introduction, but both were clearly in the first class, given the audience's near-frenzied reception. The horsehair crest on the murmillo's helmet added to his impressive height, but the other, taller still, was bare-headed. As he took his weapons from the referee, I realized he was a dimachaerus—a fighter with two swords.

My nerves were in tatters as the match began, gaze flicking between Hamitra's stone-stillness and the ferocity of the fight. The dimachaerus had attacked first, each movement a serpentine whip of power. Now the murmillo countered, cautiously jabbing his gladius, then jerking his shield forward, trying to outmaneuver the quicker blades of his opponent. Foot by foot, the murmillo gained ground.

"It's a ruse, you fool," Hamitra muttered.

The dimachaerus' move was clear a heartbeat before he made it. He struck, arcing his swords in opposite directions and prying the murmillo's sword and shield apart.

For one moment the murmillo's torso was exposed. He tried to regain his form to protect his body. *Not fast enough.* The dimachaerus continued his swing, arms circling—then thrust forward, embedding his blades into the murmillo's ribcage. Ripping the swords sideways, the dimachaerus tore the murmillo's torso nearly in half. He collapsed in on himself and fell to the sand. No time for the summa rudis to halt the match. It was grotesque and magnificent in equal measures.

Spectators shrieked approval.

"I'd say that was the finale." Hamitra's voice bristled with anger.

Without leaving me a chance to question her, she stood and walked over the seats, behind our row of cheering matrons. I followed.

Sixteen

HAMITRA AND I DESCENDED THE STAIRS ringing the outside of the amphitheatre. Petrus appeared from a lower corridor exit. He noticed me and beckoned.

"Go on," Hamitra said, still irate. "I have an errand." She strode away, vanishing into the crowded plaza surrounding the amphitheatre.

Puzzled at her sudden departure, I met up with Petrus and we entered the inner passages under the stands.

"Follow me." Petrus relied on his cane, sharp raps echoing off the stones. A guard allowed us past with a nod, and we turned into the corridors used by the entertainers. They were much less crowded, though the few people all seemed in a hurry.

Petrus led me into a small, empty room. "I'm late meeting a friend, but it's no place for a girl." He glanced up and down the corridor, taping his cane in frustration. "Hilarus was supposed to find Gavius and meet us here." *Tap tap tap.* He seemed divided as to what to do, staring at me, then the corridor. *Tap.* "Stay in this room and wait until they return." He shuffled off as quickly as he could.

I sighed, stuck until my escort arrived. If I wandered alone, Aunt Calpurnia would have a fit. I wished Petrus had kept me with him, but I supposed he knew this place far better than I did.

A loud curse followed by a groan came from the corridor. I let out a slow breath and crossed my arms. *None of my business. Stay here.*

More groaning. I peeked into the corridor. It was empty, but light shone from the cracked door of the room across. A sharp bark of pain.

I couldn't stand it any longer. Taking three quiet strides, I poked my head in.

"If you can't hold still, just drink it!" A young man wearing a stained leather apron thrust a cup toward a provocator. I recognised the wounded gladiator as one who'd won his match, though his thigh, still bleeding, had taken a deep slash in the final moments. The wrappings that offered small protection were bloodstained tatters on the floor.

"Give it," grunted the provocator, ripping the cup away and drinking in large gulps. The young surgeon took the opportunity to slap a fresh wad of bandage over the wound.

Laying back on the table, the gladiator's mumbled complaining tapered off and his breathing slowed. It seemed he'd fallen asleep.

The surgeon used the back of his hand to push blond curls off his forehead, his dark umber skin beaded with sweat, before taking up a threaded needle from where it lay on the table. He turned to peel off the already sticky mess of new bandages.

Then he noticed me at the door. "Who are you?"

"Lucilla. I'm waiting for my escort," I said, conscious that well-bred girls didn't wander anywhere without protection.

"Come in, you'll be safer in here."

"I don't want to bother you."

"You won't unless you keep peeking in that way." His brown eyes were friendly, if slightly overshadowed by bushy blond eyebrows. "Decimus Licinius Atellus." He gave me his trinomina with a nod.

I slid into the room, leaning back against the wall.

Atellus finished removing the bandages, then gently flooded the wound with the rest of the wine. Patting it with more cloths, he cleaned off clotted blood and dirt. Satisfied, he worked the needle into the flesh and through the flap on the other side of the gash. Sure fingers pulled the thread long enough that he could knot it together, the wound puckering underneath the stitch. His hands moved deftly as he completed a second, then a third.

Atellus looked over, as though surprised I was still there. "You're very quiet for a girl," he said, white teeth flashing in his dark face.

"I don't have anything to say."

His smile grew. "Tell me, were the games what you expected?" His eyebrows knit in concentration as he resumed his stitching.

"Yes. And no," I said. "Some fights were too uneven. I thought weaker fighters were paired together, not sent out to be slaughtered."

"They are. Which fight bothered you?" He made a last knot and trimmed the excess with a flick of his knife.

"The one with the dimachaerus and the murmillo. The murmillo seemed completely outmatched."

"The dimachaerus would be Marcus." Atellus's face curled in disgust. "I'm not surprised he was mis-paired. But he did fight Dorician, didn't he?"

"I couldn't hear the names."

"Well, if he did then maybe he won one fairly. Dorician has twenty-two matches—he's ranked in the first class. But he's not among the wounded. Was he killed?" Atellus seemed taken aback.

"Yes." I didn't want to describe it. "But why don't you trust this Marcus?"

"I've never had to treat him."

"Shouldn't that be a good thing?"

"Think about it." His tone made me bristle. "Every gladiator gets hurt. In training, in the amphitheatre. I've never even seen a scratch on that one. It's not right."

"If you say so." If he could be condescending, so could I.

He stared at me a little too intently.

I searched for something to fill the silence. "The executions were well done."

"Those are the only others I never have to treat," he said with severity.

"You disagree with executions? They're arsonists, murderers. Those people deserve the Emperor's justice."

"They should be executed, but it doesn't have to be so public."

"Yes it does! How else do people know they're being protected?" My eyes burned and I blinked. *Don't cry around wounded gladiators.*

Atellus began bandaging the wound, wrapping it with strips of linen. "My cousin was killed. By some thugs he owed money to. I'd like to have known they were punished, but I don't know if I would have watched. He—my cousin Publius—they cut off his hand. The physician who treated him only seemed to make it worse. The black rot set in and just a few days later he was dead." He cleared his throat.

"Is that why you became a surgeon?"

"Atellus, did you collect any—oh." A young man jerked to a stop part-way into the room, assessing me with curiosity. From the bloodstains on his tunic he was either another surgeon, or a corpse.

"Go away, Modeno," Atellus said. "I told you I'm not providing you with any blood. You have the dead—make do with them."

Modeno shook his head and shrugged. "You're passing up a fortune." With a last speculative glance at the provocator, he left.

Atellus cleared his throat uncomfortably. "Many people are willing to pay good money for gladiator blood. They believe it cures Apollo's curse—when people's bodies seize and twitch."

I nodded, having heard of it before. Aunt Calpurnia's physicians were never short of dire warnings, though they often seemed unrelated to her actual problems. "Modeno sells it and they …?"

"Yes, they drink it. Usually mixed with other ingredients."

"But you don't think it actually works?"

He finished bandaging the wound on the provocator's leg. "One person says it works, and suddenly everyone believes them. No one sees all the people it doesn't help. False cures; false hope. But we're all searching for what Asclepius lost."

"What do you mean?" I only remembered that Jupiter struck Asclepius down with a thunderbolt for his audacity in bringing the dead back to life.

"When he was still mortal, Asclepius was given two vials by his mentor, Minerva. The vials contained the blood of the gorgon Medusa." Atellus held his hands up to the lamplight, as though holding the vials himself. "In one, the blood from her left vein. A poison so powerful that a single drop could kill a man. In the other, from her right, a medicine to bring one back to life."

"Where did he lose them?" I asked, fascinated.

"No one knows. And after Asclepius became a god he no longer cared to restore mortals. We pray for his wisdom and guidance, but don't expect him to bring back the dead. That's something we must learn ourselves. But I believe every poison has an antidote. Our bodies age and die because of the poisons that infect our humours, so all I have to do is find the right antidote."

"Do you think you can?" The fates of mortals were supposed to be measured and cut with no mistakes. Wouldn't bringing back the dead mean Fate could be thwarted?

"Not likely," he said, gathering up his tools. He quickly wiped them down and packed them into a small wooden case. "Not when I spend all my time piecing carved-up gladiators back together."

"Surgeon!" Someone bellowed from down the corridor.

Atellus gave me a sly grin and wiped his hands on his apron. "See?"

After he left, I eyed the unconscious gladiator. Small droplets of blood squeezed slowly from the mend in his leg. I wondered if he would recover from his wounds, or succumb. His fingers twitched. *I should go find Petrus before he wakes.*

The room across the corridor was still empty. Either Gavius was far gone at a taberna, or he and Hilarus had been diverted by one of Pompeii's infamous brothels. Cincinnata was never short on stories about those.

A breeze blew down the long tunnel from the nearest exit, snapping my dress around my legs. Curious, I took a few slow steps, sand grating under my sandals, and stopped under the edge of the arch. The bowl of the amphitheatre opened before me. A few people remained in clusters on the stepped seats, some reliving the excitement of favourite pairings, arms flailing in imitation of winning moves. I'd thought we must all be faceless voices, high above the fighters. A confusing blend of humanity. But no, every face could be seen.

"Lucilla?" Hamitra called with relief from the bend in the corridor. "Would you be willing to accompany me to the latrines in the palaestra before we find our companions?"

"Hilarus was supposed to meet me here."

"He was busy depositing Gavius under a tree to recover from his … lunch. I told him I'd come find you."

We left the amphitheatre and crossed the plaza. The entrances to the palaestra's large field were clogged with people coming and going, and annoying groups who had stopped in everyone's way. Once we pushed inside, it was clear the bulk of the crowd from the games had the same ideas as us. The exercise lawn was packed. Some were sparring and wrestling. Others relaxed under the rows of manicured trees, sipping drinks as slaves fanned away the last of the heat. We snaked our way through the centre of the field, toward the pool.

"I've been wanting to ask you something," Hamitra said. "Would you be interested in travelling? Perhaps to Greece?"

Her question surprised me, then I realized with a jolt of panic what she implied. "You're not leaving, are you?"

"We may have to leave soon. Nikandros is near finished with the library. Now that Agrippina is to be married, your aunt will make plans for you next. I don't think they'll need us here much longer," she finished with regret.

"But I need you here. And I'm not ready to get married."

"These things are not always in a woman's power to control. Sometimes you must be like the shore, and sometimes like the sea. The difference is knowing when to be firm and when to be fluid." She gently squeezed my hand. "But perhaps I could convince your aunt and uncle that travel would help you settle more comfortably into your future life."

Future life. Husband. Children. A terrifying thought. But Hamitra had a husband, and didn't seem to mind.

"Maybe travel would help," I said, unconvinced.

"There's no telling what the future holds. And we don't want to leave, if we're able to stay longer. I've enjoyed being here far more than any place I've lived in a long time–"

Hamitra stopped suddenly, clutching her face with a grimace of pain. I reached to help her but she waved me away, withdrawing a bloody tooth from her mouth.

"I'm fine," she said, but for the first time I saw her discomposed, almost nervous. "It's been bothering me for months. I should have had it pulled sooner." She wiped her fingers with care and wrapped the tooth in her handkerchief, then tucked it into her small pouch. When she looked up, her gaze strayed behind me and widened in surprise.

"That seemed painful. You should have it looked after." The man's polite words were spoken in pure insolence and I turned, a rebuke ready to fly in Hamitra's defence.

I expected a man like Quintus, all pomp and no backbone. But this was not a man to antagonize—the dimachaerus who'd gutted his opponent. My jaw snapped shut.

Hamitra stepped between me and the gladiator. Water droplets beaded on his chest and dripped from his black hair as he climbed out of the palaestra's pool.

"Marcus," she said coolly, surprising me. "I see you've finally found an occupation which suits your temperament." Hamitra glared, echoing the look Nikandros bestowed when irritated. "I didn't realize you could sink any lower in the world." I'd never seen her display so much emotion—it verged on outright hatred. Apparently Atellus wasn't the only person to take issue with Marcus.

"You've always been easily fooled by appearances. My status is about to rise considerably," Marcus said with easy confidence.

"How odd. People with status usually wear substantially more clothing." Hamitra's disdain had the effect of drawing my attention to his bare torso. Broad shouldered and narrow-hipped, his obvious strength wasn't softened by the layer of fat many gladiators were prone to. It was difficult to shift my gaze elsewhere—there was something odd I couldn't place.

"I haven't changed for the worse, have I?" Marcus made a show of toweling off and Hamitra averted her eyes.

Atellus had been right. I couldn't see a scar. No injuries old or new. Then I realized what bothered me. He was flushed, but untanned. Skin paler than mine. Unnatural for anyone who exercised daily in the sun.

He caught my gaze. "Your friend doesn't disapprove."

Merda. I'd been staring. Fire crept up my neck. "Licinius Atellus is amazed at your ability to avoid injury." I tried to sound bored. Marcus didn't buy it—in fact what I'd hoped would seem dismissive put him on edge.

His shoulders squared, expression tightening. "Is that so?"

"My companion is very young," Hamitra said, in firm warning.

A chill ran up my spine. *How could I have been so foolish?* Hamitra wouldn't take issue with just anyone. *Eyes to see; a mind to think.*

"Yes," I said. "The surgeon mentioned how pleased he was to have one less gladiator to patch up. Though he's quite good at his work. Noticeably so." It wasn't very subtle, but I hoped it offered Atellus some protection.

Marcus grinned, a curve of lip without humour, and his azure eyes bore into mine. "Quite noticeable."

"Petrus is looking for you," Hamitra told me, pointing toward a long, shady porch. Her sharp-boned face stayed fixed on Marcus, tension crackling between them as I hurried away.

SEVENTEEN

PETRUS AND I MADE OUR WAY TO THE STABLES where we'd left our wagon. I'd pulled him away from his companions by reminding him he wouldn't be paid if I didn't make it home sometime this month. We had only to corral the others and, if we didn't stop for any more distractions, could be back at the villa before full dark.

Distractions. An inadequate word for the events of today. The spectacle in the amphitheatre was just that—frightening in intensity; glorious in triumph. I'd wanted to see the contests, imagining them to be more impressive versions of my own training. But it had been far beyond that, and I understood the attraction—the irresistible pull it had on the crowd—better than before.

And, curse Eros, attraction *is a powerful thing.* I hadn't been prepared for the way Marcus's bold gaze burned through me like lightning. It was bad enough my family threw me together with Bricus at every opportunity—at least his smile could be trusted. Marcus, on the other hand, was as trustworthy as the Trojan horse. Hamitra's distaste had poured free like water from a fountain, and it was a warning I intended to heed, no matter what darts Eros shot my way.

I could tell Petrus noticed my discomfort. "Just give me the lesson, Petrus."

"I had a lesson in mind," he said slowly, "but somehow I don't think you've taken from this day what I intended."

"Did you expect me to run screaming from the sight of blood?"

His lips twitched. "Never that. I was concerned you'd be more eager to fight."

"And now you're not?"

"Now I'm concerned about other things." Petrus halted on the curb, and I was forced to turn back to face him.

"Stop being so obtuse and speak plain."

"Oh! Uppity now are we?"

"You're here to teach me to fight, not to philosophize. I have an uncle who does enough of that."

"Words have power, too, Lucilla." Petrus frowned at my outburst, but didn't seem surprised. "Words are weapons. They act on the mind the way sword and shield do on the body. Words can pierce, or they can protect. Swords may have the power to kill, but words can make people long for death."

"Fine, fine. Words can leave a mark, same as a sword."

"So quick to dismiss me now, I see." Petrus jabbed toward a simple scrawl of graffiti on the plastered wall. "Look here, Crescens has placed his mark. 'Crescens makes the ladies sigh' — very provocative." Petrus chuckled. "The next time someone meets Crescens what are they looking for?"

I shrugged.

He glared at me, then started walking again. "They will want to know if it's true. Maybe some ladies will even want proof."

I followed. "Smart of Crescens."

"I don't want your sass, child."

"You should be teaching this to Rafa, then."

"I already have. I thought you should learn it, too. Words have the power to make things true, even though they may not have been so in the first place. Do you understand?"

He stopped again and made me face another wall — this one marked anywhere a person could reach. Some were mere scribbles, some carefully lettered and illustrated. They clustered on the plaster in manic chaos. Petrus rested beside me, hands on his walking stick.

I read. Dirty verse that made me redden. Political support for upcoming elections. Advertisements for cheap wine. All yelled their presence in reds and blacks and whites.

"What will your mark be?" he asked.

Lucilla fails the people she loves.

I almost said it — then saw him shift. I raised my arm to block his stick before it knocked the back of my head. My other fist cracked into his jaw. Petrus stumbled back against the wall, dropping his cane and catching himself against the rough plaster.

"I didn't mean ..."

With a curt gesture he waved me off. Tenderly massaging his jaw, he bent to retrieve his walking stick. "Well, you've left your mark on this old man, at least." Petrus grimaced. "You'll leave a mark on many people. Most of all your friends."

"Are you telling me to be kinder to my friends?"

"I'm making sure you know you have them. When is the last time you spoke with Rafa?"

"This is your lesson? To make me feel guilty?" So what if I hadn't spoken with Rafa over the past few weeks? I'd been distracted by Bricus, and a ship filled with dead bodies, and Agrippina's wedding plans. Rafa hadn't come to me either ... too busy with his duties to Uncle and Justa. I scratched the back of my burning neck. "He's ... making his own life Petrus. How do you talk to someone who's walking away?"

He tapped his stick on the ground, his face wrinkling deeper with his small smile. "Simple, girl. You walk beside him."

∞

The moon was a sliver in the night sky. I climbed the narrow staircase to Rafa's room under the rafters, dragging my feet. It had been a long day. Almost knocking my head against a roof-beam, I muttered under my breath. I didn't know what prompted Rafa to move here last year, nesting with the birds instead of the rest of the household, but privacy was probably even harder to come by for him than for me.

Rafa sat at a low table, lamplight illuminating his wiry form bent over a scroll. A dozen more scrolls littered the ground at his feet and lay draped over the table.

His head shot up at my approach, revealing the reed-pen in his hand and an open inkpot.

"What are you working on?"

"Why do you care?" He pushed away the scroll, rattling the ink.

"Of course I care. You're the one who's been avoiding me."

"Vitalis is dead."

I was stunned into silence. "When?" I croaked out. *How could Justa's mother die, and no one tell me?*

"Two days ago. I would have told you this morning, but you were busy," he accused.

I tried to think of something helpful to say. To let him know I felt for Justa's loss—and his as well. He had grown close to both Justa and Vitalis while helping Justa's business. Hadn't I left him to his own tasks? I could have enforced my supposed ownership and told him not to leave the villa. It looked strange to the others, allowing him so much freedom—not that Rafa cared how the other slaves saw me.

Rubbing my forehead, I sat on my knees beside him. "Will you tell me what happened?"

His eyes filled with unshed tears, dark rings exposing his fatigue. "Justa returned in the evening and found her dead, lying over her records. I think ... I haven't told Justa this ... but I think she was poisoned."

"That's a bold claim."

"I don't have proof, but things haven't been right between Vitalis and Stephanus's household lately."

Things had never been right in that household. I had no love for Stephanus, or his ambitious wife Themis, who confirmed all Aunt Calpurnia's fears about social climbers. They'd freed Vitalis and other slaves, not to recognize merit, or in gratitude, but to have freedmen support their bid for status. To have more votes during elections, and persuasive tongues arguing their case. But I didn't know if either would go so far as to poison Vitalis.

"What reason could they have to kill her?"

"You don't have to believe me," he said bitterly. "I shouldn't have told you. I have to talk to Telesphorus—Stephanus's overseer—about something I heard first."

"I believe you. Rafa, I just don't want you to get caught up in something that will drag you under. You don't have any status to protect you if—"

"I know!" He slapped his hand on the table, rattling the inkpot. "I know I have no status; I have no name. I can't help Justa. Like I couldn't help—" He cut himself short, his breathing heavy.

His hand lay on the table and I covered it with mine. "We're grown. Tell me what happened."

"I swore an oath to your uncle. I'm not to tell anyone."

"I'm not *anyone*, Rafa. I'm your friend."

At last he looked me in the eyes. They betrayed all his worry, his frustration. But even in his pain he weighed this decision carefully. Then the tension fell from his face.

"My mother was a companion to Queen Berenice," he said. I nodded, always suspecting he was the son of a wealthy family. "My father was killed during the uprising in Jerusalem and mother and I fled with the Queen and the rest of her entourage when they came under Roman protection." He paused and I waited anxiously for him to continue. "When the Queen and Titus began their affair, my mother was asked to report on their activities."

"She was an informer?"

"No. She refused. So I was abducted to ensure she followed their plan."

I opened my mouth to ask more questions, but he held up his hand.

"She died while I was being transported to wherever they were going to keep me. They received word of her death and decided to kill me. I guess I was no longer of any use. But they didn't know I'd read the letter they cast off, and that I could speak Latin and hear their scheming. I'd only ever responded to them in Greek. They got drunk, it was my first bit of luck, and I managed to sneak away. Somehow I made it from Ostia, where we landed, down the coast. My only thought was to get home." He said it in a dejected rush. "When I look back on it now, I can't believe how foolish my plan was, and how fortunate I was to end up here."

"But why couldn't you have told me this sooner? Surely no one is hunting for you now?"

"After they approached her the first time, my mother knew we were in danger. She said my best protection was to know my enemies." He paused again, and I suspected this was what Uncle had wanted to keep hidden for my safety. "She confided it was Titus's brother who wanted her services as informer."

"Domitian?" I wasn't shocked, but it was a dangerous game for an Emperor's son to play. After Nero's death it was as though the Hydra had been unleashed—kill one emperor and two more rose to take his place. In the insanity that followed I wasn't even sure Domitian's actions were wrong. Rafa and I had done our own share of spying, after all. And Titus Augustus still lived, so perhaps his brother was just being cautious, protecting their father and family legacy. But it was impossible to know. Which explained why Uncle had kept Rafa's past so guarded.

"Do you need my help getting home?" I asked, ashamed I'd not made the offer sooner.

Rafa shook his head. "Your uncle and I decided it would be best for me to stay here. The risk was greater to me if I returned home. And I had no one left." He shrugged his shoulders.

Rafa had lost; Justa had lost; I had lost.

I was tired of it.

Taking the short knife for trimming the reed pen, I made a shallow cut in the palm of my hand and extended it to Rafa. "I swear to help with your burdens, if you'll help me with mine."

He looked askance at my hand, thoughts I couldn't read flitting across his face. "Can I swear it without the blood? I'm not allowed, you know," he said, reminding me of the edicts of his god.

"Without the blood, then." I was grateful he'd finally told me the truth about his past. The air was clear between us, apart from secrets that weren't mine to tell. I wrapped my hand in a strip torn from my shawl—Aunt Calpurnia would bemoan the loss of another one—and held my hand out again.

"Wait." I withdrew it quickly. "Are you planning to kill Domitian?"

He snorted. "No, I don't blame him for my mother's death. It was a fever. It would mean more to know Justa can count on your support, since I have nothing to offer her."

As if his love counted for nothing. I nodded. "She has it."

He smiled at my extended hand and reached for his pen. "I feel inadequate, since you cut yourself," he explained. He took the pen and slashed his palm with ink.

I snorted. "Nice showmanship. Did Petrus teach you that?"

"I had to make some kind of gesture."

We clasped hands, and I felt the miles between us vanish. Petrus had been right, I should have known to speak with Rafa sooner.

Relief didn't last long. I was too aware we'd been utter failures at proving the senator was behind Father's murder. "So how are we going to prove Vitalis was poisoned?"

"I could ask Nikandros if the library has any works on herbs or poisons." His tone wasn't optimistic.

"A slave researching poisons is not the best idea."

"True. And he notices everything. I can't open a scroll without him asking what for."

"And there's hundreds of books in there. I wouldn't even know where to start. It's probably best to find another way."

He nodded, and I breathed easier. Rafa poking around in the library might make Nikandros nervous. He and Hamitra could decide to leave. Or he might decide their secret was worth more than our lives. I wouldn't risk Rafa's safety.

Feeling Rafa's perceptive gaze on me, I turned my attention to his table. I had no idea he'd been so busy, but many of the scrolls that lay open bore his handwriting. "What are you writing?"

"I'm just practicing," he said evasively. I stared at him until he gave in. "Poetry, mostly. Maybe some philosophy one day. For now, it's enough to play with the words."

"'If you build a house of words, it will last no longer than your voice carries on the wind,'" I quoted.

"'But when written, others may build monuments on the foundations I lay.'"

"I hope your words are remembered."

"Likely not. But maybe they'll linger, slowly decaying in a library somewhere like Philodemus's."

I smiled at his wistful tone. "Can I read some?"

"Not yet."

Eighteen

"With this offering, I redeem me and mine," Uncle spoke the incantation for the ninth time, throwing the last handful of black beans over his shoulder. Our entire household was gathered in the atrium and, as the beans scattered across the floor, we banged our bronze pots and dishes, making an ear-splitting racket. "Spirits of my father, my ancestors, be appeased and be gone," he said as the ringing died away.

I held my breath. Every Lemuralia, when the walls between the living and the dead were weakened, my father's spirit seemed the strongest to me. Would this be the night when he broke through, when I might see him again?

Slaves collected the pots. Norbanus hurried them on, grumbling instructions about having them all scrubbed at once. It was midnight, and I hoped we'd get something decent to eat by morning. Pherenike smiled at me as she left to accompany Norbanus to the kitchen.

I shook my head. I'd freed Pherenike as soon as she became thirty, and the first thing she did was marry herself to Norbanus. What did freedom mean, if you threw it away once you had it?

Titan, Agrippina's monstrous new dog, knocked me into a column as he ran around sniffing at the beans. My future brother, Nonius, had been bursting with pleasure after his return from Pannonia. But what kind of lover brought home a huge, hairy, mountain dog as a gift? It puzzled me as much as Norbanus and Pherenike, who I'd always known to hate each other.

I climbed the stairs to my room, hopping to avoid a fresh pile Titan had left on the landing. Undressing quickly, I threw my shawl and dress in the direction of a chair, then slid into bed. My contented yawn turned to a groan when I remembered our excursion tomorrow, traveling to Agrippina's villa near Stabiae so she could show off her fancy redecoration.

It *could* be a pleasant day, being out on the water. Though Aunt Calpurnia had taken her yacht to Baiae, so our little sailboat would be crowded. Justa was coming, as she had provided the villa's new draperies; Nonius, of course; Bricus and Quintus who were here for the summer. And I'd insisted on bringing Rafa.

From out in the hall, Quintus cursed and bellowed for water and cloths, clearly having stepped in the mess Titan left. Bricus let out a hearty guffaw that made me smile. Then I thought again of who was going to be in one small boat, and my smile vanished. No point hoping tomorrow would be pleasant. *Lares protect us … and let us all survive.*

∞

The wind lashed the boat and we tilted precariously as waves broke over the sides, flooding the bottom with water.

"We're almost at Capreae. Let's find a place to get to shore," Rafa shouted over the rising storm.

Droplets of rain began to fall. It had been clear all morning and into the afternoon, but we'd been out for barely a half-hour before the storm blew in, clouds dark and angry. I refused to look at Agrippina, whose lengthy session with Sidonia had prevented a morning departure. I refused to look at Quintus, whose expedition to Herculaneum to meet a magistrate prevented a mid-day departure.

"The harbour is right there." Nonius pointed toward the docks on the small island, but we were already speeding past.

"Take the sail down," Bricus yelled. Rafa, Quintus, and I tugged the ropes. Faster and harder the wind blew.

"We can row to Capreae." Quintus took up an oar. "I know where we can land. Look for a hole in the rocks. Small, under that tall cliff." He gestured at a high wall of pale stone, scraggy bushes lining the top.

Agrippina and Justa sat clutching the mast while Bricus and Quintus rowed for shore. Rafa and I bailed water out of the bottom as more and more waves crashed over the sides.

If we blew past the island, we'd be taken into the open sea. But rowing toward it was worse—it seemed a never-ending wall of rock.

"There!" Nonius yelled. A tiny black opening appeared, just visible above the waves. If we didn't reach it, jagged spear points of stone would break the boat apart.

Then, as if a great hand reached up from the deep, fingers of water spilled over the sides of the boat. Our foundation dropped from under us. There was no time to do anything but take a breath. The force of it pulled me down, under the rolling waves. For a moment, calm surrounded me. Noise vanished.

I struggled to reach the surface, gasping for air.

"Agrippina! Justa!" I heard faint cries in answer. Flailing arms splashed to my right. Quintus's heavy toga was caught, and he went under. Without another thought, I dove, needing two strong pulls to rip the fabric free from the metal rings of the boat. Lungs burning, I dragged Quintus to the surface and draped him over an oar. He coughed and rubbed water out of his eyes. Chest heaving, he stared at me as we floated on the choppy waves.

The burn in my muscles eased. "Let's go."

We swam, Quintus using the oar to keep him afloat. Rising on a swell, I caught sight of Rafa at the mouth of the cave, dragging Justa with him. Nonius clung to the rocks near the entrance, pointing at me. Off to my right Agrippina gripped another oar, kicking for shore. Bricus surfaced in the water beside me. Together, we helped pull Quintus, rain whipping our faces.

Every inch toward the island seemed to be against the raging water. I kept my gaze forward, locked on our destination. *Just a few more strokes.* A surge took us right as we reached the mouth of the cave. Its sudden force crashed me into the jagged rocks and my upper arm burned with pain. Fighting to not swallow water, I propelled myself into the grotto.

The cavern was completely enclosed, save for the small opening which we'd washed through. The low light reflected off the water in shimmering grey patches. My companions looked otherworldly as they dragged themselves onto shore, shedding silver skin.

Bricus grabbed my hand and dragged me onto the rocky slope. We collapsed together, gasping for breath. The waves lapped at my feet, the calm of the cave surreal after the rain and turmoil outside.

Beside me, Bricus pushed his sopping hair out of his face, his other arm warm where it cushioned my head. I smiled at him, and at the same time realized how close we were pressed together. And how my dress clung to the length of my body. Bricus's gaze traced my form, a slow smile spreading over his face.

Light flared from behind me.

"Fortune smiles on us," Quintus said, full of sarcasm.

Bricus's laugh echoed in hollow barks off the walls of the grotto. I turned to see a feast. Lamps, which Agrippina and Justa had begun lighting, were placed around the perimeter of a naturally hewn room nestled in the grotto's walls. Lush carpets were piled on the floor, and in the centre stood a low table laden with fruits, bread, and decanters of wine and water.

"What is this place, Quintus?" I looked around in awe.

"I visited here once when Father came to the island to meet with some official. There's a villa almost right above us. One of Tiberius's pleasure palaces, Mother called it."

"Well it's clearly still in use," said Nonius. "We shouldn't touch any of this. It's an offering to the gods of the grotto."

"What?" Bricus asked through a mouthful of grapes. "Bah." He waived his hand. "The gods will understand. Don't you have rules of hospitality here? They whipped up a storm to trap us in this place, they can bloody well feed us while we're here." A fistful of figs followed.

Agrippina looked longingly at the bread, a hand on her stomach. "This was supposed to be such a good day."

"Oh never mind!" Quintus's voice croaked, still raspy after swallowing seawater. "I'm eating too."

We sat on the carpets around the low table and filled our stomachs. Quintus and Nonius watered down the wine and we shared the goblets around our little circle.

My arm still bled, so I tore a strip from my damp dress and tried to wrap it—the scrape was mostly shallow, but ran shoulder to elbow. Seeing me fumble, Bricus plopped down beside me and bound it tight. He didn't seem in a hurry to return to his place near the fruit.

Gradually, the sounds of the storm eased, the howling wind through the grotto's entrance turned into a musical whistle.

"It must be dark by now," Quintus said. "We should stay here until tomorrow. It's not reasonable to be swimming or trying to climb the rock-face if we can't see what we're doing. And if we've angered the gods, they won't be placated by us leaving now, anyway."

Everyone nodded in agreement. Swimming in the dark and chill did not strike me as the least bit fun or necessary.

"I can't believe we're in this ridiculous situation," Nonius complained, but with a lazy slur that took away any sting. He took another sip of wine and passed the goblet to Agrippina. "Stranded in a grotto with a slave, a merchant, an exiled prince." He gestured to Rafa, Justa, and Bricus in turn, "… and my bride-to-be."

"At least it's not your wedding night." Bricus winked at me.

Even in the low light, I noticed Agrippina's blush as she handed the cup to Bricus. He took a gulp and offered it to me, draping his arm over my shoulders when I took it from him. I stiffened.

Quintus pursed his lips. "It's not appropriate to treat my cousin like a camp follower. No matter what encouragement she's given you."

My face burned hotter and brighter than a flame.

Bricus laughed, though it held a scornful edge I'd never heard before from him. "No Briton mistakes a warrior for a bed-warmer. That's only a problem you Romans have. She saved your life today, and I haven't heard you say a word of thanks."

"It was a selfish act," I said. "Trust me." Still burning with awkwardness, I dropped Bricus's arm from my shoulders and moved to sit next to Agrippina. "I would never have heard the end of it from Aunt Calpurnia if I'd let precious Quintus drown. Angry spirits during Lemuralia would be tame by comparison."

"That reminds me!" Agrippina said, glaring at both Bricus and Quintus. "Nonius was telling me the most interesting story the other day. Weren't you, Nonius?"

Nonius cleared his throat. "Oh? Yes. About Athenodorus the philosopher. He stopped at an inn in Athens known for being haunted. Visitors had claimed to see the spectre of a man in chains, so Athenodorus went to see if the tale was true."

"Did he find a ghost? What happened?" Bricus asked.

"Oh … let me think." Nonius gazed at the ceiling, searching for lost thoughts. I suspected he'd had too much wine. "So Athenodorus spent the night and waited in the garden where the spectre had been seen, but saw no strange sounds or sights. Then, just as Athenodorus was drifting off to sleep, he heard the clanking of metal in the distance." Nonius sat straighter, as though he heard the clank himself. "It grew louder, moving near. Finally, out from the shadows of the pillars came the ghostly form of an emaciated old man, with irons binding his wrists and ankles. They clanked as he shuffled forward."

"It could have been some sort of scheme," Quintus interjected. "To try to extract money from Athenodorus …" He trailed off at our angry gazes and we turned back to Nonius.

"The old philosopher lifted his hands in greeting. The ghost beckoned him with a bony finger and drifted down the corridor without a sound."

"If it had been an actor, he couldn't have faked that." Quintus butted in again.

"Shush," several voices answered.

"Finally the spirit stopped, gave a last look at Athenodorus, and disappeared. Marking the spot, Athenodorus dug it up the next day. They found the putrid remains of a man in chains."

"Ooh," Justa let out a shocked breath. "What did they do with the body?"

"Of course they burned it, and carried out all the proper rituals," Nonius answered.

"And the ghost?" Quintus asked.

"Never seen after that."

Everyone grew silent. The tempo of the wind seemed to increase and lamplight danced against the gouged stone walls.

"That's why it's important to observe all the proper forms for appeasing the departed," Quintus said solemnly.

"How do we know the rituals really work?" Agrippina gazed into one of the lamps, a slight frown creasing her forehead.

"They must work," Quintus said. "Otherwise we would be flooded with the ghosts of the murdered."

"Who's to say we aren't? Perhaps we can't see them because the rituals banish them from our sight, but we don't know for sure it allows them to reach the underworld."

"The traditions all say—"

Agrippina's gaze snapped to Quintus, cutting his lecture short. "The only thing we know for certain is that the wrongfully dead are appeased by blood. It's in all stories of the gods and ancestors. If the person who wronged them is sacrificed, then they can be at peace."

I'd never seen Agrippina so agitated and knew she was thinking of Father. It was a nightmare I shared—somewhere his spirit wandered the earth, looking for peace and finding none. No one to hear his pleas. He could even be here, in this grotto, demanding we avenge him. To let him rest. I put an arm around Agrippina and she leaned against me. She would be leaving me soon—not as unreachable as Father, but in a different world just the same.

"You Romans are far too afraid of your dead," Bricus said. "This time of year in my homeland, if you are fortunate enough to join the Wild Hunt, you can earn a lifetime's worth of gold and glory."

"Do they hunt the dead?" Nonius asked.

"No, they are the dead. They pursue their prey at night, across the sky and land and sea. What they hunt is known only to them, but if a mortal aids the Hunt—obeys their commands without question—the rewards are beyond reckoning."

"People seek them out?" Justa asked in disbelief.

"For nights at a time, straining to hear the sound of their horns. Though, I've never heard of someone joining the Hunt and returning." He frowned.

"Gods and ancestors can't protect you from all the evil in the world," Justa's quiet voice broke in. "Mother told me once she had to protect me from Lilit—a sprit from her homeland who feeds off the blood of newborn children. Prayer doesn't drive Lilit away, she must be tricked into taking a different life than the one she came for. Sometimes an animal works, but not always." Justa's sorrowful eyes were pinpricks in the waning lamplight.

"She feeds off blood?" My voice came out steady, but my whole body was numb. I'd not considered that the one-eyed man may come from another land. Foolish, since Hamitra wasn't Roman either.

"What's so scary about that?" Quintus asked pragmatically. "It's just an eastern superstition, anyway."

"Mother would never say what she sacrificed to keep me safe." An uneasy silence descended after Justa's confession.

"You shouldn't sneer." Rafa said to Quintus. "Romans absorb gods like bread sops up gravy. A shrine on every corner and forgiveness for a quadrans." Rafa reached out, hesitating a bit before taking Justa's hand. He gave it a slight squeeze. "I believe it's my turn to tell a tale. This one's easy, because it's mine. The night Lucilla and Bricus found the *Persephone*, I was making my way back from Misenum after delivering the message to the commander of the fleet."

I nodded, though not happy to recall the *Persephone* on a night like this.

"It was dark, but I decided to press on. Outside Neapolis, amongst the tombs, I saw a man lead a woman off the road. Normally I wouldn't even have stopped, for a man and a woman hiding in the dark is not an unusual sight." Rafa paused and gave us a broad wink. Even Quintus chuckled.

"But as he pulled her close, she began to twitch and shake in his arms." Rafa's droll expression fell away, and his eyes grew distant. "I still remember the outline of her body against the light of the moon, jerking as if on fire. And the man holding her—he could have been a statue. His stillness was more frightening than her torment ..." he trailed off.

"What happened?" Nonius asked softly. "Was she cursed? My father said Apollo's curse makes people fall and twitch violently. Sometimes vomit or swallow their tongues."

Modeno's treatment sprang to mind, and I reconsidered how it must feel to be so afflicted that drinking gladiator blood seemed a fair exchange.

"For a time," Rafa continued, "it seemed the man was embracing her. But then he let her body fall to the ground, and left. I remember standing there in the darkness, the moon high before I dared to move. When I finally worked up the courage to go to her, she was long dead." His eyes were pools, ready to spill; he blinked and frowned. "She was covered, her whole body a mass of bleeding sores—red and black."

My heart beat fast. *Father.* Apart from the Vestalis Maxima, I'd never known of another person who'd died in the same way as he. But Rafa, of all people, had seen it; for him to tell this story, on this night, was surely the work of the gods. I couldn't believe I'd never told him *how* father died. The details had been so horrifying, yet the specific poison seemed unimportant.

Now Rafa and I had something to pursue that perhaps even my uncle hadn't considered. If the senator had access to such a poison, others may have been murdered this way. And there were only so many places bodies ended up if they were to have the proper rites. It was a slim chance, but after so much waiting, so much treading water and failing to even see the shore, it was a chance I couldn't ignore.

NINETEEN

WITH THE LAST OF THE WINE GONE and the plates emptied, the others started drifting to sleep. Rafa and Justa, huddled against one of the rock walls, talked in hushed voices. I didn't want to pry, but Justa caught my gaze, then patted the floor on the other side of her from Rafa. I made my way over, careful not to disturb Agrippina, who had curled up beside me.

"How are you?" I whispered. The memory of her mother must be strong tonight.

"Surviving," she said. "I was telling Rafa that Stephanus has died. Telesphorus came to me yesterday. It's very sudden."

I understood her suspicion. "You think Themis killed your father—" Justa's face soured. "Sorry—her husband, and your mother?"

"Either her, or her lackey Marullus," Rafa said.

"Rafa told me he thought Mother was poisoned. But everything seemed normal to me when I found her. She only had a plate of fruit and an almost empty glass of wine. I tossed the last bit down the latrine, though. I never thought to check for poison," she sounded rueful.

Rafa thumped the rug with his fist. "It gets worse."

"Telesphorus didn't just bring word of my father's death," Justa said. "He brought a lawsuit. That harpy is suing me."

"On what grounds?" I asked.

"Themis claims I'm her slave. That all my property is forfeit to her as her inheritance from Stephanus."

Rafa saw my puzzled expression and explained. "Anything that was in Vitalis's name when she died would go to Stephanus as the master who granted her freedom. But any property that was in Justa's name would remain her own."

I raised my eyebrows, surprised.

"I've been reading up on inheritance laws," he said, with a hint of defensiveness. "It's actually quite interesting."

I lifted my hands in surrender. "I didn't say anything."

"You never have to," he muttered.

I ignored that, instead recalling Justa's small shop filled with expensive fabrics, the lucrative trade in dyes, even the few slaves she now owned. Vitalis had been so intent on separating herself from Justa's ownership of everything connected to the business. Obviously she'd been protecting Justa's property from any claim by Stephanus. Or his wife.

"But how could you be her slave?" I asked. "You were born after Vitalis was freed."

"Themis claims I wasn't—that I was born before Petronius Stephanus freed Mother." I didn't miss the way she stressed her father's name. It was one thing to be raised a slave by your father, it happened every day, but it was entirely different for your future to be destroyed by his grasping wife.

I took Justa's hand. "We'll just get the records of your birth and present them to the magistrate."

She shook her head. "They were destroyed. In the earthquake of Nero's eighth year."

"You don't have a copy?" my voice wavered.

Justa shook her head again and sighed. "I was certain Mother did, but I searched everywhere. I think they've been stolen."

"Juno's cleft!" I cursed and Justa's eyes bugged out. I sent a quick apology to the goddess.

"Telesphorus wants you to know he's still your friend," Rafa said, "but he's also Themis's tutor—for the time being. I know he's trying to make her see reason." He put an arm around Justa. A woman's tutor may need to sign documents to make them official, but most could only delay the inevitable for a short time. Especially with a woman like Themis.

Justa's blue-green eyes searched Rafa's face. "What should I do?"

"First, you make sure the case is moved to Rome. Telesphorus said that Curtius Lentulus was dining with Themis last night, and didn't leave until this morning." Rafa curled his lip with distaste.

"But Lentulus is the magistrate hearing the case!" Justa said in exasperation. "How am I supposed to get a fair hearing?"

Rafa and I exchanged a glance—this plan had been well thought out. "That's what your patron is for," I said. "It's time Agrippina did something useful." I had another worry. "Rafa, if Justa dies what happens to her property?"

He thought for a moment. "She has no other relatives so it would be claimed by Themis on behalf of Stephanus's heirs." He turned a frightened gaze on Justa. "But until the lawsuit is decided, you're still ranked as a citizen, not a freedwoman. Make a proper will as soon as we get back. Then be sure Themis knows you've done it."

I nodded. "It's the best protection you have, until we can prove she's behind these deaths." Justa didn't deserve the uneasy burden of a sulking enemy—Themis was not going to get away with this for long.

"How are we going to do that?" Justa asked.

"Fortune might be on our side for once," I said. "I just met someone who knows about poisons."

∞

A shuffle on the rocks and the woodsy, black smell of fennel brought my eyes springing open. Hamitra knelt, dripping on the rock slip, fresh from the water. She caught me looking and put a finger to her lips.

"Are you all right?" she whispered.

"Yes," I kept my own voice low. "We're fine. But the boat sank."

"Everyone's been looking for you since this evening when you failed to return." She glanced over the sleeping forms. "There's no need to wake the others. I'll head back and bring a boat after dawn."

Hamitra turned to leave but I had to ask, "How did you know we were here?"

She sat next to me. I pushed myself up, wincing at the bite of pain in my upper arm.

"You're bleeding," she said.

"Just a scrape." I unwound the bandage, cracking more of the scab.

"Let me." One warm hand grabbed my arm and held it still. Hamitra talked quickly as she re-bound it using the cleaner portion of the cloth. "When we learned your boat never made it to Agrippina's villa, I followed the direction of the storm. I heard about this grotto from a local. But he wouldn't bring me here, for fear of the water deities." She gave a slight smile and tied the end off with a gentle tug. "Luckily, I'm a good swimmer."

"Like Marcus?" The bay in a storm wouldn't be a challenge for him, either.

Hamitra let go of my arm, and a deep silence settled between us. "I've known Marcus a long time, but he's not a friend."

"I only wondered if he was—" I stopped, her eyes like ice. "That is, if he lived by your rules."

"Marcus has no rules." Her tone was flat, emotionless. "I've reminded him to keep his distance from me, and mine."

"Whatever your reasons, thank you for protecting me again."

Her face softened. "In so many ways you remind me of myself as a child. I've been worried that your ... talents ... wouldn't be appreciated here. Especially as you get older. Know I'm serious when I say you'll always have a place with Nikandros and myself. We may travel soon, but will come back for you if you need us. There is a whole world beyond this one." As always, she said more than I could fully understand, but it was sincere.

"I'll remember." I gave her a quick hug and she let out a sigh.

"Don't tell the others I came, but keep everyone here until the boat arrives. It would be foolish to take an unnecessary risk." Hamitra eased back into the water. The scent of her stayed with me long after she left. Cinnamon, spice, and fennel wrapped around me like soft arms as I drifted back to sleep.

∞

We slept in well past dawn. Even when we woke, there was no sense of hurry. The grotto's magic increased in the daylight and held us there, transfixed by the blossoming of pure colour as the sun filtered through the tiny entrance. The water became a rich azure, fracturing into a rainbow of deep blues.

Our rescuers came shortly after, maneuvering several small unmasted boats through the narrow entrance. It seemed they intruded on the calm of the cavern. *If only I could stay.* The rock didn't demand obedience. The waves didn't care for the future.

Then my stomach rumbled. I sighed and followed Quintus and Agrippina into the second boat. Civilization it was—and breakfast.

∞

"Of course I'll send someone to represent Justa," Uncle said to Agrippina, when I'd filled in the gaps in her tirade. "Though with only two days' notice, her advocate may be barely sufficient."

Beyond the study's statue of Minerva, Rafa paced quietly in the grand garden, throwing covert glances our way.

"And none of our family is to have anything to do with this Themis woman again." My sister vented her frustration by stamping her foot. I hid my smile. I hadn't seen her do that since we were small.

"Once the matter has been sent before the urban praetor in Rome," Uncle continued, also ignoring Agrippina's outburst, "she can find better council there." A calculating look passed over his face and he walked to his desk. The ever-present stack of parchment and papyri seemed only to grow with each year, but he quickly found whatever he'd been hunting. "Perhaps she would care to come with us."

"I beg your pardon, Uncle? Are we going to Rome?" I couldn't trust my ears. *Home.*

"But we can't go!" Agrippina protested. "It's less than a month until the wedding."

"What better time? We can take the yacht and purchase any last minute necessities for the wedding and your new villa." Uncle shot me a wink as Agrippina began muttering to Sidonia, listing must-have items that had been mysteriously forgotten until this moment.

"There are also several guests who have strongly hinted that they would enjoy coming to the wedding so long as they didn't have to take the road," Uncle continued, mostly for my benefit. Agrippina drifted from the room chattering to Sidonia. "Never go in for the army, Lucilla. You make friends who call on you for favours for the rest of your life."

"When do we leave?" I needed to visit Pompeii tomorrow and get my questions about poisons answered, but visiting the city again had made me lightheaded with excitement.

"As soon as I can convince your aunt." He saw my face fall. "Come, come, Lucilla. I can't bring you girls without your aunt as chaperone. You may come home tattooed like a barbarian."

∞

"Atellus," I called out, moving through the gladiator barracks.

Rafa accompanied me, though he wasn't the most intimidating of bodyguards. I'd convinced Gavius he'd be more useful guarding the barracks' entrance, an easy sell since he'd be standing in the shade. Bricus had offered to come, but after the grotto there'd been an intensity to his gaze that made me uneasy. It was bad enough he'd be coming with us to Rome; I hoped some distance would return things to normal.

"Lucilla," Atellus greeted me with a note of caution. "You shouldn't be here." He led me to the edge of the training grounds.

My gaze did a circuit of the large colonnaded space. Gladiators sparred in pairs, or clustered in small groups training with the same weapons. Spotting Marcus in a group at the far wall, I raised my shawl higher over my head, conscious of Hamitra's warning. Rafa followed us, his back stiff.

"Since I spent the morning getting here, I have a good reason," I countered. "You're the only person I could ask about poisons."

He raised his eyebrows. "You need a poison?"

"No, no. Not for me. I think an acquaintance has been poisoned."

"Do you need my help?" Atellus half-turned, as if to get ready to leave with me.

Rafa snorted.

"He's already dead," I said.

"May the earth lie softly on his bones," Atellus intoned formally.

"He fell sick very suddenly. Grew weak, vomited blood, and couldn't breathe properly." I ticked off Stephanus's symptoms. Vitalis's death may not have been the same poison, but Justa reasoned that if we could connect Themis to one, it may be enough to make her back down.

"He also didn't know where he was, at times," Rafa added. Atellus looked past me up at Rafa, and I realized Rafa was now a head taller, all knees and elbows.

"Hmm." Atellus frowned in concentration. "It could be arsenic, or hemlock. Both work quite quick in a large enough dose. Or with smaller doses, close together." His expression grew grave. "If he's been poisoned, other people may be in danger. Someone else may share his food or drink."

"I think this person was targeted," I said.

"I take it you suspect someone?"

Rafa and I exchanged a glance. Themis was a freeborn Roman, with the full protection of the law. We couldn't accuse her without firm proof. "I can't say more. But I do have another question." I took a slow breath to calm my anxiety. "Do you know of a poison which causes sores to break open across a person's skin? Black and filled with dark pus?" Rafa had been as shocked as I that the same poison was used in the murder he witnessed and my father's. He told me if Uncle had tried to find the poison, it hadn't been with his help. I was strangely relieved that perhaps this trail could be followed; that it was not cold already.

Atellus looked thoughtful, but shook his head. "No. But there are certain fevers which may. Are you sure it was poison?"

"It happened too fast for it to be a fever." I was disappointed, but Atellus was only the first person we'd asked. There had to be others, and Rafa would help me find them. "Thank you for your help."

"We're leaving for Rome in a few days," Atellus said hesitantly, "but if we come back for another games—"

"Do you have any idea who you're talking to?" Rafa cut in. "The domina does not associate with your sort."

My face reddened. "Hold your tongue." I turned back to Atellus.

But Rafa wouldn't be silent. "I'm here to protect your honour, even from yourself," his words clipped out, low but hard. Rafa gestured for me to precede him from the barracks.

I pressed my lips together in an effort to keep my face composed. Sidelong glances from those near us were enough to spur me into making a retreat. Sending what I hoped was a friendly parting glance at Atellus, I did my best to exit with dignity.

"What was that?" I tried to keep my voice down as Rafa and I negotiated the bustling streets.

"What in the Lord's name were you up to the last time you were here?" His simmering anger was barely contained.

"Nothing. I met Atellus while he was stitching up a gladiator. He told me about poisons. That's why I went to him for help."

"And that other one?"

"What other one?"

"You can't tell me you didn't notice. He watched you the whole time! Tall, dark hair, looks like he could kill a lion with his bare hands."

Marcus? I shouldn't have turned my back on him.

"You have to be more careful." Rafa's voice cracked. "You still have your honour, your family name. You can't risk it every time someone's friendly. Stay away from that place."

"I wouldn't have gone if we weren't helping Justa—which you asked me to do, by the way. And what do you mean you're here to protect my honour?"

Rafa couldn't seem to tear his concentration away from the swarming mass of bodies in our path.

"You're spying on me!" I was aghast.

"No. Not spying. Watching over you," he said, but the words were laced with guilt.

"Do you report on me to Uncle?"

"Of course not."

He was lying. He might as well have punched me in the gut; my stomach churned. "How long have you been doing this?"

"Your uncle wants to keep you safe, and so do I," he said. "We thought it would be best if you didn't know–"

"Know what?" I said, furious. "That you were only pretending to be my friend?"

"Lucilla," he said quietly, "you saved my life. If you didn't understand that before, understand it now. I've only ever tried to return the favour. But you aren't a child any more and other things are a danger to you now."

Gods below—it was impossible to be angry with him when he was being so reasonable. I let out a breath.

"You must be more careful," Rafa said, nearly begging.

I took another slow breath. "You're right. I'm no longer a child."

He gave me a relieved smile.

"But if you order me around again, I'll have your tongue cut off."

Rafa stuck it out, tauntingly.

TWENTY

A MILITARY CAMPAIGN WOULD BE PROUD to be as organized as our party. Aunt, delighted with Uncle's suggestion, had planned every step of the journey to Rome.

"I think your Aunt Calpurnia knows exactly how many oar-strokes it takes to reach Ostia from the villa," Bricus whispered to me as we took our place in the litter Aunt pointed to.

"And how many wheel rotations for a carriage to take us from Ostia to Rome?" I covered my laugh and dodged her gaze. Fortunately, she was busy ordering Agrippina and Justa into another litter. She'd hired a train of them to carry us from the city gates to Uncle's domus.

"Why couldn't we just take the wagons?" Bricus knocked some cushions together for me, then flopped down on a pile of his own.

I cleared my throat, affecting Quintus's tone. "No wheeled vehicles in Rome during the day. Only the Emperor and select pontiffs require them."

Bricus chuckled.

"Really, though, too many people got run over."

"Romans!" He tossed a cushion at me. I snagged it from the air before it could damage my hairstyle.

Bricus and I kept the curtains half-open, and I named the landmarks I remembered. Marble-faced temples and baths, their columns and statues painted in decadent, deep colours. Markets up and down the streets with bright awnings shading the crowded sidewalks. The arches of a new stone amphitheatre were crooked like skeletal fingers over their wooden supports.

An amazing number of changes had happened during five years

of peace. Rome seemed a living thing—seven hills humming with every accomplishment civilization had mastered. Clinking metal, rapping stone, sawing wood. And the odour. I'd forgotten how wonderfully the city stank. When the wind sat idle the smells settled between hills, a swirling mass of sweet, sour, musk, decay, spice. There was no cleansing breeze from the sea as at the villa, only the heat of the sun to boil it all together.

We reached Uncle's domus and were freed from the rocking and jostling of the litters. I breathed a little easier; the longer we traveled, the closer to me Bricus seemed to have been reclining. Agrippina hustled Justa away. Nikandros, who had some business in the city, bounded off his litter, clearly relived to be on his own two feet again. As I ascended to my room, I watched Aunt Calpurnia directing slaves in the atrium below and felt an increased respect for her situation. I'd go mad being so confined, day after day.

In the proper fashion, we waited for the most important vendors to visit us. An explosion of fabric soon covered our small chambers— shawls, dresses, silks, underthings. Jewellery was held up for inspection and then tossed aside, a sparkling rubbish pile on Agrippina's dressing table. Perfumes were sniffed and rejected until our eyes teared.

Agrippina tried to distract Justa from her upcoming ordeal in court, though this meant my sister talked about the wedding, and Nonius, and her new villa, and Nonius, quite a bit. I endured it, knowing I'd miss her chatter once she moved away; Rafa hovered in the background, impatient on Justa's behalf.

Merchants weren't the only visitors we received. The mornings were filled with a steady stream of clients come to see Uncle. His infrequent visits to the city hadn't lessened his contacts, rather it seemed every one of them needed a personal audience during his stay. The afternoons were when Aunt held court with matrons and their daughters, and every evening we hosted intimate dinners for our most important connections.

With only a few days left in our stay, I steeled myself for a task I'd been avoiding. Agrippina was being fitted for her wedding attire when I entered her room, carrying my gift in a box of dark walnut.

Sidonia was stitching up the last of Agrippina's towering hairstyle, using long strands of hair and dark thread to keep the braids and curls upright. Patting the last bits into place, Sidonia took the veil and jewelled comb from Lenoria and draped the orange silk over the back. It hung to the floor in fiery pleats.

Agrippina was biting at the nail of her little finger. "You shouldn't do that," I said. "You'll ruin your manicure."

"Nonius will just have to get used to it." Agrippina was assisted to her feet, her embroidered, golden-yellow gown smoothed out by two pairs of hands.

"Before you weigh yourself down more, I want you to have this."

Sidonia held the box as Agrippina lifted the lid. Sucking in a breath, Agrippina ran her hands over the golden strand. A dozen large emeralds cast brilliant reflections on the ceiling.

"Cincinnata didn't have a necklace half as fine when she married—even the second time," Agrippina bragged, her awed voice making me grin. Sidonia slipped it around Agrippina's neck, fastening the clasp at the back. "When did you get it?"

"Do you think I can't go shopping without you?"

"I just didn't think you would."

"So we're clear—I'm buying you nothing for your next marriage." I kissed her on the cheek. "Do you remember that awful yellow dress you wore? The day we arrived at the villa?"

Agrippina let out a burble of surprised laughter. "Oh, don't remind me! I only wore it because you were so nasty about it."

"I was only nasty because it was the ugliest dress I'd ever seen. This one's infinitely better." I held her arms out, admiring how stylish she looked.

"Do you think Nonius will like it?"

"Never ask for reassurance, or a man's opinion of fashion," Aunt Calpurnia said as she was carried in, lounging in attire only a shade less elaborate than Agrippina's. She was already dressed for our visitor this afternoon. "A woman must know her value and never look to others for approval. If you do, you'll always be forced to measure your worth by their yardstick."

Agrippina's dimples appeared.

"But, for what it *is* worth," Aunt said with a small smile, "I think you look lovely. And those emeralds go very nicely with the dress. I was worried the tones wouldn't match."

"Yes, they're perfect. Thank you, Luce." Agrippina gave me a gentle hug, being careful to not jostle her piled hair.

"Now out and start getting dressed!" Aunt directed me to the door. "And nothing like what happened last night must happen during Lanata's visit."

My method of enduring parties was to nod while everyone else talked. It was oddly successful. But last night, while mentally practicing a way of disarming Hilarus using only a rope, I'd been taken by surprise when Julia Agricola, who'd been dropping names all evening, mentioned Senator Rusticus. Overreaching for my wine, I'd tripped a slave, who dumped an entire jar of wine over Agrippina and poor Cornelius Tacitus dining beside her.

"I'll be very attentive today," I said with sincerity. "I've not had the chance to see Lanata in years."

Aunt nodded, somewhat doubtful. "Then be sure to wear something suitable for the Vestalis."

When I entered the atrium that afternoon, her smile was one of approval. Heavy bangles banded my upper and lower arms. Cording laced with gold wound under my breasts and crossed over my abdomen, holding the green silk dress tight. Combined with the towering hair, I felt more trussed than a roast bird.

"At least I'm almost married, so she can't find fault with that," Agrippina whispered in my ear, taking her place next to me. "Do I look all right?" She folded her hands together.

"You look fine." I smoothed the draping of her blue shawl over her shoulder. It matched the deep blue dress she'd changed into. Agrippina had never known what it was like to grow up with an older sister. Life would have been far different if Lanata had lived with us, instead of the Vestals.

Outside, wheels rumbled over the stone paving and I craned my neck for a view down the long corridor to the street. It must be her.

Lanata emerged from her ornate carriage with the elegance Venus being born from the foam of the sea. A golden-haired slave placed a stool for her to descend and took her outstretched hand. Another adjusted her gleaming white veil and skirt, and a third walked behind her with a palm fan. Lictors stood, wooden staffs at the ready, to hold back the curious crowd.

When Lanata entered the atrium, her gaze took the measure of each of us in turn. Taller than Agrippina, her face was similar, though more angular. Not surprising, as she was half a dozen years older and had lost the softness of childhood. She inclined her head in greeting to Uncle, standing with Galaria and Quintus, then to Aunt Calpurnia sitting in a chair with a handled platform.

"Lanata," Aunt Calpurnia said. "It's good to see you."

Lanata smiled, though it didn't reach her eyes. I understood her reservation—she barely knew us.

She opened her hands to Agrippina and me and kissed each of us stiffly on the cheeks. "Sisters," she said. "Though I shouldn't properly call you that since I renounced family to serve the goddess."

I looked at Agrippina. Neither of us had a response.

"Vestalis Maxima," said Quintus, taking her cue and using her title. "Would you care for some refreshment?" He escorted her to the garden.

"Thank you," Lanata replied. "I find the heat and crowds very tiresome this time of day."

A table had been set up on the edge of the domus' inner garden, which had a simple pattern of bushes and flowers in tidy, diagonal beds. Quintus sat between Lanata and his mother; I between Uncle and Agrippina. Aunt Calpurnia's chair-litter was lowered at the table's head. I sipped my lemon water as the quiet extended. Uncle waved the water away in favour of wine. Quintus looked sideways at his mother, but Galaria was picking at some figs, none of them meeting with her approval. I let out a long breath, wishing Bricus had been here, instead of at the baths. He'd have had no problem saying something brash to break the silence.

At last Aunt Calpurnia said, "How is Sicula?"

"Mother is well," Lanata replied. "Though she spends most of her days at home since her illness."

"I hadn't heard," Aunt Calpurnia said with sympathy. "Should I visit her?"

"Heavens, no! She still carries her resentment with pride. She never did forgive Father." She looked over and caught my eye, a small smile on her lips. "Your mother was very kind; my mother is very willful."

Uncle downed his wine and muttered into his glass. "Frigid bitch was more like it."

I bit my cheek. As I was the only one sitting next to him, he wasn't overheard. The muttering was, though.

Everyone turned and he coughed. "Love is a torment, isn't it?"

"I wouldn't know." Lanata straightened her shoulders.

"Of course." Uncle raised his glass as the slave brought more wine. "Your virtue is a credit to the goddess, and our family."

"Thank you." She clasped her hands together, fingers twitching. "Agrippina, may I extend my good wishes for your marriage. How old are you now, my dear? Sixteen?"

"Yes, Lanata ... Vestalis." Agrippina's neck flushed at the blunder.

Lanata smiled indulgently. "Sixteen is quite a good age for marriage. Mother was too old, I think. When a woman is unmarried into her thirties she becomes used to having things her own way—which doesn't make for an ideal union. Don't you agree Calpurnia?" Whether Lanata's insult was implied or accidental, it made me bristle.

Aunt Calpurnia gave a ghost of a smile. "Certainly. Though some women merely come from bad blood."

Lanata's nostrils flared. "Yes, I'm afraid that in the course of my sacred duties I have met many such women."

"Father once said how he admired your mother," I ventured into the pause, "and how dedicated she was to her duties."

"Did he?"

"Yes, just after we last met. He said he hoped you'd take as much pride in your own service as she had in hers."

Lanata's eyes at last betrayed true pleasure. "I have. I have devoted myself to Her will."

"Then I'm sure Lucius would be proud." Aunt Calpurnia said.

"That is inconsequential," Lanata said. "Our duty is the only thing that matters. If I've learned anything from my mother's mistakes, it's that sentiment often leads to unnecessary confusion. She should have remained devoted to the goddess. Love between man and wife is far more fleeting than that between ourselves and the gods."

"Wisely spoken," Quintus said. "Love is admirable, but fulfilling our duties is a more lasting tribute to our families."

I looked to the heavens for intervention.

"You are a credit to us," Quintus continued. "I was delighted when you were elected Vestalis Maxima ... though of course saddened to hear about the attempt on your life."

"It was shocking. To think, if I'd been the one to drink that wine."

Lanata gave a delicate shudder. "And it was a gift! Lady Vesta was watching over me that day, I'm certain of it."

A gift … "Who sent it to you?"

Uncle *thunked* down his empty glass. "This is not the time."

Lanata turned to me, eyebrow raised. "Didn't you know? Senator Rusticus. Of course I had my lictors question him. The slave who was sent with the wine was found murdered. Someone else intercepted it."

"Who? Did anyone see?" My hands trembled, and I hid them in my lap.

"Lucilla." Aunt and Uncle spoke together.

"The only useful description was that the man had one eye."

"How could you keep this from me?" I glared at Uncle. "It's another connection—"

He rubbed his forehead. "It's nothing of the sort. As Lanata said, we looked into this matter and found no proof."

My fingernails dug into my palms. *No proof. No proof.* Did he want it handed to him on a platter?

Lanata eyed me, a small frown creasing her forehead. "You must learn patience, sister—I'm disappointed that what our Aunt said about you still holds true. You're too reckless." Her frown deepened. "*If* the senator is behind it, he's proved to be a clever opponent. Accusing him openly without proper evidence risks tarnishing our entire family."

"And anyone who does *that* would no longer be welcome within it." Quintus's face twisted in a hostile sneer. "Some stains are impossible to remove."

I surveyed the rest of my family: Uncle staring with remorse into his wine; Aunt's glaring between Quintus and me; Agrippina wide-eyed. Only Aunt Galaria seemed unaffected, immersed in a bowl of peaches.

I stood with a jerk and exited the garden.

∞

"Judgement in her case was delayed until more testimony is brought forward," Rafa explained as he, Bricus, and I walked among the tombs of the Via Appia. We'd left Gavius with the lecticarii at the edge of the roadway. It had been many years since my last visit, but I remembered the way. "Justa's advocate is doing the best he can, I think." His forehead wrinkled with his worried frown.

I wished I'd been able to attend the courts, but Rafa had stood the best chance of understanding what was going on. While I'd been sparring with Hilarus or suffering a knock from Petrus' staff, Rafa had been making the most of the scrolls of philosophy, law, and rhetoric that had gone begging in Uncle's library. And he'd not wasted the opportunity.

"She has the truth on her side. That must count for something." I failed to curb my sarcasm.

"But she has no documents. The advocate is going to keep bringing witnesses forward and delay the praetor being able to make a judgment for as long as he can. Themis is older—if we can keep this up long enough, she may run out of funds, or become too ill to continue."

"Sounds like Justa's advocate wants a steady source of income," Bricus said.

"It's a good tactic," Rafa snapped.

I put a hand on his tense shoulder. "Especially since Agrippina can afford it."

We approached a small hill, fronted by a large stone facade resembling a temple. Two columns rose up on either side of a tall bronze door which supported a triangular roof. Red and black paint had cracked and peeled away, but the carved inscription over the door endured.

The heavy iron key was old-fashioned, long and hooked with two prongs. I slid it into the lock and rotated it until the inner bar slid free of its latch, though the ancient hinges screamed when Bricus swung it in. Sunlight shone behind us, but as we crossed the threshold Rafa lifted the lamp he carried. He sneezed.

"Careful," I said, "some of that dust is noble."

"Likely why it's so irritating," he said, though in a hushed voice.

I stepped over the threshold, but Bricus held me back. "I'll wait."

"What happened about not fearing the dead?" I teased.

"I don't fear them, but we don't invade their barrows like you do." He glanced at Rafa, and pulled me a few steps from the door.

"Rafa, if you take the left passage, I'll catch up with you."

With a shrewd gaze, Rafa stepped into the tomb and out of sight.

"What's bothering you, Bricus? Not jealous are you?"

He frowned slightly, his hand drifting down my arm to take mine.

"The only thing I'm jealous of is how you cling to your memories."

I would have jerked my hand away, if it hadn't been for his concern. His dark eyes held no amusement, no hint of mockery. "The past makes us who were are, Bricus. My ancestors are here—centuries of them. I must live up to their expectations."

"You speak of the dead as if they compel you. Lucilla, you're stronger than that. Every day is an opportunity to make the past different. To add memories that weren't there before." He paused, fingering the torc around his neck. "I didn't understand until after I left my homeland. At first I longed to return, but over time saw that so much of what seemed carved in stone at home was different in other lands. The world had changed."

"Or perhaps you had changed. But I haven't."

He frowned. "I don't know why you chase the past—and you don't have to tell me." He gripped my hand tighter. "But when you're ready to choose another direction, I would be your ... ally."

"Ally?" It was a mistake to meet his gaze, his expression full of things unsaid and unwanted. Longing. Desire. Promises I couldn't fulfill.

He leaned forward, breath soft and near. "Lucilla."

Merda, he's more blinding than staring at the sun. I lowered my gaze and withdrew my hand.

Bricus cleared his throat. "Your uncle's included me in Quintus's lessons. Learning about the politics of you *civilized* Romans. A few years from now, things might be different for both of us."

I flushed. *Different* was one of two things: either my enemies were dead, or I was. "Different isn't always better."

He flashed a brief grin. "Aren't you too young to be a cynic?"

"Better than being a stain on my family." My bitter smile no doubt looked as awful as it felt. I backed towards the tomb, ignoring both the scowl on his face and an absurd desire to walk into his arms. "Rafa's waiting."

I turned left, into a dark maze of passages hewn into the soft rock of the hill, as though it had been here since the earth was formed. The tunnel curved, but the bob of Rafa's lantern was clear ahead. My footsteps seemed loud and irregular as I passed niche after niche. They were cut at all levels, nearly as high as the arched vault of the ceiling— some rough rock, some elaborately decorated with mosaics or frescoes.

The urns of my familia rested in them. Round, squat, curved, elegant. Stone and glass and clay. Carved images told stories of lives long past. Many bore simple inscriptions—urns of devoted slaves and freedmen.

Whatever Rafa saw in my face as I caught up to him must not have been good, for he pulled me into a rare hug.

"Did you know he was going to do that?"

"No. Though for a moment yesterday I thought he was going to push Quintus in the pool after he heard what happened with Lanata." His smirk was more eerie than amusing in the orange lamplight. "You could do worse."

I rubbed my arms, trying to keep my entire body from turning scarlet. "I could. But he says the most ridiculous things. He told me, 'Every day is an opportunity to make the past different.' Nonsense. You can't change the past."

"I don't know, maybe he's right. Every day that I've spent in your household has added to my past. Made more days good than bad—"

"*Gods below,* not you too! I'm not in the mood for some strange philosophy of exiles." I marched on and Rafa had to lengthen his stride to keep up. "Raise the lantern so I know where we are … yes … middle corridor back there leads to the dining room. But we obviously haven't used it since we came to the villa." Father, Agrippina, and I had eaten the sacrificial meal here every year during Parentalia. Not just for Mother, but for all our ancestors.

"Doesn't it bother you to come here?"

"No. Never." I couldn't find any other words. All I could hear was Bricus's voice, cutting deeper with each echo. *Every day is an opportunity to make the past different.* But it wasn't. The past was solid as stone, as solid as this tomb. And the oath I'd made was just as unbreakable. My duty was clear, and could not be ignored. *No one else knows the one-eyed man is a monster. No one else knows of Hamitra and Nikandros and their kind.* There had to be a way, otherwise why would the gods send Hamitra to me? Ensure my survival? Not so I could run off to some cold island thousands of leagues away. Tamping down the churning unease Bricus's words had caused, I realized we'd arrived.

"Here." I knelt, the niche at eye level. Rafa knelt beside me, lowering the lantern to the floor and pulling violets from his satchel.

The urns were already sprinkled with rose petals. *Why does that surprise me? Spiro must come here often.* A surge of bitterness rose at the memory of his long absence.

Holding out my hands, Rafa passed me fistfuls of violet petals. I carefully blanketed Mother's urn. My brother Lucius lay with her, and the carving on the front showed her holding him, happily embracing as they never had in life.

Father's urn was square, all four sides carved with a relief of him charging through battle on horseback. I covered it with the dark petals as well, their sweet smell breaking through the mustiness of the tomb. Gently tracing Father's image, I wondered what had happened to his weapons and armour. They weren't at the villa, so they must either be at Uncle's, or at our domus here in the city. Except our old home was now mine. Agrippina had inherited the villa on the coast, and I, the property in Rome. Wherever they were, I had no doubt Spiro was taking care of my father's belongings.

For a long while I knelt on the floor, questions of duty and family roiling in my mind. Whatever Rafa's thoughts, he kept his peace.

My feet tingled as I stood. Cramped legs pulsed as the blood ran through them again. A few steps down the corridor lay another urn. Eudocia's was simple, her name stamped in the clay. Removing my blue shawl, I wound it around the tall urn several times, knocking some white rose petals to the ground.

I turned to Rafa. I had no answers, only hard choices. "Agrippina's marriage means I'm running out of time, Rafa. Finding proof against the senator may always be fruitless. I need to figure out what kind of creature the one-eyed man could be." Perhaps then I could trace him somehow, or know what to do to defeat him. Hamitra thought it impossible, but she couldn't know everything. *I hope.*

"Is this about what happened with Lanata?"

"Yes—she was right. I've been waiting, but I haven't been patient. You know the library, and you know where I can get more scrolls once we've been through what's here—in Herculaneum … Pompeii … even Rome. The smallest hint could be important. But I don't think it would be a good idea to let Nikandros know." We couldn't make him suspicious, otherwise he and Hamitra might leave. Or feel too threatened by Rafa.

"Why? He might be able to help find what we're looking for."

I took a breath, choosing my words in the hope that Rafa wouldn't become suspicious, either. "No one believes me about that man except you. I don't need Nikandros telling Uncle what I'm doing or they'll ship me off to some terrible province." I swallowed against the sudden image of Rafa's broken body on the shore. I wouldn't risk it, no matter how many secrets I had to keep or lies I had to tell.

His confusion vanished, a mischievous smile taking its place. "You realize that researching in the library means you'll have to sit still for hours at a time?"

"Ugh. I know." *What can't be changed, must be endured.* "But I must do this. Eventually we'll find something."

"Should I even ask what you plan on doing then?"

The cloudy nature of what happened then was irrelevant. The path would be clear once the time was right. Years of training and frustration and keeping the peace wouldn't be for nothing. But when I looked into Rafa's eyes, I saw none of my anger, only his worry. "Well, Lady Justice might have a sword," I said in a lighter tone than I felt. "But I have two."

He pressed his lips together, either with laughter or dismay, and turned on his heel to lead us out. "She's also blind."

"All things human hang by a slender thread."
Ovid

PART III

JUNE

Year 10 of the Emperor Vespasian

Twenty-One

I TICKLED THE SOFT SKIN AT THE BACK OF GAIUS'S KNEES. Sidonia held him as he kicked his chubby legs and giggled. When I leaned in to kiss his nose, he shot out honey-smeared hands, tangling them in my hair.

"Really, Luce! Now you're as dirty as the baby," Agrippina said.

Sidonia clutched the squirming Gaius while I peeled my hair off his chubby palms. "I'm not sorry," I whispered to my nephew. He patted my cheek with an affectionate smack.

"Sidonia." Agrippina motioned toward the yacht with a sigh, but her dimples appeared and she made silly eyes at Gaius while Sidonia carried him aboard.

Lucius, clutching his mother's skirt, regarded me steadily. His dark curls bounced in an unruly cloud around his head as he looked from the boat back to his mother.

I went down on my knee to look him in the eye. "When you come here next I'll teach you to swim." The boys were off with Nonius to the city for a few months, but I hoped they'd be back for part of the summer.

"He's still too afraid." Agrippina fussed with Lucius's curls.

"Am not," Lucius said. "I don't want fish to eat me."

"Your auntie is quite good at spearing fish." I gave him a little hug. His own dimples flashed as he smiled. A slave picked him up and sat with him on the boat.

Agrippina kissed both my cheeks in parting, then clutched at my hands. "You'll come with me to Pompeii after the Ides?" she asked yet again.

"Yes, of course," I said, giving in to her pestering.

"No need to sound so grim. I know just the thing! I'll buy you a shawl—the new style with beaded fringes."

"There's no need—"

"I insist." She gave my hands a final squeeze before boarding her yacht.

Lucius waved until they were out of sight.

Leaving the dock, I walked the long path from shore to summerhouse. Seeing Agrippina's children reminded me how quickly time was passing, something I didn't feel when on my own. One day, one season, one year. Each blended into the rest. Until I saw how much the boys changed since our last meeting.

I'd kept my promise to Uncle, keeping the peace the best I could. I'd been patient, avoiding scandal … planning for the day Rafa or Uncle or *someone* would discover proof of the Senator's guilt.

But *any day* never came. Now my nephew Lucius was nearly four. Agrippina had children and a place in society. Lanata was one of the most prominent women in Rome. Quintus had begun his political career. And I … I had nothing. I may as well have still been that girl standing scared on the road. Waiting for the man with one eye to decide my fate.

The sound of stomping feet made me turn. Bricus bounded down the path toward me, waiving a parchment in his hand.

"It's starting!" he shouted.

"What is?" I smiled reflexively at his contagious good-humour.

"I have my commission for the army—Centurion in the II Adiutrix." He saluted as though I were his commanding officer. "Just had word from your uncle. He's arranged it all." He eyed me with a glint as he rolled up the letter and stuffed it in his belt.

Catching me off guard, Bricus wrapped his hands around my waist and pulled me close.

His lips were warm and firm when he pressed them to mine, slowly deepening for more. I followed his lead, heat spiraling through my body. His tongue tasted of lemon and honey, betraying a stop in the kitchen. Strong hands caressed my back.

I brought my own hands up to rest against his shoulders, thumbs playing with the gold torc he wore against his collarbone. Pressing my palms lower onto his chest, I gently broke away.

Bricus sighed and shook his head. "Hasn't this gone on long

enough? You've kept yourself apart from everyone, even me. But we could make a life together."

I should have prepared for this. Not pretend it would never happen. "Fine thing to say now that you're unavailable for ten years. Though longer engagements have happened—" Any attempt at humour died when he brushed a strand of hair from my face with a gentle caress.

"Lucilla, marry me. As soon as possible. You belong with my people. They'll respect your strength. All your abilities that make you less Roman make you more Briganti."

"And all the ways I'm Roman would make me an outsider among your people."

"Haven't you always been an outsider? When I first arrived here you were the only person I could understand. As much of an outsider as me. Do you think I've known you for years and failed to see your frustrations?" His gaze was earnest, and he held my hands pressed to his chest, the fine linen of his tunic gentle on my palms. "We can bring what is best of Rome to my people—create unity out of warring tribes and petty factions. Your own people could do it and I see no reason why mine—ours—couldn't do the same."

He rarely spoke of his deep ambition. To restore peace to his homeland would be the work of a lifetime. Months and years of blood and fighting, politicking and bribing. Things my fortune and connections would ease.

Turning from him, I looked out over the bay. Ships sailed on the horizon for ports around the world. Soon one of those ships would take Bricus to join the imperial army in Britannia. He had a thirst for adventure, for the new and the possible. It was something which bound us together—the belief that somehow we could shape the world to be as we wanted, not just accept the harshness of Fate's yoke. But I had no future until I settled the debts of the past.

I wrenched my gaze from the sparkling water and faced him. "I can't marry you, Bricus." I knew it was the right answer, but his frustration made me want to soften its harshness. "You're excited to be going home, but you're not thinking about the future. What happens when we get to Britannia? Or when there's children?"

"Do you think I'm trying to turn you into a matron? That I'd leave you by the hearth alone? When I'm asking you to come with me, I mean for you to live by my side. There are ways to ensure children aren't a worry until we're ready." Bricus reached for my hands again, and I let him take them, his thumbs stroking my knuckles.

With a sigh, I pressed my forehead to his chest. Every word he spoke pierced me. There was no good reason for me to refuse. Except … I couldn't marry him. My feelings for Bricus would never outweigh the oath I'd made to Father; to Eudocia. He deserved better. Someone whose scales would always tip in his favour. "When do you leave?"

"The end of the month. And I promise I won't ask anyone else before then." He flashed his usual broad grin, but it didn't reach his eyes.

My resolve cracked. "I'll consider it under Uncle's guidance."

Bricus gave me a long look which I couldn't decipher, lips parting as if he wanted to say more. Then he nodded once, and turned to walk back through the grove.

∞

"You let me have that one," I said, irritation creeping into my attempt at graciousness. Sparring with Hilarus had grown hollow—he was allowing me more victories, and it was putting me on edge. I was sure Aunt Calpurnia had a hand in it.

"I must be getting old," Hilarus said with a glance at Petrus.

"Is this some new sort of lesson? Where you plan to shatter my confidence with a surprise tactic?" Panic fermented inside me. Their behaviour was definitely abnormal.

Hilarus handed his wooden gladius to a waiting slave, who began packing away the scattered training equipment. I threw my swords onto the pile.

Walking over to me, Hilarus held out his hand. I extended mine and we clasped forearms. He held my gaze for a heartbeat, and I realized he was saying farewell.

"Have I grown so fearsome?" I tried to swallow my regret. If this was the end of my lessons, it was the end of my friendship with them, too. Aunt was packing me off to either Britannia or to Rome. "You'd better buy him a drink," I said to Petrus, "so he can mourn the loss of his youth. Imagine, losing to a girl." The words sounded strange, as though I spoke from a far distance.

"There's no shame losing to a stronger opponent," Hilarus said.

"Now you tell me."

Hilarus pulled the silver ring off his finger and extended it towards me. I took it and clasped it in my fist, trying to still my trembling hand. I couldn't refuse such a token.

"Remember," he said, "you have a reason to win."

After a last look, Hilarus walked out, followed by the slave lugging the bundled weapons.

Petrus gestured for me to accompany him. We walked in silence until we reached the summerhouse, the site of Bricus's recent proposal. I wasn't sure what Aunt and Uncle were planning, but if Bricus was their choice, they would surely see sense in continuing my training. Since I wouldn't be training, that could only mean—

"I have to apologize for being blind." Petrus's joints creaked as he dropped onto a bench.

"I thought you weren't blind," I teased. But as I turned and looked down at him, I realized his gravity.

"When I first came to train you I was intrigued by what your uncle told me—and skeptical. A small girl killing a hired murderer?" He gave me a half-smile. "Not many boys have been so tested … or men either."

I knelt on the gravel at his feet, ignoring the jab of rock in my legs, ready for his lesson. Likely his last.

"Petrus, I said to myself, this will be a fine retirement. Give a girl a few drills and line your pockets with a rich man's gold. But you were such a serious little bird. You listened. You worked. Every lesson I put you through, you mastered. After even a short time, Hilarus and I both knew you were gifted in this."

It wasn't a gift. All the hours of sweat and toil weren't effortless. I'd worked until I ached; until I bruised and bled. "Why are you telling me this?"

"Because I became too proud, and vain. Your growth made me feel youthful again. Your successes made me believe I was a master. I took you far, but you went further. To watch you fight is—" he paused, searching for the right word. The moment lengthened and I dreaded what he might say. "—frightening." His eyes were heavy with sorrow and he reached to touch my head, but I spun away, standing.

"What do you mean?" I tried to keep my voice steady, my body was tense with anger. "I followed all your instructions. Am I not supposed to be good after so many years?"

"I taught you the lessons of an old man. Of a soldier and prize fighter. To fight for the kill, not just the victory. Not just for survival. I worked you too hard. But you were so good, I couldn't treat it lightly."

I looked up into the trees. Into the sky. This day was unexpected, and I wasn't handling it well. "Are you upset that I was a good student, or a poor student? After all, I haven't actually killed anyone I fought."

"Not yet. But you will. And you won't hesitate."

"So now I'm a murderer, as well as a poor student?" I blinked quickly to clear the brimming tears. *A fighter doesn't cry.*

"You're not a murderer." Petrus stood, one hand leaning on his cane, the other taking hold of my shoulder. "I'm making a mess of my own apology. Lucilla, you're frightening as a fighter the way a storm is frightening to a sailor. Unavoidable. Relentless. The sailor can't stop the storm from coming, only hope he survives. I've spent more than thirty years training soldiers and gladiators. You had some advantages which others did not ..." He glanced back toward the luxury of my home. "But I have never trained a better fighter."

I looked in his eyes and saw he spoke the truth. "Then why are you apologizing?"

"Because you're the daughter of a senator. What kind of life are you fit for?"

I'm fit to fulfill my purpose. Sorrow and fear vanished between one heartbeat and the next. I hadn't known it, but this is what I'd been waiting for. I was as ready as I could be.

"You wanted these lessons because you were afraid. Fear will always be with you when you face your opponent. But in my time as a gladiator, I learned of a thing stronger than fear—anticipation." His expression turned hungry, eyes clouding over as he saw something long past. "It was why I had to leave the sand. Why I took to the stage. The longer I fought, the more I wanted the kill. For many years after, the only thing that saved me was pretending to be human."

"I'm not heartless," I said, chafing at his tone.

"If you were, I never would have stayed." He embraced me with shaking arms, then left down the path, cane pounding on the gravel.

"So what do I do now?"

"Live, Lucilla," he said over his shoulder. "And practice!"

Twenty-Two

"This is a terrible idea, Agrippina."

She dragged me on toward Pompeii's colonnaded training ground. I checked on Gavius, heading into a taberna across the street, and wondered if he actually believed Rafa was meeting us, or if he just wanted to get off his weary feet. Agrippina gave my arm another tug, and I stumbled over a deep rut in the stone street—Pompeii's roadways were a menace.

"What possible reason can you give for coming to watch him all the time?" I asked.

"Most of the local gladiators are for sale, so I pretend I'm interested in making a purchase and am having trouble deciding. Besides, the lanista is very discreet."

I rolled my eyes. "I'm sure you're fooling everyone. Why don't you just buy Terentus and keep him at your villa? Nonius doesn't visit you there. If you have to continue this infatuation, at least be sensible."

Agrippina had adjusted to matronhood with all the ease I'd expected. She performed her duties, hosted parties, loved her sons. It was the distance between her and Nonius which surprised me. They'd been so devoted at first, but it had hardly lasted through the births of the boys. And now this.

"You're such a prude, Luce. You really haven't been in love, have you? I always thought you were keeping things from me, but you don't understand. I can't stay away from him." Her gaze became doe-eyed, and I had a hard time keeping a straight face. "Well, if you aren't going to run away with Bricus—" she stopped when I glowered at her. "You know, I was sure you'd have at least taken Rafa to bed."

"I have never considered it."

"No need to get huffy. But Justa might appreciate knowing you're not keeping him for yourself."

"I don't know where you get your foolish ideas."

Just then Rafa trotted up and fell into step behind us. We walked through the gates and into the courtyard of the gladiator barracks.

The large space was as crowded as a marketplace. People milled about the perimeter of the colonnaded rectangle, watching different pairs of gladiators spar. Some were placing bets, or eying up prospective purchases. Most seemed to be aimless gawkers enjoying a hot afternoon watching other people sweat.

"Why are we meeting here?" Rafa whispered in my ear, but Agrippina heard.

"We need your escort to be respectable," Agrippina said. "I couldn't bring any of my own slaves. I'm certain Nonius has some of them spying on me, but I'm not sure which ones yet. And you, at least, can be trusted." She craned her neck, searching past a cluster of matrons for the reason for her visit.

Rafa's eyebrows raised at her frankness.

Agrippina droned on about her lack of freedom, but I'd stopped listening.

Rafa and I gazed, rapt, at the pair in front of us—a man and a gladiatrix sparring. The man must have been a trainer, not a gladiator, as he wore a tunic instead of being bare-chested, and had no arm or leg padding. A dull bronze helmet was his only other armor. He fought with a wooden gladius in each hand. The woman was in a loincloth and chestplate, exposing the heavy muscles in her midsection and shoulders. One arm hefted the square shield of a thraex, the other swung a wooden longsword. She was fast with such a long weapon, her pale hair swishing behind her like a horsetail, but he was faster.

I found myself drawn into the fight.

"Stop shifting around," Rafa whispered to me, "you're making me edgy."

I glared at him, but he was right. I'd been moving in reaction to the fight. Countering his thrusts, for he was the one in control. Even when the gladiatrix was on the offensive, it seemed the man was almost … toying with her. Except, instead of waiting for his chance to defeat her, it was as though he was trying *not* to win. Something stirred in my memory, but vanished as I watched him scissor his rudi, using them to spring her shield from her grasp. It flipped through the air like a tossed coin and thudded in the dust at Agrippina's feet.

When I looked up from the shield, the fight was finished. He'd knocked the longsword from her hand and had both of his pointed at her neck and chest.

The gladiatrix lifted her hands in defeat, then roughly brushed his swords away. She strode to a basin, pulling her hair free of its queue before ladling water over her head.

The man removed his helmet and jogged to retrieve the shield, still at our feet. A jolt of recognition raced through me at the sight of his coal-black hair and angular features. *Marcus.* Now I understood— Terentus wasn't local, he was in the imperial troupe from Rome.

I hoped Marcus would grab the shield and walk away without noticing us.

"Just the man I wanted to see!" Agrippina called out.

Merda.

Marcus's swift glance took in our little group. With a cocky grin he tossed the reclaimed shield and his swords to a waiting slave, and strode over to Agrippina. He bowed in a way that was somehow overly familiar. My sister blushed, the blotchy red we shared.

"Marcus, this is my sister, Lucilla." She flicked her hand in my general direction. "Lucilla, this is Marcus Sertorius, the lanista of the emperor's ludus."

"Just the traveling entertainment. I'm not yet corrupt enough to manage the entire school," Marcus replied smoothly.

"Yes. We met once before," I said, "I was with Hamitra."

"Of course," he said, dismissive, though his blue eyes flashed with recognition. He returned his attention to Agrippina as she began negotiating the purchase of her latest obsession.

Bricus appeared among the mob in the colonnade, his orange hair a beacon in the crowd. Spotting us, he muscled his way through. As he approached, I realized we hadn't spoken since his proposal. Rafa gave me a quizzical look when I began edging sideways, but short of pushing him over to get away, I was hemmed in. No doubt my face was the same unfortunate colour Agrippina's had been.

"Picking up some new techniques?" Bricus's loud voice carried. "You'll have to learn to fight from a chariot." He failed to notice my furious efforts to shush him. Marcus and Agrippina both looked up, and my sister's creased brow lifted with inspiration.

"If you won't sell Terentus, how about a wager?" she said.

"I don't take sucker bets," Marcus said, giving Bricus a once-over. "Your fighter looks strong enough, but I won't lose one of the emperor's troupe on a provincial gamble."

Agrippina's dimples deepened. "But that's not my fighter. Lucilla is."

"No. No. No." My heart jolted to life.

Marcus didn't even have the good manners to keep his laughter contained. "You can't be serious?"

Both Rafa and Bricus stared at me, grinning.

"Put her up against that gladiatrix you were just sparring with," Rafa said.

"Traitor," I whispered. I grabbed Agrippina's arm and pulled her closer. "I understand how important this seems to you, but I can't do this. Aunt and Uncle have expressly forbidden any public display of …" I looked meaningfully toward the training ground. "And I won't fight on a bet designed to undermine your marriage. You and I both have more honour."

Disappointment twisted her mouth. "You got those stupid lessons. You learned to fight. Just by doing so you have dishonoured the family. Terentus could be killed in the amphitheatre any day." Her fingers bit into my hand as she broke my grasp on her arm. "Imagine, for once, that you want to spare me pain, instead of cause it."

"You know you can win." Bricus prodded. "What's the harm?"

"Keep your voice down." I hissed.

"You would be winning a man his freedom," Rafa said quietly. "Wouldn't that be worth the risk?"

My stomach felt like an iron weight. Where was Quintus when I needed some sobriety? I took in their expressions. Rafa melancholy; Bricus, amused; Agrippina, hopeful.

"Very well," I conceded. "But stop saying my name. None of these people need to know who I am." There was a chance no one would recognize me, we rarely visited Pompeii.

Agrippina nodded. "So, Marcus? Do you take my wager?"

"If your sister wins," Marcus said, grin widening, "I will let you *purchase* Terentus, but only once we've completed our contract here. I can't have a lawsuit following me home."

"Agreed."

"And what do I get when she loses?"

My humiliation wouldn't be enough? I clenched my fists against his arrogant certainty.

"Half Terentus's value in gold. Just for your trouble," Agrippina said, a small smile playing at her lips.

"We have a deal."

I followed Marcus to the sparring weapons. The stew I'd had for lunch churned in my stomach.

"I really do remember you," Marcus said, as though I should be flattered by his attention. "I couldn't forget such spirited eyes."

"It's inappropriate for you to speak to me that way."

"I didn't realize you were a fighter. Is that a regular part of the education of a senator's daughter?"

"No." I wished for a more crushing retort.

"Don't worry. Atellus is around here somewhere. I'll get him to patch you up once Veneda is done with you."

"There would be no one better." I was glad to know that Atellus was still alive, after exposing his mistrust of Marcus like a foolish child. And I might need a good surgeon. *Stop it.* I could hear Petrus snap. *Push thoughts of losing from your mind, focus on the opponent.*

Marcus paused. "You're really going through with this?"

"Of course."

He gestured to the weapons, eyeing me as though I'd sprouted a second head, before leaving to speak with Veneda. Her dark eyes widened in surprise as she looked over—then she sized me up and her face settled into a condescending grin. I did the same. As Petrus taught me, I tried to interpret what I saw. Having watched her fight, I knew she was strong. But her speed mostly came when she was swinging across her body—she wasn't as fast thrusting forward. No novel tactics either, though her high cheekbones and fair hair suggested she came from the east, perhaps as far as Scythia, Pherenike's homeland.

I turned to the pallet of weapons, breathing deep to steady my nerves, and took time selecting two of the smallest wooden rudi. I checked the balance of each, relieved to find they were lighter than the ones I normally trained with. As I walked back to Agrippina and Rafa, Marcus stepped up beside me.

"Do you need a moment to change into something more suitable for fighting?" he asked, glancing at my dress. The only thing more horrifying than what I had just gotten myself into was having to do it half-dressed. Gratitude for Aunt Calpurnia's managing ways washed over me and I raised my chin.

"That won't be necessary. Thank you for your concern." I could remember my manners, even if I was about to disgrace my family.

"Well, well." Marcus gave a mock bow. "Enjoy your fight, *domina*."

It was all I could do to keep the sword at my side.

"Agrippina, can you take my shawl?" I whispered after he left. I turned and she removed the long, gold pin which held the silk over the braids crowning my head. When I turned back, her eyes were wide but unworried as she folded the shawl over her arm.

"Don't worry, Luce. I've seen you practice for years. You can show this barbarian how a real woman fights."

How nice, now I'm a real woman. She gave my arm a squeeze. Standing behind her, Rafa nodded in encouragement. Bricus crossed his arms and smiled.

Gods above and below, what had Petrus told me about single combat?

I muttered a swift prayer to Minerva, "Wisdom may have deserted me, Lady, but bless my skill and I'll pour Uncle's best wine as libation for a month."

The loose circle of spectators parted for me to enter. Veneda was there already, pacing out her side of the sandy ground. She should be tired from the first fight, and sure enough her breathing seemed heavy. Perhaps I could outlast her. If nothing else, I could make her underestimate me. I shuffled, timid, toward the centre of the circle.

The referee held his rudi aloft as I approached, red and blue stripes on the wooden shaft glaring in the light.

Voices shouted out the odds and bets were placed. I cut out the sounds of laughter and watched Veneda play up to the crowd.

My heart hammered, almost deafening me.

This is madness.

The rudi came down and Veneda came at me.

I parried her overhand blow, arms jolting with the impact, and stepped to the side. She pressed again, both sword and shield swinging, putting me on the defensive—and I let her, backing and side-stepping around the sand.

"Come, child!" Veneda jeered. "Don't make me chase you all day." She grinned, flashing large teeth.

But I had no ear for her taunts. Only for the scrape of sand underfoot and the grunt of her breath. I let her stay on the offensive, taking the measure of each blow. No surprise, she was fast and strong.

Veneda flicked out the bottom of her shield, almost splitting my shins, and I stumbled backward. Pleased with her tactic, she strutted a few paces. But she only betrayed her fatigue—she should have followed through on her advantage. Veneda thought me an easy victory, and now I'd seen her rhythm. Her strength made her complacent; predictable.

After her next blow I countered, swords low and high at once, and drove her back. Now I set the pace, and I was faster with my smaller weapons. I forced her low, then high, then low. My arms grew more confident with each block and strike. I pressed her to the edge of the circle, spectators falling back as she shuffled sideways to gain more space. Veneda's face twisted with concentration and worry. She grunted with each blow now, and I knew she was tiring. I feinted to her shield side and she slashed down, overreaching with her sword arm.

Dress snapping at my ankles, I spun past her and cracked both swords against her back. Veneda went sprawling, face-down in the sand. The shock of the blow echoed up my arms and down my core. If the blades had been real, I would have severed her spine.

Pulling up from my half-crouch I let out a slow breath of relief. A true victory. One I knew, without a doubt, I had earned.

Smiling, I turned back to Agrippina and Rafa.

Their faces wore matching expressions of shocked disbelief. Even Bricus looked astonished. I felt my smile drop away and turned, confused, scanning the other spectators. Whatever they'd expected from our fight, this clearly was not it. One man, boisterous with pleasure, collected on his bets, but others exchanged coins in undertones.

Veneda rolled over and sat on the sand rubbing her back and glowering. Marcus's expression was inscrutable. I felt his gaze follow as I dropped my swords and strode from the grounds—it wasn't reassuring.

∞

I reached the tombs outside the walls of Pompeii before I stopped. Still shaken, I sat on a stone bench and tried to focus on the relief carved on the monument in front of me. My gaze traced the engraved letters, saw the face in marble—but it was other words I recalled. Other faces.

Petrus called me frightening, and fear was what I'd seen in the eyes of those who knew me best. *Why fear?* They knew I could fight … though none of them had seen me train for several years. Agrippina had left to be mistress of her own household for the last four. Bricus spent most of his time in Rome with Quintus, not even sparring with me since I backed him over a tree stump two years ago. And Rafa seemed to spend more and more time on Justa's eternal lawsuit, or with whatever my uncle required of him.

They had their own lives, their own dreams. Why should they care about mine? About the man haunting my nightmares and the spirits lurking at the edges of my vision? I was the one whose ambition was misplaced. Who didn't fit in the world.

Footsteps approached the forgotten tomb.

I sighed. Who would it be? Agrippina would have brought an entourage, already haranguing me for going off on my own. Bricus made much more noise. Rafa, perhaps?

"I don't like losing." *Marcus.*

I whipped off the bench and turned to face him, wary.

"Neither do I." *Why did he follow me?* For the first time, I regretted not having an escort.

"Where did you learn to fight?" he demanded.

I didn't want to answer, though after searching me out he was unlikely to leave unless I did. Besides, it wasn't a difficult question. "I had excellent trainers. And I practiced. Every day since I was twelve."

His eyebrows rose, a hint of a smile appearing under his glare. "Unusual, for a girl such as yourself."

"What do you mean by that?" It was an effort to keep my voice calm, even though I suspected he was trying to provoke me.

"Shouldn't you have been more worried about fancy parties, *domina*?" he stressed the word sarcastically and stepped forward, standing in the gap between the half-circle of benches. The tomb was at my back, Marcus in front. I didn't like feeling penned in. Leaping benches didn't seem a dignified option.

"Stop calling me that—you're not a slave." I moved to leave, expecting him to stand aside. "You have your answer. I should get back to my sister."

Marcus crossed his arms, the very image of a thwarted Hercules, and refused to give ground. "I never make a wrong bet. I need to know why I lost."

"Now you know." I pulled myself straighter and glared up at him. "Don't bet against me."

"I won't. And certainly your sister won't either," he scoffed. "She's been trying to purchase that man for a month."

"She can be very persuasive." The knot of worry in my stomach grew—there was only a slim chance Aunt wouldn't hear of the fight.

Marcus took a languid step forward, and with the quirk of one dark eyebrow his expression transformed from frustration into suggestion. "And are you easily persuaded?"

I took an instinctive step back, pulse jittery at his unnatural change in mood. "Only by people I like."

"That's not very polite. I thought senators' daughters were instructed in manners."

"I must have been busy that day."

His mouth curled in a playful smile, teeth biting one side of his lower lip. "Learning to fight is far more useful than learning manners," Marcus said without a hint of mockery. "You've spent your time wisely, if you ask me."

"Yet manners I could use everywhere … including at fancy parties." I tried to rein in my self-pity. This wasn't a man who respected pity.

"Manners are only entertaining to people who have nothing else to offer." He moved nearer. The darkening shades of blue in his eyes reminded me eerily of drowning; of being pulled against the light. "Don't insult your talent."

I shook my head, trying to clear my thoughts. He was too close, smelling of sand and salt. One deep breath and we would touch. My mind knew he was dangerous, but every other part of me wasn't in the mood to listen.

"You have your answer," I said again. "You let your own eyes deceive you and that's no fault of mine."

"Yes, I did," he admitted. "I saw what our mutual friend wanted me to see."

"Hamitra?"

"You didn't know? Now I see how desperate she was to keep you from me." Marcus raked me with his eyes, possessively. "I wonder why that would be?"

His expression was beyond bold, it was ominous. Fear drove all else away, froze me as it once did, on an abandoned stretch of road. I didn't want to be involved in a game I couldn't understand.

"Because you're a killer," I spat. "I saw you—years ago—when you cut that man in half on the sand. You enjoyed it." Memory of how he'd torn open the murmillo brought a surge of disgust to my voice.

"And the crowd? Did they enjoy it less?"

I wanted to deny it, but couldn't. We'd done everything but swing the sword.

Marcus took my silence for agreement and pressed on. "It's not the kill they enjoy, but the victory. A gladiator is the shield they raise against their own mortality. When he kills, they kill. His victory is their victory—not just over the opponent, but over death itself." His gaze searched mine for an answer to some unasked question. "You're lurking on the edge of two worlds. One day—"

"Lucilla!" Rafa called, jogging towards us from the road. I sighed with a mixture of relief and regret I didn't care to contemplate.

Marcus straightened with a jerk. "Get home safely," he said in an undertone. Exchanging watchful stares with Rafa, Marcus disappeared among the tombs.

"What are you doing alone?" Rafa challenged.

"I wasn't alone." I knew full well what he meant but ignored it. I raised my hand, stopping his coming lecture. "Let's just get back."

"You can't—"

"You talked me into this!" I pointed at him. "You and Agrippina and Bricus were all fine before I fought. And then—" I stopped before my fears tumbled free.

"You were good, Lucilla," he said, but I knew him well. I knew he was holding back.

"I would have killed her. If the swords had been real."

"You knew they weren't real. That's why you finished that way."

"Then why were you so shocked?"

Rafa hesitated. He rubbed his hands over his face, trying to hide his expression. When he lowered them, there was no mistaking his sorrow. "I saw you stand over Veneda and … the way you looked down at her …" He swallowed. "It was like I didn't know you."

How could I explain? It was never about Veneda. "Rafa, you know why I fight—"

"And I know *who* you fight," he said, interrupting. "But for the first time, I knew that if you found him, you'd really do it."

"Did you think this was a game for me? You and Uncle may have given up. Him for wine and scrolls. You for Justa. But I won't give up."

Rafa put his hands on my shoulders. "I haven't given up, but there's nothing new to trace."

He was right. He'd visited every crematorium in Rome and along the bay, searching for victims of the same poison. Questioned surgeons and charlatans. The few similar deaths he'd uncovered provided no insight. An unknown poison, and none of the other victims seemed tied to Rusticus. Our search for proof against Themis had been equally fruitless—if any of her freedmen knew her plan to kill Justa's mother, they weren't betraying her secret. No poison, no proof. Like a serpent swallowing its own tail, we were only punishing ourselves.

I let out a sigh. "You know, you're free in all but name. Able to come and go because there's no one who wants to stop you—Uncle won't. I won't. But I'm free in name only." I gestured to the tombs, wondering if Gavius had drunk his fill at the taberna yet. "I'm not even supposed to walk through town without an escort."

Rafa's lips twisted in amusement. "Between us we make a whole person."

"A whole useless person. Nothing we do succeeds." Time for a new tactic. "I must confront the senator. Perhaps I can encourage him to tell me the truth … somehow." It was a half-formed, foolish plan, but it was the only option left. "Come with me?"

Rafa nodded, knowing it wasn't a real question. He was the only one who could—he wouldn't let me down.

"Be patient, Lucilla. The senator won't be back in Rome until the fall sessions. Let's stay the summer and make our plan."

One summer. I just had to avoid marriage for one more summer.

TWENTY-THREE

"I TELL YOU, BROTHER, I don't have the words to describe the seriousness of this event." Aunt Calpurnia had been at a loss for words the whole evening.

I'd hoped—prayed—no one who knew me would have seen the fight. But Matidia had heard about it. Confronted by her mother-in-law, Agrippina had thrown me to the wolves. Of course she wouldn't admit to being the reason behind the fight. Of course she wouldn't confess to a wager which would make a mockery of her husband.

"We're fortunate it was one of Matidia's slaves who saw it, and his silence will be kept. But Lucilla has gone too far this time." Aunt fixed me with a stony gaze, waiting for her brother to pass sentence.

"You have nothing to say, Lucilla?" Uncle asked.

I shook my head. *Of course* I wouldn't betray my sister.

Uncle took another sip of wine, then carefully shuffled the parchments on his desk. "Should I exile you? I thought you didn't want to marry Bricus. But you're forcing me to choose between your wishes and the honour of our family."

"I can't explain how it happened, but I regret my actions." Almost. I didn't regret sending Veneda sprawling in the dirt.

"She's smiling!" Aunt exclaimed. "Lucilla, you're not taking this seriously." Her struggle to remain calm made her long earrings chime.

"I agree with your Aunt. I'm nearly decided to send you to Britannia. I've recommended Nikandros to a friend in Camulodunum. He and Hamitra will be leaving with Bricus, so this may be the best time. It's a long journey and perhaps you'd have time to reflect on the severity of what you've done."

"No." Aunt Calpurnia glared with grim satisfaction. "Sending her off to the edges of civilization won't correct her behaviour. It's time Lucilla marry and fulfill her duty to the family."

Exile I had expected. I could handle exile. But this ...

"Is this necessary?" I asked, nearly choking. "I'll never do anything so thoughtless again. I swear by the fire of Vesta—I'll be honourable until the end of Rome."

"It's time you became someone else's problem," Aunt said.

"Really, Calpurnia," Uncle admonished.

"Lucilla." Aunt sighed, beckoning me over to her litter. I sat stiff-backed, perched on the edge. "I've watched every foolish thing you've done for the last ten years. The fighting, the disobedience. The thought of the scandal you could bring on us at any moment has been intolerable." Aunt held my arms and forced me to look her in the eyes. Her expression softened. "There is strength in you, the same as in your father. A woman needs strength to live in this world, but make no mistake. These childish indulgences cannot continue."

I fumed at her lecture, but held my tongue. From Bricus it had been a warning. From Marcus, a threat. The path I followed had reached its end.

"We've made a match for you with Cocceius Nerva," Aunt said with a flourish, as though awarding me a triumph.

"Who?" I asked, recoiling.

"Nerva is a distinguished member of the Emperor's inner circle." She lifted her chin. "He may not be a senator, but he has been consul, and is well respected."

Oh no. Well respected *and* distinguished. "How old is he?"

"Hush, what does that matter?"

"It matters to me. I could still marry Bricus," I tried to stop the desperation from creeping into my voice. "At least—" I bit my lip. *At least I cared for him.* "... at least I know him."

"Nerva is the more secure opportunity—*your* opportunity," she continued, ignoring my outburst. "This may not be the life you would choose, but responsibility isn't a choice. And I've done my best to ensure your match will be more successful than mine. Now you must make it so." The remorse that hid in the recesses of her eyes sprang forward. Her husband had left her after their child died ... and after she lost the use of her leg. She'd endured. Could I do less?

Frowning, I surveyed the familiar room: table stacked with scrolls and parchment; polished marble gleaming on walls and floor; Minerva casting her spear into the garden.

I can't disappoint my family forever. Turning back to Aunt and Uncle, I nodded. "May I at least meet with him, before agreeing to the marriage?"

"We wouldn't have you marry someone you couldn't be content with." Aunt's body drooped with relief, no doubt expecting me to run from the room, cursing. "He's in Hispania, but wishes to meet as soon as possible after his return."

"Your life won't change so much, Lucilla." Uncle sat back down at his desk.

With a disappointed glare, I stalked from the room.

How could he know? I kicked out ineffectively and startled a few pigeons on the terrace as I stormed past. His own marriage was a sham, living apart from his wife for months on end. Or was that the reality of marriage for us? Rich in money, poor in affection. Agrippina's marriage was the same, now that her girlish infatuation with Nonius had passed.

If I had to marry, Bricus was the better choice. He'd reminded me Mother's people were Briganti. Perhaps I could make a home for myself in Britannia. Certainly all those things that came with marriage would be more enjoyable with Bricus … except I wanted none of them; they only led to a life like Agrippina's. A life chained to children and status. Compromises I wasn't ready to make.

Aunt had been perfectly clear. It was time for me to choose a future—either with my family or in exile.

Neither was appealing.

∞

Hamitra was in the library, tidying scrolls left out on the long table, the room so different from when I'd arrived as a child. Shelves neatly stacked with scrolls in their diamond-shaped grilles. Boxes tucked in wooden cupboards held the most valuable originals. The smell of dust and mold had given way to oiled wood and ink.

"Must you leave now?" I asked, though her back was to me.

"It's been too long as it is." Hamitra turned, and even in the fading light I realized she hadn't changed nearly as much as the library.

"Is there nothing more you can tell me?" The words were out before I could stop them. Perhaps it was because they were leaving and their secret, whatever it may be, was leaving with them. My heart was sure I'd never see Hamitra or Nikandros again.

"There's nothing more I could tell you that would be of use. The man with one eye is not …" Hamitra let out a slow breath, continuing on a whisper, "… human. You know that. You can't defeat him."

"But if he comes back—"

"It's been a long time. In my experience, if someone needed you dead, they wouldn't be so patient." She said it with certainty, and I wanted to believe her.

"But when you leave? What if you're the only thing keeping him away?" I couldn't keep the fear from my voice.

"You have a choice—come with us to Britannia. Be with Bricus, or not. I wouldn't force you to stay with him once we've left."

"Uncle will never let me leave without my promise to marry Bricus. I won't lie, just to run and hide. I would never do that to my family … or to Bricus." *I won't be the one to kill his smile.*

"Then you've made your decision. But promise me you won't try to find that man."

"There must be something! Every monster can be defeated. Even the Kraken—" I groaned at how foolish it sounded. Turning the man with one eye to stone was definitely out; the world didn't have an abundant supply of Medusa heads.

Hamitra clasped my hands, her own firm and warm. "The gift I have, I would share with you if I could. But every gift comes with a price." Her expression darkened, and filled with a sudden sorrow. "And the price of this would be far too high."

Hamitra turned and paced the darkened room collecting small, unlit oil lamps. She placed three of them in a line on the table. Lighting a taper from the lantern by the door, Hamitra touched it to the spout of one lamp. The flame took hold and flickered. She took the terracotta lamp and held it up, inspecting the flame. Then she used it to light the second lamp, the fire nudging brighter as the spouts kissed.

"I still don't know whether people are capable of true change." Hamitra blew out the first lamp and set it down, but the second lamp she used to light the third. "Or, as they become older, if they become better at acting out what's expected of them, remaining the same inside." She blew out the second lamp, leaving only the third burning. Hamitra arched her eyebrows as she stared at me and asked, "Is this the flame from the first lamp?"

I looked at the two discarded lamps on the table, then the flame of the third. The fire had never died, yet was it the same?

"You know I've never been good at riddles." My fingers twitched, and I had the absurd wish to bat away her riddle with my gladius.

Hamitra held the lamp out to me.

I cradled it in my hands. "I would say it depends on if a person is only the flame, or the flame and the lamp together. Fire can't burn without fuel. It has no home without the lamp."

"You're better at riddles than you think."

"No. I still have no idea what it means." I struggled to put the lamp on the table, instead of throwing it across the room. No answers. Just secrets and warnings.

It only confirmed my low opinion of riddles.

∞

"You know which legion to find me in." Bricus adjusted his tunic, still uncomfortable with the longer style worn by soldiers. "Ugh. It feels like I'm wearing a skirt ... how am I supposed to fight in this thing?" He tugged it again, stomping his foot on the wooden dock as he struggled.

"It's possible." I tapped his hand away and loosened the bunched fabric caught in his belt.

He caught my eye and a playful smile tugged at his lips. "Well, if you ever want to lose the dress, you know I wouldn't make you wear it when we're married."

I laughed, but fire crept up the back of my neck. "Make sure you fight in formation—there's a reason they train you that way. And don't forget, you're slow to parry when you're backing up."

"I wouldn't have to step back if you fought beside me." Bricus slid his hands around me and pressed a gentle kiss to my lips.

I pulled back, embarrassed at his boldness, but there were few people on the dock, and Hamitra was being very deliberate in seeing her belongings were loaded correctly.

"You had a honey cake," I accused.

"I'm going to miss them. Good thing Pherenike packed me a full bag. I'll share them with you, if you come." He lowered his head to kiss me again, but I stepped out of his hold.

"I can't, Bricus." I tried to smile, but couldn't manage it. My heart felt brittle, as though his next words would break my resolve. "You're too good for me. When I'm with you, I forget that anything else matters."

He nodded, but the light had gone from his eyes. "You have family in Britannia. Remember that."

Bricus slung a pack on his back and turned to board the ship. I crossed my arms, fighting the urge to run on board. To leave behind the expectations of my aunt; the idleness of my uncle. To leave my overwhelming fear of the task ahead.

Hamitra laid a hand on my shoulder. "We'll watch over him. I've never been to Britannia, and we might spend a few years there. I'm sure Nikandros will find something to keep his interest." She gave me a gentle smile. "You only need to write, and I'll find you."

"Thank you." The words were inadequate for all that she'd done. I embraced her. From the deck of the ship, Nikandros turned towards us, heavy eyebrows furrowed.

I was too restless to wait on the docks so I climbed the stairs in the fortified wall protecting Herculaneum from the sea. Gavius fell into step behind me, his massive girth making him grunt with each step.

I paced along the sea wall, first toward the sailors unmooring the sail, and then in the opposite direction, towards the homes perched upon the wall.

Who would make me laugh the way Bricus had?

Who would protect me, with Hamitra gone?

Rafa and I had to decide what to do next. It was one thing to confront the senator, but I had to be cautious of the man with one eye. At least we had a few months until Rusticus returned from his travels and I was forced into marrying some old, distinguished status-seeker.

I sucked on my sour mood as though it was an unsweetened lemon and watched the ship leave the harbour, then cross the bay. Its red sail was easy to follow until, at last, it slipped from sight. Adjusting my shawl, I turned from the sea. Few people were out during the mid-afternoon in Herculaneum—most visiting the baths—which suited me fine. Gavius was red-faced from standing so long in the sun.

I nodded in the direction of the taberna on the corner. "I'll wait in the temple."

With a brusque nod, he walked off. I had no qualms about dismissing him. There was nothing he could do if the man with one eye came, except die. And there were very few other threats I couldn't handle until he got back. It was refreshing that Gavius, at least, didn't doubt me.

Restraining my desire to stomp up the few steps to the Temple of Minerva, I forced myself to tread lightly. The portico was shaded by a deep roof, supported by four columns facing the bay. Crossing the porch, I paused in the entrance to the cella and waited for my eyes to adjust to the dim interior. In truth the temple served not only Minerva, but Vulcan, Neptune, and Mercury. Each deity had a separate shrine. There was enough space for a half-dozen devotees to kneel at each altar without bumping elbows, but happily for me the cella was empty.

Minerva wasn't hard to spot, the relief on the far wall bore her image with the familiar crested helmet, the snake-wreathed head of Medusa on her breastplate. I knelt and removed a small jar of wine from my pouch. Unstoppering it, I placed it on the scrubbed marble altar next to the other offerings. My promise to the Lady had been specific, and apparently it had been heard—I hadn't embarrassed myself fighting Veneda.

A shadow crossed the entrance to the cella.

"That wine smells almost as good as you." Marcus entered the temple, his mood buoyant.

I turned back to the altar, silently begging Gavius to return from his drink. *The one thing I couldn't handle.*

Marcus crossed the room in four long strides and knelt beside me. Lowering his face to my neck, he inhaled deeply, his hair tickling my jaw. His boldness left me frozen, the heat of his body next to mine seeped into my skin.

"Lemongrass. My favourite." His breath grazed my collarbone as he spoke, and I caught the scent of fennel, rich and dark.

"No doubt." His behaviour was unrestrained. What changed that he was willing to—"Hamitra," I whispered. *She's gone.*

Marcus chuckled, looking down at me as we both knelt. "I'm surprised she left you."

"This is my home—not hers. She couldn't stay forever." I shifted backward, preparing to stand.

Marcus took hold of my elbow. It didn't hurt, but if I wanted to stand my arm would have to come off. I wouldn't struggle in vain, so I swallowed my anger and waited. Apparently the protection Hamitra offered only lasted while she was present.

"She should have known better." He plucked the wine off the altar and downed it in one gulp.

"That is a sacred offering," I said, aghast. I glanced at the doorway, then back at him. Someone would come soon. The temple attendant perhaps, or Gavius.

"If Minerva wants to punish me, she will." He saluted her image with the jar before placing it back, emptied.

"If she turns you into a spider as she did Arachne, I'll be happy to step on you." I jerked my arm despite my attempt at patience. His stone-like grip didn't loosen.

"Why are you here?"

"I made a vow, I'm expected to honour it."

"No, not at the temple," he said, humouring my evasion. "Why didn't you leave?" His probing gaze left me in little doubt that he knew I might have gone with Hamitra—or rather with Bricus.

I turned to the altar, not willing to meet his eyes any longer. For a terrible instant the secrets I held inside threatened to break free. Father's death; the man with one eye; my longing to avenge the wrongs of the past. But Marcus wasn't Rafa. He wasn't to be trusted, and he'd earned no truth from me. "I belong here."

"Do you? Tell me you haven't thought about living a different life. One outside your jeweled box."

"I'm more fortunate than most, I know that. I have money, family connections, every luxury I could want."

Marcus let go of my elbow and brushed a strand of hair off my face, the passage of his fingers scalding. *Why am I letting him touch me?* I stiffened my back, leaning away.

"And yet," he said, mocking my sincerity, "you want more."

I narrowed my eyes, tired of being on the defensive. "Why are *you* here?"

"Curiosity."

"You've found out my most shocking secret already."

He smiled. "No. I've seen you fight. But that's not your secret."

I checked the door. Still no one. "My aunt would disagree."

"And you care so much what others think?"

"I care what people think of my family."

His smile turned into a sneer. "You're quite the traditionalist."

Tired of his taunts, I stood and made for the exit. *Why did I let him distract me?*

I'd reached the porch when his hand locked on my shoulder and spun me back to face him. I hadn't heard him rise, or walk. *Not good.*

"Throw away your attempt at conformity," he said roughly. "It weakens you. None of this ..." He waved a hand, as if dismissing the town, the bay—the entire world. "None of it matters."

"There's nothing wrong with knowing one's place." I shrugged his hand off my shoulder. "I won't dishonour my family."

"So you're waiting for some old senator to spill his seed in you and give you brats to call your own?"

I cringed at his coarseness, blood rising. "I can live my life with honour, even if it's not the life I would choose." The words tumbled out in feeble defence.

He looked at me with a spark burning in the depths of his eyes. "Even a blind man can preach honour, only to lead his followers off a cliff. You're not as bold as I thought." Marcus's face twisted as though disgusted. He shook his head and strode away.

Gods above and below, I should have gotten on that ship.

TWENTY-FOUR

THE CARESS OF A HAND ON MY HIP brought me to the edge of waking, its touch soft as it kneaded gently to my waist. Another hand stroked the hair away from my neck, sliding through tangles to cup the back of my head.

A burning kiss on my throat released a sigh. His hands grew urgent. The insistent press of lips and tongue on my neck roughened by the scrape of teeth.

My eyes opened in panic as I came fully awake. Hand flying under the pillow, I sat up gripping my knife.

No one. I stared into the darkness and felt my neck. *Nothing.* I didn't know what to make of it. Was it a dream, my overactive imagination—or something more? With a sigh of frustration, I ruffled my hair, releasing a hint of fennel.

Marcus.

I jumped up and searched my room. Checked under the bed — behind the curtains—out the window. Only when I realized the inside of my clothes trunk would be the last place a grown man would hide, did I stop. And Gavius or some other guard would be outside my door.

It must have been a dream.

I hadn't seen Marcus for months, since the Temple of Minerva. He'd turned his back on me then, which was for the best. I didn't want to be involved in his conflict with Hamitra. Didn't need more secrets, more deception, or more complications. Yet I had an uneasy sense I'd become a target for all three.

∞

I wandered the empty villa. Though *empty* was a bit of an exaggeration. Slaves, freedmen, clients and connections wove a complicated pattern through our home every day. But for all the companionship they provided, I'd do better living with just the statues.

It seemed life had gone from the villa in the two months since Bricus, Hamitra, and Nikandros had left. Petrus and Hilarus came no longer. Even Rafa was gone temporarily, as I'd let him journey to Rome with Justa for another of her court sessions.

I was the lamp, unlit; my spark was missing.

After spending the rest of the night in uneasy bouts of sleeplessness, I'd risen this morning with much more sympathy for Agrippina than I'd had before. She claimed what she felt for Terentus was love, but I'd seen her with Nonius. I was convinced she'd just passed from one infatuation to another. Once my sister took hold of an idea, she was like a dog on the trail of a fox. If she kept Terentus, it would lead to a scandal Nonius couldn't overlook. I had to do my best this evening to talk her out of it one more time. But a party at Cincinnata's was not the most sobering atmosphere. If I couldn't manage to convince her, I'd have to find some other way of ensuring Terentus left her life.

Which led back to Marcus.

If Agrippina wouldn't see reason, Marcus would have to break his agreement with her. It shouldn't matter much to him—no doubt easier than honouring it and having to explain the sale when he returned to Rome. But I'd have to do it quickly, the imperial gladiators were only here for a few more days.

It would be for the best. Eventually Agrippina would tire of Terentus—but by then she'd be without her sons, without her husband, and without the status which I knew she really did enjoy.

Agrippina's problem was she'd thought love and marriage were the same. Certainly not the case for the marriages I had seen. Marriage was the union of two families, two sets of connections, two estates— with all the gold, property, and obligations of each. It's what my match with Nerva would be, if I could stomach it. I'd hoped the recent death of Emperor Vespasian might reduce Nerva's status in the eyes of my Aunt, but Titus Augustus held his father's advisor in considerable esteem, so my future was all but decided.

The hanging lamps swung wildly overhead and I stared at them, uncomprehending—there was no breeze. Then the ground shook. A vase fell over and cracked open on the floor of the porch. Tremors shivered up my body, rattling my teeth, and I clutched a column, waiting for it to pass. The quakes came more frequently now, otherwise I may have considered it some sort of omen.

If it was an omen, I hoped whoever it had been for recognized its importance—I'd yet to receive such an obvious message from the gods.

∞

The lights of Cincinnata's villa sparkled in the growing darkness. Agrippina's yacht drifted toward the dock, and even from the water the stir of noise from the party above was clear. I thought this villa, outside Pompeii, belonged to Cincinnata's third husband, but it may have been her own. It was difficult keeping track of Cincinnata—a problem her husbands seemed to have as well.

We entered in a crush of guests without any of the proper formalities. A man, stark naked and very erect, walked past singing at the top of his voice while a young woman tried to straighten the leafy crown on his head. Slaves lined the corridors, each one holding a pitcher of wine, and clad only in garlands. They stood still as statues, waiting to pour wine … or be of other service.

"Agrippina," I said, for her ears alone. "This is a Bacchanalia. Besides being illegal, think what Aunt Calpurnia will say when she finds out."

"No one cares about that silly law. Mutius is even here—look." She pointed to the sallow-faced magistrate of Pompeii who enforced religious edicts. In one hand he clutched a cup of wine, and in the other the breast of the woman straddling his lap.

"It's still inappropriate," I hissed. "I'm not married yet." I knew such events happened—it was impossible to be Agrippina's sister and not know such things—but I had no desire to be part of it.

Agrippina linked her arm in mine, pulling me through the atrium. If any of our slaves had been with us, I would have left that instant. But Sidonia and Agrippina's one guard had vanished down the twisting corridors. And I had a foreboding sense that Agrippina might need me before the evening was through.

We passed a shallow pool. I narrowly avoiding stepping on a

woman who had splashed up from the water and sprawled half-out over the lip of the basin. A man emerged from behind her and massaged her thighs through the wet gown plastered to her body. I took a shaky breath.

"Don't worry, Luce," Agrippina said. "Everyone here is quite respectable. I'm sure you'll find a nice young man to entertain you." She studied me intently. "You should keep your veil over your arms. You let them get too much sun."

"I like the sun."

She tutted, patting the loose curls around my temples, and her face softened. "You know, you could be quite lovely. Just have Opelia pluck your eyebrows, then you wouldn't look so serious all the time. You're far too serious these days."

When had I been lighthearted enough for her? I shook my head and lifted my shawl to cover my hair and shoulders, though the thin silk didn't offer much protection.

"There's Cincinnata." She pulled me over to her friend.

They kissed each other on the cheeks, the flurry of questions between them drowned out by the sudden beating of a large drum. Cincinnata pointed, and Agrippina took off through the crowd. I made to follow, but Cincinnata placed her hand on my arm.

"She'll return shortly." Cincinnata snapped at a passing slave and took two glasses of wine off his tray. I took the one she offered.

"She's here to see Terentus, isn't she?" I asked numbly, taking a small sip. The wine was dry, and not to my taste, but it would be uncivilized to spit it back into the cup. I swallowed, managing to not make a face.

Cincinnata smiled her usual half-sneer, but her face transformed when she noticed someone behind me. Her lip dropped open and her large brown eyes took on a predatory shimmer.

Turning in the direction of her gaze, I wasn't surprised that Marcus, standing near the entrance, was the object of her notice. His deep green tunic was strained from the width of his torso, as though made for a smaller man. The darkness of it emphasized the odd paleness of his arms and neck. *Why hadn't I asked Hamitra more questions?* Now I was unarmed against an opponent I knew nothing about—it wouldn't be easy to have Marcus break his deal with Agrippina if I had no leverage.

As though I'd said his name out loud, Marcus's gaze snapped to mine. He approached, and I downed the rest of my wine in two large gulps. I needed to speak with him, but Petrus's lesson about controlling my enemy screamed *not now*.

The corridor seemed a safe retreat, but Cincinnata hooked my arm and turned me back. She ran her gaze over me and I realized her intent. My sleeveless arm, taut with muscle and darkened from the sun, couldn't be more different than her nearly white, statue-smooth one.

She smiled, pleased with herself. "A man wants a woman who needs his protection."

"I'll have to take your word for it. You're the one who's been married three times."

Her scowl twisted into a demure smile as Marcus neared.

"I understand you're the one I should thank for inviting the champions of the ludus," Marcus said to Cincinnata. "I'd like to thank your husband as well, is he here?"

"He's not with us this evening." Cincinnata's soft tone didn't fool me one bit. "He took the dogs and is likely at the top of Vesuvius. Deer hunting—such a thrilling sport. To race through the woods in pursuit of a noble prey." She moved from my arm to his, clutching it as though she would wilt to the floor without his support. "Tell me, do you hunt?"

"I don't hunt … deer," Marcus said, amused gaze flicking my way. "They may be swift, but not a satisfying prize. I like something with a bit more bite." He removed her grasp from his arm and pressed a gentle kiss to the palm of her hand. She looked faint with longing.

I pressed my lips together, disgusted with them both.

A slave took that moment to whisper something in Cincinnata's ear, and she gave a small pout. "Would you be kind enough to look after my friend?" she asked Marcus. "This is her first opportunity to honour Bacchus."

"I'd be happy to." His expression bore an unmistakable challenge.

With a thin smile, Cincinnata disappeared down a long corridor.

"I don't need your company," I muttered, and waved for him to leave, spilling a last few drops from my glass.

Marcus frowned, plucking it from my grasp. "Did you drink this?"

"Bacchus is honoured through wine." I gestured to the room beyond, then squinted in confusion—it seemed larger than earlier.

"And opium?" He dropped the cup on the tray of a passing slave.

I stared at him for a heartbeat. "Cincinnata." I'd given that scheming harpy the perfect opportunity to embarrass me. *She's going to be sorry*—

Marcus stepped in front of me, stopping me from following her. "It's bad manners to spill blood at a Bacchanalia," he said, as though reading my thoughts.

"Only if someone lives to tell the tale," I muttered.

He let out a soft chuckle. "That would be my kind of party."

"I should go. This has never been my kind of party." I needed to get to Agrippina's yacht before my control vanished. A tingling lightness was spreading through my body and I rubbed a hand over my eyes.

"You should stay and enjoy yourself. You worry about angering Minerva, but Bacchus can be just as unpleasant. I recall the punishment for denying Bacchus involves tearing apart a loved one. Not a pleasant thought." The quirk of his lips made me feel I missed a joke.

"Found religion have you? Very convenient."

"I'm trying to be sure you don't do anything rash."

"Me? Rash? I'm a testament to conformity, remember?" I tried to keep the frustration from my voice, upset with myself that his comment at the temple had bothered me at all. Let alone still did, weeks later. My hands went from weightless to iron, and I wiggled my fingers, trying to shake the feeling away.

Marcus reached for my hand and anchored it under his arm, his heartbeat thudding in my palm where it held his bicep. My pulse sped as though to match.

"Walk with me. I have to be sure you're looked after." He led me deeper into the villa.

I was surprised, given his disgust at the end of our last meeting. *Marcus will do what's right for Marcus*, Hamitra had warned. Now, somehow, that involved me. Frowning, I glanced up at his strong-boned profile. So different than Bricus, whose face was still rounded with youth—rounded with humour. *Why didn't I leave with Bricus?*

Marcus caught me looking and drew me closer. "I have a proposition for you."

I bit my lip. *Stay focused. I'm here to end Agrippina's madness, nothing more.* "I can't imagine you have anything I want. Unless you're willing to stop the sale of Terentus."

Marcus didn't seem surprised by my request. "The contract is finalized. I wouldn't want to face your sister's wrath in court."

"I thought those sorts of things didn't matter," I accused.

Marcus raised an eyebrow, exasperation breaking through his composure. He guided me down a long, open corridor. Columns framed each group of revelers—in twos or threes. Or more. Couches had been placed throughout the vast atrium, cushions on the floor. All occupied. A gallery of writhing worshipers of the god of the vine. Harsh grunts and soft moans filled their air, destroying the careful rhythm of drum and flute and lyre. *I need to leave. Even Quintus wouldn't have enough restraint for a party like this.*

Marcus steered us into an alcove, its curved wall covered by a mural of Actaeon in the midst of his transformation into a stag. I stared, transfixed at the agonized expression on Actaeon's face, the grotesque twisting of his limbs as they elongated into bony hooves. I pulled my hand away from Marcus's hold.

"Tell me why this business of Agrippina's bothers you." His curiosity seemed genuine.

I crossed my arms, considering what argument might sway him. "I know my sister is making a mistake. She'll regret it in a few weeks, or even a few months, but then it will be too late."

"A little high-handed, don't you think, to meddle in your sister's choices?"

"You know nothing about it. How could you possibly understand the losses a woman like Agrippina will suffer?" Parties like this one were understood, expected even. The pretense of honouring Bacchus made a night of abandon acceptable. But for Agrippina to openly flaunt a gladiator as her lover would be ruinous—his low status reducing her to a life of mockery and shame.

"Every choice comes with a sacrifice," he said, amused. "But there's nothing more liberating than when someone accepts her true nature."

"Even when that nature leads to disaster? She can't let her feelings for this man destroy her life. It's senseless."

Marcus snorted. "I never thought I'd be arguing in favour of love."

"It's not love!" I tried to keep my voice soft, but it echoed in the alcove. "It's lust—she'll grow indifferent to Terentus the way she did Nonius. Will you break the contract or not?"

"If you prove to me you know what you're talking about." He stepped closer, blocking out the room beyond, and I swayed on my feet as I looked up at him.

"What do you mean?"

His eyes trailed down my body and I felt their caress as sure as if he'd touched me. Marcus reached out and pulled at my shawl.

I grabbed his wrist. "Stop," I hissed, but I may as well have been trying to stop the tide. My hold on him had no effect. Furious, I turned from him to face the wall.

The thin silk slid free from my hair and fell with a *shush* to the floor. "Prove to me you know anything of what your sister is feeling. Otherwise let her make her choice."

I swallowed, throat dry, and tried to keep my breathing even. *Why did I drink that wine?* "If you won't help, so be it. I'm not so easy to manipulate."

"You think I'm manipulating you?" His tone was injured, but I felt the slow tug of his fingers in my hair, plucking out the binding pins.

Curls and braids tumbled down around my shoulders. My head felt lighter, tingling with relief, the way it did every night when I freed myself at last from the expectations of the day. From the costume of a lady I only pretended to be.

"I know you came to my room." I sucked in a breath. *Gods below, don't provoke him.*

Marcus closed the distance between us, pressing against my back. "Why would I do such a thing?"

"You tell me."

He slid a hand up my neck, touch scalding, and a shiver ran through my body as he traced my jaw with his thumb. "To prove I could. I can't have you underestimate me. And I thought women enjoyed being seduced."

"Women enjoy affection, not manipulation."

"You think I have no affection for you?" Tilting my head, he bared my neck and kissed my hammering pulse.

I held myself rigid, but a soft groan escaped me as his lips drifted down the vein.

Marcus inched his other hand down my hip, down my thigh. He paused, his body shaking with silent laughter as his fingers traced the outline of the knife strapped there.

Merda.

"My affection for you just doubled." His whispered breath carried the scent of fennel.

Gods above, this isn't like me at all. Leave now. Now.

"I have to get back to my sister." My feet listened at last and I turned to face him, intent on getting to the yacht. His gaze speared mine and it felt like the floor had slipped away.

"Come with me." His jaw tightened, as if he wished to bite back the words. "Come fight in Rome."

The room spun—no—that was the tainted wine. I leaned against the wall, fighting a wave of confusion. *What had Marcus said? Rome?* "This is your proposal? Are you mad? I can't fight in the amphitheatre. My family would be dishonoured for generations."

"It would be easier than you think. You would take a new name, a new appearance. No one would know who you are. I can't guarantee your safety, but I don't think you're concerned about that."

"What would you know?" But my retort was without heat, head swarmed by a thousand thoughts. The horror of my family; the chanting of the crowd. The way I felt alive when training—heart thudding, swords voicing things I had no words to say. No burdens … no worries except for the opponent in my circle.

"You would be an auctorata, not a slave. Everything would be by contract. The prize money rises if you sign for a longer term—"

"Do I look like I just gambled away the family fortune? Only disgraced sons stoop to such things, trying to win gold and stop thugs from breaking their legs."

"Some fight because it's in their blood," his voice was urgent, as though trying to convince himself as much as me.

"You have me figured out, do you?"

"No, domina. You're a mystery to me," he sounded sincere. "But I can give you what you want—the freedom to live on your own terms."

"Dying on the sand doesn't sound like freedom."

"Do you think I put such a low value on your life? If I thought you'd die, I wouldn't make the offer."

"I'm flattered," I said, sarcasm a feeble cover for the lure he dangled. For a brief instant, I'd been tempted. But Bricus had made me an honourable offer, and it wasn't enough. I couldn't let Marcus sway me from my purpose. "I have a duty to my family."

"Ah yes, I'd forgotten your desire for matronhood."

I glared at him. "Why should you care? What's in this for you?"

"I'm always appalled by the waste that … people make of their lives." His eyes burned with emotion and I wondered what he'd been about to say.

"Being dragged out of some amphitheatre by a meat hook would be a waste."

"You really are a fool." Hands rough on my shoulders, he gave me a little shake. "You're a one in a million fighter. I should know. I've never seen a woman with more skill, and very few men either."

An unexpected thrill swept through me. I wanted to believe him — to believe I was so rare — and that at last someone valued me for it. But he distracted me so easily. "You still haven't answered my question. What's in it for you?"

"The pleasure of your company in Rome, of course." Marcus bent his head and I waited, breathless. "And a manager's share of the prize money."

Gods below, he's difficult. Even with the buzzing in my head and tingling in my limbs, I knew it was a ploy. *Secrets and lies …*

My subdued frustrations flared and I ran my hands up his chest, resting them over the fast beat of his heart. "Is that all you want?"

His blue eyes darkened with intent. Hands cupping my buttocks, he lifted me without effort and pressed me back against the wall. My legs wrapped around his waist — the feel of his body against mine was nearly painful through the thin fabric of my dress.

The room faded to a dull haze. Music played, soft but relentless. Incense spiced the air. The cool plaster at my back fought the heat of Marcus's body against me. He inched his lips towards mine and I twined my fingers in the thick mass of his hair.

"Come with me," he said again.

"No." Gripping his hair, I pulled his mouth to mine.

Our lips met, then our tongues. Yet the more I sought, the gentler his kiss became, as if afraid I'd bite.

He pulled away. "You would have killed Veneda if the blades had been real."

I ran my hands along the rough stubble of his jaw and he closed his eyes, expelling a sharp breath. "You shouldn't have listened to that conversation."

"I didn't need to overhear you. I saw it in your eyes."

"Stop arguing. I'm not going with you."

"I could make you."

I froze.

Before I could blink, he had my wrists in his hands, pinning me against the wall with his body. I tried to pull away, but my arms may as well have been cemented into the plaster. His face was blank and cold as stone. Fear stopped my breath; stopped any thought of struggle. "Everything I ask, I could force you to do." His voice held no humour now.

"Then why ask at all?"

The moment lengthened, and I thought he might not answer. "Because I don't need your obedience," he said in a rush. "Tell me—why did you learn to fight?"

I jerked against his grasp. *Useless.* "Why do you care?"

"Our choices are the only thing that matter. Your skill is hard won." He rubbed his fingers along the calluses of my palms, hands like shackles around my wrists. "But unexpected."

You are unexpected. One green eye, one dark hole. They were only words. Words spoken long ago. But they still had the power to make me shudder.

I sucked in a breath, air numbing my lungs. "What did you say?"

Marcus narrowed his eyes, confused.

"Lucilla! We're leaving!" Agrippina's angry call from outside the alcove made me tear my gaze from Marcus. Arms crossed, my sister flicked her eyes over him, his body still pressed along mine.

I'm making a fool of myself. He was never an opponent I could control.

"Put me down," I hissed, cheeks and neck flaming with embarrassment. It was difficult being indignant with my legs wrapped around him.

He lowered me as though I weighed nothing. "This isn't over."

"Yes, it is." I followed Agrippina, refusing to look back.

TWENTY-FIVE

"WHEN I SAID FIND A YOUNG MAN, I meant someone of good family!" Agrippina at least waited until we'd boarded her yacht before loosing her anger.

"You're not serious! You're buying a gladiator for your own amusement." I seethed at her hypocrisy. The cool night breeze helped my head feel clearer. But the rocking of the ship didn't help the pitching in my stomach.

"I'm not just bedding Terentus. I'm in love with him. Plus, I'm married. What would happen if Marcus got you with child?"

"Nothing happened." *Not that I was in a state to stop it.*

"If Cincinnata hadn't told me where to find you —"

"Enough, Agrippina!" This wasn't about me. I glared at her swollen lips and tousled hair. She reached up to tuck a straggling lock over her ear. "You must see reason. This obsession with Terentus has to end. You wanted Nonius for so long, and you're giving him up so easily."

Her back stiffened and she cast me an exasperated look. "The reality was different from the dream, Lucilla. I was a girl—I didn't know it wouldn't last." Agrippina pulled her embroidered shawl tight across her body, rings flashing on her perfectly manicured hands—and I realized just how serious she was. All our lives, I'd never seen her smallest nail untattered; whole. My concern doubled.

"So you're willing to leave the boys with Nonius, while you live in exile?" Our feet echoed on the deck as I followed her to the couches, but neither of us sat. "You can't have thought this through. If you take up with Terentus openly, you'll lose your status. You won't be able to return to your home in Rome. Most of your friends here won't receive you anymore—"

"Don't lecture me," she snapped. "I've always done my duty. It was supposed to be enough—everyone said it would be enough. But it's pointless. My husband is indifferent. More concerned with his foolish politics than me. My sons will grow up and leave. I need more."

"More? I can't believe I'm hearing this. You have everything you said you wanted!"

"I wanted to be loved."

"The boys love you." I was shocked by her callousness. Her selfishness. "You *know* what it will do to them to grow up without their mother. How can you abandon them?"

"You're one to talk. You abandoned your future and your responsibilities a long time ago. Choosing that slave instead of your status."

"Rafa needed protection—"

"And those lessons!"

"It won you Terentus—"

"And the opportunities Uncle and Aunt would have given you, had you shown the slightest interest in being dutiful." She threw her hands up in disgust. "Now you blame me for doing the same? For following my heart?"

"You've always followed your heart. That's why you married Nonius. Everything was so easy for you, while I had to fight for every bit of what I needed."

"Oh yes, *fight*," she spat the word. "Don't you think I know why you've been training so long? Your desire to avenge father's death has turned you away from any happiness. Aunt told me you could have a brilliant match. You could try to … be normal … to have a husband and children and a life. But I know you, Lucilla," she said it like a curse, as though knowing me was a terrible thing. "You won't be happy when you've killed whoever these people are, even if …"

"Go ahead and say it!" The fury poured out of me. "Even if I could succeed." Chest burning, I walked to the rail and clutched the wood, wishing I could rip it from the deck.

Agrippina shuffled her feet as she neared. When she spoke, her tone was softer. "If anyone could it's you. But what would you do after?"

I couldn't resist the gentle hand she laid on my shoulder, and turned to face her.

Her eyes searched mine and she sucked in a breath. "You don't think there will be an *after*." She grasped both my hands. "Father wouldn't want you to throw away your life in this pointless fashion. Terrible things happen all over the world, Lucilla, without explanation and without being righted."

She didn't understand. She never had.

"This is not a 'terrible thing.' This was a deliberate act. A crime committed against our blood by someone who's tried over and over to hurt us. They could decide to strike again at any time. It could be your sons, Agrippina, who are targeted next." It was clearly the first time she'd considered this. "We don't know what caused it. We can never know if we're safe. I have to find them, make them account for what they've done."

"It's been eight years since we've been attacked," she said, trying for a reasonable tone. "Whatever reason they had must be long past. If Uncle hasn't found proof against Rusticus or whoever was behind it, how can you expect to? Lay it to rest."

"There's been no rest for me." *How could I make her see?* "Each morning, I expect it to be my last. Each morning I expect *him* to return."

To her credit, she didn't roll her eyes at the mention of a man whose existence she still doubted. "Then don't stay where he can find you," she said, inspired. "Terentus and I are leaving the day after Vulcanalia, once he's freed. The ludus is heading back to Rome, but obviously we can't live there or here. We're going to Greece. You could come with us and start new."

It was appealing. Certainly more appealing than Marcus's offer. In Greece we could make ourselves hard to find. And with me, Agrippina stood a much better chance of either sticking out this mad scheme, or making it home safely if it fell apart.

But no matter what justifications I made—Greece, Britannia, or beyond the Pillars of Hercules—if I left now, I would be running away. *I can't run away.*

Agrippina saw it in my face and her hopeful expression fell. "If you aren't coming with us, will you make me a promise?"

"Of course."

"Watch over my sons. I haven't been a very good mother to them."

She shook off my attempted protest. "I know they're Nonius' responsibility, and he'll take care of them. But I would be happier knowing you were there to protect them."

I wanted to tell her *no*. That her children needed her; that growing up without a mother would leave a hole which could never be filled. But she knew these things, as surely as I did, and was choosing to leave anyway.

"I will. You know I will. But the boys will never forgive you."

Her face crumpled with sorrow, and she wiped at her eyes. "They may not forgive me, but perhaps one day they'll understand." She gave me a small smile. "You could marry Nonius. After he divorces me, I mean."

"Don't you think he'll have had enough of the Calpurnii?"

"He's always respected your … tenacity," she said, a dimple appearing in one cheek. "And he's a good man. Just boring." She put an arm around me and we stared out over the moonlit bay.

I sighed. "It's a generous offer, but I think we wouldn't suit, in the long run."

"If you change your mind, you're always welcome to join us. Terentus has relatives in Athens. We'll be leaving from Pompeii around mid-afternoon. I'll look for you." She always hoped for the best.

"Good journey, Agrippina." I folded her into my arms and she clutched me tight.

"Good journey, Luce."

∞

"Uncle." I accosted him in his study. The morning was overcast, wind blowing from the sea fluttered curtains and ruffled parchment weighted down on the desk.

"Niece." His lips twitched and he put down his goblet. It was early … but then, he may well drink before breakfast for all I knew.

"I must go to Rome."

He stared at me. "Shopping for your betrothal? You should wait until your Aunt recovers." His tone exposed his concern for Aunt Calpurnia, still recovering from a bout of fever. Emperor Vespasian himself had been carried away by the fever just two months before.

"I no longer need a chaperone."

"A woman always needs a guardian, at least for appearances."

"I've never had a guardian when I needed one." It sounded ungrateful, but I was tired of his complacency. He'd try to put off this conversation as he'd dismissed all the others over the years.

He rolled up the scroll he'd been reading, avoiding my gaze. "I think I've done a fair job of protecting you."

"But you haven't brought us justice." My voice raised, years of resentment and frustration building inside me. "How long did you expect me to endure this isolation? To wait before punishing those who attacked us?"

Uncle clutched the scroll, hands shaking as he brandished it at me. "You have duties to this family beyond your juvenile obsession."

I recoiled as though slapped. "I won't hide here any longer, making excuses instead of taking action."

"You cannot act without proof." He flung the scroll down, sending it skidding across the desk. He stood, chair scraping against marble. "If you dishonour this family, we'll have nothing to do with you again!" As soon as the words passed his lips, his eyes widened in shock and he shut his mouth with a snap.

"Which of you made that vow?" I said, my voice a strained whisper. "You or Father?"

His face sagged, regret and sorrow weighing it down. He turned to face the statue of Minerva, hands limp at his sides.

"Would I still be here, if it had been Lucius who cast me out?" He reached for his goblet and took several long swallows, then dropped it with a clang back onto the desk. "The vows you make to yourself are far more binding than those you swear to others."

"Then why? What did you do to him?"

It seemed he warred with himself, head shaking back and forth. "You must understand," he said, voice flat. "Everyone loved your mother. But I—foolish boy—I tormented myself loving her." His shoulders hunched and his hands covered his face. "I broke faith with my brother. How could I stay—" his breathing hitched and he spent a moment that way, face in his hands.

I didn't have the heart to leave, or yell, or comfort him. *How could he? How could he keep this from me?*

"I was a disgrace, but Lucius was no better. No better than me," he said, with more than his normal slur. "He couldn't stay faithful to any woman … no matter how much he talked of love. And he talked. Gods damn him, he talked! Got every woman he wanted and kept the only one I loved." His lips twisted as though tasting a bitter fruit.

I wanted to say something—to ask the dozen questions pressing in on me—but I couldn't find the words. Only *liar. Father. Mother. It all had to be a lie.*

"We Calpurnii are a bloodline of honourable cowards," he said, recovering some of his composure and standing his goblet upright again. "We put on a good show, preserving our dignity before others. But inside we're faithless. Weak. At the mercy of our desires." Straightening his shoulders, he cleared his throat. "You'll have to be better than your father, Lucilla. Live your life with honour. Nerva is a rich man; a powerful man. But he's an old man. Do this for your family and soon you'll be mistress of your own fate."

"You tell me to live with honour, but in the next breath to plan for my husband's death," I said, shaking with rage. "The wisdom of the wisest men has passed through your hands, sits on your shelves—" I was beyond angry. I was betrayed. I'd thought him loving, but he'd been hiding all these years from his guilt. Hiding behind duty and philosophy. "I am no coward," I spat, and his back stiffened. "I won't hide here until I'm too feeble to act, waiting for a confession that will never come. I'm done with waiting."

He slammed his hand on the table. "Then you're no longer welcome here."

I stalked from the room, sandals slapping on the mosaic floor. Our raised voices had alerted the household, and I pushed past some slaves gawking in the atrium. I couldn't remember when my uncle had ever yelled, so I wasn't surprised to see Aunt Calpurnia being carried over.

"Lucilla," she called after me. Ordinarily I wouldn't have stopped, but her voice was weak, barely audible. It was only four nights ago the physician had nearly bled her dry trying to cool the fever.

I approached, brushing aside the deep orange curtain hanging from the frame. Aunt Calpurnia lay on her litter, pale and gaunt.

Fine lines creased around her eyes and across her forehead as she frowned. "Sit with me."

I did, lifting my legs so we could be carried. The litter was spacious, and the lecticarii didn't struggle with the extra weight.

"You're always welcome here, no matter what my brother may

say," she said, voice straining. "He's worried for you."

"I don't want to discuss it." I didn't know how much Aunt heard, and it didn't seem the right time to upset her further.

"Love is a terrible thing, Lucilla." I thought at first that she was trying to lift my mood, but her eyes were sombre. "It keeps us chained to the people who hurt us most. It makes us hostages to the fate of those we care for. We will do the most unspeakable things, if we can say they're done for love."

I looked away, unable to watch the pain break across her face. We'd been carried to the pool, overlooking the crescent of the bay. Patches of light shone through the thick clouds, dotting the dark waves. The high curtains of the pavilion whipped in the breeze.

Love. Agrippina thought she married for love, and now she would run away for it. Uncle claimed to have loved my mother, yet because he loved Father, it caused a break in our family which had never healed.

"Are you telling me I should be happy to marry without love?"

"If you must marry—and you must," she said, before I could argue the point, "it's far better this way. The worst pain in my life came not from the loss of my leg, but from burying my child." She picked at the cotton blanket in her lap. "He was only days old, yet he was so perfect … which of course is what all mothers say … but how can you see anything but perfection in that tiny form?" I reached for her hands to stop their trembling. "I've never loved anything so completely as my son. When he was inside me he was restless and eager to be out in the world, always moving, fluttering." Her voice was steady, but tears ran down her face. "When I held him for the last time I thought—this can't be my boy. My boy would never lay still."

I wiped the tears from her cheeks, and from mine.

"What kind of gods give me so much I don't need, and take away the one thing I wanted? What kind of gift is love?" Her voice faded, filled with genuine confusion.

It was frightening to realize that no one, it seemed, had answers. I lived my life following a road that had been mapped for me, believing they knew where it led. But Marcus had been right—they were blind.

I needed to look out for myself.

Twenty-Six

I WAS AT ODDS WITH EVERYONE.

Uncle's rejection and Aunt's candour had gutted me. I'd walked the garden, then the grove, then halfway up the tremoring body of the mountain. I'd visited the chickens, who were now quite peaceable. The kitchen, where Pherenike passed me a honey cake over the grasping hands of her little girl … and quietly collected a satchel full of food. I had no sword to call my own, but I'd gotten a knife, strong sandals, and a purse of coins. Making my way to the sandy beach, I hadn't paced the waterline as usual, but gone down the pier and into one of the boats.

At a thousand strokes I realized how foolish I was being, imagining I could row to Rome with so little provision, so little protection. *Haven't I learned anything?*

So I let the boat float in the bay. Watched the stars appear. Tried to find the perspective I desperately needed. On my back, staring at thousands of lights beyond my reach, it had been reassuring to know that *up* was one direction I couldn't go. Eventually the wind and tide drifted me southward—and I remembered the grotto.

Lighting the lantern as the cavern appeared, I rowed in. The hull scraped against rock and the sound of paint being shorn off had me reaching for the rough patch on my upper arm where the cavern mouth had skinned me years ago. I hauled the little boat onto the slippery ramp then dropped to the rock in exhaustion, watched the hanging lantern at the bow swing to a stop. Its pale light barely illuminated the water beneath the boat.

There were lamps here before.

I unhooked the lantern and surveyed the cavern. A few lamps lay forgotten on the ground, but the remaining carpets were soggy from the damp, or maybe from the flooding tide. Remnants of food, now moldy, littered the ground. A festering grape squished under my sandal and a pungent aroma wafted up. I didn't envy the slaves who had to clean up these offerings.

Fortunately, one jug of water was full, so I wouldn't die of thirst tonight. *A mind to think, Lucilla.* I hadn't even remembered a waterskin. Finding a somewhat dry corner of carpet, I curled up, pillowing my head with my wadded shawl.

In the list of foolish things I'd done, this was near the top. Rowing the bay, at night, without company—without leaving word. I could hear Aunt Calpurnia already. *My future needs serious consideration—*

The ground shook under me, more restless today than normal. The tempo of the waves increased, breaking against the rock. It was calming, the muffled rumbling of the earth, the protection of the solid dome above me, the water flowing …

∞

I awoke, cocooned in blue. Water shone as though the sun lay below the waves, rays bursting from the depths. I wondered what I would find if I swam to the bottom of the grotto. Perhaps it had no bottom at all.

Shimmering azure and silver light bounced off the statues set along the cavern walls. Neptune and his nymphs, emerging from deep halls to frolic on land, unseen by us mortals. No wonder the emperors kept it to themselves. It would be a nightmare keeping the gawkers away from the natural beauty of such a place. I could only imagine what would happen if those scribblers from Pompeii were allowed free rein in this cavern. *Crescens makes the ladies wet,* no doubt. Petrus and that graffiti lesson would haunt me my whole life.

Though hungry and sore, I had no heart to return home. I needed to find Agrippina and give her a proper farewell before she left. Being already so far south down the coast, her villa was closer.

Rowing from the cavern at last, I looked up for the sun. It was midday, the sky hazy with low clouds blowing—

I froze, staring. Those weren't clouds. Vesuvius seemed to be smoking, its peak circled by wispy plumes swept eastward by a stiff breeze. *Perhaps the slopes had been too dry for the bonfires last night.* They tended to get out of control during Vulcanalia.

The wind helped the boat along, but the oars bit into new blisters I'd inflicted on myself last night. I cursed softly, wishing I'd taken one of the small sailboats. At last I pulled past the high cliffs and tall trees surrounding Surrentum, and spied Agrippina's dock tucked in the shallow beachfront.

Mooring the boat, I dashed up the steep stairs two at a time, calling out her name.

"The domina is visiting Pompeii for the day," a round-faced slave explained. We stood on the porch overlooking the bay, and the whole time we spoke his eyes never left the mountain in the distance.

Then the ground bucked as if dropped from a height. I pitched forward, nearly falling over the low marble railing of the terrace. I cracked my knees on the tiles. The slave fell hard beside me, crying out as he landed.

A thunderclap ripped through the air as though the sky had cracked. Awestruck, I stared at Vesuvius. A massive column of smoke streamed from her peak like a jet from a fountain. But it didn't arc as a fountain's did. It kept rising higher … and higher. I tore my eyes from the plume to search along the coastline for the cluster of red-roofed buildings that marked Pompeii, lying at the foot of the mountain.

"Agrippina," I whispered.

She had horses in her stable, but the road would take me the long way around the arc of the bay—a straight line across the water was shorter. Uncle was right, mathematics had a purpose after all.

I ran for the boat.

∞

Too hasty. I'd been too hasty putting myself at the water's mercy.

Halfway to Pompeii, the bay turned violent. A massive wave had raced from the shore out to sea carrying ships large and small, and I'd exhausted myself rowing back toward the town. Most others were trying to escape, but the winds were against them, blowing south-east and trapping them in the bay. For a while I could hear drums as the fortunate boats with oarsmen pulled into the distance.

The column of smoke and ash from Vesuvius kept rising. *It must fall. But what would happen when it does?* This wasn't mist; wasn't rain.

Focus. Row. Stop looking at the cloud. But I couldn't tear my eyes away. As if reaching an invisible ceiling, smoke spread out in billowing tendrils, overshadowing the mountain. And the towns. And the villas.

Row faster.

My hands bled and my arms ached from rowing, but I was close. So close I could see when the clouds started falling. Not water, not steam, but a rain of rock turned the coastline into a grey haze. Each splash of stone falling into the water hit me like a blow to the stomach. They floated out on the waves, pock-marked like hard sponges. Some tiny as pebbles, some the size of fists.

Nature herself had betrayed us.

The ships in the harbour creaked and groaned, trying to break free from the river, their oars in disarray as they crashed into each other and the debris in their path. People ran from town down to the beach, struggling and splashing in the hard-covered surf. Cries of pain and fear echoed from all around, water carrying the sounds of panic.

Then the earth groaned and we were sucked back again—all the boats, all the people in the water—tipped back toward the open sea like a jug knocked on its side. The sandy silt under the waterline exposed fish, seaweed, garbage. I clung to the rim of the boat as the waves crested, then plunged me down.

Coughing out a mouthful of water, I rubbed the worst of the burning dirt from my eyes as the boat settled on the waves.

The oars were gone.

I was fortunate the boat was still afloat, but, as Rafa and I well knew—Fortune was a bitch.

Exhausted, I collapsed to the bottom of the boat, not caring that I sat in a pool of water. I was already soaked. In front of me, the mountain kept churning. Whatever lurked in the belly of the earth was expelled in heaving gasps. I wouldn't have been surprised if a Titan appeared in the cloud, raining destruction on us all. But the relentless flow, now darkening with streaks of grey and black, was bad enough.

Flashes of lightning and the deep rumble of thunder were unleashed under the dome of ash. The rain of stone increased, its leading edge almost at my boat. My body screamed with fatigue. But if I tried to swim I wouldn't make it to land, or to any of the vessels that hovered tantalizingly in the distance.

My chest tightened; heart and lungs squeezed by knowledge I could no longer deny.

I couldn't fight. I couldn't flee.

Helpless, I waited.

∞

I licked my cracked lips. Like a furnace, the air sucked the moisture from my pores, leaving only a burning tingle behind. I was lightheaded from hours without food or water; baked by heat.

The boat lurched, too full of debris to keep afloat much longer. Water spilled over the rim and pooled at my ankles. I cupped handfuls, my bloody palms stinging from the salt. The urge to drink nearly overwhelmed me. My hands shook as I bailed the water out.

Pumice stones grated against the hull. The entire surface of the water had transformed into churning rock. Only the odd spray, bursting up as the mounds collided, gave away the torrent beneath.

A sharp *whap* rang out to my right. I turned. A stocky man wielding an oar swung again and again, sending a larger man overboard. He struggled briefly to stay afloat, but one final thrust with the oar forced him beneath the sheet of foam and rock. The man with the oar and his remaining companions set about trying to row.

No one else was close—they might be my last chance.

Then one of their oars cracked against a floating stone and dropped out of sight. They argued again.

Frantic, I looked around, hoping any larger ships would come rescue us. A few sat beyond the line of debris—beyond the cover of cloud—a startling blue sky behind them. An image from a different world. More than one looked like a fleet vessel. Several were merchant ships. All with sails furled, oars fixed. But close enough that I could make out men climbing the rigging and lining the rails on deck, staring back toward land. We were trapped in a petrified sea, under a cover of falling rock. *Would they dare a rescue?*

I unwound my green shawl from my face and head. It hadn't protected me much anyhow. I thrust it in the air, waving it.

"Help us!" I yelled—screamed until my throat burned.

The painted eyes on the hulls stared back, impassive. A few men on the decks pointed, but no oars were lowered.

"The gods curse you for cowards!"

My boat pitched, filling with water, and I landed hard against the rim as the bottom slipped away. The swirling water twisted my skirt around my legs. I struggled to keep my head above the waves. Flailing blindly for anything to keep me afloat, I scraped my blistered hands against large pumice stones. Pain shot up my arms. I tumbled under.

The darkness was overwhelming; the silence absolute.

Thrashing for the surface, I broke free. I sucked in two hasty breaths before the rocks crowded me down, bumping my arms and head relentlessly from all sides.

I went under again. The cold waves churned me and I lost the light. If I swam now, I may only be going deeper—I had no way to know. Panic clutched my chest and I fought to hold the air in my lungs. But it was darker now—darker in every direction. And blurry.

A shape burst into view and I screamed out the last of my air in a flurry of bubbles. I was hooked by the waist and drawn up, pulled against the force of the waves. I breathed in, but the water burned my lungs. Froze my limbs.

It was so dark.

∞

The air tasted of ash and salt.

I coughed. Someone held me as my body convulsed, trying to breathe and vomit at the same time.

A bowl of water sloshed in front of my face and I took it with shaking hands, trying to gulp it down but choking. The hands guided mine and forced me to take small sips.

"You're safe." His breath carried the scent of fennel and blood.

Exhaustion claimed me.

∞

A foreign land would have been more familiar than the landscape before me.

It was gone.

From Herculaneum to Stabiae, the bay was a smoking ruin. Behind it all rose the mountain, its once lush peak a barren crater, half-hidden in a dense ash cloud. I'd heard the men on board talking—in the night, burning clouds of fire had descended the mountain, covering the slopes and land below.

I stared, but no matter how long I searched, I couldn't bring myself to understand what had happened.

I've never heard of such a thing.

Like a veil thrown over a corpse, here and there, mounds and roofs were contoured by blanketing debris, but the rest was under the shroud.

Our villa couldn't be seen. No villas could be seen. The entire coastline was altered, cut fresh with new juts and coves. No trees, or terraces, or beaches. Just raw land, dark and barren.

I prayed that Aunt and Uncle had left on her yacht. But she'd been so sick, and Uncle would never leave her.

My stomach knotted, then clenched with hunger. I hadn't eaten since … Pherenike's honey cake. I covered my eyes, but it didn't block their faces. Pherenike, Norbanus, their children. Sidonia, who'd been with Agrippina since childhood; Lenoria, who never managed to get my hair right. Gavius … and more. So many more.

Hilarus and Petrus, had they still been in Pompeii?

And Agrippina … her ship might have left before the eruption. I wanted to believe someone I loved had escaped.

But I had no hope.

My knees hit the deck, heart a lead weight dragging me down. No anger; no tears. Just emptiness. When Marcus knelt beside me, I let him hold me. His arms were warm, his body solid, but the comfort he gave was stiff. As though sympathy was a language he didn't know—or one he spoke very poorly.

TWENTY-SEVEN

WE'D CLEARED THE BAY AROUND MIDDAY, sailing well beyond the Island of Ischia before turning north toward Ostia. The captain had wanted no chance of being near the mountain if it erupted again.

Now, it was night and the deck was deserted. Only the men in charge of the aft rudders and the forward scout remained. Everyone else was clustered in the hold below. There was no place for me there—gladiators and sailors didn't make for reassuring company. At least on deck I was not confined, not stared at.

Marcus had saved me from the water, and I was on a ship for Rome, where whoever remained of my family would surely go. But any comfort from Marcus's arms had vanished when he'd spoken: He would get me to Rome, but only if I accepted his offer to join the ludus. I'd have to be faster than Mercury and evade him as soon as we docked.

Soft footfalls came up behind me.

"You can't run from me," Marcus said.

"I could." My voice was still raspy from the seawater.

"I would find you."

"I have a powerful family. They'll protect me. They always have." *If any are left.*

"And your friend?"

Rafa! I whirled around.

"Will your family protect him, too?"

Pressing my lips together, I fought to remain calm. Quintus wouldn't go out of his way for Rafa's sake. He was my responsibility now. I took a slow breath, wincing at the burning tingle in my lungs. "He's likely dead with the others."

"You and I both know he left days ago. But it's promising you lie so easily."

"Stay away from Rafa." I wanted to sound menacing, but heard desperation. "He's mine and I will protect him."

"The city is a dangerous place. Gangs during the day. Petty thieves at night. Anything could happen. Someone could even mistake his identity and take him to the amphitheatre." His voice wound its way through my imagination like a snake, spreading poisonous thoughts where it went. "Who knows? He could become a gladiator." Marcus laughed softly.

"You can't be serious. You know the law won't allow it."

"True. Though by the time you make your case it might be hard to find him, among all the other bodies."

I swallowed hard. "Why would you do this?"

"To keep you from making a terrible mistake."

How can he even pretend this is for my benefit? That I wouldn't see through his self-interested scheming? "Forsaking my honour, my family, to fight in the amphitheatre—that wouldn't be a mistake?"

He stepped closer. "Yesterday Lucilla died. Tomorrow you can be anyone. Leave her in the ashes."

He's right. The thought stole my breath. I was as good as dead. When whole towns are swallowed by the earth, what's one more missing girl? A dreadful gift—freedom to pursue dreams long denied, yet stripped of the family they'd been for. An unwilling gasp of laughter escaped me.

Marcus smiled and I shivered.

The darkness deepened, clouds crowding out the moon and stars. The water, the sky, even the light in Marcus's eyes were bathed in shadow. I tried to quiet the hammering in my heart, but it seemed compelled to race towards ruin whenever Marcus was near.

He ran his hands up my arms, up my neck. His kiss scalded as though I was still frozen from the water. Fingers biting into my hips he pulled me hard against him. Lips persuading without words that I should surrender to his strength. Keep his body between me, and the terrors of the past—and those of the future.

It would be thrilling.

Easy.

And weak.

I broke away and slapped his face. From his calm expression, I had no doubt he let me.

"You threaten my friend. Force me to abandon my future. And still think I'll give myself to you?" I croaked the words out, nearly breathless.

"I have that effect on women." His lips curved into a half-smile that made my blood burn.

"Not on me." Curiosity and anger finally burned through my reservations. "What are you?"

He froze, his cloak of humanity ripped away. Wariness etched deep lines in his face and his eyes drained of emotion.

"You want a bargain? Tell me what you are. Hamitra. Nikandros. You're different. Not human. Tell me, and I'll agree to go with you."

"I could just kill you." It was cold, humourless, and I knew he could do it. The next instant I was pressed against the mast, his hands wrapped around my throat. He constricted his fingers bit by bit, squeezing hard enough to make my eyes water.

"I'm dead already, aren't I?" I tried to keep my voice steady, but it was a struggle to get it out. My pulse thudded against his fingers and I wished I hadn't pushed him so far. It was just as well my mouth was dry—I couldn't swallow against his grasp.

"But I don't want to kill you." He seemed surprised by the confession. His hands relaxed against my neck.

"I have that effect on people," I said, willing the tension to fall away. When his hands left my body, it was all I could do to stop from running below deck.

He stood utterly still, barely rocking with the sway of the ship. "What did Hamitra tell you?"

"Nothing," I whispered. "I promised her I'd never ask." *And I'm not going to confess to what I've seen. The less he believes I know, the better.*

He eyed me with suspicion. "How about a new bargain?"

I nodded. Bargaining was better than death.

"I won't kill your friend, if you'll come and fight as auctorata. I won't kill you, and you'll never again accuse me of being anything other than human."

"This seems one-sided. Unless not killing people is a challenge for you?"

"It can be very challenging." Marcus looked at me pointedly.

"Do I have any choice?" I asked, even though I knew the answer.

His body relaxed at my defeat, shoulders rising and falling as he took several deep breaths. "Not really."

"So if Lucilla is dead, who am I now?" Yesterday I had a home—a name. Today the chain of my family was broken. I was no one. A shadow.

"Leave it to me."

"That's not reassuring."

∞

"You shouldn't use your hands for two or three days." Atellus sat with me below deck, the passengers and crew almost all disembarked now that we'd reached Ostia. He'd wrapped thick bandages around one hand, and was working on the second. I'd been relieved that he was the surgeon traveling with the gladiators—I didn't know him well, but any familiar face seemed like an island in a storm.

"Humph." My non-committal noise made him frown, but I couldn't risk more without voicing my pain. Open, bloody blisters from rowing covered both palms. Thanks to the pumice rocks, they'd been skinned and now resembled raw meat. But crying or vomiting didn't seem like good ideas if I was joining the ludus.

"They'll take at least a month to heal up. Longer if you're going to be stubborn." Atellus bent his head to his task. I distracted myself by watching the play of light through his tight-wound curls, the blond a striking contrast against his dark skin.

I hissed as he tied off the end of the bandage. "Merda."

"Sorry." His gaze slid to the ladder where Marcus leaned, observing. "Do you need an escort to find family in the city?"

"She has one," Marcus said.

Atellus waited for my answer.

I pressed my lips together. Though he knew my name, he didn't know my family, and held the mistaken belief they were from Pompeii. To keep my family name from disgrace, that was all he could ever know. "Thank you for the offer. I know where I'm going."

Unsatisfied, Atellus began collecting his tools.

Marcus straightened suddenly and vanished up the ladder.

"Lucilla?" A voice called from above. It wasn't Marcus.

I sucked in a breath and dashed up after him, biting back a groan as I put too much pressure on my palms before adjusting my grip.

"... have you seen her?" Rafa stood on the dock below, speaking with Marcus.

"Rafa!" I was elated and horrified. *How was I going to explain this to him?* I ran down the gangplank and into his arms. "Are you all right? How's Justa?"

He clutched me tight, making a sound that was part laugh, part sob, before he answered. "Justa's fine. Or she was two days ago when I left Rome. I've been searching every ship that's arrived at these godforsaken docks ever since I heard."

"Has anyone else ..." From the look on his face as he pulled away, I didn't need to finish.

"But I know Quintus is keeping watch. Well, he has a man keeping watch." Rafa let out a long breath, clutching my arm. "Let's get you home."

I stepped back and rubbed my forehead with my knuckles.

His gaze fastened on the bandages. "What happened? Lucilla?"

"I'm not going with you," I said, trying to not glance at Marcus. "You can't tell anyone you found me. Ever."

Rafa's eyes narrowed, drifting to Marcus, and I wasn't reassured by their quick calculation that flared into anger.

"I'm joining the ludus."

∞

We arrived in Rome. It was night, but it hardly mattered. Day, night—everything before my eyes was black smoke and white ash. We rode in a train of open wagons, the mood subdued. Rafa jostled along beside me, furious but silent. Once in a while a gladiator would eye me curiously, but I didn't care. Marcus had been sure none of them had known me. Even Veneda—thankfully traveling in another cart—knew nothing of my true identity.

From the fetid port at Ostia, all the way to Rome, voices in the street whispered *Vesuvius*. Rafa had told me the fleet at Misenum had been partly lost, but rescuers had still been dispatched by the emperor. Everyone, it seemed, had family on the bay. The docks had been flooded with slaves and citizens alike calling out to the arriving ships, looking for lost souls. Down the streets of the city, lamps burned in windows. Temples had fires lit and doors open. No doubt the sacrifices had been constant these last few days.

Our cart halted as the street narrowed. Dismounting, the men collected the few possessions they traveled with. A few carried the locked cases of weapons and armour that had been brought. Rafa and I stayed out of the way. This was where we parted.

A small fountain, carved as a dolphin, trickled softly in the night. The rippling water in the marble basin reflected the light of the lamps at the intersection.

Fighting back panic, I held out my hand. Rafa folded me into a quick, hard embrace.

"May the Lord protect you," he whispered in my ear.

"And the gods keep you safe," I returned.

Rafa looked over my shoulder, expression curdling with hate. "If she dies, I will kill you."

I put a warning hand on his arm and turned to face Marcus.

"Everyone dies," Marcus said complacently.

"You know this is wrong." Rafa's teeth were clenched so tight, he could barely form the words. "Lucilla doesn't know what she's agreeing to." He turned on me. "Your family might still be alive—they could come any day. I'm going to Quintus. He'll end this farce."

"No!" I held him from retreating. "Whether they came next month or next year, the damage will be done. I'll be disgraced. I … Rafa, I don't want you to find me again." I let him go and stepped back.

"What are you talking about? You'll need money. Word from your family if—when—they reach the city."

I let out a slow breath. "You and I both know they're dead."

Rafa reached for my arm, but I jerked away.

"And if they're alive, I'll only bring them shame. Dishonour. I can't do that to them—living or dead."

"This isn't your choice Lucilla, he's—"

"Haven't we always protected each other?" I held his gaze, the memories flowing between us. Some laced with tears, others with laughter, and a few with feathers. His brown eyes softened, the frustration falling away. "If you want to stay a slave, go to Quintus, and keep my secret. But this is your chance Rafa. You don't need a proper name or piece of parchment. Go back to Justa and live as a free man."

"Abandon you, you mean?" His lips twisted with anger. "Live in hiding as a nameless coward? Do you think you're the only one who cares for their name? For their honour?"

"If you tell Quintus or anyone else about me, you'll die. I can't be responsible for that." I glanced bitterly at Marcus, who didn't look contrite in the least.

"I'll come visit," Rafa said. "At least to be sure you're still alive."

"She won't even be fighting for months," Marcus said, impatiently shifting from foot to foot.

Rafa shot out his fist at Marcus but the blow never landed. Faster than thought, Marcus's hand whipped up, then slowly squeezed until Rafa was panting and down on his knees.

"Marcus, please," I begged.

Marcus flicked his gaze to me, then back to Rafa, before unclenching his hand.

I knelt down and pressed my forehead to Rafa's. "Do you understand?" I couldn't voice aloud the danger Marcus posed to us, but surely Rafa could see he was a force beyond the ordinary. "Don't come back."

He tenderly flexed his hand and we both rose. "Try to stay safe, Lucilla," Rafa said, subdued and frightened. He pointed at Marcus. "You keep her safe."

Glowering as he turned, Rafa vanished into the dark of the street.

"He thinks he can protect you," Marcus said, amusement creeping back into his voice.

I pulled my shawl up, covering my hair and shading my face. The rough-spun wool scratched at my neck. I still felt cold. Breathless.

"Come." Marcus took me by the arm, casting a wary glance at the moon. "There's much to do before morning. We were on that boat for too long."

I jerked my arm from his grasp, but fell into step beside him. The others were gone up the hill, so I had no choice but to stay close to Marcus as we made our way to the gladiator's ludus. It seemed to be in a portion of the old palace of Nero. I was surprised Nero's vanity project hadn't been completely razed, though Vespasian had been an emperor who wasted nothing.

I'd not been in this part of the city for many years and tried to make sense of my surroundings. Father had brought me to the golden house of the emperor several times. Perhaps we'd walked these very halls together, but the fluted columns and deep covered portico didn't seem familiar. I shook my head—no memories, they were stored in the heart. If I opened that part of me, I feared it might never be sealed again.

Guards at a tall entrance gate waved us through. Without slowing, Marcus raised his hand in greeting as we passed. We walked down a long, windowless corridor, which opened to a massive courtyard. Training equipment was set up in the four corners of the yard, with an open central area, but I barely had time to take it in. Marcus's pace increased as we crossed the yard. He took hold of my arm, pulling me abruptly after him.

My sandals slapped on the stone stairs as we rose up a floor and continued down a low-lit corridor set with more than a dozen doors. At the end, we finally slowed. Marcus opened the wooden door and all but threw me inside.

"Don't leave this room. Someone will be here soon," he ground out, jaw hard-set. "Let her in and follow her instructions exactly. Nothing else." Orders issued, he slammed the door in his rush to leave. I heard two heavy footsteps, then silence.

I took a breath, trying to calm my racing pulse, and surveyed Marcus's room. Oil lamps had been lit in preparation for our arrival and light bounced softly off the plaster walls, illuminating the few furnishings. In one corner was a large bed, its dark, rough-hewn posts wider than my torso. The covers glowed orange and red in the dim light. Under the high window was a table set with fruit, bread, a large jug of water and a smaller of wine. Stomach rumbling, I dropped into one of the chairs and ate.

A soft knock at the door interrupted me. I opened it to a tiny woman, not even as tall as my shoulders, holding a large copper basin. Red hairs whisped from her temples, streaking her long brown hair with flaming ribbons.

Without a word, she shut the door and set the basin on the table. Unfastening a pouch from her waist, she took out a smaller bowl of wood, burnished with use, and dumped in a sachet of red powder. Adding some water from the pitcher, she stirred it with a wooden spoon until it formed a vibrant red paste.

She turned to me at last, saying, "My name is Parsina. Sit." Her voice was soft, but demanding. She pointed to the chair.

"I was wondering if Marcus told you not to speak to me," I replied. "I am—"

"You have no name yet." She poured the rest of the water into the copper basin. "Sit."

I shut my mouth and sat down.

"Marcus told me you were born of the fire of the mountain." Parsina placed a cloth around my neck and shoulders, gently lifting my hair and brushing it back.

"How poetic of him."

"It is wrong to speak poetry?" She tilted my head back, and lowered my hair into the basin of water.

"Not wrong, just misleading," I said. *And Marcus is an expert at misleading.* "No one is born of such destruction."

"That is what poetry is for. To tell a truth that is not a truth."

"Are you a poet, or a philosopher?" I asked, dropping my head lower, to keep the water from splashing as she cupped it over the top of my head.

"Nothing so learned. Marcus calls me the Mater Luda."

"Mother of the Gladiators?"

She wiped a few drops that ran down my face. "My husband was a great fighter. A murmillo. But when he died, there was someone else to take care of. And then another, and another. So I never left." Parsina stirred the red paste and, using a wooden comb, spread it through my hair. I let myself relax, the familiar tugging of a comb through tangles just like any other night, as Opelia or Lenoria would prepare me for bed. *No, it wasn't. The past was dead. Buried. Don't open its tomb again.*

"Hold still and close your eyes," Parsina said. I focused on the coolness of the paste on my face as she rubbed it over my eyebrows.

"Do not move or touch your hair until I return. I will bring more water, hot, for rinsing." Her accent deepened as she stumbled over the words.

As Parsina latched the door behind her, I wondered what I could possibly do until she returned that didn't involve moving or thinking.

A gentle shake woke me.

"I cannot rinse without your help." Parsina chided.

"Did I move?" I asked. The words sounded wrong. I blinked, trying to clear the heaviness from my head.

"No. The sleep of the dead. Now—chin up." She rinsed the warm water over my hair, again and again until she was satisfied. Then she wrapped it in a towel and used a soft cloth to wipe my eyebrows.

Parsina held my chin with her slender fingers, turning my face right to left. The fine lines around her eyes deepened and she tsked. "You are too soft. A girl for parties."

"I never really cared for parties." And I was not soft. Petrus had trained me well. My muscles were strong, my lungs were strong, like his and Hilarus' had been—*No!*

I wanted to break away from her grasp, and her gaze, but I couldn't. She watched me for a long moment.

"Your heart bleeds. You must not let others see this."

"You know nothing of my heart," I said sharply, but her words cut me. No heart, no memories.

"I know your heart, because I have one. Have I not suffered, and lost? I am not that girl I was," she said without self-pity, only simple fact. Our noses nearly touched, but I still had to strain to hear her whisper. "You are not that girl any longer. That girl is dead. Now you must be another. Be stronger and you will become stronger." She released me.

I took a deep breath, mind reeling.

"For now, we mask your pain. When you look like another, you will act like another." Parsina grabbed the tweezers from her supplies on the table.

I groaned. *Be stronger.*

TWENTY-EIGHT

I WOKE UP SWEATING. A large, heavy someone was draped along my back, arm thrown over my body. His snore sent vibrations down my spine and the expected scent of fennel drifted around me. I inhaled, and Marcus's own scent, at once familiar and completely foreign, caused my stomach to tighten.

My knife was under the pillow. The blade, strapped uselessly beneath my dress, had nevertheless survived my ordeal, so I'd put it in easy reach before falling into an exhausted sleep. I could kill Marcus and leave all of this behind. Go to Quintus and salvage what was left of my broken family. Rafa would be safe, and he and I would work out how to prove the senator—

His thumb stroked the underside of my breast and I held myself still. The rest of his fingers twitched on my ribs. *Is he awake? I'm waiting too long.* I inched my hand under the pillow, feeling for the knife.

Marcus nuzzled at my neck, pressing his lips along my jaw. His hand cupped my breast and I closed my eyes. *This is a bad idea.* I tried to roll away but he held me tight and bit gently on my earlobe. *Definitely awake.*

"I'm not sharing a bed with you." My threat was diminished by the fact that he still fondled my breast.

"This was your idea," he said lazily.

"Liar. You weren't even here when I fell asleep." *Get up, get out of the bed.*

"When I came back you told me you were cold." He pulled me closer. He wasn't cold.

"Let me up," I said. He raised his arm and I stood, wearing only my short tunic. I snatched up a cover of red wool, wrapping myself without looking at him. "Next time give me another blanket."

He chuckled, and the bed slats groaned as he rolled off the mattress. Splashing came from the washbasin behind me.

I sat down at the table and picked up a pear. My raw palms still ached. Even just opening and closing my fist around the fruit made me shudder with pain. *How would I fight like this?* I let out a slow breath. *It must be endured, like all the rest.*

Finished with his washing, Marcus tossed a towel on the chair. "The hair is a bit bright, but it'll work."

A small mirror rested on the table and I surveyed my altered appearance. *Bright* was one way of describing my hair. *Prostitute red* might be another. My eyebrows matched. The kohl she'd adeptly applied around my eyes smudged overnight. I rubbed at it carefully to remove the smears. From the pot Parsina left behind, I applied oil to the stylus and then rubbed it in the black powder. Touching up the areas that were light, I stared into my eyes. Agrippina had always admired them—the rings of green and yellow and brown. But now they were flat. Black-rimmed and dark.

"I don't like it," Marcus volunteered.

I agreed. "Parsina said I need to appear stronger." Looking back in the mirror I tried to pretend I could be the woman reflected there. She seemed unpleasant; distant.

"You're not allowed to wander the streets like that."

"You're not my guardian."

"I don't want to kill five men a day to keep your honour intact."

"I don't need your protection." But I did. *This is dangerous.* The hair alone would brand me a whore to most people—women of good families didn't go out like this. As a gladiatrix, I'd be in the same class as one. I may as well tie a sign to my neck that advertised *body for sale.*

"I won't leave the ludus without covering my hair. And washing my face. But this …" I pointed to the reflection in the mirror. "This was your idea."

"You're the one concerned about your family name. If anyone recognizes you, deny it. Lucilla died in the eruption. It's the best way to protect your identity." He sounded sure of himself, but his eyes betrayed a flicker of concern.

I stood and found my clothes. Slipping the dress over my head, I tied the shoulder fastenings. "Have you thought of a name for me yet?" I tried to sound interested.

He'd sunk into a moody silence, brows furrowed as he watched me comb my hair.

"Vesuvia," he said.

I sucked in a breath. "No—"

"You'll have an instant appeal to the mob. They love the dramatic."

"I can't take the name of the mountain! They'll vilify me—turn against me from the start."

"Be a force of nature, not a person. Remind the crowd forces of nature can't be underestimated, can't be controlled. You're deceptively gentle-looking. Vesuvia will be your identity and your fighting style."

I stared at him, appalled and confused. "My style?"

"You'll fight like that cursed mountain. First, on the defensive. Lull your opponents into complacency. Convince them of their victory. Then, attack in swift bursts."

I could see now what his plan was. Fiddling with the straps on my sandals, I imagined how the spectators may respond to this persona. If they didn't stone me out of the amphitheatre before I drew my swords, there was a chance of winning them over. If I could, it was possible I'd survive. "You mean fool them into thinking I'm weak?"

Marcus nodded.

I let out a breath, not voicing my doubts about how strong—or weak—I may turn out to be. "And then?"

"Then you bring the fire."

My anger sparked, disgusted he would jest about the nightmare we'd lived through. But his hollow expression extinguished it just as fast.

"How much did you see?" I dared the question. Speaking of his otherness wasn't allowed but I could hint, perhaps, that I understood he experienced the world differently.

"Too much." He raked his hands through his hair, eyes unfocused. "It's a waste of an answer, I know. An evasion."

"You've made a mistake, Marcus. I'm not a killer. And I'd rather not remember …" I trailed off weakly. We both knew it wasn't something to be forgotten.

"You've never killed before?" He seemed to know the answer.

"Only to save my life."

"This is no different. Believe me when I say that if you don't make every effort to kill your opponent, you'll die."

"Matches don't always end in death." This much I knew, both from Petrus and Hilarus, and from visiting the amphitheatre. Nine times of ten, both gladiators lived, though one may be badly wounded. I grimaced. *Since when did a one in ten chance of death seem acceptable?*

"They end in death if a gladiator does his job," he said. "The summa rudis is there to see the rules are obeyed. But you must fight as though your life depends on it, because it does. When your opponent's blood is up and the crowd is chanting, she won't care if she disarms you or takes off your arm. Until a victor is crowned or a stalemate reached, there is no reason—only action."

"I can't do this." Dizzy, I sank back into the chair. *Foolish.* As though I'd have new choices today. *No more choices.* I stared at the ground, searching for inspiration in the timbers.

Then I saw the knife, hilt up, fallen between the mattress and the bed-frame. I lunged for it. Even as I stood, Marcus was already there. His hand gripped mine as the knife reached his throat and he bore me down onto the table. My back struck the wood, forcing the air from my lungs. He held me, confident as a lion with a mouse.

"You missed your chance," he said. The blade was poised at his neck and I knew it was only there because he allowed it.

"Did I ever have one?"

"Not really." He controlled my hand, using it to shave the blade against his neck.

"Showing off?" Anger surged again, fanned by my awareness of his body against mine.

"It's surprisingly tempting." He raised his eyebrows … then nicked his skin.

A drop of blood welled on the flat of the steel. For a heartbeat we were still. Then his hand trembled where it held mine and he shifted against me. I couldn't breathe. He fought not with me now, but with himself, his breath coming faster and deeper—as if the blood on the blade was the coin that tipped the scales.

In the instant he made his decision he flicked the knife away, embedding it in the door.

I drew one shallow breath. Then another. "Why am I here?"

"We have a bargain," he said, as though it made things clear.

"You wouldn't go through with it." *Stay reasonable.* What would he gain by killing Rafa? Nothing.

But that wasn't the point. Rafa's death had no meaning for him. Whatever his purpose in bringing me here, Marcus knew I couldn't live with having failed to save one of the last people I cared for. Places for refuge were non-existent. And there were none where Rafa or I would be completely safe. Not from Marcus.

He waited, certain I would realize the inevitable on my own.

I was trapped.

∞

The man talked too loudly. His nasal monotone made my jaw clench. Marcus and I walked toward him across the massive courtyard of the ludus while he droned instructions to his secretary.

"The lanista, Decimus Porcius Lurco," Marcus explained.

Lurco stood under a russet awning tapping his foot against the sand. A wide belt fixed with gold medallions and rough gems tried in vain to hold up his ample mid-section. The secretary's stylus flew across the wax tablet in his hand, wood frame clicking as he flipped the hinge to the next leaf and continued scribbling. Other slaves, two of them bodyguards, stood behind Lurco.

We stopped a few paces away and Lurco ran his deep-set eyes over us, then looked away, never slowing his relentless jabber.

Marcus leaned over and whispered in my ear, "Lurco's only thought is for the perfect spectacle. He must arrange one hundred days of games for the inauguration of the new amphitheatre. Not only gladiators, but beast hunts and creative executions as well. And there have been rumours the amphitheatre will be flooded during the first week for naval battles, as a farewell to Nero's private lake."

I had a sudden, odd pang for the young emperor. Nero had commanded the power of the empire, yet spent his days amusing his vanity until he was despised and deposed. *Gods above, who made a lake just for themselves?*

Try as he might to be indifferent, Lurco's eyes kept flicking to my bright hair and modest dress. His puzzled frown deepened. I remained still, not wanting to display my discomfort.

"Why are you telling me this?" I asked Marcus.

"Because you must convince him you're worth the effort to take on without having to resort to the usual protocol for auctorati." Marcus made a gesture at the small cluster of slaves that carried writing tablets, schedules, and boxes of scrolls. "You don't strike me as a person who'd enjoy being a slave. And you don't want to give testimony before the magistrate, do you?"

"Of course not." Keeping my family's name from scandal was essential. If I was enrolled in the lists of auctorati who had chosen to incur infamia, I'd be dishonouring my family for all time.

"Then you must understand Lurco."

Lurco finished his rambling and turned to face us. "What's this?" he asked, pointing at me as he addressed Marcus.

"Three guesses," Marcus said.

"I expect it's a replacement for the man you sold." Lurco spit on the sand. His secretary shuffled back a step.

"It could have been far worse."

"Yes, yes. I've heard. Everything destroyed." He seemed bored by the topic. He looked me up and down again. "Too bad it's a girl. We need more men, not women."

"You need first class fighters. Fighters who will capture the audience," Marcus said.

Lurco rubbed his nose, considering. He snapped his fingers and a slave brought him a cup of wine. "Yes, I do need that," Lurco conceded. "What's her name?" he asked Marcus, as though I was a horse in the market. He sipped his wine, swirling it in his mouth.

"Vesuvia."

Lurco sprayed the mouthful over his secretary. "Jupiter's cock," he said, coughing. "I can't advertise that."

"So don't advertise her first match," Marcus said. "Let her establish a reputation first."

Lurco pursed his lips, but succeeded with his next sip of wine. "Let's see what she can do," Lurco said, still addressing Marcus. "Get that Kushite, the blue one." He snapped his fingers again. One of the slaves jogged away. Lurco gestured for me to take my pick from the selection of wooden weapons on the rack in front of the columns, and waited.

"You don't get out of our bargain by failing," Marcus warned as I walked away. He didn't know me well if he thought I would lose on purpose—not with so much at stake.

I stood by the weapons, eying the courtyard where dozens of gladiators were training, divided into groups based on fighting style. Separating herself from a group, my opponent stepped forward. Her skin was the darkest I'd seen, far darker than Atellus, and streaked indigo—clearly dyed. Her gaze was thoughtful as she assessed me, with none of the swagger Veneda displayed. Noting Veneda's twisted scowl in the background I guessed that she, or one of the other witnesses, had already been spreading stories.

The woman reached the rack of weapons and we faced each other. She wore a short brown tunic partly covered by a leather breastplate. With a confident grip, she took a net and a wooden trident. I tried to hide my apprehension. It was lousy to spar against a net. Weights hung from the edges, and it was next to impossible to get out once entangled. Especially if you were only using wooden weapons. At least with a sharp blade you could sever a portion of net to free a trapped arm—if you were lucky. I racked my brains for tips from the few times Hilarus used one.

In the end I decided to fight with the weapons I knew, and find an opportunity to outmaneuver the net. I chose two rudi, one curved, and one straight, ignoring the jolt of pain in my bandaged hands as I tested my grip.

"Trust you to find a dimachaerus," Lurco brayed at Marcus, eyeing my choice of two weapons, instead of blade and shield.

Marcus stared at him until Lurco turned away, shoving his thumbs into his belt with a huff.

"What's your name?" I asked the woman.

She looked at me in faint surprise. "Don't you know? Every dark woman in the amphitheatre is Nubia." Despite her heavy accent, her Latin was clear. I wondered how long she had been here.

"Not very creative."

A hint of a smile appeared. "But practical."

Marcus gave me a warning frown as Nubia and I walked to the open area in front of Lurco. *Too much Lucilla, not enough Vesuvia.* I stiffened my shoulders. Groups of gladiators broke off their training and shuffled closer to watch.

"Go ahead, go ahead," Lurco yelled at us.

Nubia cast her net with a sharp flick. I ducked and slid sideways, one sword knocking down the point of the trident as she thrust it out. I wanted to press her back, but curbed my instinct to find the fastest victory. It was Lurco I had to impress—I needed to draw Nubia out slowly, and spin the fight into a performance.

I let her attack, giving her the opportunity to retrieve her net instead of forcing her to abandon it. Parrying, rather than disarming her. Again and again we tested each other. She moved with fast jabs, sliding around the sand instead of moving forward and back.

The fight lengthened. More gladiators and guards joined the loose circle, some shouting encouragement, some observing critically.

Feinting left, but casting across her body, Nubia caught my left arm in the net. I grunted as the weights dragged at me, sword slipping nearly out of reach. I clutched it with a grunt of pain. Winding my arm around the net, I yanked her forward—the strap ripped free from Nubia's arm and she fell, rolling in the sand. The net trapped my arm like an unyielding sleeve, but at least I still had both my weapons.

Nubia recovered her feet with an agile spring. We circled again. Two hands on her trident, she pressed forward, using both ends of the shaft to attack. Unable to bend my left arm, I used the protection of the net as a shield, ignoring her raps and countering with my right sword. Swinging the net up, I smashed the dangling weights into her body and knocked her head backward. She stumbled—her trident whipped out of her right hand, tines pointing at me as though in invitation.

If it was a show Lurco wanted, this was my opportunity.

Left arm high, right arm tucked, I spun towards her along the shaft—then slashed at her unprotected body. I stopped my swords just as they kissed her skin.

We stood, toe to toe, breathing hard. Her eyes looked down at the first wooden blade poised to remove her head, then lower to the second pressing her ribs at the bottom of the breastplate.

"I've not been cut in three before," she said, eyes wide.

I stepped back. *How would Vesuvia respond?* "Your opponents must not be much of a challenge."

Nubia snorted.

"Fine, fine." Lurco raised his hands. "Marcus—terms?"

Marcus nodded at me and turned to Lurco. The secretary held his stylus poised for dictation.

Nubia placed a hand on my arm, stopping me from leaving, and began unwinding the net. "You're more creative than Veneda. She thinks you beat her by trickery." Nubia disentangled the weights and slid the net free.

"I did." I forced a smile. "I tricked her into thinking she was better than me. It's not my fault the truth knocked her ass in the sand."

Nubia flashed a grin.

"Making friends, little girl?" Veneda strode over, her long hair swishing behind her in its high queue.

"If you're afraid to use my name, I understand," I said, in Aunt Calpurnia's voice of disdain.

Her eyes narrowed. "What ludus are you from—Germania? Hispania? No one tricks Marcus. Or makes a fool of me."

She thinks I'm already a gladiator. "Just trying to make a name for myself. It's Vesuvia—you'll remember it in time."

Veneda clenched her fist. "Someone is going to rough you up, little one, and you won't be able to run home to your mother."

"I killed my mother," I said, without emotion. Playing loose with the past seemed the best way to avoid tripping myself up with lies. I took childish glee in Veneda's darkening expression. Nubia glanced between us with interest, and I suppressed my desire to wink at her — there was no room for Lucilla here.

"You don't frighten me," Veneda said. "I've defeated more ferocious opponents. Those who fight for freedom, not just because they're bored children."

"Do you want me to free you, Veneda?" I asked with mock sweetness. "I suppose I could arrange it, since you're scared to die on the sand." I spat at her feet. "Coward."

Her face contorted with rage. I shifted my weight to the balls of my feet, thinking she might take a swing. *Perhaps I'd gotten carried away.*

"Vesuvia," Marcus called from behind me.

I gave a thin smile to Veneda and Nubia, then I walked to where Marcus and Lurco stood under the awning, waiting for Vesuvia to sign her freedom over to the ludus.

Twenty-Nine

I HAD A ROOM OF MY OWN ON THE UPPER FLOOR, three strides across, five deep, with a bar to throw across the door at night and a cot with a lumpy straw mattress. Each auctorati had the same, it was the only benefit of our status. Well that, and the bonus in silver we received for signing on. The slaves, of which there were far more, slept in shared quarters on the lower floor. And those who'd achieved fame—and prize money that came with it—had private rooms, some housing their wives and children. Between the three interconnected barracks which made up the gladiatorial ludus there had to be roughly a thousand of us, and perhaps thirty were women. My new familia.

Slave or auctorati, we trained alike in one of the three courtyards, ate our bland meals together, and all except the potential runaways, who remained chained, had free hours in the afternoon to visit the city baths, or markets, or brothels. I was tempted, if only to provoke Marcus into action—he'd cast me off completely in the three months since our arrival. As trainer of the small group of dimachaeri, he worked us without mercy during the day, but otherwise avoided me. I wanted to be relieved by his absence, but only felt betrayed. He'd turned me into someone new, without care for the consequences. What did Vesuvia care for Senator Rusticus or the man with one eye? She had to spar and train and prepare for the chalk circle. Each day, I poured more of myself into making Vesuvia stronger. Into making sure I didn't walk around with a bleeding heart and a target on my back.

But at night, on my lousy excuse for a bed, I sometimes remembered Lucilla. Her memories were only for the lost. Long walks in the gardens with Uncle. Petrus and Hilarus in a grove scented with lemon. Late nights with Rafa in the library, surrounded by scrolls and dim lamps. On those nights, silent sobs racked my body until sleep came at last. When I woke, I sent Lucilla away.

In all the ways that didn't matter my life was much the same as the villa. I had food, a roof, and time to train. The routine was single-minded—make us better fighters and ready to face death when it came. Even the petty taunts of Veneda and her clique were arrows shot wide; no one knew me well enough to know where to aim. There was a soothing simplicity to it all.

But there was no beauty, no variety, no call for kindness.

Except with Atellus. Though he'd been dismayed at my joining the ludus, he'd reassured me he wouldn't reveal the little he knew of my identity. Now I saw him most days as he tended the mosaic of injuries I received during training. His surgery was on the ground floor of my barracks, almost as small as my room, but with shelves filling one wall. They were stacked with jars, bandages, and implements I couldn't name. One large window let in plenty of daylight.

Atellus pulled a round pot off the shelf and returned to the tall table where I sat. "Luc—"

I clamped my hand over his mouth, bandages dangling off my palm.

He rolled his eyes at my dramatics and I let go.

"Ves-u-via." He stretched out the name. "You need to return to your family. This is no place for you." Not the first time he'd given me this advice. I'd always ignored it, not wanting to reveal too much of my true situation, but gave in a little today. Maybe he'd drop it at last.

"They're dead, save one." I thrust my mangled palm back at him for more torture. "And I would hate to disappoint him and turn up alive." Now that he was the closest family I had, my mind often wandered to Quintus. He was pater of our familia, whatever that meant. *Probably spends all day counting his inheritance.*

Atellus finished unwrapping the bandage and I winced at the sight. My mangled palms had improved from looking like raw meat, though they were now a mess of new pink skin and broken blisters.

I hissed as he washed my hand with what felt like vinegar, but sat patiently on the edge of the table while he worked. He dabbed my palm with a wad of cloth. "Veneda's been talking—"

"Veneda is always talking."

"She influences others. Galla and Kore are new, but she's good at recruiting her cellmates. And she's friends with Achilles."

That gave me pause. All but the most inexperienced of the novices had killed before, and all made worthy opponents. But Achilles was different. Hungry to kill. To injure. If I'd never met the one-eyed man, Achilles would have the most chilling gaze of anyone I'd seen. I might call it animal, but it held too much madness, too little reason. Animals didn't kill for sport.

"I won't be matched against a man."

"But you must live here among them." Atellus pulled the bandage off the other hand and I ground my teeth. "Sorry," he said, contrite and annoyed at the same time.

"Marcus watches out for me," I said, in feeble argument.

"Marcus cares only for himself, don't forget that." He gripped my arms, brown eyes serious. "If he cared for you, you wouldn't be here."

I looked away and Atellus resumed his torture, washing my second palm. Then, pouring oil from a small jar, began messaging it gently into my hands. I tried allowing the muscles to relax, even as the pressure of his fingers stung the tender skin. The tang of olive oil filled my nostrils.

Someone coughed. Rafa stood at the door, frowning.

"I told you to stay away," I snapped. "Twice."

"If you're not Lucilla, I'm not your slave."

I snorted and held my hands out for Atellus to wrap. "How's Justa?"

"None of your business for now," Rafa said. "Concentrate on staying alive—no distractions."

I chafed at how he brushed aside my concern for Justa. Though she, at least, had benefited from Vesuvius. Themis was gone—the lawsuit had been dismissed—and the sword dangling over Justa's head vanished. A blessing instead of a tragedy. But hers was the only good news Rafa had brought. No one from the villa survived. I'd refused to hear more, so he'd offered to keep his attention on Rusticus.

"And the senator?" I asked.

"No unusual guests. Though I think he's dined with every pontiff at least once during the past month. The emperor also." Rafa glanced at Atellus, but we hadn't said anything compromising.

That rankled. My fortunes were at their lowest, but Rusticus now moved in the highest circles. There must be some way of putting pressure on him to reveal the truth. But I no longer had even a family name to support me.

Atellus finished the bandaging and I put my hand on his arm. "Thank you for the warning about Veneda."

He shook off my touch and turned to Rafa. "Can't you make her see reason?"

"I never have before."

"Surgeon!" Priscus banged through Atellus's door, supporting a bloody-faced Verus. Both gladiators were fuming with anger.

"Lay him on the table," Atellus said.

I jumped off and stood aside.

Verus lay with a groan, both eyes swollen nearly shut. "I'll kill that cheating coward!"

"Achilles attacked him," Priscus ground out in explanation, expression murderous. "After Verus was down."

Atellus gathered more bandages while Priscus tried to get Verus to lay still and stop cursing so he could be treated.

I jerked my head at Rafa and we left. From across the courtyard, Achilles stared at the surgery with a smirk while he talked with Veneda.

I walked with long strides in the other direction, towards the exit. *Rafa shouldn't be here.*

"Vesuvia, wait," Rafa called, jogging to catch up. "I have a plan."

I pulled him into the narrow corridor which connected one courtyard with another. "What are you talking about?" I quickly checked both ways down the hall.

"You don't fight for more than a month," he said in a whisper. "That's plenty of time for you to get away."

"I told you all I could. There's no getting away from this bargain. Trust me." I silently motioned as though writing, reminding him of the letter I'd had him send to Hamitra—the only person I knew who could oppose Marcus. The letter could take months to reach Britannia, if it made it at all, with no guarantee Hamitra would still be with Bricus to receive it. An act of desperation, but if Rafa wouldn't leave me be, I couldn't give in without trying for a solution.

"This will work," Rafa continued. "You're not a prisoner. One afternoon, head out for a visit to the baths, then keep going. We can all ride to Ostia. Board a ship for Hispania."

"Hispania?"

"We can go into hiding." Rafa nodded, confident in his plan.

I sighed. I couldn't tell him Marcus was some sort of demigod. After all my reading and endless speculation, it was the only conclusion I'd been able to reach which seemed halfway sane. I also couldn't tell Rafa how the one-eyed man had drunk Sylos's blood, or how Hamitra fought him off. Confessing such things out loud was too risky in this place. I had to be careful how much I revealed. "Do you remember the night we were stranded in the grotto?"

Rafa nodded, puzzled at my change of topic.

"Before dawn Hamitra found us. She swam in the dark, in the storm, and found us in the grotto. Then she swam back to tell the searchers where we were."

Rafa's eyes were wide. "Why didn't you tell me this?"

"I needed her protection."

"Yes, but—"

"It was more important it remain a secret." I could see the hurt on his face that I'd not told him, but didn't regret my choice. "Then they left and it no longer mattered."

Rafa's face grew sombre. "And Marcus ..."

"Is not a protector."

"What do we do?" Rafa's face sank as he joined the pieces together. The question didn't need an answer.

We made our way down the covered hall toward the exit. Rafa looked uneasily over his shoulder as one of the lions gave a low-throated growl.

He shuddered. "I'll never get used to those things."

Several cells on the ground floor had been turned into cages for the huge number of animals being carted into the city—they couldn't all be contained in the Ludus Matutinus with the beast hunters. Lions, elephants, gazelles, crocodiles from Africa. Bear, deer, and boar from Gaul. Tigers and panthers from the east. The world was being drawn into Rome for the emperor to supply an endless parade of exotic death.

"The animals aren't the worst part." I nodded at the cells on the other side of the lions.

Rafa's face thinned in disgust. In a rare edict, the emperor required condemned prisoners, normally executed right after sentencing, to be held in the Carcer. But the smelly pit-like prison at the base of the Capitoline Hill had become so crowded that additional noxii were kept confined here at the ludus. Now they waited for the games to start, and their executions to come.

Rafa and I were both in low spirits by the time we parted at the gate. At least he would go home to Justa.

"Wise decision," Marcus said from behind me.

I nearly jumped out of my skin. *Of course. He'd heard.* "I won't risk his life, as you know," I said, weary of the trap I was in. "But I won't be intimidated by you forever."

His lips twitched. "I hope not—"

Whatever Marcus would have said next was lost—my attention had snapped to the new recruits who marched through the gate and he followed my gaze, frowning.

I recognize that bulk. But I didn't let myself believe until I saw his face.

Hilarus surveyed the yard, his eyes as wide as mine when our gazes met. Bringing his expression back under control he came over, steps unhurried. We clasped arms, his massive hand swallowing my forearm as usual. Marcus stared at us with a peculiar expression.

"If I was any more surprised to see you," Hilarus said, "I'd be using this courtyard as a latrine."

"Pleased to see you, too." I grinned, feeling weightless for the first time in months. "But I'm afraid your ring didn't make it with me."

Hilarus shrugged. "Lady Nemesis doesn't need a ring to know her true followers."

"What are you doing here?"

"Searching for Petrus, and others. I'm without Fortune, as usual. But there's always room for me at the ludus. Lurco's taken me on as a trainer." Hilarus gave Marcus a hard look before asking me, "Now your turn. What are *you* doing here?"

I cleared my throat. Hilarus knew me too well for me to lie; I needed a distraction.

Marcus put a heavy hand on my shoulder. "Training later, don't forget." He strode away down the corridor, past the cells.

"So," I said, "have you seen the lions?"

∞

Marcus swung, clipping my thigh and sending me into the sand. "Not fast enough."

"You're cheating and you know it," I muttered under my breath.

He gave a lazy grin and waited for me to stand, then advanced again. Shield extended from his body, he jabbed his sword from behind its protection. I parried. He swung his shield and I only just avoided another fall.

Nothing was more demoralizing than sparring with Marcus — I felt like a child again, fighting Hilarus. Slow and weak.

"Your first match is in two days, and you expect to survive, fighting like that?" He shook his head.

I charged, trying to break through his form with quick thrusts at different heights. He brought his shield down and knocked one wooden blade from my hand, then forced me to a halt when his sword reached my throat.

"Done?" I asked, panting.

"Since you're dead, I'd say so." He tossed his equipment to a slave.

He could fight me all day and not break a sweat. Trying not to let my irritation show, I returned my own weapons and stalked off to meet Parsina. She had a small shrine in one of the ground floor rooms, and had made me promise to visit before my first match.

As one of the few novices, I'd been paired against Galla. She'd drawn my attention because her hair was the same burnt-orange shade as Bricus. And also because Veneda had taken extra time to prepare her, going so far as to spar against her using two swords. It made me uneasy — they were cellmates, and Veneda seemed far more protective of Galla than any of her other companions.

"You've left it long enough," Hilarus said as I entered. I wasn't surprised to see him — Parsina seemed to have found a new cause to care for. She stood next to him, barely as tall as his chest.

I crossed my arms. "I could have waited until tomorrow. I know you're both devoted to Nemesis, but I don't think She'll be much help."

Parsina brushed a strand of dark hair behind her ear. "The Lady needs to be asked, before She will answer."

"You must be specific," Hilarus said. "Asking Her for victory is good, but it could still include death. I've always asked for victory, honour, and my life."

"Does it have to be in that order?" I couldn't stop my cynicism from creeping out. A small statue of Nemesis sat on the altar and I clutched it tight, not sure I wanted to bargain with Her. *Lady, I could ask for victory, but why should it matter?* "Why should I be spared, when so many others weren't?" I muttered.

Parsina laid her hands on mine, and I let her take the statue from my grasp. "You have much anger. Do not fear it."

I glanced at Hilarus. "Petrus always said it would get me killed."

"Trying to avoid anger is lesson for a girl, not a woman," Parsina scoffed. "Yoke your anger. Make it serve your purpose. The way it strengthens Lady Nemesis."

Hilarus frowned, thoughtful. "Petrus was wise, and Vesuvia is strong already."

"Strong in body, perhaps. This I have seen." Parsina replaced the statue next to a bowl of incense. "But her heart still bleeds. The girl inside lingers—she must go."

"Maybe I should ask the Lady for that, instead."

Hilarus nodded and clapped me on the shoulder. "Your prayers are for Her ears. Ask wisely." He made his way out.

"He loves my Lady," Parsina said, "but he does not see Her true form. Lady Justice threatens the sword, but when it must be bloodied, Nemesis wields it. She would not swing without the anger of Justice behind Her."

I sighed. "Galla hasn't done anything to me. Justice isn't needed."

"Poor child," Parsina mocked gently. She reached into a hutch beside the altar and passed me a rabbit with brown silken fur. "You think today is tomorrow."

The rabbit's heart beat fast between my palms. "Does it have to be this sacrifice? Surely some wine would do." Vesuvia was a shell. Did the goddess really need a life, in exchange for helping a shadow?

"You must get Her attention," Parsina said. "How many others call on Her tonight? And more again tomorrow."

I nodded, resigned. The world was never short on demands for revenge. I contemplated my plea. *Banish Lucilla. An honourable victory. And, if She had time, maybe my life.* That should do it.

At least rabbits were easier to kill than chickens.

THIRTY

MY NERVES TIGHTENED WITH EACH FLARE OF THE TRUMPETS, until it was a struggle to keep from twitching. I waited with the thirteen other fighters assigned to the evening's entertainment. Some paced, some brooded in silence, some prayed. Galla rocked on her haunches, eying me with suspicion. Achilles threw jabs at the wall of the dark tunnel. Zepharos, a veteran of twenty-six matches, stood calm, helmet under his arm as he faced the archway to the amphitheatre floor. It was packed again tonight, as it had been every night since its inauguration. This was my first opportunity inside.

After the formal parade around the sand, we'd stretched our tense muscles, sparring with our opponent using wooden practice weapons. The referees looked on to ensure no one tried to gain advantage by injuring their competition early.

My contract allowed my choice of armour, and I'd selected a gilded breastplate over my pale yellow dress. Marcus said I was foolish to wear the dress, but it was the one point I refused to concede. If I was to make a name for myself, Aunt Calpurnia's edict might be the only way to do it. In any case, I wouldn't have been entitled to much more armour or costuming—like a retiarius, I was classed as a light fighter, with a bare minimum of padding.

Parsina had braided my hair, freshly reddened, and wrapped the plaits around the crown of my head. I didn't look very fearsome. But that was the point. So I ignored the laughter I felt directed at me while Galla and I warmed up. Galla didn't laugh. None of the gladiators laughed. That was enough.

Now we waited in the tunnel. Gold and silver armour; red

feathered helmets; studded leather belts—a pageant worthy of the emperor. Most of it resembled the heavy, decorated parade armour my father had worn for celebrations, not meant for serious combat. For the first time I realized how Petrus would have enjoyed the stage, after the arena. All the pomp; none of the death.

Trumpets flared again and my heart sprang to life. The chalk had been spread, marking our field of contest. They were ready.

We're first.

As novices, the nuntius only bothered to announce our names, and I hoped the hush in the crowd was for the lack of excitement we presented, not simmering hostility.

We entered the sand through the gate for the living. Opposite us, at the far end of the oval, was the gate for the dead—a gate for exits only. *Not tonight. Not for me.*

The immense crowd spiraled around us, from the lower wooden podium for the emperor and his chosen, up to the peak near the canvas awning. I felt like a dormouse, trapped at the bottom of a deep jar, kept away from the light until it was time to be devoured. The crowd hummed like a hive. Galla and I exchanged a glance which might have been bewilderment.

I couldn't control the arena. It wasn't a field of combat I'd choose. No avenues of escape, no places to hide. Remembering advice Hilarus gave long ago, I smiled: there were no places to swim either.

Galla's brown eyes narrowed and I realized I was grinning like a fool. *Focus. You're not being Vesuvia.* I twisted my grin into a sneer, daring her to best me. Her mouth pinched in anger.

Then the weapons were in our hands and we faced each other, the summa rudis between us. I exhaled, letting the crowd around me fade. Eyes for the only person who mattered. Galla held a wide gladius and a small shield, her legs protected by high greaves which flared above her knees. Her sword arm was padded but her breastplate was short, leaving her midsection exposed. I needed to get past the padding, either by cutting deep into it, or striking where she was unprotected. The voice that was Lucilla surfaced, telling me I didn't want to kill Galla—I had no reason to. But I had to draw blood.

I adjusted my grip on my swords, ignoring the irritation of my still-bandaged hands.

The staff dropped. We circled.

Galla tested me, her thrusts slow but powerful as they rang against my blades. She was a head taller than me, her reach long. But she was uncreative; a true novice. I blocked and countered her attacks, easily taking her measure.

Diving, I rolled away from one of her better strikes and she stepped on the trailing hem of my dress, ripping a portion of it loose. I made a show of spinning away, playing up for the crowd.

Then she hit me.

I reeled, head ringing from the shield strike to the back of my skull—reverberations clanged behind my eyes.

Merda.

Wake up, Lucilla—this isn't a game.

I'd spun enough out of the way that the summa rudis didn't let Galla press forward. She paced in jerky struts behind him. The referee checked my skull. No blood.

We engaged again.

Yoke your anger, Parsina said. I swallowed my frustration and let her attack for one heartbeat. Two. Three … then bore down on her, swords carrying my fury. I forced her to retreat right, then left. Her eyes grew wide with panic as she understood how impotent she was against me. I could steer Galla whichever way I wanted and pressed until her breathing rasped from exertion, her blocks pitiful and slow.

Galla had no thought left for tactic, pure instinct drove her—it wasn't enough. Our blades crossed and, her shield forgotten, she didn't even try to stop me as I slashed up with my left, raking her thigh. She cried out in pain; the crowd roared.

Fingers splayed over her wound, she collapsed to one knee. The summa rudis stepped forward to signal my victory.

Galla had other plans. She grabbed a fistful of sand and flung it, spraying both me and the summa rudis with dirt and blood. I tried to duck, but her shield was already in flight—it cracked into my temple and I fell sideways to my knees.

She was coming, but my eyes were useless, head spinning.

The scrape of sand. A shuffle.

A grunt.

Blind, I thrust my sword up from where I knelt and felt it pierce flesh, then break bone. I hoped it wasn't the summa rudis—it was bad fortune to kill a referee.

Eyes streaming, I finally saw through the grit. Galla hung limp on the end of my sword, head pierced through, chin to crown. The point of my gladius protruded from her skull, her helmet rocked on the ground where it had fallen. Glassy-eyed, Galla collapsed and I pulled my sword free. I groped in the sand for my second blade. The summa rudis approached, still wiping blood and dirt from his eyes. He stopped just short of spitting on Galla as he kicked her sword away from her body. I didn't wait for him.

I raised my arms, both blades skyward in an iron V. My heart raced, blood tingled in every fibre of my body. I knew Marcus hadn't been lying—the thought burned through every part of my body, echoed back from the screams of the crowd: *I'm alive.*

The summa rudis crowned me with a laurel wreath while the nuntius announced my victory. The crowd was a sea of cheers. If anyone laughed now, I couldn't hear it.

I walked back through the gate for the living.

"You did well. She fought without honour," Zepharos said as I came down the tunnel. His bare torso was a vicious hash of old scars and he pointed to one down the center of his chest. "I would know."

I started to nod, but stopped before my brains could slide out my ears, the golden edges of victory slipping away.

Keeping my head up and ignoring the keening in my skull, I pressed on down the hall. I passed Achilles, a feral gleam in his eyes as he looked over my ripped and bloody dress. It made my stomach heave—or perhaps that was just the blow to the head. *Don't be sick here.*

Was the hall always this long? Shaking, my skin turned cold and beaded with moisture. At last I staggered into a tiny cubicle near the exit and vomited on the dusty stones.

Stupid. Senseless.

Atellus, out of breath, came close to tripping over me as I sat shuddering in the doorway.

"Let me see your head." He probed with his cool fingertips to feel the bones. Then he ran his hands through my hair, loosening the braids and checking his fingers for blood. He took my face in his hands and looked in my eyes, turning my head side to side.

"I'm—"

"You need to stay awake tonight," he said. "I'll tell Lurco you won't be training tomorrow."

Taking my arm, he helped me to my feet. When he steered me to the exit, I shrugged him off. "I can walk."

The guards waved us past and I realized he was going to escort me back to the ludus.

"What about the rest of the fighters?" I asked.

"I was only in charge of the corpses," he said with a dismissive wave. "Modeno can handle them without me."

"Is that where you ran from? The other gate?"

He nodded, then we walked in silence.

Rafa was waiting outside the ludus. He'd seen. "You had no choice, Luce," he said quietly. His eyes flicked to Atellus.

"I'm not a child, Rafa. I had a choice."

"Then I'm glad you chose yourself."

My eyes spun and I put my hand on his shoulder, vision hazy.

"You should rest." Rafa shuffled away from the gate.

Atellus draped my arm over his shoulder, supporting my sagging weight. Somehow we made it up the stairs and to my room. I only had water and some fruit on the small table, but didn't have the stomach for either. Atellus propped me into the corner where the bed met the walls. I sighed as all my weight sank into the mattress.

The wooden latch *thunked* into place and I stared at Atellus, confused why he was still in the room.

"I'm spending the night," he said.

"I'm not very good company." I hoped he didn't notice how my voice slurred.

"That's because you don't know how to have a proper conversation about anything that isn't miserable."

"You're in for a long night then." My eyes drifted shut, and I startled when he clapped his hands in my face, the sound splintering.

"What do you know about …" He scratched his head. "… the Trojan War?"

Quite a lot, it turned out.

∞

By dawn, Atellus was satisfied my mind wasn't knotted beyond normal. He yawned, opening the door. "*Odyssey* or *Aeneid* next time?"

"How about the *Metamorphosis*? It's nice and long," Marcus said, standing outside the doorway, arms crossed.

I frowned at Marcus, resenting his intrusion, and embraced Atellus. "Thank you." Instead of being tormented by guilt, I'd spent the night feeling human. It was an unexpected gift.

Atellus looked from Marcus back to me, and I could read the silent question in his eyes. I shook my head. With sigh, he left.

I blocked the doorway, not wanting Marcus to enter and shatter the brittle peace I'd found.

"You didn't wait at the amphitheatre," he snapped.

"I was injured."

"You seem fine."

"I was well taken care of."

"Were you?" The insinuation was clear.

I froze. "I killed a girl last night because you brought me here. You have no other claim on what I do."

"It's common enough to take a lover after a victory. Especially after a kill."

I let out a huff of disgust. "And you were going to volunteer were you?" Atellus wasn't even the sort to pursue a woman's affections. No doubt Marcus thought I'd be desperate.

He crossed his arms. "I came to make sure you didn't do anything rash and compromise your position in the ludus."

"Take your concern elsewhere." *This was all his fault.* I swung the door closed—but he thrust his arm out and held it open. After a half-hearted attempt at trying to force it closed, I gave up and dropped onto the one chair in my room. Exhaustion swept over me and I put my elbows on my knees, holding my head in my hands. Marcus closed the door behind him with a rattle that made my teeth ache.

"I didn't bring you here to—" He stopped when I flipped my finger at him. "Glad to see you're picking up the language."

"What *did* you bring me here for?" He'd pushed so hard for me to enter the ludus, to fight, to kill. "Why not let me drown?" Gods knew, life would be easier if I was dead.

"Because you're like me. A survivor. I couldn't let you die needlessly."

"And when I die on the sand? Won't that be needless?"

"Don't be so dramatic. What good are you if I have to worry about you all the time?" His tone was full of contempt.

"I don't know what's more disturbing—your complete selfishness or the fact that you're oblivious to it." And a sudden suspicion took root. "Are you testing me?" Bitterness crept into the accusation.

Marcus set his mouth in a thin line. "Should I try to make life easy for you, domina?" He'd not called me that since coming here, and I knew I'd caught him out.

"Yes! That's exactly what you should do. You should piss off and let me live my life." I stood and pointed at the door.

He clenched his fists, expression flickering between frustration and confusion. "I cannot."

But as soon as the words were said he stalked out, banging the door in a way that left me satisfied I'd pierced his coldness.

Closing the bouncing door, I dropped the latch and fell into bed.

∞

Nubia lowered herself onto the bench beside me, cup and bowl clattering on the wooden table as she settled in.

"I wasn't expecting company," I said. I'd eaten most of my meals alone since arriving at the ludus. The other tables had clusters of gladiators and trainers eating together.

"You're ranked now. It's no longer embarrassing to sit with you." She spooned herself a mouthful of the thick porridge.

"I hadn't heard." I turned back to my figs.

"That's because you've been lazy, sleeping all day."

Either she was trying to be friendly, or trying to rattle me.

"Don't you want to know?" she asked.

I shrugged.

"Secundus palus—like me," she said, her tone guarded.

I was a bit surprised to be ranked only one notch down from the deadliest fighters. Usually novices became fourth or third class fighters, then moved up as they gained victories.

Nubia stared at me, waiting for my response.

"Which other women are with us?"

She tilted her chin toward the courtyard where Veneda was sparring with Achilles. Her long blonde hair, in a high braid, whipped around behind her as she attacked.

Nubia looked back at me. "Just us three."

"Who do I fight next?" I wasn't sure I wanted the answer.

"Rigea. She's a class lower. Veneda and I almost always fight against the thirds because we can only fight each other so many times. Gets boring. Until I kill her." She smirked.

"Doesn't explain why you're sitting with me."

Nubia turned her attention back to Veneda, who was approaching. Achilles swaggered behind her.

Veneda slammed her hands on the table, rattling the bowls. "Enjoy your victory while it lasts."

I took a slow sip of wine. "How kind. Off you go."

She leaned forward, sneering. "You don't see how it works here. But you will. For everything you take, you'll lose something in return."

Lose something? All I could do was smile—I had nothing left. "I took nothing. Just gave Galla what she deserved."

Veneda glowered and turned on her heel, braid whipping through the air, and stormed away. The tense silence at the tables nearby turned into a babble of talk.

"She knows she fights you soon. She fears it," Nubia said, her mouth full of porridge.

"And you don't?" I ripped my eyes away from Veneda's retreating form. "You planning to kill me too?"

"Don't have to. We're both light class." She was right. It was unlikely a retiarius and dimachaerus would ever be paired together. "Lurco likes to pair me with novices to scare them."

"It didn't work." I pushed my half-finished porridge over to her.

Her hand, still streaked blue, caught my attention as she grabbed a fistful of figs from my plate and dropped them into the sludgy mass.

"Why do you dye your skin?" It must itch like mad whenever she did it—I would know.

"For the crowd," she said. "You live longer if you're noticed. Colours are good." Nubia eyed my hair. "I'm blue, you're red."

"And Veneda?"

"Depends. Is *bitch* a colour?"

∞

I used to think a month was a long time. A time for watching the vines blossom on the hill. For working my way through volumes of scrolls in the garden. Even for patiently enduring Agrippina's unending trials of hairstyles and beauty treatments.

That was before the ludus.

The days between my matches against Galla and Rigea didn't seem so leisurely. The one good thing to come from that month were my hands returning to normal, at long last. Still a bit stiff, but calluses had formed, toughening the skin.

It was a relief when I defeated Rigea without having to kill her. Or Cynae who came the month after. Though I made an attempt to fight it, the victories made me feel far better than they should have, diminishing my nightmares and shielding me with an armour that none of Veneda's schemes could pierce. She tried harder with each passing week—bumping me in passing; having rocks thrown through my shutters at night; a beheaded chicken nailed to my door, blood staining the wood as it drained. I'd not laughed so hard since Vesuvius.

Now it was two days before our match.

Body aching, I dragged my way down the long open corridor from the training area to the stairs. Marcus had intensified my routine this last month and, despite our strained—sometimes hostile—relationship, I knew he was preparing me as best he could.

The sky was darkening as I forced my legs to make the climb to my room, the door protesting on its mangled hinges. Unbuckling my leather breastplate, I let it thud to the floor.

A shadow blocked the light. I turned as Achilles walked in, his thickset body filling the doorway. "Get out before—"

His arm arced up, a metal greave glinting in the fading sun, and struck my face. My head snapped sideways and pain lanced through my cheek. I crashed into the wall.

In my small room, there was no retreat. No time to think. I raised my arms to block, but he knocked them aside, following through with a fist to my jaw. I tasted blood and coughed—a tooth rattled across the floorboards.

Achilles picked me up and threw me against the bed, cracking my ribs on the side of the wooden frame. My breath left in a burst. He knelt behind me, pushing my face into the straw mattress, the coarse blanket grating the wound on my cheek. I tried to cry out; tried to get air into my lungs, and raked at his hands with my nails. Achilles ground my face deeper, holding me as my limbs shuddered and weakened.

He ripped at the back of my dress—and I realized his true intent. In a desperate burst, I kicked out at his knee, but the action only let him force my legs further apart. I spasmed when he thrust inside me. But I couldn't draw a breath. Couldn't swim free. Black and white flashes eclipsed my vision.

I thought I heard shouting.

THIRTY-ONE

THE FEEL OF SOFT SILK WAS UNEXPECTED. I'd not worn anything but rough wool for months. Someone, Parsina perhaps, had taken the trouble of washing me. My skin was sponged clean, even my fingernails had been scrubbed. But despite the blue silk dress, despite the bath, I felt tainted.

The bed frame creaked as I gingerly pushed myself upright, narrowing my eyes against the dim light filtering through the shuttered window. Swelling on my face forced my eye closed. I ran a hand along my jaw and winced as my fingers found the raw scab that spread up my cheek. Tongue probing, I felt the hole where my molar had been. Gods above—it had been a perfectly good tooth.

Marcus entered his room carrying a plate of food and glass of wine, his expression unreadable. Closing the door, he walked over to the table and put down the plate with quiet precision, as if he didn't want to startle me. He sat at the foot of the bed, not touching me, and held out the wine. It was bitter, but I kept drinking.

"I should have foreseen this," he said. I didn't think his expression of frustration was an act, but with Marcus I could never be sure. *Could he have known?*

It was clear now that Veneda had recruited Achilles to her cause, wanting to remove me as competition. To shame me as I'd shamed her. All the cues had been there—I'd known Achilles was dangerous, I knew Veneda hated me. But I'd thought they would act like me. Provoke a fight. Perhaps try to kill me. I should have anticipated this.

"I'm a fighter, Marcus. I'm supposed to protect myself." I hadn't seen, and now I would have to live with the consequences.

"Atellus heard first," he said. "He was checking on Priscus's leg and heard the scuffle. We threw Achilles down the stairs, but there were too many others by then. If I'd gotten there first—" He set his jaw.

"Fortunate for Achilles." I downed the rest of the foul wine.

Marcus took the glass and looked at it pointedly. "Parsina said there's no chance of a child."

"I see." I counted the slats in the shutter to avoid considering the monstrosity that would come from two such tainted parents.

Marcus brought me the plate of honeyed figs, another rare luxury. I ate with deliberation, torn between wanting him to leave me alone and hoping he would stay. It seemed a long time that I was eating but, once finished, couldn't remember the taste.

He tossed the plate to the floor with a clatter. "I've been told," Marcus said, breaking the uneasy silence, "that the best cure for what you've gone through is to jump into bed with the first man you see."

His face was impossibly innocent, and the fact he was trying to bait me even now drew an unwilling snort. "You've been told the worst piece of advice in all history," I said. "Well, perhaps second to Helen being told to flee with Paris. That started a rather long war."

"Or to Brutus, being told that killing Caesar would restore the Republic." His lightness helped to ease the pressure in my chest, but I still felt short of breath. "Several people have asked after you—"

"Let me guess. Nubia. Hilarus. Atellus. I don't want to see them." My cheek and eye throbbed with pain as I tried to keep a torrent of emotion from breaking across my face. "Tell them to leave Achilles alone. I don't need them to do something foolish." If we weren't careful, this would lead to all our deaths. *You take mine, I'll take yours* was what Veneda had all but said. "Achilles will pay, sooner or later."

Marcus laid a gentle hand on my swollen face. "You may be bruised, Lucilla. But they haven't broken you. Don't let them break you." He lowered his face, eyes inches from mine. "Would you like me to kill him, or can I trust you'll do it yourself?"

∞

I hit the palus with my sword. *Neck. Hip. Chest.*

Again, Lucilla. Practice. But even Petrus's chorus couldn't help me focus. It was all I could do to go through the motions.

What was I doing?

My old life was gone. No—not just gone. Destroyed. I could go to Quintus and throw myself on his mercy. He was pater of our family now, his responsibility was to protect me. But I'd abandoned my duties as a daughter of our house. My whole family would be shamed if my life as Vesuvia was discovered. Too great a risk for a man as cautious—and ambitious—as Quintus.

So what was I doing?

Training. Despite the sore ribs and bruised face. I ignored the covert glances of those around me; pretended my every action wasn't being scrutinized. Did they see me as dangerous ... or damaged?

I hit the palus again. *Leg. Arm. Neck.*

If I didn't train, Veneda would know she'd won.

Veneda—the thought of her ignited a fire in my chest. I'd been marked too injured to compete, so our fight had been postponed. But it would come soon enough.

Chest. Thigh. Arm.

I was weak. I needed protection—again. I felt more exposed than when burning rocks threatened to suffocate me. Almost as helpless as that ten-year-old girl standing alone before a killer.

I'd trained for years to defend myself. Protect myself.

Useless.

Parsina stared at me from across the courtyard, eyes like pools, trying to suck me in. I didn't need Nemesis right now, I knew who my foes were and what they deserved. The goddess knew I had made my offerings, but even the shrine to Nemesis was tainted by Achilles's presence. The ludus stank of Achilles. Of his sweat and filth.

Neck. Groin. Head.

If Nemesis wouldn't help me, perhaps another goddess would.

∞

Hilarus and I pressed through the crowded streets. I wore the blue silk dress Marcus had given me, and a shawl draped into a deep hood over my face and hair. With Hilarus behind, I could be any matron of modest wealth, not rich enough for a litter, but able to have a bodyguard. I'd offered to walk beside Hilarus, but he wouldn't hear it, only having agreed to escort me to the Temple of Vesta if I left Vesuvia in the ludus. I'd reluctantly agreed—in any case, this wasn't her errand.

Apartments rose six and seven stories above our heads, their second and third floors precariously overhanging their foundations. Graffiti on a plastered wall drew my gaze. Scrawled near a doorway, I recognized verses from a poem about Vesuvia:

> *The gods in their wisdom*
> *Made peacocks beautiful,*
> *And owls wise,*
> *And the phoenix who triumphs*
> *With sand in her eyes.*

Beneath it was a charcoal phoenix, wings unfurled, talons holding two crossed swords. Most of the verses I'd heard or read were similar—some compared her to predatory birds, some to the mountain. They weren't beautiful, like the flowing verse of Horatius, but had inexplicably caught on. I didn't know if I should be upset or pleased.

At last we reached the old Forum, temples vibrant with painted and gilded columns. Statues, each generation's larger than the last, scowled down upon knots of people catching up on the day's news.

Hilarus stopped beside me at the base of the stairs leading to the Temple of Vesta. "You won't find what you need in there."

"How do you know what I need?"

"I learned to fight from my father. Numerius won the rudius three times," Hilarus said with rightful pride. Even auctorati were released from their contracts if they had a fight worthy of the rudius. Three such wins marked a true champion.

"You've never told me about your family."

Hilarus shrugged. "Petrus didn't like to share the stage."

"So why now?"

He crossed his arms, considering me. "My father has grown feeble. No longer a warrior. Doesn't even remember his own name. His body has become a prison."

I rubbed my forehead, realizing where this was going.

"You're more than your sheath, as I'm more than my sword," he said with candour. "You will never be free from your body. You can only be free in your heart."

"I'm not fighting for my freedom, Hilarus."

"No." He placed a hand on my arm. "You're fighting for your spirit. That's the only thing that lasts."

I shook my head. "Parsina's a bad influence on you. So you don't think I should fall on my sword?"

"I think that sword is meant for someone else, don't you?"

I readjusted my veil, shading my eyes, and left him in the plaza below as I carried my pot of honey up the steps of the temple.

Uncle told me to endure what couldn't be changed, but how much could one person bear? I had a sword; knew how to use it. Petrus's prediction had come to pass—I did use it. But my arms felt leaden, lifeless. Despite Hilarus's disapproval, I'd come to ask for a different gift than vengeance. Endurance. Only the Lady of the eternal flame could rekindle the fire I lacked.

Her temple was small and circular, columns separating the inner sanctuary from the outer porch. A mosaic of light spread across the floor as the early evening sun shone though the lattice-work walls between the columns. Air was musky with incense and smoke from the perpetual flame—it burned in a high, bowl-shaped hearth centered inside. I walked around it solemnly, searching the embers and the tongues of light, hoping they would give away something of their divine nature.

"Lucilla!" The softness of the voice didn't hide the disbelief of the speaker.

I turned, half-expecting to see Agrippina, the tone was so similar. But my rising excitement faded. *Wrong sister.*

Lanata's silhouette was lit by the sun in the temple door. Beautiful and straight-backed, she resembled Agrippina, though her features had none of the softness. Vesta had found a worthy representative.

She walked towards me, hands open, her white shawl and full skirt swaying around her. "But you were in Herculaneum during the disaster! How did you survive?" Instead of embracing me, she circled instead, her gaze heavy with disbelief. Or maybe disappointment.

"I was rescued. I'd been on the water," I said without emotion, trying to shake the specter of Agrippina from my eyes.

"Quintus never said a word." She continued to look at me apprehensively. Perhaps she also saw a ghost today.

"Quintus doesn't know. He can't know."

"But—"

I lowered my shawl. Her lips pursed as she noticed the unnatural shade of my hair. "I've joined the emperor's ludus." I didn't want or need to explain the rest.

Her shock was expected—but also gratifying. She'd always been everything I couldn't be. The pinnacle of the slope Aunt Calpurnia and Agrippina had been so intent on climbing. Powerful, honourable, respected. Many an empress had held less sway than the Vestalis Maxima.

"I had not heard …" Her voice died as she made the connection at last. "Vesuvia … that's who you've become."

Nodding once, I waited for her reaction.

Her frown seemed to deepen until, unexpectedly, she smiled—the same dimpling grin Agrippina gave when a situation was too ridiculous for words. My heart ached for that smile.

"Why have you come?" she asked.

I hesitated. Surveying the temple and finding it still empty I made my confession. "I've been dishonoured, Vestalis, taken in violence. I ask Vesta to remove my shame and restore my honour."

Lanata's posture changed, the dignity of her office wiping away all emotion. "By your own choice you have moved yourself out of the goddess's protection. You have incurred infamia. Your body is no longer inviolate—I cannot cleanse you of that."

"I know, but I had to come. I felt She was calling me here." I held out the pot of honey, my forgotten offering.

Lanata took it from me, placing the pot on the hearth before clasping my hands. "Maybe She was, though not as you might expect. Vesta can't help you in this, but perhaps I can." Her gaze stayed rooted to mine. "You can avenge your honour. This man, is he a gladiator?"

I nodded. "Achilles."

"Achilles. If you defeat him, you may redeem yourself. Though it might be too dangerous for you."

"Don't coddle me. You don't know what I'm capable of."

"I didn't mean to insult you," Lanata said, "and you're right. Neither of us had much of a childhood. We've walked different paths, you and I, neither of them easy." Her brows creased, and I noticed how they'd been carefully narrowed. She saw the direction of my gaze and ran her fingertips over one eyebrow. "Our father gave us quite the gift."

"You should have heard Agrippina moan about her eyebrows." I sighed. I couldn't avoid remembering her, no matter how hard I tried.

Lanata's expression became grave and she folded her hands across her body. "Facing a man in the arena would be suicide. If you're set on death, it would be better to kill yourself for your dishonour, than to be shamed before the whole of Rome."

"I won't give up. But you and I both know that women don't fight men in the arena."

"I've heard many men say pretty words about honour, when often what they speak of is pride. Of the way others see them. Honour is so much more ... It is how we see ourselves." Her eyes strayed to the flickering fire. "Women are the ones who understand the perilous nature of honour. We are the ones who guard our bodies, and our minds, and our actions. Who are judged for the slightest misstep. It's we who face the harder road of reining in our natures, while men pursue their whims and call it bravery, or spirit."

I reached for her hands. "I know you've sacrificed to be the woman you are today. You've not had a family, not had your freedom. But you have your honour. Please, Lanata, I need mine back again."

She let out a slow breath and her face tightened with resolve. "I tell you, Lucilla, I didn't enjoy being a Vestal at first. It took many years of training and struggle and patience to become the Vestalis Maxima. But now there are certain advantages I have over every other woman in Rome. And many men too, come to think of it." A grim satisfaction entered her voice. "I can arrange this for you. Leave it to me, little sister. You will have your revenge."

THIRTY-TWO

LANATA WAS GOOD TO HER WORD. It didn't hurt that her circle of acquaintance included the Emperor, the college of pontiffs, and the most prominent members of Roman society.

Vesuvia versus Achilles. I shouldn't have fought a man, especially one a class above me, but Lurco, in a stroke of Roman practicality, promoted me to primus palus. His inspiration seemed to largely come from a heavy gold medallion that appeared around his neck.

Achilles had taken the pairing with nothing but a grunt, but it caused waves in the ludus. He and I became islands, a sea of bodies always separating us. At first words, then fists, were exchanged between Veneda and Nubia, or others in our factions. Only an increase in guards kept an all-out war from erupting.

It wouldn't be an easy victory. No matter how many rabbits I sacrificed to Nemesis, I wouldn't put my fate entirely in Her hands. Before now, death either threatened without warning, or seemed a distant possibility. This was the first time I had the chance to consider the consequences of my death, and had time to plan my course.

There was something I needed to do.

I paused on the stoop of my domus. Hilarus waited for me to enter. Shaking out my hands, I tried to compose myself. This wouldn't be fun.

I walked in, Hilarus' footsteps following behind. My shawl was pulled up over my head and wrapped to show only my eyes, which I'd washed of the kohl. It was afternoon—the time a patron expected privacy, and maybe a trip to the baths. But I knew Quintus enjoyed working in the afternoons and had bet he'd be in. A slave bustled off to announce that *a friend of his cousin* had arrived.

The atrium—I'd not been here since Father's death. It seemed smaller than I remembered, and grubbier. Paint faded on the walls and chipped tiles in the mosaic floor. But we hadn't lived here for a decade. Quintus would likely refurbish it soon. I shouldn't have been surprised to learn that Quintus was here, instead of his father's domus. After all, that was where his mother lived—and this was a prime location.

I paced toward the shallow pool, water gleaming in the soft light. The alcove to my right held the death masks of our ancestors, the same disapproving faces staring out from the past. Yet the two most important were missing. Father's face had been so disfigured that no mask had been made. Uncle hadn't been found.

If I had to wait much longer, something would end up broken. I strode down the hall toward my father's—Quintus's—study.

Quintus, sitting at the desk, rose with a jolt as I stormed in.

"If you don't wish to speak with me," I said with false sweetness, "then you'll have to leave my house at once."

His eyes widened comically and he shouted at the slaves for privacy. I raised my finger to my lips before he could speak my name.

"Where have you been?" he asked in a hush. "There were rescuers scouring the area for months—is Agrippina with you? The boys don't really understand what's happened."

"The boys are in the city?" An unexpected lightness overtook me. I'd not known … and been too afraid to ask if they'd made it to safety.

"Nonius had taken them to Misenum for the day. He's convinced that Mars gave him a portent in a dream." Quintus waved this away. "He's been so spiritless lately, I'm trying to be patient with him. Agrippina, his family … his home was destroyed."

"It was all destroyed, Quintus. All of it."

"I know," he replied, subdued. This new, humbled Quintus seemed too good to last.

"I'm not coming back." I fiddled with my veil, lowering it around my shoulders. Being here was like feeling for the absent tooth in my mouth—it only reminded me of what was lost.

"But you have to. Where would you go?" Then his eyes narrowed as if he'd just noticed my appearance. "Where have you been?"

"Do you want to know, or do you want to keep this domus?"

His eyes sparked, the Quintus I remembered resurfacing. Always moving in the direction of the gold.

"I want to make a new will," I said.

He looked about to protest.

I held up a hand. "You can still have almost everything, except for that small farm north of the city and five hundred thousand."

He was doing the math and knew it was only a small percentage. "I don't see how I can stop you. You're still alive, after all."

"I need to date it before Vesuvius, so that if anything happens to me, the bequests have already come to pass."

"What's going to happen to you?" He pulled out parchment, ink, and a reed pen.

"Death, likely."

"You've never been funny." He sounded tired.

"I am Vesuvia."

"Juno riding Jupiter!" He recovered quickly. "You're fighting Achilles—for the love of Minerva, why?"

I didn't answer, but told him what he needed to hear. "I don't expect to return to your protection. I would do nothing to dishonour our family. You can maintain that Lucilla died in the eruption. But I need to make these changes before the fight."

"At least now I know when to distribute your property."

"No. Don't wait. Do it as soon as possible." I knew Emperor Titus had required a one-year period before anyone lost in the eruption could be declared dead, but the time was only half gone.

He sighed. "After all that happened between us as children, I wasn't expecting you to even remember me in your will. Thank you for that, by the way," he said, with genuine feeling.

"I made it when I was twelve. And I didn't think it would be such a windfall for you."

He had the grace to look regretful. Everyone else who had been due to inherit had died. "I would not have it this way for the world."

Quintus being human—I was at a loss for words. "One—no—two more things," I said, once I'd collected myself. "Rafa is to be freed by my will."

"Ah. I thought that may be the case." He eyed me coolly, but I didn't care what sort of conclusion he was drawing. "And the other?"

"I need a sword."

∞

It was late when we returned, the guards waving Hilarus and I through the gate. Torches cast irregular light along the corridors.

Hilarus gave me a nod before heading to Parsina's quarters in another barracks. I walked softly, not wanting to draw unnecessary attention to myself as I carried my burden to the armoury. My caution was why I heard the voices, and crept to the intersecting corridor. I pressed against the wall.

"You said you would take care of her," Rafa accused in a hush. I froze, surprised.

"Have you met her?" Marcus asked with amusement. "She needs as much taking care of as a tiger in a henhouse."

"You're a fool—"

"Careful."

"You have no idea who she is," Rafa pressed on. "Do you think her training was the whim of a bored, rich girl?"

"Enlighten me."

No, no, no. I felt fixed to the ground in horror. The last thing I needed was for Marcus to start interfering in my life—Lucilla's life. I didn't want him there.

"She's searching for her father's murderer. For years she's had one purpose in mind."

Curse Rafa. How was I going to handle this mess?

"She wants to kill this man," Marcus said, and at least there was no mockery in his voice.

"If we can prove who they are. One of them is certainly a trained killer. That's why she fights. To be ready when she finds him. But you've pulled her into this circus of yours, and now she's trapped. Trapped by your threats, trapped by her honour."

"She chooses to stay."

"You've threatened my life, and that's likely the only thing you could have done to make her give in."

"Everyone has a weakness. Why hers should be for you I don't understand." I expected sarcasm, but Marcus's voice bit with jealousy.

"She rejected you." The realization seemed to please Rafa. He went on, bold, "We'll find your weakness, and she'll be free of this."

"She won't be free of her own nature. Throw away your notion of the kind of life she should lead. Watch her fight—would you cage her? Weigh her down with the pettiness of bath-house gossip and endless parties? Is that the world she belongs in?" I recognized that tone, and knew the smug look that would accompany it, but strangely, I found myself agreeing with him.

"She's more than the sword—but that's all she lets people see," Rafa countered.

"Swords can be such effective shields, don't you think?" I couldn't tell if Marcus was truly indifferent, or simply trying to antagonize Rafa.

"She's always been heedless of danger," Rafa said, louder. "And worse, she refuses to ask for help, or take it when it's offered."

I grimaced. *Unfair.* Rafa was helping me find proof against the senator, had helped me for years and kept my secrets. I relied on him. Clearly, he didn't feel the same about me.

"She knew the risks, and you underestimate her strength. She'll move past this."

"If she survives!" Rafa's angry hiss ended on a note of terror. If I hadn't been furious with him, I may have felt guilty. "How can you let her fight that monster? I saw what he did to her without being armed. That's why I ..."

Marcus grunted. "You're the one writing those little poems."

I bit my lip. The poems about Vesuvia, like the on the apartment wall. *Why didn't Rafa tell me?*

"It was the only thing I could do to help her. Try to ensure the mob wouldn't turn against her for being ..." Rafa trailed off, apparently unsure what I was.

"The woman they fear their wives could be." Marcus was laughing now. "It's clever ... and it's been effective."

"For now."

I was barely breathing.

"You tell me she's more than the sword," Marcus said. "But it's you who doesn't appreciate how much. Tell me she hasn't fought every obstacle in her way. Even her friendship with you was a battle most wouldn't take on."

"Then don't let her waste her life," Rafa pled. "You've manipulated this situation—for what benefit I don't understand—but you're putting her in mortal danger. Of all the people to trust with her safety, I don't know why she relies on you. You clearly want her dead more than—" A brief shuffle and Rafa's voice became strangled. "Go ahead ... kill me now and Lucilla will be free of this farce."

My heart pounded, but I couldn't move, furious with both of them. Feet scuffled, and I assumed Marcus had released Rafa, as the sound of rasping breaths echoed from the hall.

"Don't question my motives. She doesn't need me to protect her from her choices. I'm ensuring she makes the right ones."

"Right for who—you?"

I couldn't reveal myself. I couldn't listen any longer. So I backed down the corridor.

∞

Parsina came to collect me for the ritual.

"I'm not killing another rabbit."

"We do not have to, not for this one. This is not a contest, it is a reckoning. Vengeance is what the Lady loves best." Her face was wan, despite her certainty. "Others—many others—have been wronged by Achilles. He has earned retribution time and again."

She led me to the shrine. Incense pooled in the small room and the scent washed over me, earth and spice. More people than usual had come this evening—more than just the fighters who were on the roster for the next day. Some wives and children were also gathered. Most I knew only by sight. I'd not wanted attachments in my new familia.

Nubia was leaning against a wall, half-hidden in a dark corner next to Atellus and Hilarus. She nodded as I passed; Atellus's face was solemn.

The eyes of the devout bored into me; I didn't want to carry their burdens. Yet I couldn't force them to take their pitiful hopes elsewhere. Even though I wasn't fighting for them, I understood why they wanted Achilles dead.

Ignoring the crowd, I knelt before the offerings on the altar. They seemed scant, only bread and honey.

"Nemesis, I call upon you," Parsina began, laying a hand on my head. "Lady of righteous resentment, balance the scales Justice will not. We give so that you may give, Adrasteia, and guide your faithful daughter to recover her honour, wrongly taken. Let her wield your sword and strike for you to the heart of the undeserving." Parsina paused, waiting for me to bind myself with my own oath.

I mumbled it low, under my breath. If the goddess couldn't hear me, then She wasn't worth the effort. "Lady Nemesis, I call upon you to witness my suffering. I have suffered much — but I have endured." I swallowed. "I beg you to turn my endurance into strength. I can't swear to build you a temple on a hill or buy a statue of gold, as I might once have been able to do. But I can swear to devote my sword to your cause. To use my strength to punish the undeserving, and balance the scales of justice." I said the words with sincerity but, once uttered, worried they may have been too vague. Perhaps I should have specifically mentioned Achilles.

Parsina repeated the ritual, allowing each gladiator to send their own pleas and promises to the goddess. The room filled with hums of hope. Of victory and honour.

Time and again, I'd pursued that which was impossible. Rusticus. The man with one eye. The injustice of their freedom still haunted me. Yet today I wasn't surrounded by disappointment and disapproval. Today others knew my course and stood behind me. I didn't know this feeling. But somehow, as Vesuvia, I was strong where Lucilla had been weak.

Finishing with Zepharos, Parsina returned to me, placing her hand on my hair again and speaking words I couldn't hear.

I stayed kneeling while the others murmured a few parting words to the goddess, some touching my dress or hair as they left the small room.

"I know the Lady will favour you." Parsina's liquid eyes were dark and distant.

Yes. Tomorrow would be a different day.

THIRTY-THREE

MERDA, HE WAS STRONG.

We circled again. Achilles wasn't the fastest fighter, but his blows sent shockwaves down my arms as I parried. No doubt my slashes were like a soft breeze. I needed to end it soon, or he would best me.

His helmet jutted out low over his brow, obscuring his eyes. I didn't want to look in them anyway. He used a small shield, but his long reach turned it into as much of a weapon as his sword. If I thrust far enough to cut his body, I'd become an easy target.

Rallying my strength, I used short movements, thrusting with all my speed, forcing him to give ground to avoid a cut to his thigh or exposed shield arm. Neither of us wanted to end the fight at first blood.

He knocked me back with a push of his shield, taking an odd half-step in the wrong direction before recovering to advance again.

Achilles swung out his shield, forcing me to dodge sideways — I tripped over a dangling rip in my skirt and fell, rolling just in time to avoid the rim of his shield as he crunched it into the sand. Part of my skirt tore free as I gained my feet, the crowd roaring at the close shave. Achilles smiled and I kicked the fallen skirt towards his face. He retreated from the cloud of fabric and dirt.

With a quick jerk, I tucked my remaining skirt into the belt of my loincloth. *Gods curse Aunt and her respectability. I'm going to cut that smile off his face.*

I moved toward his shield-side, forcing him to stretch farther for each blow, his vision of my second sword limited by heavy helmet and shield. With each step, I lowered my stance, bending my knees until I was fighting from a wide crouch, like a spider before it jumps. Hamitra and I had once worked for months on this maneuver.

Achilles followed, a slow pivot, needing to turn or swing across his body to reach me. He wanted to hurt me, but was failing. And growing impatient.

My timing had to be exact, his reach had to be fully extended. If only he would—

And then he did—Achilles swung his sword in a low arc at my legs. I sprang up, knees to chest, over his sword and away from the momentum of his arm. Bringing both swords together, I chopped down, throwing the full force of my body behind the blades as I landed. Steel grunted through flesh and I severed his sword hand. It lay on the sand, still clutching his blade.

Achilles sank to his knees, soundless in his shock.

I lifted my sword—my father's sword that I'd reclaimed from Quintus—and rested the point at the base of Achilles's throat.

The summa rudis rushed forward, baton out, to wait for the verdict. We looked toward the emperor's box. Augustus Titus stood, arms extended out to the crowd, jovial expression on his round face.

The crowd was shouting. Cries of, "He's down! He's had it!" were picked up and carried in waves through the mob. They turned their thumbs and the emperor obliged them.

Achilles removed his helmet and let it clatter to the sand, contemptuous gaze burning the crowd. His maimed arm hung at his side, blood draining out into a grit-filled pool beside him.

"With honour," Achilles said. It was the first time I'd heard him speak.

The summa rudis lifted his baton and nodded. I looked back to Achilles, his eyes still defiant. I sheathed my sword down his throat and into his body.

The crowd roared.

I drew out my sword and watched him fall.

Breathing deep, satisfaction surging through me, I waited for the summa rudis to place the crown on my head. But his attention stayed fixed on the emperor's box. Someone rose on the platform and made his way past senators in their purple-banded, white togas. Descending to the sand, the Emperor's Praetorian guards made a protective square around him. One approached and removed my swords. I took a knee.

"Vesuvia." Caesar Domitian, the emperor's brother, greeted me with a smile. "I have wanted to meet you for many days now." He tapped my shoulder and I rose. "My good friend Marcus told me this bout was significant for you. Congratulations on a notable victory. And on winning me a hefty purse." His face was round, like his brother's, the features pinched toward the middle. He reminded me of Quintus, though perhaps that was the carefully pomaded and styled hair.

"Thank you, Caesar. Marcus likes to talk a great deal," I blurted out. *What was all this about? Good friend—since when?*

Domitian chuckled, though it sounded forced. "He says a great many nothings I find." Frustration curled his small mouth so that it almost disappeared beneath his bulbous nose.

"I couldn't agree more, Caesar."

He gave me a thin smile. "My brother has put on some splendid games hasn't he?" He was annoyed, though whether with the emperor or still with Marcus I couldn't tell.

"It takes more than one man to organize such an event," I said, taking a stab at it being sibling rivalry.

"It certainly does. A great deal of planning goes into each day. And often many details are beneath an emperor's notice." He was grateful for the chance to point it out. Definitely sibling rivalry.

"It is to the glory of our empire to have such an honourable family at her head." It was far beyond Vesuvia's place to even breach this territory, but he'd started this odd exchange.

"Yes. Rome above all," he said, sincere. Domitian fixed me with a straightforward gaze. "Are you still loyal to Rome, Vesuvia?"

"I will be eternally loyal to Rome. And she will be an empire without end." If Marcus wanted to draw Domitian's attention my way, then there may be a good reason.

He gave a quizzical smile and slicked a hand carefully over his hair. "The *Aeneid*? Interesting quote for a gladiatrix. Now one for you:

> *Fair Ilium plundered by Grecian might,*
> *No honour gained—betrayal not fight.*
> *A brazen strike, a base desire.*
> *Behold his fate: consumed by fire."*

Domitian clasped his hands together once, as though pleased with his performance. "It was being passed around by my guards—I had to draw lots for who would accompany me today." He flicked his eyes over the Praetorians standing around him. Most of them were regarding me with the same expressionless face Hilarus relied on when he tried not to smile.

I'd have to thank Rafa for his quick pen. He'd turned the humiliation of a man losing to a woman into a contest of honour — one which would satisfy even a Roman.

"So, daughter of Ilium," Domitian said, waving his hand, "is it safe for me to crown you?" A slave stepped forward bearing the victor's laurel crown. Caesar raised it high and the crowds, who'd grown silent trying to hear our exchange, erupted into cheers again.

I went down on one knee. Domitian placed the wreath on my head. When I stood, chants ringing around me, he handed me the palm branch. He nodded, then ascended to the emperor's box followed by his escort.

Swords returned, I saluted the emperor, then the crowd.

∞

The fight spun again and again through my mind as I marched back to the ludus with the rest of the gladiators. *It wasn't right — too easy. Why aren't I dead?*

I nearly knocked over Parsina when she stepped into my path.

"How did you do it?" She ran her hands down my arms, turning me around as she searched for injuries.

A bitter suspicion sprung to life. That incoherent half-step Achilles made had either been a ploy, or something more sinister. Only one person had the knowledge — and opportunity — to poison Achilles. I scanned the courtyard and saw Atellus observing our return. He met my eye for half a heartbeat, then ducked inside his surgery. *Gods below.*

Parsina held me back from following. "We prayed for you, and the goddess answered."

Somebody answered. I forced a weak smile. "She did."

Conscious that most everyone in the courtyard was staring at me, I kept my pace steady as I headed for the surgery. Half-way across, next to a rack of shields, Veneda stood with Kore, her cellmate, her face a mask of unflattering disbelief. I changed my direction.

"Who's next, Veneda?" I called out, stretching my arms wide. "Or are you done hiding?"

She swallowed, eyes darting around the scattered crowed. "I don't set matches. And," she raised her voice, "Achilles never listened to anyone. So don't pretend I had anything—"

"And Galla decided to break the rules just for fun, did she?" My neck flushed with anger. Did she think I'd let the blame die with Achilles? "What did you tell her? Take any chance to kill me?"

"We all know you love to humiliate your opponents." Veneda's voice snapped like a whip.

"Not all of them—just the weak ones."

Veneda charged me, and I was aching to kill her instead of waiting for more treachery. She took a swing, a meaty fist arcing over my head as I ducked and shouldered her in the gut. I tackled her hard and she hit the sand with a grunt. Before either of us could land any blows, stomping footsteps surrounded us and someone lifted me away.

"You're next, Veneda!" I yelled, Hilarus pushing me out of the crowd. I glared at Veneda as Kore helped her to her feet. "Coward!"

Hilarus nudged me every time I slowed my pace, until we were out of the courtyard. "Save it for the circle," he grumbled.

"I'm tired of saving it. She doesn't deserve the honour of a match." I brushed some grit off my ruined dress and entered the surgery, leaving a disapproving Hilarus in the corridor.

Atellus was cleaning implements—they were laid out on the long wooden table. He barely glanced at me when I entered.

I slammed the door. "If anyone finds out, they'll kill you."

"I don't know what you mean." He wouldn't meet my gaze.

Taking a deep breath, I tried to calm my agitation. Atellus wasn't Veneda. I took another breath and looked heavenward for inspiration, then stared at him. The silence stretched. He scrubbed at one of his knives. It was thin, with a delicate blade. I thought he might bend the metal, he rubbed so hard.

He set the knife down with a sudden *smack*. "I hoped you wouldn't be able to tell."

"How did you do it?"

"Olives. He liked to eat olives right before a match." If he had any regret, it didn't show.

"I guess his heel wasn't his weak spot after all."

He grunted, perhaps with amusement, and picked up some

fiendish-looking pincers. "I don't think it was the poison that killed him—you were far quicker than I thought."

"First you try to save my life, then you flatter my skill. You make it hard to stay angry with you." I moved to the other side of the table from him. "But why? Why did you do it?"

He stared at the pincers. "You shouldn't die for such a man."

"I'm not afraid of dying." I leaned on the table. *Why wouldn't he look at me?* "You diminished the honour of combat. My honour."

"That's the problem! You don't even care that it might have meant your death!" He dropped the pincers and wiped his hands roughly on a towel.

"Of course I care," I shot back, blood rising again. "I have a very good reason to live. But I'm not afraid. I've already been dead." It was strange, how hollow and feeble the words were. Fear used to bite my heart like a wolf, gnawing at it until I struggled for breath. But somehow, after the match with Galla, the wolf was tamed, the intensity diminished. How could I explain such a thing without sounding like I'd given up?

His head snapped up and he stared at me. "What reason?"

"An unfinished duty." *Don't ask more.*

"A burden shared is a burden halved." He held his hands out, offering.

"I'm already sharing it," I said, thinking of Rafa with a twinge of disappointment. "But lately it's seemed to grow, instead of shrink."

Atellus ruffled his hair his posture screaming *guilt*.

"What aren't you telling me?" I walked around the table and took his arm, trying to catch his gaze. "Atellus—what?"

The door creaked. "Poisoning Achilles wasn't his idea," Rafa said softly. He shut the door and leaned back against it.

I crossed my arms, looking between them and trying not to curse them for traitors. "How nice. Sharing my secrets, are you?"

"No secrets," Atellus said. "We both want to keep you alive."

"I didn't ask either of you to interfere." They'd thought I couldn't do it. That I was too weak. I'd have rather taken Veneda's fist in my face than hear another word.

"Lucilla, you're in too much danger here," Rafa said with more firmness than usual.

"I haven't lost a match yet."

"You haven't." He glanced at Atellus, then back to me, eyes taking in my ripped dress, bloodstained and crusted with sand. "Except with yourself."

Striding to the door, I glared at Rafa. "You learned too many riddles from Petrus. I don't have time for this."

Rafa blocked my exit. "But you have time for what? Finding someone else to kill?"

I sucked in a breath. "Just what does that mean?"

Atellus stepped around the table. "This isn't you, Lucilla," Atellus said. "The girl I met—the one who was rescued from the mountain— she didn't want to be a killer."

My lips curled in bitterness. "You barely knew her, Atellus."

"I did know her." His brown eyes were sad. "Not for long. But even from our first meeting, you were easy to like. You tried, but you could never hide your true feelings—and it's a rare person that lets you see who they really are."

I swallowed, throat thick. "Apparently, what I am is a killer."

"Vesuvia is," Rafa said, jaw fixed and tone unbending. "But not Lucilla. You have to leave this place before she consumes you."

"It's easy for you to judge me. Going home to Justa each day. But you forget why I'm here."

Rafa turned to Atellus. "Can we have a moment?"

Atellus nodded, downcast, and slid out the door.

Rafa resumed his role as doorstop, so I paced towards the shelves. I couldn't look at his mulish expression any longer without throwing something, so I turned my attention to the jars and pots scenting up the room. "What more can you have to say? I'm a killer. I'm too weak to fight my own battles. And apparently it means nothing to you that I've endured all this to save your life."

"Quintus came by yesterday before your match."

"Did he?" I kept my voice flat. "How did he find you?"

"Justa's new business is doing well—likely he heard about her. He made me feel very honoured to receive him, he even drank my cheap wine." His light tone was forced.

I sighed. "Quintus always was a pompous ass."

"His ego is so big that when he's in Rome, the city has eight hills."

"Writing comedy now? Get to the point, Rafa."

"Quintus felt obligated to inform me that you'd left me freedom and a fortune in your will. By September, I'll be a wealthy man."

The edge in his voice made me turn. He was stiff with anger. "Sorry you have to wait so long. I can't change it now."

"What are you playing at, Lucilla? Do you think I want a farm and some gold, instead of your friendship?"

I let out a long breath. *It's Rafa that doesn't belong here, in this world of hate and death. He doesn't belong with me.* "My friendship hasn't done you much good. You've been chasing ghosts for me, but for what? We'll never have proof against the Senator. The one-eyed man has disappeared into the ether. He may have returned once Hamitra left. Now I'll never know. And my family ..."

"Staying here—letting Marcus control you—won't bring them back. Remember what Bricus said about changing the past? All you're doing is making your past darker and bloodier. For what? You can't get revenge against the mountain—"

"I know! I can't control anything except to keep you alive." I slammed shut the memory of Bricus; of smiles and futures that could never be. At least, not for me. "Rafa, you're the one with the future ..." I stopped at the look on his face.

His expression put Atellus's guilt to shame. "Justa's with child," he said, proud and disheartened. And I knew why—he couldn't be his own man while still tied to me. And with the inheritance, I'd finally given him the opportunity to walk away.

"Is this part of what was *none of my business*?" My stomach no longer felt sick, it was stone. "I see. You no longer want my protection or need my family's money. At long last you're ready to be free of me." It was hateful, and I was glad at the hurt in his eyes. Let him be the one to hurt, for a change.

Rafa's lips set in a thin line. "You can be free—but you're choosing to stay caged. Leave this city. Let the past go and start again."

I shook with rage, ready to strike him for the first time since I threw that cursed egg.

"Twice I've had to start again. Twice I've failed." I couldn't swallow, my throat was too tight. I pushed him aside and threw open the door. "Enjoy being a new man."

He couldn't have stopped me if he tried.

THIRTY-FOUR

THREE SMALL LAMPS HUNG, lit, over the table in my dark room. Their flames flickered from my relentless pacing—if three steps in each direction could be considered pacing. In any event, it wasn't helping. The word *traitor* became the beat to which I marched.

How could Rafa? *Traitor.* And Atellus? *Traitor.* Of all people, they should have understood—winning wasn't the most important part of the fight. It wasn't worth this dishonor.

One soft rap on the door made me pause.

"Lucilla?"

I pressed my hand to the wooden crosspiece, a feeble instinct to keep the door barred. I hadn't seen Marcus all evening, since returning to the ludus, and I wasn't in the mood for a lecture about my sloppy fight. Or to tell him Achilles had been poisoned. "What do you want?"

"Not to stand in the corridor," he said with a soft laugh.

I didn't know which was worse, Marcus angry or Marcus amused. "You could just leave."

The door groaned, and I knew he was pressing against it. "I could just break it open."

"Lurco would make you pay for a new one," I muttered, but removed the crosspiece so he could enter. No one was likely to attack me with Marcus here, but I secured it again to avoid any possible retribution for killing Achilles.

Marcus was busy at the small table pouring two cups of wine from the pitcher he'd brought. He set it down with a thud and turned to hand a cup to me. His black hair was damp and disheveled, as though he'd just bathed, dripping onto the shoulders of his tunic.

I took the cup but didn't drink. "I don't enjoy wine around you."

"No opium this time." Marcus grinned. "But you should revel in the afterglow of the death of your enemy."

"You have an unfortunate way with words." *Afterglow.* I felt both liberated and empty. I could have felt content, except for Atellus and Rafa's betrayal. I closed my eyes and leaned against the wall.

Marcus downed his drink in a long gulp. "Why aren't you pleased? I don't think you appreciate how extraordinary that fight was. It's all the city is talking of tonight."

I shook my head. No use pretending. "It wasn't extraordinary. Atellus poisoned Achilles before the fight."

"No, he didn't."

My hand leapt of its own will to grab Marcus's arm. "What?"

He looked down where I gripped him, and I pulled my hand away. A lazy smile tugged at the corners of his mouth. "I switched the poisoned olives before Achilles could eat them. Do you really think I'd let those fools interfere with your triumph?"

My throat was suddenly dry and I took a few slow sips of wine. "How did you know?"

"I don't like surprises—Veneda and Achilles fooled me once. That was more than enough." Marcus lifted the pitcher and refilled both our cups, a frown darkening his expression.

I paced toward the door. It didn't make sense. Achilles hadn't been poisoned … "So why did he stumble?"

Marcus snorted into his wine. "Why did he stumble?" He wiped his mouth with the back of his hand and dropped his cup on the table. "I don't think he's ever had to move so fast in his life. You nearly had him on that third advance. You shouldn't doubt your talent. I don't."

"Was that a compliment?"

"It wasn't as hard to say as I thought."

I put down my cup and looked up at him, suspicious. Marcus seemed flushed, his blue eyes distant. "How much have you drunk tonight?"

"Just enough." Standing toe to toe, the scent of fennel on his breath nearly overwhelmed me. "You should probably have another."

I didn't like his ominous tone. "Why?"

"Because I have news."

"I knew it." I threw my hands up in irritation. "I knew you

wouldn't bother coming here just to—" *Eyes to see, a mind to think, and hands to act.* Nothing about letting your mouth blabber.

"Just to … what?" He leaned forward.

I stepped away. "Tell me."

"You're fighting Veneda tomorrow."

A cold rush passed through me and I sank onto the bed. "I can't. I fought today—I get a month to recover."

"You'll find the time between matches shrinks in proportion to the amount of new jewelry Lurco wears."

It wasn't enough time—not to recover, not to train. My hair itched my scalp, and I raked my fingers through, releasing the tight braids. "Who would bribe Lurco to make me fight tomorrow?"

The bedframe creaked as Marcus sat next to me. "You tell me."

"Besides you, Veneda, and the god of the mountain, no one else has tried to kill me in nearly a year."

Marcus scrutinized my face. "And before this past year?"

I clenched my jaw, not wanting more foolish words to tumble out. Someday I would get part of my old life back. Until then, I couldn't give Marcus any more knowledge of what that life entailed. "Lucilla's dead, remember? And if you want Vesuvia alive past sunset tomorrow, I need some rest." I gave an obvious yawn and stretched my arms up over my head, then winced at the flash of pain in my left shoulder.

"What happened?"

I rolled the joint slowly. *I shouldn't have tackled Veneda.* "It's fine. A pull, nothing more."

"It'll be tight tomorrow if you don't attend to it. Let me?"

I hesitated, then nodded. He unfastened the left shoulder tie, and I used my free hand to keep the dress from gaping at the front, as it did in the back. It was an old one of Parsina's—faded and too short to be worn out of the ludus, but soft.

Marcus brushed my hair to one side and massaged with careful pressure along my shoulder blade. "Why didn't Atellus help you?"

"I was too busy being told off for my bloodthirsty ways." The argument still rankled. Achilles was dead, and so he should be. Tomorrow I would have the chance to kill Veneda. Then I could put all this behind me—focus on finding a way out of this trap. And I would have to do it alone, now that Rafa had abandoned me.

"Don't let your desire for friendship make you weak." Marcus stroked repeatedly down my neck and over the tight muscle, gentling his touch when I twitched.

Bit by bit, the ache in my shoulder eased, but my awareness of him grew. His fingers burned like a brand along my skin and I fought to keep my breathing even. "Seeing as how you don't have any friends, you can keep your opinions to yourself."

"I made sure Achilles wasn't poisoned," he said, as though he deserved a statue. Without warning, he lifted me and settled me on the edge of the bed, between his legs. Marcus clamped his hands over my hips as I made to stand. "Don't struggle, you'll pull something else."

He was behind me, so I couldn't read his expression. Just as well, I had no desire to be mocked. "Don't do that," I said, each word precise.

"What?" He resumed massaging my shoulder, harder than before, kneading deep enough to make my eyes water.

I gasped and tried to stand again. "Don't treat me like a toy."

Marcus wrapped his hands around my arms, holding my body immobile, thighs rigid against mine. "I give you more consideration than anyone. Do you know how hard it was to leave Achilles alive?" His soft breath tickled my ear. "To let you face him, alone, before all of Rome, when I could do nothing if you lost? And you aren't the slightest bit grateful."

"I'm fighting for my life again tomorrow because of you—"

"Don't be petty. You made an enemy of Veneda yourself. I had nothing to do with it."

"I'm not here because I want to be." I jerked against his hold to no effect. "Let me out of this bargain. What more do I need to do?"

His hands constricted. "And where would you go? To Rafa and his new family? Your cousin? Perhaps you think to escape to Britannia." Out of his mouth, each choice sounded more foolish than the last.

The dread I carried in my stomach surged, infusing my voice with disgust. "At least I'd be free of you."

In a burst, Marcus stood, pulling me with him. I stumbled, unable to break his hold as he turned me to face him. "You will never be free of me. Accept it. This is exactly where you want to be."

The depths of his eyes captured me as always—but in the near-dark of my room, their blue had given way to inky black, reminding me of the night of Vesuvius. A night without stars, when the sky was filled with clouds and death. It was all he could offer—the ludus, the killing—the darkness of being Vesuvia. It was too much, and far from being enough. "Don't expect me to step off the sand tomorrow."

Marcus blinked, his expression angry and surprised all at once, and gave me a shake. "This is not your chance at suicide."

"You're leaving me with no options—"

"You will fight, and you will win. Those are your options."

"Those aren't options—they're orders."

For the first time, Marcus seemed at a loss for words, jaw working as though he wanted to speak, but couldn't. With a curt nod he said, "Then obey."

I barred the door again after he left.

∞

The stone arches of the amphitheatre tunnel seemed to pin me down, like a bird caught under a cage of fingers. And I was caged—trapped—in a disaster of my own making. *I should have married Bricus. I should have thought of my future, instead of the past.*

Rafa had made a life—it was the one thing I fought hard to protect which had succeeded. So why was I upset with him? I couldn't remember.

My mind was numb.

I shouldn't be thinking this way; feeling this way. I was moments from being called out, the pairing ahead well started. I could hear the blades singing and the crowd chanting. But I couldn't shake the terrible burden of failure from my shoulders. I was a better fighter than my childish dreams could have imagined. Yet I'd never find the one-eyed man. Never have proof that Rusticus killed my father.

I must have made a sound because Marcus, waiting deep in the tunnel with me, turned.

He saw my agitation and walked over, laying his hands on my shoulders. "Forget yesterday. Clear your thoughts, and focus on what's in the circle. Just you and Veneda."

I tried to fill my lungs, but the air seemed thin. How could he possibly understand? "I'm hollow, Marcus. A brazier when the coal has been used up. Ash and embers." It sounded pitiful. Weak. I didn't care.

Marcus slapped me. It wasn't hard, but it stung my cheek.

My eyes flew to his and I saw the anger surge in them.

"Lucilla can be hollow if she wants," he said roughly. "Vesuvia is not. You're named for the mountain—be the fire." He pointed his finger at me. "Remember your oath: To be burned, to be beaten …"

The oath of a gladiator. To give your body over for your duration in the ludus. If you didn't fight, you could be punished and killed. Trust Marcus to hold me to such an oath.

"You may not care for yourself any longer," he continued without mercy, "but consider your friends. Because I will visit your punishment on them."

I couldn't read him, whether bluffing or serious, but I knew he could do it. And even in my anger for Rafa—for myself—I wouldn't take that risk. "You're a monster."

"Yes, I am." He gave a thin smile. "But I'm still alive."

∞

Jangling my hands at my sides, I walked out onto the familiar sand. I ran my eyes over the crowd as Veneda and I approached the assistant for our weapons. The emperor's chair was vacant, but his box was crowded with senators. Slaves and guards hovered in the background. On the opposite side from the emperor's podium sat the Vestals, at least five of them, shining in their white dresses and veils. Senators flanked them as well.

Has Rusticus seen me fight? Why hadn't I considered it sooner? I couldn't continue to rely on Rafa, and if Vesuvia was consuming me, I might as well make use of her. Perhaps a visit from her would put the fear of the gods in Rusticus. He was doubtless a coward.

Veneda had taken her blade and shield, so I collected my own swords and moved to the circle. The nuntius was working the crowd, announcing the epic contests that Veneda and I had each fought.

Ignoring him, I paced the chalk circle and considered the senators more carefully. There—beside the Vestals—was that Rusticus? It had been many years since I'd last seen him, but his fleshy body and square head made him distinctive against the other, thinner men.

Focus—we're ready to start.

The summa rudis lowered the baton and Veneda and I circled. She was wearing the particular snarl she saved just for me.

And she'd gotten better. Or perhaps she'd always been this good and had badly underestimated me the first time. She moved in quick bursts, with no predictable pattern to her thrusts or blocks.

We came at each other again and again, the *ring* of steel growing louder and sharper. Harrying her shield-arm, I tried to break her form, but she kept her shield tight to her body, striking out only when she had a clear thrust. I gave her a false opening on my right, then my left—but she avoided any possible trap.

The match dragged on, heat from the sun ferocious even though it was late in the day. The padding under my breastplate became soaked with sweat.

Veneda lunged low and broke through my defenses, blade whispering past my leg and slitting my skirt as I leapt away. The summa rudis intervened, forcing Veneda back. No blood. He raised his baton, preparing us to continue, and I saw past, into the crowd—

One bright green eye smiled; one black hole.

No. Not now.

The baton dropped.

In that very moment when I was distracted staring into his face, Veneda struck. I shifted my body, trying to force my arm up in time to protect my exposed left side, but too slow. Her blade snagged on the edge of my thin breastplate, then slid past, between my ribs. I spun away. My next breath brought a slice of pain through my chest and I knew—it was deep enough.

Triumph glowed in Veneda's eyes, a malicious sparkle that called my anger up past the pain. She stared, expecting I would fall.

In a haze I heard the crowd chanting, shouting. A swirl of noise and colour, like storm waves crashing on the shore.

In mere heartbeats the summa rudis would know I was injured. Veneda would face the crowd in victory and have the pleasure of deciding my fate. And there, just beyond my reach, the man with one eye would watch me fail.

They won't triumph over me.

What does she think? I'm beaten, weakened on the left—that's where she'll attack.

Her sword was ready, but on her own left the shield hung low, almost relaxed in her confidence and exposing her exhaustion. She was tired; I was dying.

She'd forgotten I had two swords. I never did.

I cut up with my left, and her sword came down on mine with a *clang*. But her shield was too slow for the straight lunge of my right blade into her abdomen. It lodged and I twisted it, burying the steel hilt-deep as her body crumpled forward. She knelt and then fell, blood blooming across the sand.

The crowd's roar mingled with the rush of blood in my ears. I coughed, the taste of metal coating my tongue. The summa rudis signaled my victory and it took all my focus to lift my swords. Acknowledge the crowd for the last time. I smiled.

Holding my left arm pressed against my side, I made my way with a stiff stride to the gate. Eyes finding Marcus, I expected disappointment, but his face was etched with fear.

"Was I that bad?" I coughed again. Blood splattered his tunic.

"You always did lack concentration," he said, voice harsh.

I pitched forward and braced to meet the floor. Weightlessness overtook me. I passed through shadow and light; shadow and light. Then darkness.

THIRTY-FIVE

PAIN. ONLY PAIN. How many more heartbeats would I have?

"Lucilla." Marcus's gentle shake of my arm made me gasp.

"Marcus … please. Bury me at home. Under the new soil of the mountain. I don't belong in the tomb." *I failed. I have no honour.*

Pain lessened. My body grew heavy. *Almost time.*

"No." His voice was hard. Uncompromising. "I'm not giving you up, even if you do ruin my plans."

I shook my head, confused. "Marcus. Enough. I need peace." *Why couldn't he give me this last thing?*

"Peace? Not yet." He nuzzled at my neck, breath hot on my ear. "You can't deny me now."

I ached at the longing in his voice.

His teeth at my neck brought a new, sharp pain. Fingers, then hands, began to tingle. *He's drinking from me.* I struggled against his hold, feeble and weak. Black rings misted the edge of my vision.

His breath quickened. A hiss. The pressure of his wrist opened my mouth and the hot copper of blood filled my senses. I gagged, but he held me down. I swallowed, and again. He murmured in my ear, voice flush with triumph:

> *"From beginning bound.*
> *From ending freed.*
> *What you are,*
> *Once I was.*
> *What I am,*
> *You will be."*

I was spinning, drowning, choking on blood. I thought I knew pain—the pain of loss, of injury, of suffering.

I'd known nothing of pain.

Burning rivers of fire sped through my body. From my chest and deep in my core they radiated in flashes, lightning strikes, trying to turn my insides out.

I writhed. Marcus held me, like waves breaking against a rock.

My heart sped.

∞

I opened my eyes to angry voices, jumbled and distant.

... don't care for your questions ...

... outcome was more important ...

... hard to keep quiet ...

A blur of words and pain.

∞

Every move was agony.

I sank like stone.

Blood sparked and seared. Bones were icy slivers, ready to shatter.

A hand over my mouth—I couldn't struggle against it.

The only release from torture was darkness.

∞

Sounds of a scuffle awakened me.

Past the rushing heartbeat in my ears, the convulsing in my limbs, I made out their voices.

"Let me see her." An angry demand.

"Lucilla's resting. I've told you already, she's not badly hurt."

"If she wasn't hurt, she'd be training. Where is she?" Atellus spat.

The door slammed and the voices faded.

I was unraveling like ripped fabric—grateful I couldn't see the pieces falling away.

∞

Sunlight. I opened my eyes and felt … whole. The absence of pain was unexpected. I waited for the fire.

For a long while I lay there, basking in the sun and letting my gaze trace the trowel-strokes in the plaster ceiling. I followed whorls in the grain of the great beams that held the storey above; saw the floorboards shiver as someone crossed the room. Felt their heartbeat echo along my skin, slow and steady.

Wait.

I sat up so fast I was standing.

What's wrong with me? I shook my head to clear it of the cacophony of sounds. The *thunk* of wood on wood—I spun at the noise, expecting it beside me. No—it was outside. Footsteps in the corridor. Murmured voices all around.

I surveyed the room and almost fell with the overwhelming sensation of colour. How had so many colours escaped my notice? The brightness and play of sunlight flowed like a river. I'd thought the cover on the bed was red, but now seemed flecked with maroon and rust and hues I'd never named. Notch-marks on the chairs screamed their presence in wood I knew was smooth to the touch. Or was it? I ran my fingertips over the back, each tiny imperfection a ravine.

Don't panic, maybe I'm dead. That would be reassuring—it would make some sort of sense.

A mirror! If I was dead, I wouldn't have a reflection. The dead were only shadows.

The air billowed around me as I stalked the room looking for my reflection. Fennel, yeast, wood, wine, ash, rot. Blood—my gut clenched. Its tangy sweetness caressed my tongue, leaving me dry and dizzy and weak. I stood, hands balled at my sides, willing the intensity to pass.

Please, Minerva, tell me what's happening.

Rushed footsteps in the hallway snapped my attention to the door. The fast beat of a heart sang across my skin, making the hairs on my arm stand. But my arm was wrong—it was too pale, the hairs too fine. I clutched the table for support.

Marcus entered and shut the door, dropping the latch. His eyes raked my form and I realized two things in quick succession.

One: he could see me, so I wasn't dead.

Two: I was naked.

"Merda! Marcus where are my clothes and what in Juno's name

has happened to me?"

"Don't panic. I have clothes for you over there." He pointed to a chest by the brazier.

I slipped on the blue dress and turned back to face him, flushed with agitation and absolutely confused.

"You need to tell me now," I said.

"You were a disaster after the match with Veneda, so I had to burn those clothes." He was trying not to smile and fury overtook me in an instant.

Breathe, let your blood cool. I gulped down air and it tickled my lungs. I grabbed the back of a chair to keep something between us. "And you never bothered to dress me again?"

"Why would I want to do that? I had to check you were changing properly. Well done, by the way." Now he *was* smiling.

Riddles and jests. Begging me to smash in those beautiful teeth—

Crack. The chair splintered in my hands and brought a stab of pain. Startled, I looked down. Bits of wood rained to the ground, except for a finger-sized shard, lodged in my palm. With a curse, I yanked it out and dropped it.

I gasped as a warm rush spread through my hand. Marcus chuckled.

Blood dripped from the wound, then slowed. My skin knit back together. Within heartbeats the hand was unmarked.

Trembling, I ran my fingers over the nonexistent injury. Feeling up my arm I searched for the scar from the grotto, but it too had vanished. Ribcage—my death-wound—nothing.

I sat on the bed and closed my eyes. I was dead. Marcus was dead. This was some kind of underworld for the disgraced.

"Am I dead or have I gone mad?" Perhaps this was an illusion—a trick of the Furies. If so, I deserved it.

"How much do you remember?" Marcus knelt in front of me, eye to eye. His scent surrounded me and I fought the familiar lurch of desire that struck whenever he was near. But now it came with more. Underneath the sweat and spice and fennel, I could smell blood. I wanted nothing so much as to sink my teeth into his throat. It was so close, inches away.

"Lucilla." He shook my shoulders. "What do you remember?"

What is he saying? Focus, Lucilla. I closed my eyes, taking shallow breaths through my mouth. "In the arena, fighting Veneda." Memory broke to the surface. The man with one eye—how could I have forgotten? But it seemed I had a more pressing concern, one which needed answering without delay. I opened my eyes.

He raised his brows, waiting for me to continue.

"We killed each other. You brought me here." I sucked in a breath. My hand flew to my neck as I remembered. "What did you do to me?" I tried to recoil from him, but he grabbed my face between his hands and forced me to look at him.

His eyes, burning pools of azure, pulled me.

What I am, you will be.

"What are you?" I asked in a hush.

"What are we, you mean?" He gave me a true smile and it left me breathless. I'd seen him use his charm before, on me and on others. But I knew now those expressions were only masks. Not like this—pure, happy. How long since I'd been happy?

"All right. What are we?" I tried to smile back.

"Immortal."

Madness. Pure madness.

"You don't look convinced," he said. "Let me explain, then I'll answer all your questions."

At my nod he stood back, leaving me space to breathe.

My eyes flicked between chair and table, window and door. Everything so familiar, yet somehow unrecognizable. Marcus watched me intently and I stilled my twitching fingers. Slowed my breathing. When my wandering eyes finally met his, he began.

"We don't age. We don't get sick. We can be killed, but only with much carnage." He laughed. I didn't understand the joke. He gestured to the fragments of the chair scattered on the floor. "You'll heal any injury that doesn't kill you outright."

"Is that all?" I asked, wary, searching my memory for stories that fit his description. "I've never heard of a creature like this. It sounds more like ... a god." It was blasphemous to even suggest it.

"You're not the first to think so. It's certainly a gift."

"What's the price?" I asked, and he frowned. "Every coin has two sides. Apollo gifted Cassandra with prophecy—but with the curse of never being believed."

"There is a ... limitation." He narrowed his eyes as if to gauge my reaction. "We must drink blood to survive."

Blood. The mention of it made my throat constrict. Dread washed over me. "What kind of blood?"

"Human blood."

No. Father's throat torn out; Sylos bitten and drained by the man with one eye. *I couldn't be like him.*

Springing to my feet, I paced the room. *Marcus must not be telling me everything.* "I need to drink human blood to survive? I can live forever if I'm willing to feed on people?"

"Keep your voice down." He eyed my progress as I passed the table one way, then the other. "It's the most natural thing there is. Humans eat flesh. Pig, chicken, even human when they're desperate enough. We drink from them. Understand—you're not human any longer. Your old life is past. You must drink, or you will die." Marcus gave me a sardonic smile. "I've worked hard to be sure you wouldn't die. You're mine now to protect, even from yourself."

"What do you mean 'I'm yours'?" I snapped. I was out of my depth. Not a daughter, not a niece, not a sister. *Not a human.*

"You're of my blood now. We're bound." He made it sound simple, though I sensed he was holding back. But I couldn't wrap my mind around half of what he'd told me.

"But Hamitra … I thought you were like her. She told me she hunted creatures like—" I stopped my pacing and sank into the unbroken chair. *Nothing was as I'd thought.* Could Marcus know of the one-eyed man?

Marcus crossed his arms, a slight smile tugging at the corners of his mouth. "She really didn't tell you?" His voice was thick with surprise. "For all that humans have vast imaginations, it seems nature is far more limited in her creations. We're all the same. In fact, it was Hamitra who made me what I am."

Why didn't she tell me? How could she let me think she was *better* than that monster? Too many questions. *Focus.* Focus on the ones Marcus could answer. "Why are we this way?"

He shrugged, still amused. "Why does a caterpillar become a butterfly?"

"So I was fated to become this thing?" I tried to swallow against the bile in my throat.

"No." He knelt in front of me. "Your own choices led you here.

And mine. If we'd never met, you would have remained human."

I pressed my hands to my eyes, not wanting to recall all the choices which led to this moment. Every one a thoughtless step down the path which led me here, instead of to a normal life; a human life. "Marcus, I can't do this. It's unnatural."

"No more so than for any other animal. A lion has no qualms about eating a baby." He raised his hands at my horrified expression. "I don't eat babies. See—I'm far better than a lion."

I wasn't so sure.

"Don't fight what you are." He laid his hands on my knees, his heartbeat resonating where we touched and pulsing along my skin. "Only human blood will sustain you. Immortals who live together can feed from each other for a short time, but not indefinitely."

"Have you ever lived with another … immortal?" The word stuck in my mouth, but it was better than *blood-drinking monster*.

"I have." His face and voice drained of emotion. "But I haven't found someone I'm compatible with."

It was visible to me now, how he mastered his expression, locking emotions away behind his mask of calm. I'd lived a miserable two decades. How heavy were the years of pain he carried?

Could I bear to know Marcus for eternity, but always as a stranger? I closed the sliver of space between us and pressed my lips to his.

He hesitated, but only for a moment. The instant our tongues met I ignited like tinder. But the taste of him was no release from the call of blood; it was there, too strong to be ignored. From where he knelt before me I rode him to the floor. Lips finding his jaw. His throat. Then my teeth sank into his neck.

The heat and sweetness of his blood filled my senses. I gave myself over to mindless pleasure—until I was thrown.

I tumbled through the air, striking the wall and landing hard on the bed. Head whirling, I looked up to see Marcus standing over me, his own breath heavy. The skin on his neck had already healed.

"No blood yet," he said, with frightening satisfaction.

∞

It had been an agonizing afternoon. Atellus tried again to visit, but Marcus had me convinced it would be better if I fed before I met anyone

I'd like to keep alive. The thought turned my stomach, and I stayed hidden.

"When were you going to tell me about your father's murder?" Marcus asked, watching me eat dinner.

I glared at him, barely pausing as I worked my way through a chicken. I'd been consuming enormous amounts of food since I'd awoken. An after-effect of the change, Marcus said. My body was depleted, but he'd been evasive about exactly what happened during the transformation—his willingness to answer questions had vanished.

"Rafa told me you're hunting the murderer," he continued, heat growing in his voice.

I glared some more and drank my wine. Wine was fun. It changed flavours four times along my tongue before I swallowed. But, I recalled with dread, blood had been better.

"And perhaps you'd tell me," he slammed his hand down on the table, "why a one-eyed immortal would come looking for you after your fight with Veneda."

I snapped my gaze to his, shocked. "He came here?"

"I told him you died after the fight. And he was interrupting my … dinner," Marcus said, still angry. "But I don't think he believed me."

Chewing some grapes, I stalled. "Do you know where he went?"

"I was too busy keeping you from shaking the ludus to the ground with your screaming." But it was he who looked shaken now, anger draining away. "What is he to you?"

"He was one of the men who killed my father, and our nurse. She died trying to protect me and Agrippina." It made even less sense now. *Why had he left me alive?*

Marcus looked surprised also. "Cyclops attacked you as a child, but you escaped?"

"Is that his name," I asked, smiling a bit at this description, "or did you just make it up?"

"It seemed fitting." He grinned.

It was more than fitting. The nameless monster who haunted my dreams faded. He may not be human, but he was no longer invincible. And the Marcus who'd manipulated this insanity also seemed to vanish. He'd not dropped his high-handed ways, but now that his secret was mine as well, perhaps we could be allies. So long as I didn't go for his throat again.

"I think Cyclops was hired by—or is somehow loyal to—Senator Gaius Commidius Rusticus. My father had an affair with the Senator's wife."

He tilted his head, mulling this over. "But you have no proof?"

"No, only bits of conversations. And during my fight with Veneda, Rusticus was there at the amphitheatre—Cyclops on the podium behind him. Rafa's been searching for years and never found a trace of him." Idly, I spun a grape stem between my fingers. "Father's death was the worst thing I'd seen until Bricus and I found a ship filled with bodies. They'd been torn to pieces."

Marcus's face had gone carefully blank. "When was this?"

The stem fell to the plate and I watched him through narrowed eyes. "About five years ago. Right before we met."

He scratched his jaw, contrite as a wolf among lambs.

"*Persephone*," I accused. "That was you."

"Sea travel is difficult at the best of times, and it was an inconvenient time for me to be confined."

"That's your explanation?"

"How's your tooth?"

I frowned. "Don't change the subject." But my tongue had already felt for the hole. Still missing. "I thought you said I'd heal."

"Heal, but not regrow. Except for teeth." Marcus took an apple, biting into it with satisfaction. "Every few decades they'll fall out. When they return, they bring an appetite."

"Appetite?" The word turned my mouth dry. Men ripped limb from joint. Reduced to meat. "No wonder Hamitra despises you."

The instant he sprang out his chair I was out of mine. Clutching the edges of the table between us, Marcus tried to rein in his anger. The wood groaned. "Hamitra is no different than me, for all her attempts at playing human. And I wouldn't have been on that boat if it wasn't for her foolish scheming."

I stared, unsure what to say.

Marcus pushed the table and it skidded toward me. "If you eat much more you'll make yourself sick," he said, and I looked down at the scattered remains of the food. "Stay here." He stalked out.

Grabbing my glass of wine, I drank in long gulps. I was like a child again, stumbling over things I didn't fully understand. Hamitra and Marcus had a past which was far longer than I'd thought.

Stomach roiling, I decided to follow Marcus's advice and stop eating. Instead, I turned my chair to face the window and sat, watching through new eyes as the sun sank below the horizon. Waves of colours, some familiar, some dazzling and fresh, painted the sky.

I heard Marcus return, but didn't tear my eyes from the city. Bright lanterns and dark corners; old brick and gleaming marble. A city of a thousand years. And I could see the next thousand. *But at what cost?*

"I'd forgotten what it was like," Marcus said, no longer upset.

"What?" I asked.

"The change."

I waited. If he wanted to tell me he would.

"You're becoming more patient," he said at last.

"It's about time, don't you think?"

"And funnier."

"There's no need to be sarcastic." I turned to him.

Marcus's eyes shone with amusement. "You really aren't going to ask?"

"I'm not sure I want to know how old you are. It's too strange."

"You could ask about people you know of, and I'll tell you if I am older or younger."

Always games. Would I become so annoying, if I lived long enough? "Fine. Caesar Augustus."

"Older."

Older than a hundred years. "Alexandros the Great."

"Older."

Older than four hundred. "This isn't fun if you're older than Zeus."

"Younger, I think. Though I've never met any gods, so that might be up for debate."

"Have you met any heroes—Odysseus or Hercules?"

"Not them, but I've met others." He may have been teasing me, I couldn't be sure.

"What were they like?"

"Delicious."

"Go away, Marcus."

"We hunt after midnight," he said. Then he left again.

Thirty-Six

"Marcus," I whispered. "Faster."

He quickened his pace, leading me through the city. Steps fast but silent, we kept to the shadows of deep porticos, weaving through a forest of columns and statues.

Noises from the buildings swirled around me like falling leaves. We pressed on in the darkness and I worked to pull my wayward senses under control—it was jarring, as though the entire city had been condensed into the street around me. Sounds came in bursts: an argument between lovers; a brawl in a taberna; the rutting of dogs; of people; a child crying.

Odours pressed in with shocking clarity, yet complete disorder. They battled each other for my attention. The perfumed sweetness of incense knocked away by rank bile. Spiced sausage overwhelmed by the burning coals that cooked it. Stinking bodies of human and animal. And like a knife through it all, the undercurrent of blood.

How can I endure an eternity of this? Of all the changes to my body, this visceral response was by far the most unsettling. My new-found speed and stamina made running effortless. Sound seemed to reverberate along my skin, turning the very air alive. Night was no longer dark, but a range of vivid shades I couldn't name. Yet the driving need for blood had no comparison. I'd never longed for anything with such intensity—it had me panting with desire.

Marcus paused at the side of a building, out of the light, and I focused all my attention on him. Traced his form with my eyes, smelled his scent, felt his heartbeat. His voice was a low rumble as he spoke, "I wouldn't cage you, but I do insist on one thing."

"Interesting. Hamitra was sure you didn't have any rules at all."

"Rules are too confining, and constantly broken. Can't say I have much use for them. But you must only let a human know your true nature if it's to your advantage. Otherwise, keep it hidden."

"Hidden? It's impossible to live in the open and hope our differences won't be noticed. I could tell, and I was just a child."

"Your childhood was far from normal. And you're in a very small minority—it's always amazed me how people only choose to see what they expect to see."

"The victims are a bit obvious," I said, refusing to consider the implications of this night.

"Hamitra and Nikandros decided long ago that human bite marks were far more suspicious than the carnage of ripping the throat out," Marcus said in a detached way, as though we were discussing the weather, not murder.

"And you?"

"Once your dinner is dead, it doesn't matter what the corpse looks like, so long as it doesn't land suspicion on you."

I felt ill. "It matters to me."

"Death is death," he whispered, running his hands through his hair. "Surely you know that by now. I won't apologize for what I am— I've seen humans do much worse."

"Why did you do this to me?" I asked, the weight of my conscience bearing down. "You could have let me die. Twice."

"*Thank you* is the appropriate response when someone saves your life." His anger carried on the air as though it was incense, a new scent, yet unmistakeable.

And, as always, he was half-right. I wanted to be alive. If this was the only way, so be it. "Thank you."

"I didn't want to change you so young," he said with regret. "If I could, I would have waited until your body was fully mature—at least twenty. Far longer if I'd the patience and opportunity."

"Why?"

"The more you've seen of life, the easier the bargain of this one becomes." He gave a sharp sigh. "And children don't make the change."

I narrowed my eyes. "Just what does that mean?"

"Nothing important for now. But I'd have preferred you didn't make such a mess of your fight with Veneda."

"I'm touched by your concern," I said with as much scorn as I could. "It was misplaced, though. I'm twenty-one." My birthday had passed unmarked a few weeks ago.

He stared at me, surprised. "Hamitra," he cursed softly.

I didn't even try to stop my smirk. "How old did she say I was?"

"When we met the first time she told me you were thirteen."

I shook my head. "Fifteen. I'm lucky to have made it this long in the ludus," I accused.

"That's your opinion. I'm glad you were too young for her to risk trying to change you. She's always wanted a child. It must have tortured her to leave you behind." He sounded too happy about it. "Why did she leave?"

"They agreed to escort a friend back to his homeland in Britannia. But I think they'd stayed in one place too long." It made sense, now, that Nikandros had wanted to leave years ago. It was risky staying long enough that people might notice you didn't age—or that all their neighbours were killed. Bodies in Pompeii, then Neapolis, then Surrentum. Eventually the rumours of wild animals and rival factions had dwindled. Had they … hunted … further inland? It was a disquieting thought but, then again, so was everything about this.

"How long do you stay in one place?" I asked.

"If the food is in good supply, perhaps four or five years. When we first met in Pompeii, I'd just joined the emperor's ludus as auctoratus, so my time here is up. And Atellus is too close to realizing I have even less conscience than he thought."

Five years. Hamitra spent almost ten with us.

"Don't let it trouble you. You'll get used to it." He gave a snort. "*Iteri*, Nikandros calls us. Wanderers. We travel where there is no path, and leave no trail. A little pretentious, if you ask me, but it fits with his pretentious mission—to collect all the knowledge of the world and preserve it from destruction."

"Is that why they were interested in our library?"

"It's how I knew where to find Hamitra. They've spent years planning an introduction to your family. Your uncle's collection was well known. Bloody waste of time, though. Who are they saving such knowledge for? Humans? If humans go out of their way to remain ignorant, nothing Nikandros can do will change that." His expression was more puzzled than angry. "What are you smiling at?"

"Just a thought. Perhaps Uncle's library isn't lost, after all. They must have copied all the important manuscripts years ago. It would be a small consolation."

"You too?" He lifted his hands in mock surrender. "We're not scouring the world for scrolls." I didn't miss that he spoke of us as a unit. It was too certain for my liking.

"So what's your mission?" I asked.

Marcus turned from scanning the street to look at me, suspicious.

"If Nikandros and Hamitra have a mission, you must have one too. What have you been doing with eternity?"

He gave me half a smile and closed the distance between us, robbing me of air. "Waiting."

I drew a shallow breath. "For what?"

He reached to take my arms, but I pushed away and backed up. "Stop it, Marcus! I'm sick of these games."

"This is no game. You don't understand yet—" He exhaled in a sharp burst. "I shouldn't be so foolish, lack of blood does things to the mind. You need to feed." He sped on suddenly and I had to push to keep up with him.

He stopped outside Senator Rusticus's domus. "You can be as messy as you need, just be silent," Marcus whispered in my ear. He passed me a small pouch and I could smell its contents without opening it. Fennel. He gave a wry smile. "For after. It's stronger than mint— better at disguising the scent on your breath."

Gods above and below.

I turned back to the domus, trying to calm my racing pulse. Preposterous that after all these years, vengeance would be so easy. It was night. Everyone slept. All I had to do was walk in and drain the bastard who killed my father. No more sleepless nights; no more haunted dreams. My thirst would be satisfied at last.

∞

Marcus remained in the alley while I approached the domus and leapt to the first floor roof. Walking without the sound of footfalls, I crept over the tiles and dropped into the garden below. Hyacinth blossoms pooled on the ground and their aroma puffed up around me, sickly-sweet. The garden was criss-crossed by a dizzying array of odours. With practice, it may be possible to trace someone's path long after they'd left it. Right now though, it was just confusing.

Stalking through the garden I let my heightened senses reach out into the rooms beyond. Heartbeats flickered to life, pulsing along my skin as though they were my own. No sign of Cyclops—perhaps he was searching the city for me.

Inside all was quiet. I peered in one room, then the next, eyes tracing sleeping shapes for the rotund figure of Rusticus. The pull of blood was strong, the familiar scents of humanity making my body shake as though I'd been starving for weeks. It was all I could do to pass so many defenceless people.

At last I found him.

I stood over his bed, watching as he took his last breaths.

His chest rose and fell rhythmically, peacefully. Not like Eudocia. Chest shuddering as she struggled for air.

Not like Father. A grotesque mockery of the man I loved.

Not like this.

It was too kind. Achilles fell by my hand in combat; Veneda also. To kill a murderer in his sleep wasn't justice.

He needs to know.

I struck—the soft flesh of his flabby neck offered no resistance to my teeth. A warm gush of blood destroyed all other senses. More satisfying than anything I'd ever tasted. Even more than Marcus's blood.

Rusticus moved, as if to sit up or call out, and I clamped a hand over his face. He struggled, trying to break my hold, arms beating against my grasp like feeble wings—

Like an animal.

The thought ripped through me and I pulled away. Lungs heaving, I stared into his stricken eyes. Each heartbeat pulsed more blood free from his torn neck—as it must have from my father's, where fingers had ripped open flesh and fat.

"Do you know why I'm here?" I asked.

His eyes rolled back, and I slapped him, gently, before he could pass out.

Rusticus drew his gaze to mine.

"You killed my father."

He choked. *No*, he mouthed.

"Lucius Calpurnius Piso. You had him killed like a dog in the street. To be brought home to two daughters!"

"No." He coughed. "You … are mistaken." His voice came out harsh and cracked. He tried to staunch the flow of blood from his neck, but it trickled through his fingers.

"No? He was fucking your wife!" Rage burned white hot. *He won't do this. He won't deny his crime.*

"… the box." He pointed, hand shaking.

An inlaid mahogany box sat on a table. His breaths came slower. I tried to slow my own, my heartbeat violent in my ears.

I broke the lid off, splintering the delicate pattern. Pieces of the lock thudded on the plush carpet. Rifling through bits of parchment, Father's name blazed like a lantern in a dark night.

Horrified, I turned to Rusticus, his face ashen, the cushions around his head dark and slick. My stomach constricted.

Eyes sped past the words as I read it over, and slowly unravelled its meaning. He and Father had agreed on terms for his divorce from Junilla. Father would be free to marry her, so long as Junilla left all her dowry with the senator. She'd consented. It had been all but done.

"You knew? But you said it would be the death of him."

"Her spending drains … every man she marries." A thought fluttered in his eyes as he looked at me and his dry chuckle turned into a bloody cough.

"I don't understand." My head spun. All this time I'd been convinced it was Rusticus, but … "Then who?"

"Who else?" Rusticus asked, as arrogantly as a dying man could.

He knew. The bastard knew.

"Tell me!" I screamed.

Voices rang in the hall. I flew to his bedside but he coughed again, a strangled gurgle, and convulsed. Footsteps approached the door — when I turned back, he was dead.

I dove through the wooden shutters of a high window and fled into the darkness. Shouts rang out in the domus, now far behind.

If I'd still been human, my feet would have pounded on the paving stones. But, for all my speed, their tread was silent.

If I'd still been human, my muscles would have begged for rest blocks ago. But my strides stayed long; breaths steady.

I ran until I was near the gates, then jumped onto balconies and over rooftops until I launched myself beyond the city's wall.

I ran on.

When I stopped, it was as though my feet knew where they should take me. Peach trees lined a roadway to a fine villa, only a single storey, but with a sprawling tangle of rooms.

If I'd been human, this might have been my life.

The sweet aroma of fruit mingled with dew in the grass and I inhaled deep, trying to drive away the cloying scent of blood. Then I remembered the fennel. Taking a handful from the pouch at my belt, I chewed the seeds, releasing their heavy flavour.

Cautiously, I approached Nonius' villa.

Creeping past window after window, I hunted this time for those I knew were innocent. Lucius and Gaius. A wave of sadness gripped me. It was a kindness they'd never know Agrippina decided to abandon them for her lover. So many had lost mothers to Vesuvius, they could remember her without taint.

The boys slept, arms and legs flung at all angles. Their nurse was on a mat by the door, so I didn't enter, but stood at the window and fixed them in my memory. Their fast heartbeats worried me for a moment, then I realized it was normal for children.

I'd sworn to right the wrongs against my family. A hasty plan—a foolish plan. Thought up by an ignorant child. *And now I've killed an innocent man.* If the Furies hadn't been hunting me before today, ready to inflict madness and torment, they would certainly pursue me tomorrow. I'd plunged ahead, reckless as usual, failing to do the things within my power. Failing in my promise to my sister.

I watched my nephews, not caring for time or the world around me. Bit by bit, the turmoil within me eased, replaced by something I'd not felt since before Father's death; before I believed myself set to lose against an impossible future.

Hope.

Its sweetness pierced me, tainted by how hard and cruel I knew the world to be. Lucius and Gaius couldn't replace my sister, but they could bring new life to our family. Their futures were not yet measured or cut … so long as I found Cyclops. I needed to keep them safe. Free to grow up in as much peace as anyone could hope to have.

I knew now why Uncle let me learn the sword, instead of denying me. Hoping to make peace with my father's spirit and perhaps keep part of his brother alive, and with him. Why Aunt hadn't pushed me into marriage earlier. Shielding me, in her own way, from the same youthful misfortunes she'd suffered. Hoping in time I might see marriage as my duty, not a punishment.

I held on to the feeling, trying to lock it in with other emotions—anger, guilt, pain—which I knew far better. I'd had hope once, before the threads of my family had been unravelled. Perhaps, if I could protect those who were left, I could have it back again.

Thirty-Seven

VAULTING OVER THE WALL and down into the dark training ground, I silently made my way to Marcus's room.

I was silent, but unfortunately not invisible. Atellus blocked the door. Despite the dim light I could tell he noticed my bloodstained clothes. I rubbed my face, hoping the blood was gone from my mouth.

"By the gods, what's happened to you?" Atellus demanded.

I couldn't ignore his frustration. Urging him into the room, I shut the door behind us. "I don't know what to tell you. I can hardly explain it to myself." I turned toward the basin, desperate to wash the tackiness from my hands, but not for the first time misjudged an opponent. He wasn't just frustrated, he was furious.

Atellus grabbed my arm and spun me to face him. My body reacted before my mind could reason. I flung him away, and it was as though I tossed a doll across the room. He hit the stone wall with a sickening thud and fell in a crumpled heap to the floor. I stifled a gasp, shocked into stillness.

He was conscious, but his breaths were laboured. His expression was a mirror of my thoughts. Shock, confusion, pain.

And then the smell of blood hit. Its sweetness invaded my senses and I held myself rigid for fear of making things worse.

Marcus entered the room—definitely worse. He wasn't surprised to see Atellus laid out on the floor, but barred the door. Atellus tried to jerk away as Marcus knelt beside him and began assessing his injuries.

"He's bleeding—" was all I managed to croak out.

Marcus gazed up at me and I expected anger for betraying our secret. He withdrew his hand from behind Atellus's head, fingers smeared with blood. "Does it still call to you? You didn't have enough."

Beads of sweat broke over my skin. Marcus extended his hand toward me, a silent temptation against my better judgement.

Lips parting, my body jerked forward of its own will.

Atellus's eyes locked with mine, but our expressions were nothing alike anymore. Fear and disgust warred on his face as he tried to understand what Marcus implied.

"He's not going to live the night," Marcus told me as I knelt beside them.

Atellus shot him a look of contempt. "I think I'll survive a blow to the head, even if it is bleeding."

"It's not your injury that will kill you."

"Enough, Marcus," I snapped, anger overpowering the gnawing hunger. "Atellus won't tell anyone what happened. Why would he?"

"Because he hates me more than he cares for you. He'd do anything to drive me away."

"I could say you were the one who threw me into the wall in a jealous rage," Atellus offered, stumbling to his feet and inching away from Marcus's reach. "In fact, that's exactly what I'll do."

Marcus moved so fast Atellus had no opportunity to even turn for the door, but was forced to his knees. Marcus stood behind him, trapping his arms backward at an awkward angle.

"No!" I moved forward to intervene.

"Not any closer Lucilla, or I'll pull his arms off."

"Marcus, don't do this. He doesn't know anything."

Marcus regarded me for a long moment, impassive, then sent Atellus stumbling away from the door. Crossing his arms over his chest, Marcus glared. "I've already cleaned up one mess tonight, I don't need another." He pointed at Atellus. "How do you think this will end? He'll betray us. They always do. I won't let that happen."

"Lucilla." Atellus pulled a short dagger from his tunic. "Come away. Let me take you back to your family. You don't belong here." He brandished the dagger at an unconcerned Marcus.

I groaned. "Atellus, put that away." He needed to calm down. And he looked ridiculous, holding it like a surgeon, not a killer.

"Whatever he's threatening you with, I can help." Atellus moved himself between me and Marcus.

"You don't need to protect me. I can leave any time I choose." I moved for the door, hand stretched towards him. *Please.*

Relief washed over me as Atellus edged around Marcus.

"She's trying to save you, fool, and you're not even clever enough to see it," Marcus taunted.

Atellus stopped, his nostrils flaring like a bull about to charge.

"Not a clever boy at all are you? Rafa had to tell you to take care of Achilles—would you even have thought of that yourself?" Marcus snorted. "That's why you're here, stitching up gladiators, instead of working with your father in the imperial household."

That Marcus knew these things didn't surprise me; Atellus's blind rage did. He quivered where he stood. "How did …?" He stumbled over the words.

The smile that slid across Marcus's face was pure poison. "Not. Clever. Enough."

"Shut it, Marcus!" I snapped at him, but it was too late. Atellus made to plunge the dagger in Marcus's chest. I raced to intervene, the cool blade slicing into my shoulder.

"Gods below," I cursed.

Atellus stared transfixed at the dagger imbedded in my shoulder, mouth gaping in shock.

Marcus pulled the blade free and dropped it with disdain. "That wasn't necessary."

"The dress was ruined anyway." I flicked at the sagging shoulder ties, not meeting Marcus's gaze. Wishing my instinct hadn't been to protect his vicious, scheming hide.

Atellus snapped his mouth shut and took my arm, though his hand trembled against me. "Lucilla, sit down and I'll …" His heavy eyebrows notched higher and higher as he saw the impossible.

A tingling rush passed through my shoulder as it healed, skin weaving like fabric on a loom. Atellus reached to touch the vanished wound; Marcus pulled him away and struck, teeth bared, at the pulse in Atellus's neck.

"No!" I kicked Marcus's knee, snapping it backwards.

Cursing, he dropped Atellus and I rushed to catch his limp body.

Another crack, and then a hiss as Marcus righted his leg. "We can't be exposed. I won't risk it."

"But you can save him. You saved me." I tried to staunch the bleeding with a strip off my skirt, but it was already soaked through.

Blood gushed from Atellus's mangled vein.

"I cannot," Marcus replied.

"Can I?" I begged. His gaze held no reassurance. "Please—can I save him?"

"Give him your blood. It would be the only way."

Turning back to Atellus, I grabbed the knife from where it had landed and cut my wrist, letting the few drops which escaped fall into his mouth.

I stared, stricken, as Atellus struggled for breath. His eyes widened in pain and he clutched at my hand. I held him as his body began to jerk and twist, spasming as whatever untold horror I'd unleashed inside took hold. His mouth opened and closed, gasping, and I wept when his gasps turned to gurgling. I held on, his body unbearably hot to touch, trying to comfort him as blood trickled from his eyes and nose.

I hadn't thought it could get worse—and then it did.

Small, dark sores bloomed and opened on his arms and torso, a snaking growth along his body. I fought the urge to retch when they opened, overflowing with blood and black fluids. *Just like Father.*

My heart raced, but his slowed, every beat weaker than the last. The space between them lengthened, and I hated how I felt it with such clarity.

Atellus didn't seem to know where he was or what was happening, his eyes glassy and distant. But when I called his name he turned, so I bent my head to his ear and whispered, "Be at peace."

He mouthed some words, but I could only make out *antidote.*

Body shuddering, he convulsed in my arms, the sores at last having covered every inch of skin. His heart stopped.

No.

There has to be more.

He can't be dead.

I sat, covered in blood and gore, tears running down my face. Waiting for the change. A miracle. Life.

"Atellus," I whispered.

Marcus tried to pull me upright. "It's over, Lucilla."

I shook him off and ran for the basin, heaving and sobbing. At the sounds of shuffling, I raised my head. Marcus had wrapped Atellus in the carpet. Blood seeped through the bottom, smearing the floorboards. Colours swam before my eyes, a blur of reds.

Marcus saw my fixation on the dark stain. "You must hunt, Lucilla." He neared and took my chin in his hand, forcing me to look away from the body. "Hunt, and you'll be able to control yourself."

"How could you?" I choked on the words. "How could you let me do that to him?"

"You had to understand. This secret we keep isn't a game," he said, voice sharp. "Do you understand now?"

He shook my shoulders and I looked into his eyes. They reflected my grief, but I suspected for an entirely different reason.

My gaze was pulled back to the rug-wrapped body, my mind in chaos. "Why didn't he change?" I asked. "How many don't—"

"Almost all," he snapped. "For me, all. Before you."

I stared up at Marcus, the horror of what he said slowly washing over me.

"All …" I could barely form the word.

All. Echoed in my head. Driving away the hope, the light. Half-formed dreams of changing Rafa, changing Justa, living in some sort of peace—vanished in that echo.

All. Marcus was older than four hundred years, perhaps far older—how many friends, lovers, how many lives lost?

All.

His eyes followed as I backed away, expression hardening into an impassive mask, watchful but emotionless.

Dizzy, lightheaded, I made for the hall.

What am I?

A killer.

A monster.

Before me lay a void, a never ending sea. I was trapped again on the water. Humanity didn't live on the waves, or under them, or in the sky above. Waves didn't care for you, didn't care if they pulled you into a darkness so complete it froze your flesh and froze your blood—

Blood. Marcus said I needed blood.

I clutched at my hands, what was left of my dress. Covered in red and brown and black.

How much more blood do I need?

Down the hall, down the stairs I stumbled. The lower floor was dark. Slaves didn't need light. Condemned didn't need light. This was their fate, whether by my hand today or in the amphitheatre tomorrow.

A guard raised his hand as I approached the cell door. I knew him—Cassius. Perhaps he was going to call out a greeting, but it didn't make it out his throat. I tore the flesh free from his neck. Ripping the keys off his belt, I opened the door to a cell of noxii. They were to go to the beasts. What difference, really?

I'd killed four before one woke enough to scream. His neck snapped like a chicken bone. The rest went with barely a whimper.

A noise at the cell gate had me spinning to face the intruder. Marcus slapped me across the face, but I was so flushed there was no pain. He shook my shoulders and I dropped the head I was holding.

"Lucilla, breathe." Marcus shook me again.

"I'm dizzy." I stumbled.

He righted me. "You can't go so long without a proper feeding." His words pulsed as if from the end of a tunnel. "It's my fault. I thought you wouldn't hesitate if the thirst was nearly uncontrollable. I made you wait too long."

Contentment rippled, slowing the fire in my heart; the echo in my head.

Then I saw what I'd done. Pairs of dead, glassy eyes stared up at me, expressions frozen in fear and agony.

"I'll let one of the lions out," Marcus said. "It'll seem the guards had some sport that got out of control." He surveyed the carnage. "Or perhaps two lions."

I was sprinting across the courtyard.

"Clean up before you get back." He didn't need to raise his voice for me to hear him.

∞

I ran down an alley and vaulted onto the roof of the nearest building. Terracotta tiles crunched as I landed too hard, then regained my footing. I kept running, leaping over streets and fountains, using balconies and ridge beams to ease my path onto the highest rooftops I could find. It was full dark. The new moon cast no light. Only torchlight in the streets and lamps burning in the few windows rich enough to spare oil made a dent in the darkness. Not that I needed their guidance.

Reaching the Arx, the smaller of the two peaks of the Capitoline Hill, I stopped. I sent a swift prayer to Juno, hoping She wouldn't be upset at me joining the birds atop Her temple.

Rome was spread before me. A sea of shimmering lights, dark shapes, grotesque odours. More than a million people lived in my city. And I could kill any of them. From the condemned prisoners in the Carcer to the Emperor himself—I could end any life I chose.

How many could I save?

The only thing I could deliver was death. Not hope, not healing. Just death—like those of my father and Atellus. Violent and painful.

How many fathers would I kill?

Half my life I'd been obsessed with revenge. There'd been no doubt in my mind—so sure Rusticus was responsible I'd been closed to all other possibilities. Now I would have to live with my mistake. And Atellus. And the men I'd ripped apart.

I exhaled sharply. *Breathe.* Think for once, before acting. I'd had eyes to see and hands to act—but I'd not been doing any thinking.

Find Cyclops. He'd lead to the person responsible. Then I could throw myself from the highest mountain if I wanted. Gods—if Fortune had Her way, maybe I'd survive that, too.

Returning to that moment again, when I'd seen the one-eyed man in the amphitheatre, I tried to recall every detail, pushing aside thoughts of Veneda; the chaos; the crowd.

He'd been on the podium, but wasn't a senator, so would have no reason to be there unless guarding someone else. I'd assumed that person was Rusticus, seated to his left. On his right there had been a mass of white, where some of the Vestals—

It couldn't be.

She wouldn't.

Lanata. But why would she have Father murdered? Or me and Agrippina? And how would she and Cyclops be connected? I shook my head—more questions. I wasn't good at this. My mind raced like a chariot around an endless track.

Think. I knew more about Father's death than before. Cyclops had given Father his blood, that's what caused the sores, the appearance of poison. It could have been an accident—perhaps Father managed to cut Cyclops and blood entered the wound on his throat. Or … Cyclops had given him the blood on purpose.

But what reason would he have? Father would never have escaped Cyclops's attack even without being poisoned. It only made sense if

Cyclops wanted to see if Father survived—if he could become immortal. But why would he care?

Your sister's fate hangs by a thread.

I'd thought he spoke of Agrippina, screaming from the villa. But what if he'd meant Lanata? That night on the beach, when he'd drunk from Sylos, Cyclops had drawn his sword on me. He didn't break my neck, or drain my blood. He was going to see if I could be changed. Because that might mean—

Lanata could be turned immortal.

If it was true the blood brought death to nearly everyone, perhaps Cyclops was hoping for a companion of his own. For signs that someone would survive. I had to speak with Marcus and learn if the change was common among relatives.

I rubbed my forehead. It still didn't explain why Lanata would kill our father. Is it possible she didn't even know what Cyclops was doing? If she did, it was too risky to confront her with Cyclops on the loose. If she didn't, I might cause the death of another innocent person by speaking against her without proof.

I needed help, but had no one to turn to.

Atellus was dead.

Marcus was heartless.

Rafa was … human.

I sat, deflated, perched on the temple roof. Sunlight inched above the horizon, breaking in ripples over the city, slowly filling every dark corner. Eudocia had been right: the sun had not yet set forever. The day began as it always did, with no concern for what happened in the night.

What can't be changed, must be endured.

A croak of laughter escaped me, scaring away the nearest birds. *Endurance.* I silently cursed philosophers, with their trite answers that explained nothing. I was beyond mere endurance now. And while it was possible I'd gone mad beyond repair, I was more than that, too.

I was powerful.

It was time to live another day, but this day was one for answers.

I knew who I had to visit.

Thirty-Eight

I DROPPED INTO THE ATRIUM of my domus—Quintus's domus.

Conscious of my grisly appearance, I took care no one noticed me on the way to the bath. My sodden dress clung like a second skin as I peeled it off and flung it into a corner. The pool was shaped like an inverted pyramid, steps leading down on all sides, and I let the warm water soothe my skin. As a child I'd had to swim if I went past the fourth step, but now I stood in the centre, the water below my shoulders.

Rubbing myself raw with the pumice stone, I scoured off the blood and flakes of black flesh that clung to my skin, my hair. Then I lay back, floating, immersed everywhere but my face. I sighed and shut my eyes. The rippling sensations along my skin eased. Sounds in my ears lessened. All that remained was the steady rhythm of my heart echoing back at me.

Then a shift in the air warned me I wasn't alone.

I stood to see Spiro holding a towel, a clean blue dress hung over one arm. He looked far older than he should have, the stubble on his shaved head a steely grey, bushy eyebrows speckled with white.

"I didn't believe Quintus at first, when he came to me with your amended will." It was the same voice I remembered, the one which would interject during father's stories, or argue with Eudocia. I should have known Quintus would go to Spiro. He needed more signatures for my will, signatures from people he trusted. Spiro averted his eyes and extended the towel as I left the water.

"Thank you." I reached for the towel slowly—slow for me, normal for him—and ignored the flash of instinct branding him as food. I was definitely not eating Spiro this morning.

"You could have come home." He passed me the dress.

I slipped on the dress, belting it around my hips, then took a pinch of fennel before tying Marcus's pouch to my belt. "Come home and done what? I'm a terrible weaver and my flute playing is dreadful—"

Spiro held up a hand. "I couldn't protect you," he said, almost more for himself than me. "I pray you never know a failure as complete as mine. I failed Lucius twice. And I knew you realized it too."

I rubbed my arms, fighting my response to the rise in his pulse, the anguish in his voice. "I was just a child, Spiro." But he was right. I'd felt he failed us. Today I understood his burden.

"Why have you returned?"

"Do you remember the man with one eye?"

He gave a slow nod. "Of course. Quintus had me searching the city for months."

"So Uncle believed me?"

"He did. But we couldn't find him."

"I saw him. Two days ago."

Spiro's eyes narrowed, calculating.

"I think, perhaps ..." Voicing this aloud would give it a power I couldn't retract, like my mistaken convictions about Rusticus. "I think Lanata might have sent him and his accomplice to kill us."

Spiro didn't appear surprised. "Your uncle suspected Lanata for a time, though I couldn't believe it. When she was nearly poisoned, we discounted her. What have you learned?"

"I saw them together. I thought Quintus might know some reason why Lanata would do this." *The simplest answer is usually correct.* Veneda sending Achilles to stop me from defeating her again; Themis grasping for Justa's wealth, kept away from her by Vitalis's careful planning. "I need to see Father's will. Does Quintus still have it?"

∞

It was so early Quintus hadn't been shaved, the growth of brown stubble thick on his face and neck. His pulse jumped below the skin. He surveyed my own unkempt appearance—red hair hanging loose and damp, dress belted inelegantly around my hips. I'd have to remember to take a shawl when I left.

I read the will, then passed it to Quintus for inspection, running over the implications.

"If either Agrippina or I died before we reached our majority," I said, "our portion of Father's estate would have been split by the remaining sisters, correct?"

Quintus nodded.

Lanata had been an adult when Father died, her share secure. But we'd been attacked fleeing Rome a month before Agrippina's twelfth birthday—if we'd died with Eudocia, Lanata would have taken it all. And if Hamitra hadn't saved me on the beach, my sisters would split my share. "Did Father tell her? How could she have known?"

Spiro rubbed his forehead with his knuckles, deeply upset. "He didn't have to tell her. Lucius was traditional. He left his will with the Vestals for safekeeping. If Lanata had wanted to read it, she certainly could have found the opportunity. But why would she do it?" Spiro asked, subdued. "She was already inheriting so much."

"Three times *much*," Quintus said thinly, "is *more*."

"Aunt Calpurnia implied she used her wealth to buy her position," I said. "What if she also murdered the former Vestalis Maxima? She could have made it look as though the poison was meant for her, to keep herself from suspicion." It was devious—the more I thought it through, the more certain I was of Lanata's guilt. But I couldn't be positive until I'd spoken to her.

I turned to leave.

"You have no proof," Quintus said. "If Lanata is as clever as you think, all she has to do is send this man away, and you have nothing."

He was right, but this wasn't about the law—this was justice.

"I'll be careful." I tried for demure. Quintus wasn't buying it.

"Spiro, leave us." Quintus nodded towards the door.

I stopped Spiro before he left and embraced him. I couldn't be careless with my goodbyes any longer. He gave me a melancholy smile, then closed the door.

"You've never liked me," Quintus said with a shadow of a grin. "I didn't like you either when we were children. But I'm not the same spoiled boy I was. I used to hate visiting Father, especially after you and Agrippina arrived. I began calling it the Villa of the Misfits." His tone was apologetic.

"I suppose it was," I admitted. An escape for Uncle, who couldn't bear the city. For Aunt, who refused to risk pursing another marriage. And for me.

Quintus's eyes became unfocused and he dropped into his chair. "I regret it. Vesuvius took everything from me. My father. My family. And more than that—it took away who I thought I was." The bitterness in his voice was unmistakable.

An unwanted surge of sympathy swept me. It was easier to think of him as my enemy. He'd never been that, though. Only ... family.

"You weren't there. You didn't see it, smell it—" I almost gagged, the memory of ash heavy in my lungs, and sat with a jerk in the opposite chair.

He cleared his throat. "Several of my friends also inherited their fortunes that day. At first I was like them. Shocked. Saddened. But also secretly, disgustingly, gleeful."

"So what happened?"

"You." His gaze was piercing. "You appeared like a spirit, and I saw in your eyes how everything had changed. You weren't just a rebellious child, trying to be difficult." I frowned, but he continued. "Your impulsiveness had been tempered. At first I thought you no longer cared about living, embarking on this life. Then I saw you fight."

"When?" I asked, surprised.

"The day you fought Achilles. I needed to be there." Quintus's simple statement was tinged with both duty and emotion. "I realized you fought not because you wanted to die, but because it made you feel alive." He stood abruptly, the chair scraping across the tile. "And I hated you more than ever! For weeks I'd been feeling lost, purposeless. I thought at last I could be my own man, and with the money—" He took a slow breath. "Now it all seemed meaningless. But you—you had nothing, yet had found yourself."

He resented saying it; I refused to consider how true it might be. "What of it?"

"I don't know what will happen to you, Lucilla, and I ..." Quintus walked to the brazier and used the iron poker to stab at the red coals. "Lanata came looking for you."

My head snapped up.

"Yesterday. She asked if I'd seen you since Vesuvius. I was curious why she would care, so worked on gaining her confidence. She's never liked you, or Agrippina, and it was easy to convince her I shared her resentment." A small smile appeared in his eyes, then they sobered. "I know you're right about her. But if it was gold that motivated her in the past, it's something else now. She wants you dead, Lucilla. Any way she can. No—not any way. She wants to see you suffer."

How much more suffering could she need? I clenched my fists. "Why warn me? Everything is easier for you if I'm truly dead." He wouldn't have to help Rafa; not have to worry I may come back some day to reclaim my inheritance.

"I had to. I can't be in your debt any longer."

"My debt? You mean … that day our boat sank?"

"Of course the boat!"

"But you never said anything!" We'd never spoken of it, even when Bricus had taken him to task that night in the grotto.

His agitation grew and he paced toward the door. "What could I say? I hated you, worried you would shame our family. But even after all the animosity between us, you saved my life. Now we're even."

"You didn't owe me for that, Quintus. There's no debt between family." I gave a small smile.

His lips twitched. "You should leave, Lucilla. There's nothing more for you here. We made our deal and I'll uphold my end. Leave before Lanata decides to act against you."

But she already had, and I wouldn't let her defeat me. I stood. "You won't hear from me again."

"You said that last time," he couldn't quite hide his frustration.

"I can't come back, now."

We surveyed each other for a moment. The scent of oil reeked from his tousled hair, and he reached up, like always, to self-consciously pat the errant curl above his ear. But he was far different from the boy who tormented me in my thoughts. I'd have to fix this Quintus in my mind instead, though he wouldn't like to be remembered so untidily.

He extended his hand. "Good journey."

I shook it, gently. "Health and prosperity to your family, Quintus Calpurnius Piso."

∞

I remembered a shawl. Drawing it over my face and hair I took to the street, walking without purpose. I wanted to confront Lanata, but she'd proven how clever she was, always one step ahead. It would have been easy for her to bribe Lurco into matching me against Veneda right after I'd fought Achilles. Achilles … the fight with him was a trap I'd been too willing to enter. She'd tried to recruit Quintus to her cause, had Cyclops searching for me, and though I could easily kill her, I had to know why she'd done this to our family. Without a plan of my own, I'd be at her mercy again.

But first, I needed rest. I'd had no sleep since my *change*, as Marcus put it, and was bone-weary. After last night, I didn't know if the ludus would be safe. But where else could I go?

I could go anywhere. Survive anything. Eat anyone.

A laugh bubbled up, but it sounded strange, strangled.

"That's how I knew you were right for this life," Marcus said from behind, making me jolt and chastise myself for not being more aware — it could have been Cyclops.

"What? My obvious insanity?"

"You smile at inappropriate times. It's a good sign." He fell into step with me. "I knew it when you laughed on the ship, after I told you Lucilla was dead."

"She should be dead."

"I was wrong."

"I know."

"Stop being difficult." Marcus stepped into the alcove of a boarded up doorway and I followed with a sigh. "Lucilla is not dead. You'll regret it if you don't let her finish her life. You'll never be this person again." There was a note of longing in his voice, and I knew he was thinking of whoever he'd once been, in the beginning. "After a few centuries, you won't even be able to explain her actions. She'll be a life from a story, not your own."

I wanted to argue, but whether or not it would be true for me, it was true for him. "Marcus, I can't trust you. Atellus's death proved that."

"It proved nothing," he snapped. With a quick glance to see if we were unobserved, Marcus cracked a board off the entrance and ushered me inside, following me down a musty corridor and into a small atrium. Tendrils of vines ran wild up the crumbling plaster of a dozen columns, twining to nest over the open roof. Sunlight shone through in scattered patches.

"Blame me for Atellus. Blame me for the noxii you killed," Marcus said, and I turned from the light to face him. He was sincere, as though I could wash away the memories as I'd washed the blood from my mouth.

"I do blame you! There was no need for you to kill him."

"He would have betrayed us. I'll do the same as often as it takes to keep us safe. There have been thousands of men like him, and will be thousands more."

"No. There won't."

Marcus glared, face set in hard lines. "Humans will always betray me—us. Always."

He was certain, as though certainty made him right. Atellus had paid the price for that belief. Just as Rusticus had paid the price for my convictions. I couldn't dwell on this now. I needed answers. "Why didn't you tell me our blood was poison? Why make me believe it could heal him?"

"It was possible, just unlikely. You had to learn what we are."

"It was how my father died." I tried and failed to keep the grief from my voice.

His eyes searched mine, brows snapping together in a deep scowl. "You said your father was poisoned."

"I didn't know it was immortal blood!"

"You should have trusted me to help you."

"Trust you?" My amazement echoed around the dank room. I stepped closer, the words escaping through gritted teeth. "You've manipulated me time and again for your own benefit. Threatened my friends. Killed someone I cared for—"

"I saved you." His pointed finger was inches from my face. "Kept you from breaking under adversity. Prepared you for a life beyond any human aspirations. No man could have done more."

"And I'm in your debt." My admission brought an infuriating flash of satisfaction to his eyes. "But once I've paid it there's nothing more between us."

Marcus pulled me against him, threading a hand through my hair as he kissed me with a rough urgency. No pretense. No practiced seduction.

He broke away, staring at me defiantly. "Nothing?"

I punched him in the stomach with my right fist; when he doubled over, my left to his chin sent him sprawling.

"I'm not your plaything," I snarled. He'd toyed with me; toyed with Atellus, all while planning to kill him. One honest moment would never atone for the anguish he'd caused.

By the time Marcus gained his feet, the bruise on his face had already bloomed and faded. "*Fene,*" he cursed. "I don't wish to be your enemy." His voice was thick with an accent I'd never heard.

"Then stop treating me like one." Holding my arms rigid at my sides, I tried to smother the resentment burning though me.

Marcus paced the atrium like a caged lion, his steps cracking the decrepit mosaic of black and white tiles. "I've never met a woman I couldn't reason with. Or seduce."

"Or intimidate?"

"Intimidation works on reasonable people."

"I'm not sympathetic."

"Then how about the truth? As soon as I saw you fight Veneda, this was your fate," he said, the confession reluctant. "Yes, I manipulated. Spied. Did everything I could to keep you alive, and keep you near, until I had no choice but to act." Marcus ran a hand through his hair, face drawn. "I'd like to say I regret not giving you a choice in the matter, but I don't regret it."

Reaching into a pouch on his belt, he withdrew something. He opened his palm to reveal two rings, one gold, one silver.

I stared at them, baffled. They looked like my rings. But those had been in my room on the night —

"How did you get these?" My voice trembled and I snatched the rings from his hand. Golden ram, inscribed *to the very end*; silver griffin, symbol of Nemesis. I thought they'd been long lost.

"You had them on a cord around your neck, the day you fought Veneda in Pompeii. The night before we left I came to … persuade you to come with me."

"So you stole my property? That's not flattering," I said bitterly.

He rubbed his neck. "You accused me once of testing you."

"I remember."

"You were right."

"I could get used to you saying that."

His half-smile appeared. "I had to test you. These bodies of ours — they're easy to keep alive. But it's not an easy life to live. It never will be. If I'd known about Achilles before he attacked you, I would have spared you that. But I can't be everywhere at once."

I stared at the rings, cupped in my hands. "I've never counted on you to protect me."

Marcus gestured to the rings. "Try them."

"They're too big." Looking at them again, I saw seams where they'd been altered. They fit on my tallest fingers—one on each hand.

I stared at the rings, resized; at my hands, now free of scars, skin pale and unmarked. I clenched my fists.

I didn't know Marcus. Had never known him. I'd only known the parts he needed me to see. More troubling was the worry that I no longer knew myself. Was I Lucilla, Vesuvia, or someone new? Whatever the answer, it would have to wait. I must reach Lanata before she moved against me again. But I couldn't do it alone.

Crossing my arms, I forced the words out. "I was wrong about Rusticus. It seems my half-sister Lanata was behind it from the beginning. My cousin all but confirmed it."

"I could kill her today, though if Cyclops is with her, it may be impossible without an unwanted spectacle."

I shook my head. "She must confess. I can't do to family what I did to Rusticus," I said, disgusted.

"There's no sense acting before we have a chance to plan. I'll get you back into the ludus. Rest. Or would you rather feed again to regain some strength?"

"No." I wanted to say *never again*, but knew it would be pointless.

"Come," he said. "While everyone is still distracted by the lions."

∞

Marcus waited until I was through his window before making his way in by the gate. He entered a short while later carrying a small wood-framed tablet, its wax inset only large enough for a few lines. "A message. Left for you."

I took it from him, reading the careful lettering. "'Jupiter's temple during the sacrifice.' It must be from Lanata."

"You know it's a trap," he said.

"I've been in far too many to expect it's anything else." My tone was laced with accusation.

"It's not my fault you're so easy to manipulate."

"But what's her plan? If she wanted to have Cyclops kill me, it would be easier to send him tonight. Why meet first?"

"You forget, I'm here. I've warned him from my territory."

I gave him an obvious once-over. "I'm sure he was terrified." I rubbed my face, fatigue setting in, but no time to rest. "The sacrifice is mid-day, and will stretch until evening. Lanata is part of the ceremony, so why would she want me to come before the end?"

"Does it matter? She doesn't know what you've become. And she doesn't realize you have an ally stronger than hers." His lips stretched into a smug smile. "Her plan won't work."

"So we're allies, are we?"

"Now that I've gotten what I wanted from our bargain."

And I've gotten far more than I'd bargained for. I frowned. "Then I'll be confident you won't let Cyclops ambush me."

He walked to a corner of the room, removing a floorboard under a cupboard to reveal a cache of weapons—our weapons. "I'll scout the area. If he nears, I'll be sure he doesn't surprise you, and dispatch him if I can without a spectacle." He passed my sheathed knife.

I wrapped my fingers around the familiar hilt, not bothering to ask when or how he retrieved it from the armoury. "After all this time, it seems wrong to let you kill him for me."

"I won't, if you'd rather hunt him yourself."

"Actually, I'd rather you not put yourself in danger." I smiled at his look of surprise. "I'd like to be certain of his death—going against him one at a time doesn't seem the best way to do that." He'd moved my belongings to his room and I quickly changed from the blue dress into a short tunic.

"You don't think I'm equal to the task?" Marcus buckled on a sword belt, expression unreadable.

"I've seen Hamitra fight unchecked, but not you. Maybe she's better." I ignored his grunt of annoyance and strapped the knife to my thigh. "Kill him if you think it's the right course, but otherwise, wait. Unless you have some secret talent you've not told me about—is there more about what we are that you're hiding?"

"Nothing relevant." He raised his hands at my attempted protest. "Nothing that isn't better spoken of tomorrow. I'm more concerned you'll do something foolish if Cyclops crosses your path. If you do, it'll be your skill against his. Feed if you need more strength—especially if you've been injured. But remember, you can't expose what we are."

"I have no intention to. I only need answers from my sister."

Marcus's eyebrows snapped lower. "Your oath. I need your oath you won't expose us unless you have no other choice."

I sighed. "Very well, what gods would you have me swear to?"

"No gods. Just your word." He extended a hand.

I clasped it. "Then you have my word. Now, help me with these sheaths would you?" With some difficulty, and more adjusting around my chest than seemed necessary, Marcus helped buckle the sword sheaths so they lay down the back of my tunic. I slipped the blue dress overtop, then braided my hair and pinned it in a crown around my head. "I can't sit here all day, wondering what she's planning. Waiting for the next disaster. Maybe I can get her alone before the ceremony starts."

He nodded. "I'll follow, but don't look for me."

The hilts of the swords rested within reach—and view—at the base of my neck. I snatched up a blue shawl to drape over my head and shoulders. Stepping up on the window ledge, I surveyed the narrow alley a storey below. A woman was pushing a handcart of vegetables toward the intersection. Once she turned, the way would be clear.

"Allies, right?"

"Trust me," he said.

I snorted. *Why did this feel like a colossal error?*

The woman with the cart turned. I dropped.

THIRTY-NINE

THE PROCESSION ENTERED AT NOON through the bronze gate of the Capitoline Hill, leading a white ram for Jupiter.

Cymbals rang out as the lesser priests approached the pontiffs, arranged in front of the altar at the wide base of the temple's stairs. The High Priest of Jupiter, in his white toga with broad purple boarder, stood in the middle. Domitian on his right, clothed all in purple, seemed pleased to be standing in the Emperor's place. To the left of the High Priest was Lanata, her white dress and veil gleaming in the sunlight.

I'd observed from a distance all morning while she performed her daily rituals in Vesta's temple. Marcus's words a constant irritation, like a fly around my head: *You can't expose what we are.* So I'd waited as Vestals in white gowns and shawls floated in and out on errands. Slaves and guards seemed to number in the hundreds. Inside, my sister, mistress of them all, attended to each task with infuriating serenity.

It should have been easy to catch her alone; to force her to confess. But if she didn't, what then? Torture? Could I stoop so low? The idea turned my stomach in more ways than one. With torture, there'd be blood. After last night, I knew I didn't have the strength to resist.

Several dozen people had come for today's ritual. Guards herded us to one side of the shallow pool in the centre of the courtyard. My frustration had burned hotter with each passing hour. Vesuvia would never stand for this. She would kill Lanata and be done with it.

My feet jerked forwards.

Stop. You can't expose what we are.

That was Marcus's rule. It didn't have to be mine.

Hamitra's rule, too, to guard a dangerous secret. And I need answers more than blood.

Answers. I needed Lanata for answers. Cyclops too—or I'd never know why he spared me. That question had festered throughout my childhood; a riddle that deepened now I fully understood what he was. I scanned the citadel for any sign of him, edging my way toward the outside of the crowd for a better view. The Temple of Jupiter was on my left, doors standing open. Other temples walled the courtyard, their deep porches and wide columns offering plenty of places to hide, but couldn't make out any sign of him. No sign of Marcus either.

I swallowed against a sudden doubt. What if Cyclops had been watching the ludus the whole time? I'd never know if Marcus had been killed. Surely Cyclops was no match for him. Gods damn Lanata and her scheming—it was me who wasn't equal to this kind of task.

Cymbals rang out again. The High Priest began the ritual.

And, as though conjured by the sound, a slave approached me. He bowed and handed me a small wooden box, then twisted his way out through the crowd.

I stared at the box, dumbfounded, and a tremor ran through me. The scent was unmistakable. My hand shook as I opened the lid, dreading what I'd find inside.

A finger, stained with ink and blood.

And a note.

Wait, or more will follow.

A haze spread over my vision and I crumpled the parchment in my fist. *Breathe ... just breathe.*

But every breath cut to my core, infused with Rafa's scent. The same scent from a thousand days together, amplified by my new senses, and tainted by his blood. A molten river burned my veins.

My eyes snapped to the altar, to my sister. Her smile was tight as she met my gaze.

Guilty. Guilty as Achilles, as Veneda. Drain her and be done.

I made an oath. I can't expose what we are.

Gods below, I shouldn't have let Marcus bind my actions. Lanata had broken all the laws of gods and men. Why shouldn't I do the same?

I need Rafa alive.

Merda. I twisted the silver ring again and again around my finger.

With a hollow thud, one of the sacrificers felled the ram. The animal made no noise of protest. Wet sounds of butchery filled the courtyard as the ram was slit open, neck to groin, the same sounds as when I'd torn apart the noxii last night.

My arms and legs trembled from the effort of remaining still — of doing nothing while knowing I had the power to rend Lanata's limbs from her body. The High Priest took his time, prodding at the heart and lungs before declaring the sacrifice accepted by the god. Then the organs were spitted and placed over a hearth by the altar to cook.

The sun was past its height, shining in a cloudless sky — it would be hours until the end of the ceremonial banquet. My shawl and extra tunic wrapped me in heat. Beads of sweat gathered in my hair. Bodies seemed to close in around me from all directions, shifting and coughing and stinking, their heartbeats a riot along my skin.

Smoke rose in wispy tendrils. I cast my eyes about, desperate for a distraction from the scents of flesh and blood and food. Domitian brought his hand up to stifle a yawn. The High Priest ran his fingers along the edge of his felted cap. My gaze locked with Lanata's again, and when she suppressed a smile by sucking on her lip, I knew she enjoyed every moment of my helplessness.

Where would she have hidden Rafa? With Cyclops? Is that why he's not here?

I shouldn't have trusted Marcus ... her plan would fail? We'd never truly considered what it was. I'd counted on strength, when time and again Lanata had proven her cunning. *Why did every choice end up the wrong one?* Perspiration itched down my head and neck.

The burnt offerings turned to ash at last. The High Priest knelt and placed his weathered hand on the red-flecked fleece of the ram, returning it to us from Jupiter. Taking up fresh tools, the sacrificers butchered the carcass in a torment of fresh scents.

Couches were placed in front of the temple for the banquet. The pontiffs and dignitaries moved to recline under awnings held by slaves, fanned by large palm branches. Sweat trickled down my back.

The ram was spitted and placed on the hearth to roast. Some of the crowd left for their own dinners. Domitian entertained the pontiffs with a story of how he once escaped Vitellius's forces by barricading himself and his supporters here, on the Capitoline Hill. Lanata nibbled at the ram, dabbing at her mouth between bites as they dined. I swallowed, trying to stifle the heat burning my throat.

The sun crept lower, inching behind the temple next to me, each degree painfully obvious. At long last I was covered in shade.

Cymbals and horns sounded. The pontiffs rose and the crowd dispersed across the courtyard, finally allowed to collect the parts of the ram that hadn't been offered or eaten.

Limbs rigid, I approached Lanata. Around her, slaves tidied what was left of the feast, collecting plates, returning furniture and awnings to wherever they were hidden between holy days. A few lictors remained to protect the pontiffs, and Praetorians to protect Domitian. Guards posted on the Hill changed their positions for the evening watch.

Lanata nodded to her lictors, who joined the departing dignitaries. She crossed her hands in front of her and eyed me with smug satisfaction.

"So, you can control yourself after all." Dimples flashed with her small smile.

Domitian glanced over at the sound of her voice, eyes flickering with recognition as he noticed me. "Will you be joining us, Vestalis?"

Lanata adjusted her shoulders, surprised by his presence behind her. The emperor's brother wasn't a complication either of us needed. "Once I have completed some outstanding duties." Her tone was light, as if I was a matter of no importance.

Domitian considered us, then inclined his head in farewell. As the thundering steps of his Praetorian escort faded down the stairs to the gate, Lanata turned back, her shoulders straight.

She smiled down at the box I still held. "I couldn't believe when Quintus told me you cared for that slave. But apparently he was right."

I placed the box on the altar beside us, taking a deep breath. "Release Rafa at once."

"You know he's well looked after. I think I'll keep him awhile."

"For what purpose?"

Lanata sighed, as though laying off a heavy burden. "You've always been a selfish child. Father allowed you too many freedoms — something Uncle failed to correct. I'm done enduring such disgrace."

"And you think to humble me?" I choked out a laugh, and her eyes sparked with anger. "You're worried about *your* honour?"

Her nostrils flared. "Not just mine. You risk the honour of our entire family, past and future —"

"Is that why you killed Father?" Her face grew pale at my accusation, but I was in no mood for games. "He would never have dishonoured the family."

Lanata let out a harsh cackle. "No? He was about to marry that whore Junilla. She'd already been fucked by half the Senate. She'd have made Father a laughingstock. Spent our fortune without a thought."

"Ah," I said with a grimace. "Our fortune. But why would you need it? You never have to give up your position with the Vestals."

"Would you be tied to such a Fate? After my vows are over should I be content to dwindle and die without a life of my own?"

"You can't blame Father —"

"Why not? Mother sacrificed her independence just to be loved, and he threw her away at the first sign of discord. He would have done the same to your mother, too, if she hadn't died. And if Junilla wasted our fortune, he would have happily left us with nothing. He was fickle. Faithless." Her expression thinned, eyes tightening with long-suppressed sorrow.

For a moment I glimpsed the child she must have been, resentful at being sent to the Vestals; betrayed when Father married my mother after the sudden divorce of hers. "But murder?"

"What would you have done? Mother was broken. No longer honoured as a Vestal. No longer respected as she had been. That would not be my future."

"Broken pride doesn't deserve death."

"Achilles will be comforted by that."

I gritted my teeth. "It's not the same."

"Isn't it?"

"So taking our lives was going to set you free?"

Her dark eyes glittered. "The money would. As Vestalis Maxima I could do as I pleased. Under no one's command but the Emperor." Lanata pressed her lips together, face cold as marble. "My champion failed to secure your fortunes for me, with his stubborn insistence on the Lady's *signs* — as if he knew Her better than I did. But at least he used that poison on the Vestalis. Maybe your friend would like a taste?"

I let out a breath. *She doesn't know. Cyclops may do her bidding, but he hasn't shared his secret.* I shifted my stance, comforted by the press of sheaths on my back. "Do you think I'd let you go free, now that I know all you've done?"

Her light laugh made the hair on my arms quiver. "You think to kill me. You can't shed the blood of a Vestal without violating sacred law. And if you try, my champion will ensure your friend dies tonight."

"You murdered our father," I said, revolted by her cool manner. "You murdered the Vestalis who came before you. It's you who have broken the laws of nature." Every death I'd caused was etched upon my conscience, but she dismissed my accusations like someone tossing a pebble from their shoe.

Pulse thundering in my ears, I almost missed the sound I'd been yearning for. The thrum of a racing heartbeat.

Cyclops approached from the direction of the gate.

Thank you, gods above.

I glanced over the courtyard, temples casting long shadows in the waning light. No guards in the open. Slaves had finished lighting the lamps and torches. No one left but us.

Anticipation sparked in me.

Lanata had followed my gaze, face flushed with victory as the one-eyed man took his place at her side. "You thought yourself free to do whatever foolish thing popped into your head—but no more. You'll return to the ludus and if, by some miracle, you manage to defeat your next few opponents, you'll face my champion."

His green eye fixed on me—it narrowed, but the lidless, hollow socket of his missing eye didn't. His nostrils twitched and an intrigued comprehension broke over his face.

"We've met before," I said to Cyclops. "But I don't know your name."

"I gave it up, long ago." His voice was as I remembered. Slow. Practiced.

"Where's my friend?"

"He lives for now. I was sure you would come for him, but now I see why you did not."

Marcus hadn't warned me—he was either dead, or he'd better be saving Rafa somehow. Otherwise I'd hunt his treacherous hide to the end of the world. *If I survive.*

Cyclops rested his hands on the hilts of his sword and dagger, cocking his head as though considering what my altered state meant.

"I have long been a servant of Lady Vesta. Now you will serve too."

"You're a lousy servant," I taunted. "You failed to kill two small girls. Twice."

"Do not mock me, young one. Warnings of the gods must be obeyed. To rush is the slowest way to ruin … and it is as I had hoped." He glanced at Lanata, and in that instant I knew he hoped to change my sister.

"The question is," I said, "can you save her before I kill her?"

Lanata stared at each of us in turn, brows snapping together in a sharp frown. "What is she talking about?"

"She doesn't know, does she?" I asked Cyclops. "She thinks you failed—but you wanted to be as certain as you could that it would work. Why choose me?"

"It failed with her father, and I thought all was lost. Then I saw your eyes," he said, lips pulling apart, not quite a smile. "Like mine. Like hers. Vesta would not torment me with such a coincidence."

His remaining eye spiraled in three deepening greens. Lanata's eyes, wide with confusion, were three shades of brown. And I'd inherited my father's—yellow, green, brown. Apparently they'd saved my life, at least until Lanata had forced him to attack again.

Lanata pounded her fist on the altar. "Tell me what this is about!"

"I'm not waiting to fight your champion." I dropped my veil and drew my blades.

Cyclops drew his sword, faster than human.

Lanata gasped and stepped backward, banging into the altar.

"What is this?" her voice was panicked.

"Nemesis has taken exception to Vesta's meddling," I said.

Cyclops nodded once, the merest jerk of his head. "The goddess knows I am faithful. She spared my life. The sacred fire cleansed me of my weaknesses."

I looked him over. "You really believe that?"

"Why else would I be as I am? We are the chosen of the gods." His voice rang out, proud, and his sincerity made me wonder if delusion was a requirement for immortals.

Cyclops took a slow step to his right in an effort to shield Lanata. His face tightened, gaze uneasy as he flicked his eye over each of my swords. He'd seen me fight as a mortal; seen me in the amphitheatre. Taking another slow step, his left hand eased his dagger from its sheath.

I grimaced. This man haunted my thoughts for years but, for all my plans, if I'd found him two days ago it would have meant my death. He'd have made the countless hours of sweat and toil I endured fail within moments. I'd had no time to practice since the change, but Petrus' lessons held true. My body knew how to react. And today, I may be strong enough.

Cyclops came at me. Our blades rang out in the courtyard, sharp-pitched. Lanata found enough sense to flee around the altar and up the stairs to the temple's porch, calling out for help.

I pressed him back on his left, where his dagger offered less protection. He kicked out at the hearth, toppling it over and scattering burning coals. I leapt toward the stairs after Lanata, but Cyclops kicked out again and caught me mid-air, knocking the breath from my lungs. I fell hard to the pavement.

A gust of air was my only warning and I rolled before he could land—his dagger plunged between the cobbles where my head had been. With a grunt, I swung my knee up and sent him sprawling. We rolled away from each other, gaining our feet.

I spared a look for Lanata. She was pointing at me, yelling at guards who had come running from the gate.

Cyclops faced me with a snarl, teeth exposed, all pretense gone. Our blades clashed again, clanging in a fiery staccato. Six guards—no, ten—stood poised to attack. But instead of joining the fight, they stared. Some fell to their knees, begging Jupiter to intercede. I knew what they saw—we fought too fast to be believed.

We reached the temple stairs again. Lanata flung a lantern, apparently not caring who she hit. It streaked between us, shattering against an ambitious guard who'd approached at last. Drenched with burning oil, he screamed. Cyclops ran for him. For a heartbeat I thought he meant to throw him into the shallow pool. Instead, he flung him over the wall fortifying the back of the Hill. I shouldn't have been surprised.

"Are you mad?" I yelled. "You'll set the Field of Mars on fire!" Buildings clustered all the way up that side of the Hill. The image of fire spreading through the Field's dilapidated apartments sickened me.

"We are not here to protect humanity, young one." His green eye blazed with fervor. "We are the hands that cull the herd. It is only the gods we must obey."

For a horrible moment, his absolute conviction swayed me. *If the gods made us this way, who was I to scorn it?*

Then, like a hound on a hunt, he brought down a guard who'd raced for the gate. Cyclops sank his teeth into the man's neck and drank in sickening gulps. *He means to kill them all.* It didn't help knowing Marcus would agree.

I hesitated, torn between wanting to save the guards from his unrestrained madness or reaching Lanata at last. She stood on the temple porch, forgetting me as she gazed, rapt, at Cyclops.

Merda.

I sprinted towards the guards.

"Run, fools! Unless you're ready to be dinner." I pointed a sword in the direction of the gate as I ran for Cyclops. He raised his head, mouth covered in gore, the man in his arms gasping. The handful of guards nearest me began backing away, making for safety.

Cyclops had dropped his swords, but was holding the guard's body in front of his own. In a heroic last effort, the dying guard stabbed backward with his dagger into Cyclops's stomach. I attacked, blades raised, but Cyclops recovered from his surprise, moving even faster than before. He dropped the guard and gripped my forearms, using my momentum to heave me through the air.

I smashed against one of the temple's columns, pain lancing through my ribs. A blur came streaking toward me and I ducked in time to avoid a marble statue. It shattered into a column behind me. With a grinding groan, segments of the stacked column broke free. A torrent of plaster and marble crashed down as I scrambled away, throwing up my arms to protect my head. Bones cracked and I cried out—but had no time to consider the pain. He was on me. Dodging behind another column, I avoided his fist. And then I was healed.

His longer reach got the better of me and he sent me tumbling down the stairs, knocking aside a cluster of guards.

I rolled—and found swords thrust into my hands by a soft-faced boy whose armour looked a size too big.

"Thanks," I said, between laboured breaths. "Now go." I shoved him away and heard his footsteps make for the gate.

I adjusted my grip on my swords, waiting as Cyclops approached, armed again. The remaining guards lay in broken heaps on the stairs behind him.

Letting him attack, I countered, and observed. He used his size to his advantage, thundering blows as though trying to pound me into the earth. But others had tried the same. I shifted low and his momentum on the next swing forced him off-balance. Sliding to my knees I thrust up with one blade through his ribs; then I was behind him. I slashed his leg before he could turn, cutting it off below the knee. He went down and tried to roll away.

He made it back onto his knees but I was there to meet him, swords crossed at his neck, blades biting into the skin.

My breaths rasped loud in my ears. Cyclops grimaced in pain, gasping unevenly.

"Perhaps I mistook the will of the goddess." He swallowed against the press of steel. "Perhaps She wanted me to find you, instead of kill you."

"Are you offering me something?" My arms ached to close the blades, but I stared into his dark gaze, hesitating.

"Our coming together is not a mistake. It is no coincidence that a child I allowed to survive became blessed as I am."

The gods damn him and his blessings. "You—and Lanata—cursed my childhood. Cursed me to a lifetime of being that girl, helpless and afraid."

"But you are no longer her. You have the same power as I. That is no curse." He regarded me steadily, conviction unwavering. "Let us change your sister. We will be unstoppable."

I laughed, angry. "To murder? To feed off humanity? Is that what the gods want for us?"

"My death will not redeem you." His eye blazed orange in the firelight. "If you deny what you are, you will never have peace."

"Then I don't choose peace."

I scissored the blades.

His head landed at my feet; body fell backward with a splash into the shallow pool. Breathing deep, I waited to be sure his heart stopped beating. Silence. Only the crackling of fire remained.

I searched the ruins of the courtyard for Lanata. She was gone from the porch, but I knew where she'd be hiding. I strode toward the Temple of Jupiter.

FORTY

SMALL FIRES BURNED where coal and oil had spilled in the courtyard and along the porch. Bright curtains, torn from their brackets and trapped under rubble, rippled as the wind rose. To my left, a dark cloud was underlit by an orange glow—fire had spread down the Hill. I hadn't been able to control Cyclops's actions, and now I wouldn't be able to control the blaze. Guilt burned through me and I kicked aside the arm of a statue from my path up the stairs.

My feet froze. I stood next to a guard, his neck bent at an unnatural angle. Still warm.

Already dead ...

My hands clenched around my sword hilts. I swallowed hard.

He died trying to stop Cyclops. The guard may have only delayed him for a heartbeat, but that was all it took. I was in his debt.

I sprinted up the stairs to the ruined porch.

Barely pausing, I considered the three sets of massive wooden double-doors muting the rapid heartbeats of those within. The largest set, in the centre, marked the entrance to the cella of Jupiter; to the left, of Juno; to the right, of Minerva. Father, Mother, Daughter.

I opened the centre doors. Whimpering came from behind the statue of Jupiter at the end of the room. I tugged back the god's robes. A frightened slave cowered on the floor.

I sheathed one sword and hauled him to his feet. "Where is she?"

"M-M-Minerva." He'd barely squeaked out the word when I pushed him toward the door.

"Run." His frightened heartbeat called to me and I could scarce restrain myself from following.

Back through the crumbled remains of the porch, I turned and threw open the doors to the cella of Minerva. Lanata stood before the statue of the helmeted goddess. A slave trembled in front of her, protecting her with his body. His thinning hair was flecked with silver in the lamplight. Pulse fluttered under his leathery skin, pulled taught over a bony frame.

Quick as lightning, thirst claimed me; teeth poised at his neck.

Stop!

Lanata's face, so much like Agrippina's, had frozen in shock, gaze riveted on us.

My throat burned—the merest pressure of my teeth promised release from the torment.

This isn't how it's supposed to be.

I dropped the man and he skittered out the door, footsteps crunching in the rubble as he dashed down the stairs. I was inches from Lanata. From vengeance for Father. For Eudocia, who gave her life to save us. Yet that had all been stripped away, leaving only the mindless drive for blood. If I moved, I would drink.

How do you control your enemy, when your enemy lies within?

Am I the lamp, or am I the light?

The girl I'd been surfaced, as terrified as the day Eudocia died, clutching the dagger that meant the difference between life and death. But this time she wasn't weak; wasn't crippled by failure. Instead she was the girl who made vows beyond her years. Who rolled in chicken shit with a runaway. Boarded a ship of death with an exile. Who would always remember her sister dressed for her wedding—a vision in gold and emerald, smelling of roses and smiling as though her heart would burst.

If I drank now, she'd burn. I'd become Vesuvia in truth—living only for the kill. For the moment of victory. Vesuvia had cost my humanity. Could I survive losing Lucilla too?

I won't drink. But I couldn't stop from licking my lips.

Lanata's eyes widened.

"I have a dilemma, sister." I took shallow gasps through my mouth in an effort to stop the scent; focused on the crackle of the burning fires to mute her heartbeat.

"I can't imagine," she drawled sarcastically.

"I've wanted to kill father's murderer for a very long time. But I never imagined it would be someone of my blood."

"And that's a dilemma because …?"

"You see what I've become. If I feed from you as an animal, I'll be no better than one." My voice was ragged, lungs burning for a deep breath.

"I won't make my death easy for you, Lucilla."

I choked back a laugh. "You misunderstand. Killing you *will* be easy. But I can't have the taste of you on my tongue for eternity." Of their own volition my lips parted, teeth bared. I was failing; the thirst was winning.

Her face remained calm, but her fear was obvious in the ripple of her gown; the quiver of ribbons in her disheveled hair. Lanata glanced toward the door. "He told me he was a servant of Vesta and I knew he was gifted. But you think he wanted to …" she paused, biting on her lip and eyeing me with a glint. "To give me this gift?"

"He must have thought you were worthy. I wonder how he got that idea?" I didn't bother to hide my contempt.

Her lips twisted into a sly smile. "When I first came to the house of the Vestals, he was nearly invisible, serving from the shadows as he saw fit. But he saw how devout I was. Knew I had Vesta's favour. That I was *more* than the rest of them."

I saw her hope … and how to control her. If only I could control myself. "You don't understand yet what the gift means. Not just speed. Not just power …"

Lanata's heart beat faster.

I glanced up at the statue of Minerva behind Lanata and let go of all my turmoil. Infused my voice with wonder. "Immortality."

Her poise slipped, mouth falling open with naked longing. "How?" she whispered.

"It's in our blood. Father wasn't worthy of it." I hated saying the words, though they were the ones she wanted to hear.

She nodded, solemn, and I could see her mind working furiously. "But you lived."

"After all you've done to me, you expect me to give you a chance at eternal life?"

"You said it yourself, you don't want to kill me like an animal." She glanced at the sword I still held. Father's sword. "You wouldn't dishonour Father by using his sword on his own daughter. And you can't shed my blood without incurring the wrath of the gods. But if my death is by my choice, you won't be to blame."

I kept my face still as the statue in front of me. It was risky; perhaps as risky as the flip of a coin. Marcus, had better be right about the odds. I couldn't stand here any longer without giving in and draining her dry.

I dropped Father's sword, not willing to taint it further. Taking the knife strapped to my thigh, I ran the blade across my wrist. "Drink it," I hissed.

Lanata wrinkled her nose, but put her mouth to the wound before it healed over. When she came away, her lips were reddened. She took a cautious breath. Her heartbeat rose.

"What should it feel like?" she asked.

"Fire."

"I don't feel any—" She clutched her stomach. Expression contorted with pain, she fell to her knees and a flushed glow spread across her skin. She collapsed to the mosaic floor, writhing in a nest of sparkling scales—Medusa's serpentine hair twining around her.

Minerva loomed over us and I cursed her inconstancy. She'd turned Medusa into a hideous monstrosity for being raped by Poseidon in her sanctuary. But Lanata—who'd betrayed all the bonds of honour, blood, and decency—would be granted immortal life?

"No," I whispered.

Heat radiated from Lanata's body and she began to screech—an eerie ballad of pain. Blossoming sores broke open. Blood stained her white dress, flowing onto the floor. I watched her body decay from the inside out. The echoes of her shrieks attacked from wall and ceiling and floor, filling my ears and raking along my skin. Until at last they faded. Her body stopped fighting; her breathing slowed.

Lanata's heartbeat faded, surged, then beat no more.

I could breathe.

Her body lay sprawled, slick with fluids. I wasn't about to carry her away, yet Domitian had seen us—knew who I was. There were already guards and slaves who might talk of what they'd seen tonight. I didn't care for them, though Marcus would. But giving the Emperor's brother more information than necessary would be a mistake.

I reclaimed Father's sword. Taking a torch from the wall, I set Lanata's dress on fire. Then the hangings, the offerings on the altar, anything that would burn. Flames climbed to the wooden timbers of the roof.

I closed the door as I left, ignoring a stab of guilt at burning the sanctuary—it had just been rebuilt from its destruction a decade ago, when Vespasian's forces had taken the capital. Jupiter hadn't punished the Emperor for that, and I hoped he'd overlook this now.

The Vestalis deserved a noble pyre, after all.

∞

Three figures moved in the courtyard. Relief flooded me as I recognized them.

Rafa looked me up and down as we met at the bottom of the broken stairs, his right eye swollen shut. He reached for it when he saw me staring.

I caught his wrist, examining the blood-soaked bandage over the knuckle of his lost first finger. "You paid a high price for friendship."

He stared at my hand, frowning, and I released him quickly.

"Friendship is paying each other's debts." He gave me a sad smile. "As you've done for me."

I gestured to his eye. "Fight your way free?" I asked, awkwardly trying to bridge the chasm between us.

"Me? From the Carcer?" he scoffed.

My face twisted with disgust. "She put you with the condemned criminals?"

"I thought I'd lose more than my finger." Rafa looked down at his maimed hand, anger spicing the air.

"That man … he did Lanata's bidding. Or rather what he thought was Vesta's bidding."

Rafa nodded. "Once he left, Marcus got me out. I was in the lowest level and I didn't know if I was strong enough to make it past the guards." Rafa glanced over his shoulder at Marcus, busy moving bodies into a pile, and cleared his throat. "But there wasn't anyone left to fight against. Actually, it looked a lot like here." Despite his attempt at humour, I heard a tremor of fear. Rafa touched his purple eyelid and gave me a fleeting smile. "I got this convincing Marcus to bring us to you."

"He should have got you to safety. And Justa."

Rafa made a wry face. "I've always been safest with you. Do you really think I'd leave you behind?"

"The vigiles will be here soon to stop the fire," Marcus warned, voice carrying from where he worked.

I walked over to him, glad to escape Rafa's scrutiny.

"Then why did you bar the gates when we arrived?" Rafa followed, moving to Justa's side. Her blue-green eyes darkened with concern and I realized I'd been staring at her swollen belly, mesmerized by the tingling flutter of her child's heartbeat.

"It all needs to burn first," Marcus replied.

I rubbed at my forehead. I'd thought Lanata's death would pay for the wrongs of the past, but the cost of my anger had been high. Fire had already spread down the back slope of the hill. How many people would it kill? Rome was notoriously combustible.

"If the gates are barred," Justa said with a hint of panic, "how are we getting out?"

"The wall nearest the Arx." Marcus pointed at the Temple of Juno on the second peak.

Rafa and Justa exchanged a look that was both question and answer. Decided, they made their way toward the wall.

Marcus grabbed a torch from its bracket on a small temple. I pulled Cyclops's body from the pool and added him to the pyre. Lifting the head, Marcus looked Cyclops in the eye.

"He was old. At least a few hundred from what little he said when he came looking for you." He dropped the head with the body and set the corpses alight.

"If you were concerned, you could have helped me. Or was this another test?"

"No test of mine," he said. "After you received the finger, I realized what it meant and followed the slave. Should I have left your friend to the mercies of the Carcer? It was either fight Cyclops or stop the guards from their orders to kill Rafa. And I'm not enduring eternity with you believing I failed."

A deep metallic pounding came from the bronze gate. Vigiles had finally arrived to contain the blaze and were trying to force it open. They would find a way over the gates soon.

"Marcus, the pool is tainted with Cyclops's blood." I stared with horror at the pink-tinged water. "What if the vigiles drink from it while putting out the fire?"

He shrugged. "Plagues have happened before. As long as they don't share blood with anyone else, it'll be over quickly. Not every death is your fault."

I gestured in the direction of the blaze. "So I'm only responsible for half the people who die tonight?"

"Time heals many wounds. You'll learn to accept what you've become." Marcus's tone was heavy with sincerity, and I wanted to believe him. He raised an eyebrow. "You might even tame yourself somewhat. I, myself, haven't caused the destruction of a major landmark for several decades."

"Brag some other time." I jerked my chin towards Rafa and Justa. "We have to help them over the wall."

He crossed his arms. "You want to stay with your friends, but you no longer belong with them. I can teach you how to survive this life. Come with me."

"Is that an order?"

His lips curled in a half-smile. "As long as you hold those swords—it's a request."

I shook my head, exasperated, and made for the wall. He followed with a muttered curse.

"Marcus, help them?" I asked, not willing to reveal more to Rafa than I may have already.

He nodded, the three of them making their way over the old fortification.

When they were gone, I turned to face the ruined courtyard, kneeling and planting my sword before me. Smoke curled from the tiled roof of the Temple of Jupiter; from the bonfire of bodies. And from beyond the Hill. Cries echoed over the city.

I had a debt to repay. I'd made a vow to Nemesis which now bound me. *To use my strength to punish the undeserving, and balance the scales of justice.*

Gods below, I should have been more specific. Revenge may bring justice, but at what cost? I could spend eternity trailing pain behind me, laying waste to the world as I had to the temple. It had been easy—and selfish. But to balance the scales, perhaps Bricus had it right—each day was a chance to add good to my past. There were few, precious few, who I'd saved. To fulfil my oath, I needed to be better.

But the blood will be a problem.

I exhaled sharply, then rose and sheathed my sword.

The others had reached the Temple of Juno by the time I joined them. We made our way to a narrow flight of stairs down the Hill. The fire had spread faster than I expected and voices rang loud in the distance, some to stop the blaze, some to flee. We reached the bottom, where Justa stood at Rafa's side, hands entwined. I didn't want this goodbye.

Justa gave me her shawl, and a swift hug. I tried not to notice how she trembled. Rafa did better at hiding his fear, but couldn't hide its scent.

"You were wrong," Rafa said. "I still need you. I don't suppose you'd swear that blood oath now?" His eyes were solemn, but then, he'd always been far cleverer than me.

He held out his bandaged hand. I embraced him.

"You're leaving, aren't you?" he said in my ear.

I pulled away and glanced at Marcus. "Yes."

"How will I find you?"

A low rumble reverberated across the Hill, then a flurry of sharp snaps—the roof of Jupiter's temple cracked and groaned as the fire broke through and the great beams collapsed. I sighed. "I have a talent for trouble, you know."

Rafa closed his eyes with a pained expression. "I'll find you."

"For now live—live with Justa. Have a dozen children."

I removed the gold ring from my finger and passed it to him. "Once Quintus finalizes my will, you'll have a new name."

He nodded, staring at the ram. "Lucius Calpurnius Rafa. I'll bear it with pride." He slid the ring on his smallest finger.

"Don't let Quintus convince you to take his name instead."

Rafa grunted in disgust. Justa came up behind and he stole his arm around her waist, hand moving to her belly. "Good journey."

"Good journey." There was no more to say.

Marcus followed me, mercifully silent, as we passed through the forum. Sunlight had faded, but the dark no longer hindered my sight. I pulled Justa's shawl higher over my head, its long folds obscuring the sheaths on my back and my bloodstained dress. So much savagery masked in an instant by respectable clothing. Few people in the streets scrutinized us. Most were too busy either heading for the gates, as we were, or bringing supplies to the Field of Mars to battle the blaze.

I grimaced. "We can't leave without helping."

"You forget, I did some redecorating at the Carcer. The bodies there will raise enough suspicion. If we stay, you risk feeding on the ones you're trying to rescue. The city will survive this night better without you. Trust me—" He raised his hand at my attempted protest. "—at least for now. You're too conspicuous as Vesuvia."

I swallowed my distaste at abandoning the city, but had to concede, since I'd barely contained myself with Lanata. "I'll need another new name, I suppose."

He grinned, a satisfied glint in his eye. "You'd be surprised how far I've gotten with Marcus. Lucilla should be fine, unless you'd prefer to remain Vesuvia?"

"No. Let her die. I never liked her anyway."

"A noble ending then—mortally wounded in the amphitheatre?"

"Yes. A fitting end for her."

Just not the end for me.

HISTORICAL NOTES

DECEMBER OF 69 C.E.
Fighting between the forces of Vitellius and Vespasian,
who each style themselves Emperor, results in the
burning and destruction of the Temple of Jupiter.

AUGUST OF 79 C.E.
Mount Vesuvius erupts, destroying, among others, the
towns of Herculaneum and Pompeii.

SPRING, 80 C.E.
The Temple of Jupiter burns again and a plague
breaks out in Rome. Cause unknown.

ACKNOWLEDGEMENTS

This book was a mistake. It was the first book I attempted (apart from my lost Grade 3 masterpiece), and from the minute I began writing, it consumed my life in a way I could not have predicted. But a worse mistake would have been to leave it unfinished.

Many thanks go out to all those in the Scribophile writing community who took the time to read early, crappier versions and offer their amazingly helpful feedback. I know I'll forget someone (*bad record-keeping, me*), but I do remember: Anne Louise Pepper, Dawn Chapman, Jeff Judkins, Ken Loomes, Lelia Rose Foreman, Michaël Wertenberg, Paylor (you know who you are!), Tina Chan, and the authorial gauntlet that is the Ubergroup.

A special mention, as always, to Calliope (Alexander Qi, Rebecca Carter, and Erin Merrill), my steadfast writing anchors. You remind me that I'm doing this for a reason, and that my voice is as important as anyone else's. Plus, all those last minute crits … sooooo many last minute crits.

This book wouldn't be *this book* without Erin, who never let me give up, even when I wanted to imitate Virgil and burn the whole thing.

First drafts are where all things are possible, and Kevin was the one to push me to discover those things. Even when they sucked. Thank you always.

So much patience and encouragement was provided by my kids, Tessa and Cedric, who are all kinds of wonderful, and the rest of my family, who raised me to love to read, write, and believe that words can change the world. What more could I ask for?

About the Author

Aliya Smyth lives on the Canadian prairies, a land so flat you can see your dog run away for six days. When she's not daydreaming about visiting countries with visible topography, she writes speculative historical fiction and fantasy. She is a huge fan of all things fairy tale, topsy-turvy history, gritty literary, and anything that fires up her imagination.

Read about the history behind the story, forthcoming books, and other strange musings, at www.aliyasmyth.com.